THE CHILL OF THE IRRAWADDY

THE SOLDIER'S SON
BOOK III

MALCOLM ARCHIBALD

For Cathy

The Burman give us Irrawaddy chills.
Rudyard Kipling

Come you back to Mandalay,
Where the old Flotilla lay:
Can't you 'ear their paddles chunkin' from Rangoon to
Mandalay?
Rudyard Kipling

A large force of Dacoits attacked the Kyike Police Station, which was defended by Mr. Shaw, assistant commissioner, and Mr. Sladden, police inspector, very courageously. On the sound of the enemy's gongs and drums, their twenty Burmese policemen bolted, leaving them with twenty Sikhs and natives of India, with whom they defended the station for three days and nights, repulsing numerous attacks. When the ammunition was exhausted, they brought off their men safely by a long night march.
Newcastle Chronicle, 26 December 1885

PRELUDE

POLICE POST, BAN HTEIK CHAUNG, BURMA, JANUARY 1886

"Here they come again," Captain Andrew Baird looked around at the remaining defenders of the post. Of the original twenty Sikh policemen, only fifteen remained, while their commander, Lieutenant Hanley, lay in a corner of the building, bleeding from three wounds. Bo Thura sat under the window with a cheroot in his mouth, loading his Martini-Henry. He looked up when Andrew spoke, thumbed a cartridge into the breech, and nodded.

"They are coming," he agreed.

The Sikhs lifted their Snider rifles, waiting for the attack with their customary professionalism.

Sukhbir Singh, closest to Andrew, grinned through his beard and stamped his boots on the ground. "*Unhāṁ nū ā'uṇa di'ō*," he said. "Let them come."

Another policeman slapped the butt of his rifle. "*Birdh ki Paij Panth ki jit!*" he shouted. "Rout of the Enemy and Victory of the Sikh Path!"

"I am not sure what you said, but it sounds good!" Andrew knew his father had always admired the Sikhs, and he now understood why. They were the most stolidly brave fighting men he had ever met.

Andrew lifted his head to peer out the window, ready to duck when he saw movement. Although the police had cut back the forest to a radius of a hundred yards, the dacoits haunted the fringes, watching everything the police did and sniping whenever they saw an opportunity. The dull green trees seemed sinister in the gloomy light, with the constant humming of insects a backdrop and the cries of unknown birds a distraction rather than a pleasure.

"How many are there, do you think?" Hanley asked, lifting himself to a more comfortable position. Blood had dried around the two bullet holes in his tunic and the *dha* gash on his thigh. He coughed, dribbling more blood from the corner of his mouth.

"I'm not sure," Andrew replied. "A couple of hundred, perhaps. Maybe more." He glimpsed the yellow umbrella through a gap in the trees and wondered if a snapshot might end the affair. Lifting his Martini-Henry, he aimed and cursed as the umbrella moved deeper into the forest. With limited ammunition, Andrew could not afford to waste a bullet.

"A couple of hundred," Hanley repeated. He coughed up more blood. "Was that an umbrella I saw out there?"

"It was," Andrew confirmed.

Hanley grinned, showing blood-stained teeth. "You remember what Wellington said when he saw a couple of Guards officers with umbrellas during the Peninsular War? He said, 'Lord Wellington does not approve of the use of umbrellas during the enemy's firing and will not allow the gentleman's sons to make themselves ridiculous in the eyes of the Army.'"

"Trust Wellington to have a quote for every occasion," Andrew replied. "There may be more than a couple of hundred. It's hard to tell when they move around all the time."

There are more than two hundred men out there. I'd estimate between four and five hundred, a mixture of raggedy-arsed dacoits and remnants of Thibaw's Army. It's best not to tell Hanley how bad the odds are.

The gongs began again, with their brassy clamour reverberating through the trees to bombard the post. Andrew glanced at the men. The stolid Sikhs appeared unmoved by the sound, but the local Burmese were uneasy, perhaps because they knew what the sound signified. One man spoke to Bo Thura, who replied with a short sentence. Hanley looked up, coughed again, and checked his revolver. Andrew noticed the butt was sticky with blood.

That poor lad hasn't got much time left to live. He'll fill another lonely grave thousands of miles from home in a squalid skirmish he had no part in starting.

The gongs continued, stopped for a moment, and started again.

One of the Sikhs grunted and spat on the ground. "Are they trying to scare us with their little gongs?" He grinned, showing white teeth behind his beard. "Maybe they think we are children, to be frightened by noise."

The sound increased all around the police post, and a drum added resonance to the racket. Andrew checked how many cartridges he had left in his pouch and stared at the surrounding forest.

"Here they come," Bo Thura said quietly as the dacoits slipped quietly from the trees. One second, the clearing was empty, and the next, a hundred dacoits were walking purposefully towards the post.

"There are more," Bo Thura said, and Andrew saw movement on the left. He lifted his Martini and aimed at the nearest, a squat man with the remains of a light red jacket uniform on his shoulders and a dha in his fist.

As the Sikhs prepared to fire, a volley came from the forest, with a second quickly following.

"How many rifles do these dacoits have?" Hanley asked. He struggled to the nearest window, gasping with pain. "I thought the Burmese Army had handed in all their weapons."

"Apparently not," Andrew said as bullets whistled and crackled around him. He swore as a group of dacoits stepped in front of the squat man. With only a few cartridges remaining, Andrew wanted to ensure he used them on leaders rather than followers.

"What the devil?" Andrew stared as the dacoit behind the squat man lifted a rifle. "That's a Winchester repeater, one of those fancy American rifles that can fire multiple rounds without reloading."

"These dacoits are better armed than we are," Hanley said.

The dacoits spread out to surround the police post, some with rifles, others with the wicked Burmese *dha*. The gongs continued their brassy clamour, a canopy of sound encompassing the handful of British and Sikhs.

"This will be their final assault," Sukhbir Singh said. "They're coming for the kill."

"And their leader has arrived," Andrew said. He pointed to a man on a hardy Burmese pony. The rider held a white flag surmounted by a blue peacock, the symbol of Burmese royalty. "These lads are still fighting for the Kingdom of Ava. Don't they know they've lost the war?"

At the sight of the peacock flag, the remaining Burmese policemen in the post shouted and ran to the door.

"Stop!" Hanley shouted and collapsed, coughing up blood.

Andrew shook his head. "Let them go," he advised. "They'd not be reliable."

Sukhbir grabbed one of the panicking men by the throat until Andrew intervened. "No, Sukhbir."

The Burmese policemen dragged away the barricades from the door and fled outside, leaving the post strangely hollow.

Sukhbir spat on the ground.

"Here they come," Bo Thura said as Andrew lifted his rifle. "And there are more." He pointed to the right, where another force of dacoits filtered through the trees. "Where the devil did these lads come from?"

CHAPTER 1

BERWICKSHIRE, SCOTLAND, SUMMER 1884

Andrew guided the dog cart to a twisted rowan tree at the side of the macadamised road and pulled Mariana's cape tighter across her shoulders. An easterly wind carried rain from the German Ocean to spatter on Mariana as she sheltered under the tree.

"It's lovely here," Mariana said, looking over the damp fields towards the River Tweed.

"Apart from the foul weather," Andrew replied.

"Oh, I don't mind the rain," Mariana said. "When we were young in Inglenook, Elaine and I always left the house when it was wet. We enjoyed the rain after all the dry weather."

Andrew smiled, thinking of Mariana back in her

home in Natal. "I could imagine you two dancing in the rain," he said. He still thought of Mariana's sister, Elaine, from time to time, even though it was five years since a force of renegades had murdered her and her parents on their farm on the Natal-Zululand border.

"Elaine would love it here," Mariana looked over the green, fertile Border countryside, with the solid stone buildings nestling against swaying trees and cattle grazing in the fields. "It all looks so peaceful."

"It does," Andrew agreed. "It's hard to believe this was once the most contested frontier in Europe, with Scots and English having battles, raids and skirmishes for hundreds of years."

Mariana took a deep breath. "If you stand still and listen," she said. "You can hear the tension."

"Can you hear tension?" Andrew asked.

"Undoubtedly," Mariana smiled at him, brushing back a loose strand of hair that had escaped from her hat. "Can't you hear the voices of the old people?"

Andrew lifted his head. "All I hear is the wind in the trees and the rain pattering in the puddles!"

"Oh, Andrew!" Mariana tapped his arm. "You need to use your imagination! You can taste the tension in the wind and sense the old reivers and warriors." She surveyed the landscape, from the rippling Tweed to the broad fields and distant green Cheviot

Hills. "There is poetry in this land, Andrew; can you not sense the romance?"

"Can you sense Sir Lancelot?" Andrew asked. "According to some legends, he lived at Bamborough Castle; that was his Joyous Gard."

"That's quite a few miles south of here," Mariana replied.

"He was a travelling man, a knight errant, and would go riding and hunting," Andrew said. "We don't know how extensive his lands would be, but I think he'd know this area well."

They stood two hundred yards from the River Tweed, five miles west of Berwick. A stone's throw away, a pair of stone buildings dominated a grassy knoll and sheltered behind a group of trees. One was a Georgian house, two storeys tall, with rain weeping from its grey slate roof and classically proportioned windows and doors. The other was much older, a crumbling ruin of a tower that had stood guard over a ford across the river for centuries.

"Can we look at the castle?" Mariana asked.

"We can," Andrew told her. "Come on!" Taking Mariana's hand, he helped her from the dog cart and guided her through the open five-barred gate and onto the rough track that curved upwards to the grey buildings.

"I hope the owner doesn't mind us nosing his property," Mariana said as they avoided the puddles and accidentally kicked loose stones up the path.

"He won't mind. I know him," Andrew replied.

Grass grew on the central ridge of the track, and a mouse scuttled in front of them. Andrew glanced sideways at Mariana, saw her genuine interest in the tower and nodded.

This idea might work. I have captured Mariana's attention; I hope I have set the scene for tomorrow's question. Andrew looked at her fondly, lifted a hand to touch her shoulder and dropped it again.

"What is the castle called?" Mariana hardly glanced at the Georgian farmhouse. Her eyes were busy on the grey-stoned tower, where a rowan tree clung precariously to the upper wall, and moss furred the lower layers. A bevy of pigeons exploded from the ruin, wings flapping noisily, with a single crow observing them from the topmost height.

"Corbiestane Tower," Andrew stopped at the apex of the curve, where a group of whins whispered in the breeze. "A corbie is a crow, so it means the Tower of the Crow's Stone."

"There's the corbie up there," Mariana nodded to the crow.

"The tower guards a ford across the Tweed," Andrew indicated the river. "On this bank, we are in Scotland, while the opposite side is England; this ford would be an important crossing point for both countries."

Miraculously, the rain stopped, and a shaft of sun

landed on the tower's doorway, showing a carved stone above the entrance.

"What's the carving?" Mariana asked. She stepped closer, craning her neck to see. "It looks like," she turned away, facing Andrew with new colour flushing her cheeks. "It's not, Andrew! It can't be."

"It's a phallic symbol," Andrew hid his smile. "The Romans used it as a sign of good luck, which means either the original building here is very old, or the builder cannibalised a Roman ruin for his tower."

"So, this tower might have been here in King Arthur's time?" Mariana asked, glancing sideways at the symbol and then looking away.

"Not this particular tower, but I'd say there's been a building guarding the ford for centuries, perhaps back to Roman times. In that case, something would have been here in Arthurian times and perhaps owned by Sir Lancelot. He'd appoint one of his knights to watch for raiders, either Scots or English."

"Oh," Mariana lifted her skirt higher and walked to the tower, touching the stones as if to recapture the legends of King Arthur. "To think that Arthur, Guinevere or Lancelot might have been here." She looked over her shoulder at Andrew. "Do you think the present owner would mind if I went inside?"

"I am sure he wouldn't mind at all," Andrew replied. "But be careful; it's a bit tumbledown."

Avoiding looking at the carved stone, Mariana stepped through the battered doorway and looked up. The tower was a hollowed-out ruin, with bare walls reaching to the silver-grey sky, knee-high weeds sprouting on the ground and vegetation thrusting between the stonework. Birds had nested in the arrow-slit windows, and the wind moaned through the gaps.

"It's lovely," Mariana said. "To think Lancelot might have been here."

"This tower was built long after his time," Andrew reminded her. "He might have visited the site, though, if he ever existed."

"Of course, he existed," Mariana retorted.

Andrew smiled at her passion. "Of course he did," he agreed.

Mariana smoothed her hand over the rough stonework. "But Lancelot mused a little space; He said, "She has a lovely face; God in his mercy lend her grace, The Lady of Shalott."

"Indeed," Andrew recognised Tennyson's poetry.

"Maybe Tennyson visited here before he thought of the Lady," Mariana said. "He wasn't far away, was he?"

"I know he loves the Lake District," Andrew said. "I don't know about the Tweed." He changed the subject. "Would you like to see the house?"

"You know I love looking at other people's houses," Mariana replied. "Will the owner not object to two strangers dropping in unannounced?"

"The house is empty," Andrew replied. "And I have the key."

Mariana took his arm. "Oh, you clever thing! Come on then, Andrew! What are we waiting for?"

The key turned smoothly in the lock, and Andrew pushed the door open and stepped aside so Mariana could enter first.

"It's completely empty," Mariana said. She strode into the house, looking around her. "What a lovely place, and so fortunate being so close to Lancelot's tower."

Mariana has convinced herself that Lancelot lived on the tower, Andrew thought. *Maybe that's no bad thing.*

"What do you think of this house?" Andrew asked. He closed the door and stepped back to allow her a better view.

"It's beautiful," Mariana replied. Lifting the hem of her skirt, she raced to the landing upstairs, with the sound of her boots echoing in the hallway. "There are four rooms up here," she said.

Andrew followed her upstairs, checking the walls and ceilings for signs of dampness and black mould.

"What would you do with this house if it was yours?"

"Oh, that's easy," Mariana replied. "I'd have this room overlooking the tower, and your bedroom would be over there, with a view to the river." She hesitated for a moment. "I nearly said the Tugela River."

"I guessed that," Andrew said. "The house's situation is similar to Inglenook." He allowed Mariana a moment to recover from her memories. "Except for the possible Arthurian connection. Would you like to live here?"

"I'd love to," Mariana replied. "I'd see Lancelot and Arthur every day."

"Good," Andrew said. "That's why I bought it. Farming is currently going through a slump and prices have dropped, so it was dirt cheap."

"Oh," Mariana put a hand over her mouth, staring at him. "So it's yours?"

"Ours, if you want to share it," Andrew said. "Unless you have some secret sweetheart you want to run off with."

Mariana turned away. "You know very well that I do not have a sweetheart."

You used to think you loved me, Mariana. What happened?

"Indeed," Andrew said, hiding his disappointment. "When you've had your fill of Corbiestane, Mariana, we'll return to Berwick."

"When can we move in?" Mariana asked.

"When all the legal paperwork is completed, and I have the workmen install modern plumbing and lighting," Andrew said. "After that, you can do what you will to the house."

When Mariana smiled quietly, Andrew knew she was already planning her alterations.

"The stone," Mariana said. "Where is the Corbiestane?"

"At the back," Andrew led her outside, carefully locking the door behind him. The Corbiestane was a large lump of rock with the crudely carved figure of a bird inscribed on one side.

Mariana ran her hands over the carving. "What was it for?"

"Nobody knows," Andrew told her. "There are many legends, but nothing is certain."

"I think Lancelot's knight had a corbie on his shield, and he carved the stone to let everybody know he was guarding the ford," Mariana said.

"That's as good an explanation as any," Andrew agreed. "Now, shall we get away before the heavens open again? Tomorrow, I am taking you to Edinburgh to see Saint Margaret's Chapel." He saw Mariana looking at him but did not explain further. Mariana was studying Corbiestane farmhouse, deciding what type of wallpaper she wanted.

EDINBURGH CASTLE, SCOTLAND, SUMMER 1884

"It's very romantic," Mariana said, holding her hat against Edinburgh Castle's eternal wind. "Who was Saint Margaret?"

"She was Queen of Scotland in the eleventh century," Andrew said. "Married to Malcolm the Third, Malcolm Canmore. She brought the Roman Catholic faith to Scotland to replace the old Celtic Christianity."

"Oh," Mariana nodded. "Was this chapel named after her?"

They stood outside the small, stone-built chapel, recently restored after being used as a storeroom for years. Even Andrew could sense the history as he touched the ancient doorway and wondered how many people had been in this spot over the past seven hundred years. He thought of the long, long line of Scotland's kings and queens, the knights and nobles, and the thousands of soldiers who had garrisoned the castle.

"I said, was the chapel named after Saint Margaret?" Mariana raised her eyebrows.

"I think Margaret's son, King David, had it built," Andrew said, "so it's 12th century, about 750 years old." He saw that the age did not impress her. "It's also the oldest remaining building in Edinburgh

Castle. King David was a very religious man who had half the abbeys in Scotland built."

Andrew realised that Mariana's attention had wandered. He allowed her to enjoy the vista of Edinburgh's New Town, with the Scott Monument arrowing skyward and the austerely regular streets contrasting with the blue Firth of Forth behind.

"It's a very nice chapel," Mariana agreed.

"I knew you'd like it with the Arthurian connection," Andrew watched as Mariana took the bait.

"What Arthurian connection?" Mariana lost all interest in Edinburgh's grey streets as she swivelled towards him.

"I thought you would already know," Andrew teased her. "One of the earliest mentions of Arthur might have been written here."

"In Edinburgh?"

"In Edinburgh Castle," Andrew replied. "Have you heard of the *Gododdin*?" He enjoyed Mariana's look of interested confusion.

"The what?" She shook her head. "What is it?"

"The *Gododdin* is a sixth or seventh-century poem about a band of warriors fighting against the invading Saxons," Andrew explained. "The warriors spent a year in the hall or fort of a king called Mynddog Mwynfawr before they rode south to fight the invaders."

Mariana persisted in her pet love. "Did Arthur lead them?"

"No," Andrew shook his head. "But the poet mentioned him. Listen." Aware that a dozen garrison soldiers were watching him curiously, Andrew quoted from the *Gododdin*.

"He fed black ravens on the rampart of a fortress,

Though he was no Arthur

Among the powerful ones in battle

In the front rank, Gwawrddur was a palisade."

Mariana smiled. "Though he was no Arthur," she repeated. "That meant that Arthur was a greater warrior than Gwawrddur."

"That's how I interpret the words," Andrew agreed. "Somebody wrote the *Gododdin* here, in Edinburgh Castle, about five hundred years before King David built this chapel." He tapped his boot on the volcanic rock.

"Oh," Mariana's interest increased as she looked around.

Andrew placed both hands on Mariana's shoulders and gently guided her to the ramparts, where she had a better view. "Do you see that hill?" He asked, pointing to the great volcanic hill that overlooked Edinburgh's Old Town.

"Yes," Mariana said. "It's a very nice hill."

"That's called Arthur's Seat," Andrew told her. "Some say it was the site of Camelot, others that people just named it after King Arthur. Some identify this castle with the Castle of Maidens in

Arthurian legend, and others that Lothian was named after King Lot, Arthur's brother."

Mariana's interest grew with each myth. "Is that why you brought me here, Andrew? To tell me Edinburgh's connections with Arthur?"

"That was one reason," Andrew said, taking a deep breath before continuing. "How would you like to get married in a site with such an Arthurian connection?" He put his right hand in his pocket, holding the small box he had carried for days.

Mariana was silent for a moment as she digested Andrew's question. "Was that a proposal?" she asked quietly.

"Yes," Andrew said. "Most people think we're already married."

"They do," Mariana said. "But we're not." She looked at him as the wind whipped her hair around her face. "You know I've loved you since we first met."

"You had a teenage crush on me," Andrew said.

"I loved you," Mariana corrected gently. "But you preferred my sister."

"I've got to know you better since then," Andrew said. "We've grown up together."

"Maybe," Mariana lifted her chin. "I wonder if you would have proposed if Elaine was still alive."

Mariana's sister Elaine had died at the beginning of the Zulu War of 1879 when a gang of renegades had attacked Inglenook. The raiders had kidnapped

Mariana, holding her prisoner until Andrew had led a force to rescue her. The ordeal had traumatised Mariana, and Andrew had looked after her through a long recovery process.

"Have you proposed because you feel obliged to care for Elaine's little sister?" Mariana held Andrew's gaze.

"No," Andrew shook his head. "I proposed because I want you as my wife. I want to spend the rest of my life with you."

Mariana was silent for half a minute, then touched Andrew's arm. "Thank you, Andrew," she said quietly. "I wish I could believe that."

Andrew stepped back. He had planned his proposal for weeks, buying a house with spurious Arthurian connections, bringing Mariana to Edinburgh Castle, showing her Saint Margaret's Chapel, and unveiling the Arthurian legends. He had never anticipated her hesitation. "Are you turning me down?"

"It's not that, Andrew," Mariana said. "I don't want you to tie yourself to me for the wrong reasons."

Andrew nodded, deflated. "My intentions are honourable," he told her miserably.

"Of that, I have no doubt," Mariana replied gently. "You are the most honourable and kindest man I have ever met. I love you dearly, but I don't want you to marry me because of Elaine."

"I want to marry you because of you," Andrew felt his position was slipping away. He wished he had never asked. He wanted to run away and hide.

"You are a good man," Mariana told him, smiling. "I wish I could agree, Andrew, but, you see, I think you are just being kind."

And there is that shadow, Mariana thought. *That horror that waits at the back of my mind. I cannot release it, Andrew, and if I marry you, it will emerge.*

Andrew felt the small box as a weight in his pocket. "Will you think about my proposal?" He knew that half the castle garrison and the civilian visitors were staring at him, everyone amused at his embarrassment. He wanted to run away and hide.

"I will," Mariana told him solemnly. "Of course, I will think about it." She took hold of his arm. "Come on, now, Andrew. Let's just be friends as we have been for years. Show me the rest of this castle of yours." She favoured him with a bright smile. "Tell me tales of Arthur and the Scottish kings and queens." She held his arm like a younger sister. "Come on now, Andrew. No more long faces."

The journey back to Berwick-upon-Tweed was long, with Andrew brooding over the day's events and Mariana quiet. Both were glad when the train pulled up at the platform under the ruins of Berwick Castle, and they walked the few hundred yards to Andrew's house on the town walls.

Andrew opened his front door, and while Mariana removed her coat, he lifted the brown-paper-wrapped parcel from the side table, carried it to his desk, and placed it inside the bottom drawer, adding the small box from inside his coat. When he returned downstairs, Mariana stood before the slowly ticking longcase clock.

"Have you forgiven me?" Mariana asked quietly.

"There's nothing to forgive," Andrew forced a smile. "I asked a question, and you gave an honest answer."

"I hurt you," Mariana said. "I didn't want to hurt you."

Andrew looked at her. "I know," he replied. "My proposition stands, Mariana. I will not force the issue, I will not withdraw it, and I won't mention it again." He had been considering his response on the long, dismal journey home.

"Andrew," Mariana leaned forward and touched his hand.

Andrew never knew what Mariana was going to say, for at that moment, somebody knocked heavily on the door.

"Who the devil can that be?" Andrew asked, glancing at the clock. "It's past ten at night, far too late for visitors." Stepping to the door, he hauled it open and glared outside.

The man who stood there was gaunt and heavily tanned, huddled into a long greatcoat and with a bowler hat jammed on his head.

"Captain Baird?" he asked. "Are you Captain Andrew Baird?"

"I am," Andrew admitted. "I don't think I know you."

"You don't know me," the man said. "I am Captain Walter Kerr of the Royal Scots Fusiliers. I must talk to you."

CHAPTER 2

BERWICK-UPON-TWEED, ENGLAND,
SUMMER 1884

"Who is it?" Mariana appeared behind Andrew, holding a poker and glowering at her visitor.

"It's a Captain Walter Kerr," Andrew said. "Of the Royal Scots Fusiliers."

Mariana lowered the poker, glanced outside where rain was beginning to fall, decided their visitor was harmless, and frowned. "Well, bring the poor fellow in. It's wet out there."

When Captain Kerr stepped inside the front room under the glare of the gas lights, Andrew thought he looked rather the worse for wear. He was even thinner than he had first appeared and had a

yellowish tinge to his face that was decidedly un-
healthy.

*It looks like Captain Kerr has had malaria. He's prob-
ably been out East.*

"Sit down, Captain," Andrew invited. "Would
you like a drink? Whisky? Brandy?"

"Brandy, thank you," Kerr replied, trying to suppress a shiver.

"Sit down, Captain Kerr," Mariana ushered him
to a seat. "You look cold. Shall we light the fire?"

"Don't go to any bother, Mrs. Baird," Kerr said,
looking up.

"It's Miss Maxwell," Mariana corrected mildly.
"And it's no bother."

"I do apologise, Miss Maxwell." Captain Kerr
spoke with a strangely sing-song intonation that Andrew thought was Welsh.

"No need to apologise," Mariana said. "It's an
easy mistake to make."

Andrew poured a generous glass of brandy for
Kerr, then a whisky for himself and one for Mariana,
adding water to the latter. "Now, Captain Kerr,
what's it all about? Why do you wish to see me?"

"It may be rather a delicate matter, Captain
Baird," Kerr glanced at Mariana.

"Miss Maxwell and I are old friends," Andrew
said. "We met during the Frontier Wars in South
Africa and have known each other ever since. Anything you say to me, you can say to Miss Maxwell."

He felt Mariana's gaze on him and wondered what she was thinking.

"As you wish," Kerr said. "Can we drop the formality? Call me Kerr."

"Kerr, it is," Andrew agreed. "And I am Baird." He sipped at his whisky, waiting for Kerr to explain why he was there.

"How well do you know India?" Kerr asked.

"I don't know it at all," Andrew admitted. "All my travelling has been in Africa."

"I see," Kerr finished his brandy and glanced at the decanter. Andrew recognised a serious drinker and passed it over. He watched as Kerr half-filled his glass with a trembling hand, with a stump in place of his index finger.

"Some people call India the Jewel of the Empire," Kerr said at length, "but if so, it is a jewel with rough edges. On one side, we have the Northwest Frontier, the section facing Afghanistan, which has some of the wildest tribes in the world."

Andrew nodded. "So I believe," he agreed.

"On the other side, we have a jungly frontier with Burma. The southern part of Burma, Lower Burma, is British territory. The northern section, Upper Burma, or the Kingdom of Ava, is an independent nation ruled by a savage tyrant called King Thibaw."

Andrew sat opposite Kerr and noticed Mariana listening avidly.

"To get to the throne," Kerr continued, "Thibaw had to massacre scores of his relatives in a blood-bath that makes Nero look like a choirboy. That was in 1878. Before Thibaw swam to the throne in a wave of blood, one of his father's queens, a charming lady known as Hsinbyaumashin, had increased her influence. When Hsinbyaumashin's husband, King Mindon, was dying, she informed all the heirs, potential heirs, and possible rivals that Mindon wanted to say farewell. She gathered them together and killed the whole bunch, except Thibaw, whose main wife, Supayagi, is Hsinbyaumashin's daughter."

"Lovely people," Andrew murmured.

Kerr sipped more brandy. "England's Henry the Eighth would have recognised a fellow monster," he said.

"When the coronation occurred, Supayagi was due to be anointed, and her sister, Supayalat, barged in and also became queen."

"One king and two queens?" Mariana asked.

"And a royal mother-in-law," Kerr said. He failed to suppress a shiver. "The thought could put one off marriage forever."

"Are you cold, Captain Kerr?" Mariana interrupted. "You still look cold."

Kerr shook his head. "It's just the fever," he said. "I lived in the tropics for the past twenty years, and even a touch of cool damp wakes the blasted fever."

"Andrew will put a match to the fire," Mariana said, raising her eyebrows.

When the flames took hold and spread a modicum of warmth around the room, Kerr shifted closer to the fire and continued.

"Thank you, Baird and Miss Maxwell. King Thibaw, or perhaps Maung Thandar, one of his ministers, is creating havoc in Upper Burma, killing, robbing, and sending armed bands over the border into British-controlled Burma. There is hardly a week without these fellows committing some outrage or other in our territory."

Andrew watched as Kerr filled his glass again, replaced the decanter's stopper, and placed it at his side.

"King Thibaw has declared his intention to retake all the land that Britain conquered from his equally disreputable ancestors," Kerr said.

"How does all this concern me, Kerr?" Andrew asked.

"I'm coming to that." Kerr inched even closer to the fire. He glanced at Mariana before speaking again. "You may not be aware that a member of your family, Baird, a distant relative, married a Burmese woman."

Andrew remembered the array of family portraits on the wall of Wychwood Manor, his father's house in Herefordshire. Most were military men, salted with a few seamen, while one stood out as neither one nor the other. Andrew's grandmother had hidden the portrait behind a heavy curtain until her son, General Jack Windrush, had ripped the screen away.

When Andrew asked about the sitter's identity, his father had smiled.

"That's Uncle George," he said. "He went native in Burma and preferred to stay there rather than return home."

"Why?" Andrew had asked.

Jack Windrush's smile broadened. "The East can be an alluring place," he explained. "I know Uncle George had a Burmese wife and at least one son, but apart from that, who can say."

Andrew realised that Kerr was staring at him, awaiting a reply. He jerked himself away from his childhood past.

"I was aware of Great Uncle George," he said, "although I never met him."

"Very well," Kerr said, helping himself to more brandy. "Your great uncle had a son who is as Burmese as teak, without a trace of British in him except his blood."

"I've heard about him," Andrew admitted. He knew Mariana was watching him yet kept his gaze firmly on Kerr. He could discuss things with Mariana later, once they were alone.

The fire hissed as rain fell down the chimney. A spark shot from the coal, hit the inside of the fire-

guard, glimmered for a second and faded into darkness. Andrew heard a rising wind blow across the
stone pavement at the front of the house. The sultry
heat of Burma seemed a different world.

"This fellow, your distant relative, is called Bo
Thura," Kerr shifted closer to the fire as the rain
outside increased, hammering on the window as if
determined to find shelter inside the house. Kerr
looked over the rim of his glass at Andrew. "He is a
notorious badmash, a horse thief and robber of re-
pute and possibly a murderer as well." He glanced at
Mariana again. "In fact, Bo Thura has the reputation
of being the best horse thief in Burma. Are you certain you wish me to discuss such matters before a
lady?"

"I've heard worse, Captain Kerr," Mariana said
quietly. "I grew up beside the Tugela River on the
border with Zululand."

Andrew nodded. "Carry on, Kerr. I've no secrets
from Miss Maxwell." At such times, he valued Mariana's support.

"As you wish. Bo Thura, your distant relative, has
now added kidnapping to his list of crimes. You may
have heard of the kidnapping of young Mary Mac-
Connacher."

"I have not," Andrew confessed.

Kerr looked surprised for a moment. "Have you
not? It is the topic of conversation in India; perhaps

not such an important event here, with all the furore over this trouble in the Balkans."[1]

"There's always trouble in the Balkans," Mariana murmured. "I try to ignore it." She lifted the poker, stirred the fire, and added two pieces of coal. "I read a little about Mary MacConnacher's kidnapping. She was five years old, I think."

"That's correct," Kerr was nearly huddled over the fire as the flames licked around the fresh coal. "A five-year-old little blonde girl and Bo Thura stole her and her *ayah* - her nurse - away. Two days later, we found the *ayah* unharmed but badly shaken, with a note addressed to Sir Charles Crossthwaite, the Chief Commissioner of British Burma, in Rangoon."

"That wasn't in the papers," Mariana said. "What was in the note?"

Again, Kerr glanced at Andrew as if for permission to speak. Andrew nodded.

"The note said that Bo Thura would hold young Mary MacConnacher hostage until General Jack Windrush or a member of his family came to speak to him."

"Why?" Andrew asked. "Why involve my father?

---

1. In the latter part of the nineteenth century, the Balkans were a hotbed of wars and rumours of wars as the Austrian, Ottoman and Russian Empires competed for power and influence. In 1884 and 1885, the trouble was between Bulgaria and Serbia, with the Bulgarians emerging as victors in 1885.

As far as I am aware, he hasn't been in Burma since the war there in 1852."

Kerr shook his head. "We don't know why," he admitted.

"Who are we?" Mariana had been following the conversation closely. "When you arrived, Captain Kerr, you said you were from the Royal Scots Fusiliers. What have the Fusiliers to do with this situation?"

"I am presently with the Fusiliers," Kerr said. "I am also Sir Charles's aide-de-camp." He poured himself more brandy, looked at the decreasing level in the decanter, and sighed.

"Have you come from Burma to tell us about Mary MacConnacher?" Andrew asked. "A telegram would have been faster."

"It would," Kerr agreed, "but there are other factors." He faced Andrew directly. "When will you be ready to go to Burma to meet Bo Thura and rescue this little girl?"

Andrew closed his eyes. *This day has been bad enough. Burma is on the other side of the world.*

"Would General Windrush not be a better choice?" Mariana asked. "He's been to Burma before, and a man of his rank has more power and influence."

"Yes," Kerr said. "But General Windrush may be needed in another part of the world soon." He nodded at Mariana once more. "I think ladies should withdraw."

"The lady is staying," Andrew said. "You have more to tell us, Captain Kerr."

"What I say must remain within these four walls," Kerr looked at Mariana. "You must not repeat any of it."

"We won't," Andrew promised.

"We believe the Russians have reawakened their interest in Afghanistan," Kerr said. "We want to retain some of our men with recent experience in that area, including General Windrush." He finished his brandy and placed the empty glass on the hearth.

"I see," Andrew said.

"Compared to the possible Russian threat to India through the passes," Kerr said, "King Thibaw's Burma is a bit of a backwater." He huddled even closer to the fire, extending his hands to the flames. "We won't be sending Sir Garnet, Bobs Roberts or Fighting Jack Windrush into the jungle when the Russian Bear is threatening."

"Of course not," Andrew agreed.

I see the logic, unfortunately. If Father is tied up in the middle of nowhere, it would be tricky to recall him if a Cossack horde threatens Peshawar.

"On the other hand, the British public will be upset if we allow little golden-haired Mary Mac-Connacher to languish unrescued in the hands of an unprincipled rogue like Bo Thura." Kerr stood up, paced to the window, and glanced at the hammering rain. "No familial offence intended, Captain Baird."

"None taken, Captain," Andrew replied.

"And I mean no offence when I say that having a lower-ranked officer stuck in Burma is less important than sending one of our most distinguished generals there."

Andrew smiled. "I have no illusions about my lack of importance in the Army, Captain."

Kerr smiled. "We share the same rank, Baird. As you'll know, the country is going to the voting booths shortly, and the public won't like a Prime Minister who allows a little English girl to remain a captive."

"Mary MacConnacher is Irish," Mariana murmured. "The daughter of an Army sergeant based in Rangoon."

Kerr shrugged. "A detail. According to the press, she's a golden-haired Anglo-Saxon angel, so that's what the public believes. Public perception is important when the elections come around, especially with this new craze for democracy." He shook his hand. "Damn Disraeli's leap in the dark. It's causing us all sorts of trouble." [2] He returned to his seat and

---

2. Disraeli's "Leap in the Dark" – Disraeli was the Conservative Prime Minister, and his Second Reform Act of 1867 increased the franchise to include some working-class men. Disraeli believed working-class men would always vote Conservative. Many people

controlled his shivering. "So, Baird, when can you leave for Burma?" There was little humour in his smile. "You can refuse, of course, but that would be damaging for your military career, as well as leaving poor little Mary a captive."

Andrew shook his head. "I don't care a twopenny damn about my military career," he said. "I never wanted to be a soldier in the first place. But I don't like to think of a little girl as a captive in Burma."

"Of course you don't," Kerr said. "Nobody with an ounce of humanity would want that. And we don't want the opposition to get into power, either."

"I care even less which political party is in power," Andrew replied. "I'll have to work out shipping times and prices."

"We'll arrange all that," Kerr told him. "And we'll find you a place to stay in Rangoon."

"How can I contact Bo Thura when I get to Rangoon?" Andrew asked.

"We will place you in a certain hotel, and Bo Thura will contact you there," Kerr said. "I don't know how."

Andrew grunted. "It seems that Bo Thura is in charge of this operation." He glanced at Mariana. "The move to Corbiestane will have to wait," he said. "Will you be all right on your own here?"

---

believed the idea of allowing ordinary people to vote was a radical leap in the dark.

"You're not going to Burma and leaving me here," Mariana said.

Remembering Mariana's recent refusal in Edinburgh Castle, Andrew was about to ask why not but bit off the bitter retort. "This Bo Thura seems a dangerous man," he said. "I'm not putting you in danger."

"I'll be in less danger there than I was in Natal," Mariana replied.

"You'll go then," Kerr seemed relieved.

"Yes, I'll go," Andrew said. He glanced at Mariana, who lifted a defiant chin.

"I'll keep a journal of our adventures," Mariana said.

CHAPTER 3

RANGOON, BURMA, AUGUST 1884

The British India Steam Navigation Company flag hung limply from the stern, the white swallowtail boasting a red saltire that seemed vaguely out of place in the oppressive heat. Andrew wiped a film of sweat from his forehead and stared at his surroundings.

I'm used to heat after Africa, but the humidity here is terrific.

Andrew watched the anchor slide into the river with a dull splash that reverberated in the heavy air.

Now, we have officially arrived in Burma. That anchor sounded like the full stop for the story of the voyage.

"Where are we?" Mariana asked, adjusting her parasol to shade her face from the sun.

"We're in the Irrawaddy River," Andrew said. "A few miles downstream from Rangoon."

"We're certainly seeing the world," Mariana said. "It's only taken four days to get here from Calcutta." She twisted Andrew's wrist and glanced at his watch. "Four days to the minute. We cast off from Calcutta at ten minutes after three, and it's now three o'clock."

"I didn't realise you were taking notes," Andrew said.

"Oh, yes," Mariana said. "I write everything down in my journal. Everything."

"What have you written?"

"Do you want to hear?" Mariana looked pleased. "I haven't read it to anybody."

Andrew nodded. "Of course, I want to hear."

"I'll be back in a minute." Mariana disappeared to her cabin below decks and returned with a slightly battered blue notebook. "Here we are," she said. "Are you sure you want to hear?"

"Quite sure," Andrew replied.

Mariana opened the notebook, flicked through to her last entry, and read, looking up occasionally to ensure that Andrew was paying attention.

"We arrived at the mouth of a large river ten minutes since. The coastline has a very peculiar appearance, very much like what I've heard about a mirage in the desert. It appeared like a line of coconut trees, and palms were floating in the sky, a hands-breadth above the line of the horizon. The trees could have been growing in the air, without soil or land, and that was my first sight of the magical land of Burma."

Andrew nodded. "That is very poetic," he approved. "Let's hope that Burma continues to be a magical land for you."

"Thank you, Andrew." Mariana reclaimed her notebook and tucked it under her arm.

"It's only the truth," Andrew said.

"Mother used to say that my writing was too flowery and that I should only put down practical things. I stopped writing after that."

"You can start again," Andrew smiled. "There's nothing at all wrong with what you showed me." He watched as a pilot left the pilot ship, *The Guide*, and rowed towards them. The pilot, a local man with a distinct swagger, swarmed up a rope ladder to the deck, greeted the captain with a hearty handshake and issued orders to the helmsman.

"Do we need a pilot?" Andrew asked Ross, the second mate.

"We do, sir," Ross replied. "The Irrawaddy is a dangerous river, with the current constantly changing the safe deep-water channels." He pointed to the pilot boat. "There are sixty-four official river pilots, Captain Baird, most from Chittagong. Even the great Irrawaddy Flotilla vessels rely on Chittagong pilots, who each know one area of the river.

Hence, the ships must use seventeen different pilots between Rangoon and Mandalay."

"I see," Andrew said, storing the information for future use. He knew that Rangoon was the capital of British Burma and Mandalay the capital of the Kingdom of Ava, or Upper Burma, where King Thibaw held sway.

"We're hoisting anchor again!" Mariana said.

Andrew saw the ship begin to move and glanced upstream as she steamed at increasing speed under the pilot's directions, with the muddy brown water surging against the hull. On either side was scrubby jungle, with the sun reflecting from something golden.

"What's that?" Mariana asked.

"That's the Shwedagon Pagoda or the Golden Pagoda," Andrew had been reading about Burma during the voyage from Britain. "I believe my father helped capture it back in fifty-two."

"Oh, did he?" Mariana answered dutifully.

"He did," Andrew watched as the ship passed a small flotilla of fishing boats. The boats had an open, double-winged stern, and a man that Andrew supposed to be the skipper was sheltering under a shade while the crew worked in the open. *Is that the Burmese version of democracy? There's little difference from ours, then.*

"Is the pagoda made of gold?" Mariana asked.

"I think it's gold leaf over timber," Andrew replied. "Burma is full of golden pagodas."

When Mariana opened her notebook and began to write, Andrew thought it best to leave her in peace. After what seemed only a few minutes, the ship moored at the port of Rangoon.

"We've arrived," Andrew said.

"It's busy here," Mariana wrote a few words and closed her notebook with a decisive snap.

Andrew agreed as he watched a score of ships moored or moving, most under steam but some with sail, both European and Oriental. Tall chimneys spoke of industry, but the giant Golden Pagoda dominated the city.

Religion is essential to this land, Andrew thought. *I wonder how Bo Thura will contact me.*

"A woman is coming aboard," Mariana said as one of the ubiquitous small Burmese boats drew alongside.

"That's Mary of Rangoon," Ross said as the elderly woman clambered easily onto the deck. "She comes to every ship that docks here and has been for a quarter of a century."

Mary of Rangoon approached Mariana and offered a selection of trinkets from a canvas bag.

"Could I have this, please?" Mariana selected a tiny carved Buddha.

Mary smiled as Mariana scooped a handful of

mixed British and Indian coins from her pocket. "How much?"

Mary picked a single rupee, bowed, said "thank you," and presented Andrew with a rose before moving on to Ross and the other officers.

"That's a nice welcome to Burma," Mariana said, holding her purchase. "I wonder who carved this Buddha. Perhaps some dedicated monk in that golden temple over there, whittling away as he contemplated the meaning of life."

"Perhaps so," Andrew said. *Or a five-year-old child working in a gutter for a penny a day.* "Look, here's the boat to take us ashore, so get yourself ready, Mariana."

RANGOON WAS LOUD, BUSTLING, BUSY AND HECTIC, as befitted Burma's largest port. Andrew kept Mariana close by as he hailed a decorated bullock cart that seemed to do duty as a taxicab.

"Do you speak English?" he asked the driver.

"Yes, Sahib!" the man was a grinning Indian with betel-nut-stained teeth.

"Do you know the Wells Britannia Hotel?" Andrew asked.

"Yes, Sahib!" the driver nodded.

"Take us there, then. And give us a hand with the luggage."

The driver was helpful, piling in their bags with a smile as Mariana supervised.

"You're new to Rangoon?" A tall civilian stopped, lifted his hat to Mariana and watched Andrew and the driver loading the luggage.

"We are," Mariana answered. "We have just arrived."

"Trade? Or military?" the civilian asked.

"Personal business," Andrew replied, remembering that in some corners of the Empire, strangers spoke to each other without any formal introduction. He changed the subject before the man asked any more questions. "What are these vessels?" Andrew indicated the group of large, double-decked paddle steamers that lay in the river.

"Irrawaddy Flotilla Company ships," the civilian said. "It's a Scottish company managed by Henderson in Glasgow, although the operational headquarters are here in Rangoon," he jerked a thumb to a light-coloured, colonnaded building.

"Interesting vessels," Andrew said.

"They are," the civilian seemed happy to talk, including Mariana in his answer. "The company builds them in Glasgow, dismantles them and sends them over here. They put them back together in the company's shipyard at Dalla, across the river."

"That's a clever system," Andrew said. He saw the driver place the final case in the back of the bullock cart. "Good day to you."

"And to you, sir," the man lifted his hat to Mariana again, smiled and strode away, straight-backed and swinging his cane.

"What a pleasant man," Mariana remarked.

"He was," Andrew said. "On we go, driver."

The Wells Britannia Hotel stood near the northern edge of Rangoon, with a Union Flag hanging from a pole in front and a smartly uniformed commissionaire standing at the entrance. The driver pulled the bullock cart to a stop on the street outside, allowing Andrew and Mariana time to view the building. Teak built and two storeys high, it had large windows with verandas facing the front, a garden extending around the sides and back, and three European civilians waiting outside.

"It looks all right," Mariana had wondered about the hotel since they left Berwick. "I rather thought it might be an Army barracks."

"I'm glad it's not," Andrew replied.

"I'll take your baggage," the commissionaire announced, snapped his fingers, and handed the luggage to two small boys who ran eagerly forward. They lifted the bags with a skill that told of long experience.

"Thank you," Mariana responded with a tired smile as Andrew fished in his pocket for a tip. Unsure of the local customs, he handed a British penny to each youngster and a silver threepenny bit to the commissionaire, which seemed to satisfy everybody.

The hotel interior was impressive, with a mixture of traditional Burmese and British architecture, palm trees in large pots and a fan spinning slowly from the ceiling. A teak pillar stretched to the ceiling, with the lower third beautifully carved into the figure of a long-eared Buddha. An elderly Burmese woman sat straight-backed on a teak chair beside the Buddha, watching everything and everybody.

"This is nice," Mariana commented, looking around.

Andrew thought of the punkah-wallah hidden in some corner, whose endless job was to pull the cord that rotated the fan. "It is nice," he agreed.

"Is Buddha their god?" Mariana asked.

"Burmese Buddhists are atheists," Andrew had studied all he could of the country while on the ship. "They don't worship Buddha, and the images represent a perfect being, with Buddhists aiming to enter Nirvana."

Mariana smiled at the elderly lady, who inclined her head gravely, inspected Andrew with bright eyes and resumed her placid scrutiny of the reception area.

Two or three military officers and a plump civilian sat at an array of cane tables and chairs. Only the civilian looked up as Andrew and Mariana walked to the reception desk while the officers read the newspapers and drank from long glasses. Andrew was surprised to see that the receptionist was female. She was also efficient and friendly.

I suspect Burma will be different from anywhere else I have visited.

"I believe we have reservations," Andrew said. "The names are Baird and Maxwell."

"Two separate and adjoining rooms," the receptionist confirmed. "Captain Andrew Baird and Miss Mariana Maxwell."

"That's correct," Andrew said.

"I have a message about you, Captain Baird," the receptionist said, reaching under the counter. She produced a slip of paper with Burmese writing on it. "I have orders to contact Mr Wells when you book in. Excuse me, please."

Perhaps Bo Thura already knows we have arrived. Andrew glanced around the reception area, searching for anybody who might look suspicious. Nobody caught his attention.

"Mr Wells?" Mariana repeated.

"Please wait here, Captain Baird and Miss Maxwell." When the receptionist rang a small brass handbell, a teenage boy dressed in a scarlet uniform appeared. The receptionist spoke sharply to him in Burmese, and he scampered away to a carved side door.

"I won't keep you a moment," the receptionist promised.

"Find a seat," Andrew said, guiding Mariana to

one of the empty tables and pulling back a chair for her. They sat under the fan, with the palm trees giving the reception area a calm atmosphere. The civilian smiled and raised a hand in acknowledgement as the elderly lady watched everything.

After three minutes, the side door opened.

"Captain Baird!"

The man who approached had a face tanned by the sun and a military bearing despite his sixty or so years. He wore a European-style suit and extended his hand in greeting.

"That's correct," Andrew admitted.

"Edmund Wells," the man shook Andrew's hand with a powerful grip. His eyes were old and wise yet bright with life. Andrew realised he had underestimated the man's age by at least a decade. "I had a telegram telling me you were on your way."

"And Miss Maxwell," Edmund Wells bowed, took Mariana's hand, and held it gently.

"A telegram?" Mariana repeated. "Who sent a telegram?"

"General Windrush," Wells said. "I knew him when he was a lieutenant in the 113th Foot. We fought together back in '52." He grinned, showing surprisingly white teeth. "I was a sergeant then."

"What did the general say?" Andrew asked cautiously. He wondered what tales ex-Sergeant Wells had to tell.

Wells remained standing beside the table until Andrew gestured for him to sit down.

"General Windrush told me his son and his son's lady friend were coming to stay," Wells slid into one of the cane chairs with all the suppleness of youth. "He asked me to ensure you were comfortable and well looked after."

"That was kind of him," Andrew said.

"I have your room ready, Captain," Wells said.

"Two rooms," Andrew reminded as Mariana glanced at him.

"Two adjacent rooms," Wells agreed. "Please come with me, Captain and Miss Maxwell."

As Andrew passed the elderly lady, he saw her smile briefly at Wells before resuming her serene gaze over the reception area. Wells led them up the highly polished teak stairs to the upper floor, where a dozen numbered doors gleamed, and the scent of sandalwood lingered.

"This is lovely," Mariana approved.

"Mrs Wells ensures everything is to a high standard," Wells murmured as he walked, soft-footed, to the end of the corridor.

The rooms were clean and as well-appointed as any quality hotel in Britain. Both enjoyed views over the impressive Shwedagon Pagoda, with the sun reflecting from the gilding.

"That's beautiful," Mariana said.

"It is rather, isn't it?" Wells agreed. "Ask my wife

about it; Myat knows far more about that sort of thing than I do."

"Is your wife Burmese?" Mariana did not hide her surprise.

"She is," Wells said. "Myat Lay Phyu's her name and she's the best businesswoman you'll ever meet. I may be the face of the hotel, but Myat makes all the decisions. You'll see her sitting beside the Buddha in the hallway, seeing everything without intruding."

Andrew nodded. "I read that Burmese women are skilled at business."

Wells smiled. "Britain could learn a lot from Burma," he said. "The societies for women's suffrage could come here and learn what potential women can have in the commercial world."[1]

Andrew watched as a couple of young porters deposited their luggage on the floor and left without expecting a gratuity. Wells waited until the porters had vacated the room.

"We don't want our customers to think they are obliged to pay extra," Wells said. "It's Myat's idea. That's one reason why businessmen return here time after time." He held Andrew's gaze and added meaningfully. "We are also the most discreet hotel in Ran-

---

1. Societies for women's suffrage were founded in Edinburgh, Manchester, and London in 1867 following the 1866 Reform Bill, which failed to grant women the vote.

goon. What happens in the Wells Britannia stays within these walls."

Wells knows about Bo Thura. "I understand, Mr Wells," Andrew said.

"You have a lovely hotel, Mr Wells," Mariana said.

"Thank you, Miss Maxwell," Wells replied with a smile and a slight bow.

"Now, Captain Baird, I doubt you are here as a tourist," Wells turned his bright eyes onto Andrew. "I followed your father's career as he advanced to his present position, and I suspect you are made in the same mould. After over thirty years of living in Burma, there's not much I don't know about the place, so if you have any questions, don't hesitate to ask." He smiled. "Nothing you say or ask will go any further, Captain. As I said, discretion is another reason this hotel is successful."

Wells extracted a small envelope from his inside pocket as he spoke, and pressed it into Andrew's hand. "This arrived for you, Captain."

"Thank you." Andrew had half-expected a message. He ripped open the envelope, with Mariana watching curiously.

"What is it, Andrew?" Mariana asked.

Andrew handed her the single slip of paper inside, with the name *Mandalay* written, together with *immediately*.

"Thank you, Mr Wells. I must get to Mandalay

as soon as possible," Andrew said. "What is the best way?"

"The best way or the fastest way?" Wells asked. "The two are not the same."

"The fastest way. It may be a matter of life or death."

Wells only considered for a moment. "If you choose the fastest way, you are only twenty-four hours from the Frontier of Upper Burma," he said. "If you take the nine o'clock train from Rangoon in the evening, you'll reach the railhead at Prome at six tomorrow morning. From Prome, you can catch the Flotilla steamer up the Irrawaddy at ten, giving you four hours to kick your heels in the town. The steamer reaches Thayetmyo at four in the evening, and you are about nine miles from the frontier. You can hire a boat from Thayetmyo to Mandalay. The alternative is to wait for the direct steamer from Rangoon to Mandalay. It takes days longer, but it's far more comfortable."

Andrew glanced at Mariana, who looked suddenly nervous. "How hard is it to hire a boat at Thayetmyo?"

"That depends on how much money you have," Wells replied. "There's a man named Jamieson who runs a launch and doesn't ask questions."

"Jamieson," Andrew filed the name in his mind. "Are there border posts for inspections, customs and the like?"

Wells shook his head. "Nothing like that. Look for a line of white conoid pillars; that's all that marks the frontier. You might see a police post here and there if you are lucky. They are thin on the ground, as are the Army patrols. A couple of companies of the 21st Foot, the Royal Scots Fusiliers, guard the border with about one man for every hundred miles."

Andrew nodded. "Thank you, Mr Wells. I'll stay here for a day to ensure Mariana is settled in and then head for Mandalay."

Wells nodded. "Myat and I will keep an eye on Miss Maxwell," he said. "Be careful up there. King Thibaw does not love us."

"I'll do my best," Andrew felt Mariana's gaze.

I am not concerned about myself; I have been in wild and hostile territory before. I am worried about leaving Mariana alone in Rangoon. I am glad that Wells knew my father, although he is rather old to care for Mariana; he's more like a grandfather than a father figure.

"I hoped we might have more time in Rangoon before you left," Mariana said when Wells left the room.

"So did I," Andrew replied. "The sooner I leave, the sooner I return."

"Yes," Mariana said and retreated to her room.

CHAPTER 4

RANGOON, BURMA, SEPTEMBER 1884

They spent the next day unpacking Mariana's baggage and getting to know the hotel's immediate surroundings. Andrew felt guilty about leaving Mariana behind and kept close to her, wishing he had left her safely in Berwick yet paradoxically glad they had the few extra weeks together.

"I hope you are not away too long," Mariana said as they viewed the Golden Pagoda.

"I'll be as quick as possible," Andrew assured her.

"I'll be waiting for you," Mariana told him.

Andrew nodded. He hated partings but knew he had no choice. As Kerr had said, people in Rangoon discussed Mary MacConnacher's disappearance, expressing genuine concern about her welfare.

"I hear some terrible dacoit kidnapped her," a plump, red-faced man said. "By God, if I got my hands on him, he'd be sorry, I'll tell you!"

"Where's the Army? Why aren't they doing anything?" a thin-faced, malarial-yellow man complained. "We pay plenty of taxes for them. They are a waste of money, drunken scoundrels, the lot of them."

Andrew listened to the complaints without comment, advising Mariana never to be out at night and to remain in the safe parts of town.

"I'll be all right," Mariana assured him. "I grew up beside Zululand, remember? Rangoon is a civilised town, and Mr Wells will look after me."

In the evening, with Andrew ready for the morning's journey towards Mandalay, they ate in the hotel and settled in the lounge. Large windows afforded them a view overlooking the Golden Pagoda, where the setting sun reflected from the gold.

"That's a lovely building," Mariana said. "I imagined Burma would be like Zululand, with savage tribes, but people who can create such architecture are to be admired."

"We often learn from the people of the Empire," Andrew said. He looked around the room, not sure what to say when leaving Mariana for an indefinite period. Most of the people present were British or

European civilians, with three moustached military officers waiting to either travel up country or return to Britain on leave.

Andrew hoped to spend as much time as possible with Mariana before he left, but the tall civilian from the quayside joined them.

"Good evening to you both," the civilian said. "I didn't have time to introduce myself the other day." He held out his hand. "Jennings. Stephen Jennings of Jennings and Stanley. You may have heard the name."

"We have now," Andrew said, cursing Rangoon's informality but unwilling to appear churlish by ignoring the man. "I am Captain Andrew Baird; the lady is Miss Mariana Maxwell."

"Captain Baird and Miss Mariana Maxwell," Jennings repeated the names, slightly emphasising the word "Miss". "What a lovely name you have, Mariana."

"Why, thank you, sir," Mariana bobbed. "I was rather young to choose it myself, so I let my parents decide."

"They made a good choice," Jennings told her. "We don't often see such beauty as yours in Rangoon," he said as he sat on one of the padded cane chairs and signalled for a gin and tonic. "Oh, the Burman women are fine, up to a point."

"Up to a point?" Mariana asked, smiling at the compliment.

"Burman women are elegant, debonair, and intelligent," Jennings said. "But they lack that certain something that European women have." He sipped at his coffee and smiled at Andrew. "I am sure you agree, Captain Baird."

"I have not met many Burman women," Andrew said curtly. "Nor do I expect to meet any. I am here for one purpose, and once I have achieved that, we'll be on the next ship home."

Jennings nodded. "Perhaps," he said. "Perhaps. The East has a way of drawing one in, Captain Baird. It has a certain unexplained magnetism that holds one captive." He drank more of his coffee, smiling at Mariana. "There is a saying that one hates India for a month and then loves it forever. I can say Burma is the same; you will never forget your time here, and even if you leave, the memories, the colours, the sounds, and the atmosphere will remain with you."

Andrew saw Mariana listening intently. "Is that what happened to you, Mr Jennings?" she asked.

Jennings placed his drink on the table. "That's what happened to me," he agreed. "I came for a few weeks and can't see me ever leaving now." He smiled. "Burma has been good to me in some ways."

"In some ways? That is intriguing," Mariana said. "Do you live in Mr Wells' hotel all the time?"

"Good heavens, no!" Jennings smiled at the idea. "No. I'm meeting somebody here." He lowered his voice. "Trade is dull at present with all these dacoit raids, and King Thibaw no longer takes us seriously."

"Does he not?" Andrew thought of his impending visit to Mandalay. "What makes you say that, Jennings?"

"Our reputation is not as high as it used to be," Jennings signalled to a waiter and ordered a second cup of coffee. "Do you wish anything, Miss Maxwell? Captain Baird? No?"

"No, thank you," Mariana replied. "Excuse me, please. I must look out the window."

Jennings and Andrew rose as she swept away.

Jennings waited until Mariana was out of earshot before he spoke again. "We need a successful war to restore British prestige in Asia and Europe," he said. "It's been a bad few years for the British Army. The Zulus destroyed us at Isandlwana, the Boers humiliated us at Majuba, we withdrew from Afghanistan a few months after defeat at Maiwand, and when the Mahdi murdered Gordon, we retreated from the Sudan."

Andrew nodded. "All this is true," he said. "Up to a point." He used Jennings' terminology, remembering the slaughter and bravery in Southern Africa.

Jennings continued. "Our Army is a laughing-stock among the powers. I've heard that when some European fellows saw a unit of rather bedraggled-looking Swiss artillery returning from a field exercise, they joked that it was the British retreating from Sudan."

"We'll get back our prestige," Andrew said. "We were unfortunate at Isandlwana but redeemed ourselves at Khambula and Ulundi."

"Did we?" Jennings asked. "I don't know these battles."

Andrew did not say he had been present at both. "They were hard fought," he said, "and victorious."

"Our glorious Gordons ran away at Majuba," Jennings said. "So much for the pride of the British Army."

"Some ran," Andrew admitted. "Others fought, and many died fighting. Have you ever been in uniform?"

Jennings smiled. "Not me, old boy. I am a merchant, not a fighter."

"I see," Andrew said. He looked up as Mariana entered the room.

Jennings rose at once and pulled back a chair with a flourish. "Welcome back, Miss Maxwell. The table felt desolate without you."

"Why, thank you, sir," Mariana gave a graceful curtsey before she sat down. "One can tell the measure of a man by the compliments he gives."

Jennings bowed and sat. "Which regiment do you honour, Captain Baird?"

"The Natal Dragoons," Andrew said. "That is a colonial regiment from Natal in Southern Africa."

"Ah," Jennings nodded. "You must have seen action in the late wars."

"Some," Andrew did not elaborate. He saw Mariana lean forward with her mouth open and guessed she was going to explain what had happened. "No more than anybody else."

"Andrew saved my life," Mariana began before Andrew put a restraining hand on her shoulder.

"That was a long time ago. If you'll excuse us, Jennings, we have had rather a long day, and I fear we must retire for the night."

Jennings stood politely. "Of course, Captain. Good night, Miss Maxwell. Good night, Captain Baird."

"Good night," they replied as Andrew guided Mariana past the carved teak pillar, nodded to the ever-present Myat Lay Phyu and negotiated the curved stairs to the upper floor.

"What a charming gentleman Mr Jennings is," Mariana said as they reached their rooms. She allowed Andrew to open her door, took her key, stepped inside, and lit the lantern. Warm light reflected from the mirror over the dressing table to the comfortable bed. "How fortunate to meet a friend so soon after arrival."

"Fortunate indeed," Andrew murmured. "Goodnight, Mariana."

"Goodnight." Mariana closed the door quietly,

turned, leaned her back against it, and smiled, watching her reflection in the mirror.

We don't often see such beauty as yours in Rangoon. Mariana smoothed a hand over her hair. *What a charming man. And so handsome.*

ANDREW HEARD THE SHARP CRACK OF A FIREARM and reacted instinctively. He rolled from his bed, grabbed the revolver from its holster and glanced around the dark room. He lay on the floor for a moment with his pistol in his hand, thinking himself on the Zululand frontier or deep in the Transvaal.

Mariana!

"Mariana!" he shouted her name, and jerked himself upright, threw open the door, and dashed to Mariana's room. "Are you all right?" He heard quiet footsteps inside the room, and Mariana opened the door.

"Are you all right, Mariana?" Andrew repeated. He heard noises from within the other rooms on the landing.

Mariana stood, her nightgown reaching to her bare ankles and her hair an explosion. "Of course, I am all right. What else would I be?" She blinked at Andrew through tired eyes.

Andrew stepped inside the room and pushed the door closed as other guests peered into the corridor to see who was disturbing their peace. Jennings looked concerned as he hugged a quilted dressing gown over his broad shoulders.

I thought Jennings was only meeting somebody at the hotel. What's he up to?

Andrew stood with his back to the door. "Didn't you hear the shot?"

Mariana shook her head, causing further disarray to her hair. "I was fast asleep until you started banging on the door and shouting like a lunatic," she said irritably. "Now go back to your bed and let me get back to mine."

"As long as you are all right."

"Just go," Mariana pointed to the door.

Andrew left, feeling foolish. The revolver seemed out of place in this civilised hotel, and Jennings stood outside his door watching until Andrew returned to his room.

Was that a gunshot I heard? Or was I dreaming of past campaigns? Andrew lay on his bed, knowing he would not sleep again that night.

THE BREAKFAST ROOM WAS BUSY THE FOLLOWING morning, with Andrew and Mariana finding the last vacant table.

"Are you still grumpy?" Andrew asked Mariana.

"No," she shook her head. "I was a bit alarmed when you hammered on the door, that's all."

"Did you hear a gunshot last night?" Andrew asked Wells as he supervised the breakfast orders.

"I did not hear anything," Wells replied, shaking his head. "It might have been trouble with one of the dacoit bands. They sometimes come into Rangoon itself and run before the police arrive. Excuse me, Captain." Wells strode to the kitchen to answer another query.

"Do you mind if I join you?" Jennings stood beside the table. "You appear to have the only space available in the room."

"You are welcome, Mr Jennings," Mariana replied before Andrew spoke.

"That's very civil of you," Jennings sat down gracefully. "One feels a bit out of it sometimes."

"You told us you were here on business," Mariana reminded. "Did your business last all night?"

Jennings raised his eyebrows as if surprised Mariana had remembered. "It does occasionally. As well as a director of Jennings and Stanley, I am the Oriental agent for the British, Burma and Chinese Shipping Company," he said.

"That sounds very important," Mariana told him.

Jennings laughed self-deprecatingly. "It's not as grand as it sounds," he said. "I saw you out of your room last night, Captain Baird. Was there something I missed?"

"I thought I heard a gunshot," Andrew said.

"You may have done, although I didn't hear anything," Jennings said. "It may have been the police or the Army dealing with a *loosewallah* or a gang of dacoits."[1]

"I have heard vague rumours about dacoits," Andrew probed for as much information as possible. "I am not sure what they are."

Jennings sat back, produced a cheroot, and raised his eyebrows to Mariana. "Do you mind?"

"Not at all, Mr Jennings," Mariana said. "I rather like the aroma."

"A lady after my own heart," Jennings said, lit up and blew aromatic smoke into the air. "A dacoit can be many things," he said. "Most are ordinary villagers who have fallen on hard times, men forced to resort to stealing or brigandage to live. Once they can eat again, they may well return to the straight and narrow, at least until the next paddy failure." He smiled bleakly. "There is neither a Poor Law nor a workhouse in Burma for the desperately poor to seek sanctuary."

Mariana nodded. "Poverty is a terrible thing," she said. "If the dacoits are only desperate paupers, they can't be so bad."

Jennings drew on his cheroot. "I said that most were ordinary villagers. Others are quite the reverse.

---

1. Loosewallah – bandit, thief or general lawbreaker

Some are professional thieves and bandits, the very scum of society. They may have been outlawed for some terrible crime, or perhaps they chose a life outside society for the love of plunder and," he hesitated, "forgive my language, please, rape."

Mariana looked away. "I have heard the word before, sir," she said.

Jennings glanced at Andrew before he continued. "You have a very understanding and intelligent lady there, Baird."

"I know," Andrew agreed.

"The professional or habit-and-repute dacoit is a much more dangerous fellow than his destitute companion," Jennings said. "He will gather a band of like-minded and equally desperate men around him and select a village to plunder."

"Rather like the old Border Reivers that Sir Walter Scott wrote about," Mariana said.

"Much in the same mould," Jennings agreed. "When he has selected his intended victim village, he will approach the headman and demand a ransom or blackmail payment. If the village refuses, then the dacoit band will fall upon it with fire and sword, looting, robbing, destroying, and murdering. They may also set it on fire, and Burmese villages burn exceedingly well." He paused. "They are built of timber and bamboo, you see."

Andrew saw the interest on Mariana's face and

hoped she was not reliving the day when renegades raided and burned Inglenook.

"The dacoits won't live well if they burn everything to the ground," Mariana said.

Jennings nodded. "Quite so, Mariana, quite so. If they fail to find sufficient booty in the form of money, cattle, cloth, or valuables, they will choose some unfortunate victims and put them to the torture."

"Oh!" Mariana put a hand over her mouth.

"You may well say, oh," Jennings continued. "If they are pressed for time because, say, the police are approaching, or the villagers are reluctant to part with money, they will simply push a man's face against a tree. Once they have him secure, they'll lash his shoulders and back with a dha, their savage swords, until he has a crosscut down to the bone. After that, the unfortunate man tells all. If, however, they have time to spare, they will strip their victim of his clothes," again Jennings glanced at Mariana.

"It's all right, Mr Jennings," Mariana said quietly. "I am aware of the procedure of undressing."

"They will strip a man of his clothes, cover him from head to toe in earth oil – unrefined petroleum – and lay him in the sun. When he is cooked long enough, he will tell all he knows."

"Oh, how terrible," Mariana said. "What awful people."

"Terrible and awful indeed," Jennings agreed. He again glanced at Mariana and Andrew before continuing. "They do not restrict their endeavours to men, of course. They can also subject the gentle sex to terrible torments."

"I can only imagine," Mariana said.

"I don't want to imagine," Andrew said. "Perhaps you had better keep that intelligence to yourself."

"Pray continue, Mr Jennings," Mariana insisted, "I am not a child."

Now he was on the subject, Jennings seemed reluctant to stop. "The dacoits strip their victim quite naked and stretch her on a bamboo frame eighteen inches or so above the ground, then soak cotton in earth oil, place it beneath her and set light to it to slowly roast her."

"That's enough!" Andrew interjected roughly. "I don't wish Mariana to be subjected to any more horror stories of that kind."

Jennings leaned back. "I was merely educating the lady in the habits of the Burmese dacoits," he said. "On a less gruesome note, the dacoits also like to kidnap people and hold them to ransom, and sometimes they set fire to buildings. In fact, they are masters of every sort of crime known to man."

I know about the kidnapping. What sort of monster is Bo Thura? What sort of place have I brought Mariana to?

Mariana frowned. "What about the authorities?"

66

she asked. "Does King Thibaw permit this sort of behaviour in his land? Do the British authorities not curb such barbarities?"

"Our police and soldiers do what they can," Jennings said. "And Thibaw sends out the occasional column to exert some sort of justice," he pulled on his cheroot, "When his soldiers capture the dacoits, they summarily execute them without the tedious process of a trial or any of that civilised nonsense."

"A good hanging works wonders," Andrew murmured. "Or so I am told."

"The poor devils would welcome the noose," Jennings said. "Thibaw's soldiers crucify them."

Andrew closed his eyes. "I should have guessed it would be something like that." He put a hand on Mariana's arm.

"I am all right," Mariana smiled at his concern. "You don't need to worry about me anymore, Andrew. I am perfectly fine now."

"You look perfectly perfect to me," Jennings said.

"Why, thank you, sir," Mariana replied with a broad smile. She turned a cold shoulder to Andrew. "You had better get ready for your train, Andrew."

"Your train? Whither are you bound, my good Captain?" Jennings asked.

"Northward to Mandalay," Andrew replied.

"Ah, the Kingdom of Ava, home of the Lord of the White Elephant, the King of all Umbrella

Bearing Chiefs and so on," Jennings said. "Well, the best of British luck to you."

"Thank you," Andrew said and walked away, bowing to Myat Lay Phyu beside the pillar. She watched him go and settled back down, lighting a long cheroot.

CHAPTER 5

LOWER BURMA, SEPTEMBER 1884

Mariana stood on the platform as Andrew boarded the train for the first leg of his journey to Upper Burma. She watched him store his travelling case in the rack above the seat, then roll down the window to talk to her.

"You be careful here on your own," Andrew said. "I don't like to leave you alone."

"I'll be all right with Mr Wells," Mariana consoled him. "You're the one going into dangerous Upper Burma, not me."

Andrew smiled. "There is a sizeable European community in Mandalay. It's a civilised city with strong trading links and a regular paddle steamer service to Rangoon. Remember that Bo Thura wants to see me, so I'm in no danger."

"I hope not." Mariana took hold of her hat and stepped back as the engine emitted a whistle and a great cloud of steam. A moment later, she emerged smiling. "I always get a fright when they do that."

"So, I see. Now get back to the hotel and keep safe," Andrew said. "I expect to be a couple of weeks. No more than three, and then we'll be together again and get back to Corbiestane Tower."

"Take care!" Mariana shouted as the guard made his way down the platform, banging shut the doors and checking the passengers. There was a mixture of Burmese and European, with most of the latter British businessmen sprinkled with soldiers in uniform. As Andrew was not on official military business and would soon enter Upper Burma, he wore a light civilian suit with a broad hat. He had packed his second-best uniform safely in his travelling case.

"You take care as well," Andrew said as the train began to pull away.

Mariana saw him lean out the window, waving as the train slowly gathered speed. Then clouding steam obscured him, and all she saw was his extended arm.

"Good luck, Andrew," Mariana whispered. "I'll miss you."

Standing on the platform in an alien town, she suddenly felt devastatingly lonely. Mariana watched the train disappear into the distance, heard a last whistle of steam, and knew she was all alone.

Oh, Elaine, I wish you were with me. Mariana looked around at the bustle of the station, folded her arms, closed her eyes, and talked quietly to herself. *It's all right, Mariana. I survived captivity and the aftermath. I am in a civilised city under British control. All I must do is wait for three weeks, and Andrew will be back.*

Mariana slowly returned to the hotel, wary of anybody coming too close to her. Men, Burmese, Chinese and European, looked at her, a lone woman walking the streets, and for a moment, she wished she had remained in Berwick rather than travelled halfway across the world.

"Miss Maxwell?"

Mariana started and lengthened her stride when somebody called her name.

"Miss Maxwell? It's me, Stephen Jennings."

Without slowing down, Mariana glanced over her shoulder. Jennings smiled at her from five yards away, lifting his cane in acknowledgement.

"Good evening, Miss Maxwell. What on earth are you doing out alone?"

Mariana smiled, slowing to allow Jennings to catch up with her. "I am returning to the hotel," she said.

"Alone?" Jennings asked, raising his broad-brimmed hat. "Is Captain Baird already away to Mandalay?"

"Yes, I am alone," Mariana replied. "Captain Baird left on the morning train." She decided not to provide more details.

"Then permit me to accompany you," Jennings said. "I am also returning to the hotel."

Mariana smiled, relieved to have some company. "Thank you, Mr Jennings," she said.

Jennings nodded, swinging his cane. "Ah, I see, and you were waving goodbye to the good captain."

"Just so," Mariana agreed.

Jennings stepped beside her, keeping a respectable couple of feet between them. "When do you expect him back?"

"Whenever he completes his business," Mariana said.

Jennings smiled. "Ah, you are unsure."

"That's correct," Mariana met the smile. She was beginning to like this man with his easy manners.

"You are also unsure about me," Jennings said. "I am quite harmless, you know. If you doubt me, ask Mr Wells."

"Do you know him well?" Mariana asked.

"I know Mr Wells very well," Jennings smiled at the coincidence of words. "Most people in Rangoon know each other, you see. It's not a huge European community, so we tend to bump into one another every few days."

"Oh," Mariana moved aside, allowing a hurrying man carrying a great load of sacks to pass. "In that case, I will undoubtedly see you from time to time, Mr Jennings."

"I hope you do not find the prospect too displeasing," Jennings said.

Mariana shook her head. "I do not," she replied.

"Here we are," Jennings said. "The Wells Britannia Hotel. If you are unsure, look for the pagoda. Wells is the closest hotel to the Golden Pagoda."

"I'll remember." Talking to the affable Jennings had made the journey shorter. "Thank you for your company, Mr Jennings," Mariana said with a slight curtsey.

"You are most welcome, ma'am," Jennings responded with a quick bow. "I hope we can meet at breakfast tomorrow."

"I am sure we will," Mariana said. "In fact, I rather look forward to it."

Jennings straightened up, smiling. "So do I, Miss Maxwell. So do I. Shall I accompany you to the door of your room?"

"Thank you," Mariana said. "I think I remember the way. Until tomorrow."

"Until tomorrow, then," Jennings replied.

Mariana withdrew to her room, closed the door, and sat on her bed. She drew a map from her case and traced the route to Mandalay.

Keep safe, Andrew, she prayed. *Don't have any ad-*

ventures up there. She remembered Jennings telling them he did not stay in the hotel, wondered why he had changed his mind and brushed the thought away. *It is unimportant.*

Pulling out her journal, she wrote the morning's events, made a three-week table, and prepared to score out each day. Twenty-one seemed a great many days.

AFTER A LONG NIGHT-TIME JOURNEY BY A LESS-than-comfortable train, followed by a voyage on a crowded boat, Andrew was tired when he arrived at Thayetmyo. A bustling port on the western bank of the Irrawaddy River, the town was strategically placed between the Arakan Mountains to the west and the Pegu Hills to the east. Andrew had already come to expect the local gold-covered pagoda and the busy market, but the size of the British population was reassuring. Merchants lived in comfortable houses, with carriages and buffalo carts in the streets, traders in teak and rice chatting in small groups, and people seemingly contented. The small garrison of British soldiers and Sikh and Burmese policemen moved around the streets without fuss, quietly keeping order without seeming to intrude in civilians' lives.

Leaving his luggage in the care of the red-faced

harbour master, Andrew sought a reliable boatman to take him to Mandalay. As Wells had recommended a man named Jamieson, Andrew asked for him along the riverside.

The merchants seemed eager to help and equally willing to talk.

"Welcome to Thayetmyo," a cheerful rice merchant greeted Andrew. "The finest little town in the East."

"Is it fine?" Andrew asked. "Are you not afraid that Thibaw will invade?"

"Not a bit of it, my boy," the merchant replied. "If Thibaw comes, the Army will sort him out. The dacoits are a nuisance, but they'll fade away once we annex Upper Burma."

"Will we annex Upper Burma?" Andrew asked. He had heard other Europeans voice the same opinion.

"Eventually," the merchant said, "we can't allow such an unpleasant neighbour as Thibaw to remain on our borders, can we?"

Andrew had not responded, remembering similar statements about Cetshwayo of Zululand. Hiring a boat proved simple, with Burmese and British boatmen plying for custom.

"I'm looking for a Mr Jamieson," Andrew said as he stood at the riverside.

"Where are you bound?" a sandy-haired boatman asked.

"Mandalay," Andrew said. He expected a negative response, but the boatman didn't flinch.

"That's a fair journey. You'll need a decent vessel." The boatman glanced at his steam launch. "Like *Little Salamander* there. She'll take you anywhere you want to go."

"*Little Salamander*," Andrew examined the steam launch. Thirty-five feet long, she had a tall funnel in the stern, space for cargo and coal, and a couple of cabins. A canvas canopy shaded the deck from the sun. "She looks handy."

"She is," the boatman said, "named after HMS *Salamander*." He smiled. "She's a smaller version of the ship where I learned my trade."

"Are you Captain Jamieson?" Andrew asked.

"I am Captain Jamieson," the boatman said and pointed at a thin-faced man in his late fifties. "This gentleman is Sinclair, my mate and engineer."

Andrew nodded. He trusted Wells to give good advice. "Good afternoon to you both. I am Andrew Baird. How much would you charge to take me to Mandalay, Captain?"

Jamieson surveyed Andrew through calculating eyes. "When do you want to leave, Mr Baird?"

"As soon as possible," Andrew said.

"Tomorrow?" Jamieson sounded hopeful.

"Today would be better," Andrew said. "If you have sufficient fuel and supplies."

"We're fully loaded with both," Jamieson said.

"We can leave in an hour." He looked Andrew up and down. "Do you have the readies?"

"How much?" Andrew liked Jamieson's direct approach.

"Shall we say five guineas?" Jamieson sat in the stern of *Little Salamander*, smiling. Broad-faced and bulky in body, his beard was more grey than black.

Andrew shook his head. "Shall we say two?"

Jamieson's smile widened. "How about four guineas, then?"

"Two guineas and ten shillings?" Andrew knew he had found his boatman.

They settled on three guineas, and Andrew carried his baggage to the steam launch. Years of campaigning had taught him to travel light, so he took up little space in the minuscule cabin.

"Welcome aboard, Mr Baird," Jamieson said. "Don't get underfoot, and we'll get along fine."

"I'll keep out of your way," Andrew promised.

He heard the brassy notes of a gong in the background, wondered what they meant, and took a last look at Thayetmyo. He saw a slender Burmese man watching him from the quay and lifted a hand in acknowledgement. The man did not respond but shouted something over his shoulder and stood beside a warehouse, gazing intently at *Little Salamander*.

"Ignore him," Jamieson advised. "Many of these Burmans have nothing better to do than sit in the sun, smoke and gamble. The women are their better workers." He raised his voice and shouted to a toiling labourer carrying a heavy box, speaking fluent Burmese. "We have a long journey ahead of us, and you'll be sleeping on board at night, Mr Baird."

"Do we travel at night?"

"No," Jamieson shook his head. "Nobody sails the Irrawaddy at night. The currents are too treacherous, and what was a deep-water channel on Monday could be a sandbank on Wednesday. I won't be running *Little Salamander* aground, Mr Baird, no matter how urgent your business in Mandalay."

"I understand, Captain Jamieson," Andrew said. "Mr Wells of Rangoon recommended you, and I trust you will get me to Mandalay faster than anybody else."

Jamieson grunted. "Edmund Wells, eh? He's a good man. I'll do my best, Mr Baird. Except it isn't Mister, is it? What's your rank, soldier?"

"Captain," Andrew replied.

"You have the look and the snap of a military man," Jamieson said. "If you want to pass as a civilian in Mandalay, Captain Baird, look less efficient."

Andrew found a space on the deck where the overhead canopy provided the most shade. "I'll do my best to look inefficient," he said, listening to the regular beat of the gong. The slender Burmese man remained on the quay, watching and puffing at a long cigar.

Little Salamander left an hour later with Jamieson in the bow. The minute the steam launch eased into the river, the slender man vanished, but the gong continued.

"What do the gongs mean?" Andrew asked.

Jamieson screwed up his face. "It's a message of some sort," he said. "Maybe telling somebody that we're on our way."

"Telling who?"

Jamieson shook his head. "I don't know," he said. "The Burmans live separate lives from us. We live, and they live; we are in the same country, in the same towns, and often in the same streets, yet we are apart. Except for the people we employ or the village officials, we hardly speak, let alone discuss our businesses."

"You don't seem to employ many people," Andrew nodded to the two silent Burmese who coiled the landing line and hoisted the anchor. "Don't you need a pilot?"

"I've been working the river for thirty years," Jamieson replied. "I know it as well as any Burmese."

"I see," Andrew said, turning away to allow Jamieson to concentrate on *Little Salamander.* The Irrawaddy was busy with boats, primarily small fishing craft but also a few larger vessels. Andrew saw Jamieson move to the stern and take over the helm from a middle-aged, serious Burmese man. Jamieson steered around patches of lighter-coloured water where sandbanks had appeared and avoided stray branches that twisted and turned a few feet from the launch.

"There must have been a storm up in the hills," Jamieson said casually, gesturing to a tree trunk swirling past them. "The Irrawaddy has a strong current, but often the deep-water channel is quite narrow, so we have to be careful not to run aground."

The sound of gongs continued as they chugged upriver, with the echoes of one clanging gong no sooner fading than another took its place.

Andrew found the riverbanks interesting, with patches of dense forest between extensive paddy fields. He saw men in broad hats working with water buffalo, ignoring the river traffic as they guided the giant beasts. *Little Salamander* passed villages of bamboo-built, palm-thatched houses that sat on long poles above the river, presumably to escape the flood season, with fishing boats busy on the water. Men either worked on the river, in the fields or sat smoking or gambling, while women constantly worked or tended to the children. The more prosperous women wore satin longyis, a ubiquitous garment resembling a long skirt that men also sported. The poorer or harder working wore less clothing, as in most cultures.

Andrew began to relax into the voyage. Sinclair

was busy with the engine; Jamieson was skilled on the river, and the two Burmese boatmen were efficient and quiet. Monkeys chattered among the trees, brightly coloured birds fluttered overhead or squawked from the branches, and the thoughts of dacoits seemed like a different world from the somnolent life of the river.

I will be in Mandalay in a few days, and Bo Thura will contact me. I must try to free young Mary Mac-Connacher, but what does Bo Thura want in exchange? He shrugged. *Well, I'll find out in Mandalay. There's no sense fretting until I know the problem. That damned gong is still sounding, though.*

Andrew realised the regular beat of the gong had never stopped. Whether *Little Salamander* was moving or berthed, the single stroke had followed them along the river. *What the devil does that mean?*

Andrew lifted his head, sniffing. He smelled smoke drifting from ahead. Andrew knew immediately that it was not the smell of a cooking fire. He looked forward, seeing a few blue-grey trails across the water's surface. There were no fishing boats on this section of the river, only overhanging trees, the call of monkeys and the repetitive, single, sonorous boom of the gong.

The smoke smell increased as the boat rounded the bend of the river.

"What's happening?" Andrew felt for the pistol in the holster under his jacket.

"God knows," Jamieson replied, a cigar jammed between his teeth and his eyes focused on the water. "As I said, the Burmans have separate lives from us."

"I tell you what's happening. There's trouble ahead," Sinclair poked his head up from the engine compartment, wiping a dirty rag across his sooty forehead. "After a while out here in the East, you develop a sixth sense for trouble. The birds are quiet for a start, and the air feels heavier. Can't you feel it?"

"I can," Andrew agreed as Jamieson spat into the wind and steered *Little Salamander* around a patch of shoal water. "It was the same on the frontier in Africa. We felt the tension before anything happened."

"Aye, mebbe, aye." Jamieson slowed the steamer as a waft of smoke drifted from the bend, and Sinclair withdrew into the diminutive steer house to reappear, holding a Snider rifle. He glanced at the forest, deep green and tangled. "I don't like that gong," he said. "It's been with us since we left Thayetmyo, just the one gong passing on a message."

"What do you reckon?" Andrew asked.

"I reckon we'd better be careful," Sinclair said as he loaded the Snider, lifted it to his shoulder and aimed at the bank. "She'll do." He nodded to the revolver in Andrew's hand. "You'd better have that ready, Captain. The dacoits are not averse to attacking British boats if they think they can get away with it."

"Dacoits? Would they operate on the Irrawaddy?"

"They'd operate in the Chief Commissioner's mansion, Captain Baird," Sinclair replied. "Open a cupboard, and one could pop out, slice you open with his dha, and run off with your wallet and your wife. Except Bo Thura."

"Except Bo Thura? What's different about him?"

Sinclair grinned, holding the Snider in capable hands. "He'd prefer your horse to your wife. Bo Thura is Burma's greatest horse thief, although God knows what he does with them."

"Is that all he does?" The smoke was denser as they reached the apex of the bend, an acrid stink that nipped Andrew's eyes.

"God, no. He's like the rest; murder, rape, robbery," Sinclair nodded to the smoke. "And arson."

"Kidnapping?" Andrew asked.

"Not that I'm aware of," Sinclair replied.

Andrew shoved cartridges into his revolver as the steam launch rounded the bend. He heard chattering above and saw a troop of monkeys clinging to an overhanging branch.

"The monkeys don't look too concerned," he said.

"They're watching us too closely," Sinclair replied. "They want to see what we're up to."

"Ease up further, Sincs," Jamieson ordered. "Keep to the deep-water channel midstream."

"Aye, aye, sir," Sinclair replied formally, placed the Snider nearby and slowed the launch. The smoke grew thicker, wafting in billows across the water.

"Now you'll see what the dacoits are like," Jamieson murmured.

The village sat in smouldering ruin, with a scatter of dead bodies on the ground and the smoking remains of bamboo houses. Three fishing boats lay on the bank, one with a man's body inside it. All three were wrecked, with holes torn in the bottom. A small patrol of khaki-clad soldiers moved slowly between the buildings, with half a dozen Sikh policemen amongst them.

"You in the launch!" A slender officer waded into the river and gestured to them. "Come ashore! I want to talk to you!" He snapped an order, and the British soldiers splashed into the shallows, aiming their rifles at *Little Salamander*.

"Get in here!" the officer shouted.

CHAPTER 6

LOWER BURMA, SEPTEMBER 1884

"Here we go," Jamieson said, steering for the village. The soldiers kept their rifles trained on the launch until a worn-looking sergeant barked an order.

"Get that boat tied up."

"I'm Jamieson, captain of *Little Salamander*," Jamieson announced.

"They're British," the sergeant said. "Smith, stay with the launch. Corporal Rowan, take a patrol along the riverbank. Shoot anybody that looks suspicious."

"Yes, Sergeant." Rowan looked equally exhausted. He called up a section of eight men and headed north beside the Irrawaddy.

"Come ashore," the officer ordered. "I want to speak to you!"

"We're coming," Jamieson said. "That must mean you, too, Captain Baird."

Andrew was first in the village, followed by Sinclair and Jamieson.

The officer, a middle-aged major, eyed them sourly from behind his drooping moustache. "Who the devil are you, and where are you going?"

"Andrew Baird," Andrew said, then introduced Jamieson and Sinclair.

"Major Goudie, 21st Foot, Royal Scots Fusiliers. Can you vouch for the Burmans in your boat, Captain Jamieson?"

"I can, sir," Jamieson replied. "They've been with me for years."

"What happened here?" Andrew asked.

"Dacoits," Goudie replied laconically, glancing at the destruction. "They are getting bolder now, crossing from Upper Burma as if they can do as they like on our side of the frontier."

"What happened?" Andrew repeated.

Goudie pulled a face. "I don't know for certain," he said. "It looks as if they came last night, looted the place from Monday to Christmas, killed every man who resisted and escaped with the women." He faced Jamieson. "Did you see anything along the riverbank on your voyage upriver, Captain?"

"Nothing out of the ordinary," Jamieson replied.

"All right. They must have gone inland or upriver to Upper Burma. Be careful."

"We will," Jamieson replied.

"We never saw anything suspicious, sir," Sinclair said, "but we heard something strange."

"What was that, Sinclair?" Goudie asked. "Anything strange might signify some new trick these devils have up their sleeve."

"A gong, sir," Sinclair said. "I've been out East long enough to know that gongs are part of the culture, but I've never heard one quite like this before."

"What was it like?" the major asked.

"A single gong that followed us along the riverbank," Sinclair explained. "Just the one gong, as if it was passing a message, telling somebody where we were."

The major sighed. "I've never heard of that before. You'd better be careful out there."

"It's still sounding," Andrew lifted a hand. "Listen."

Goudie lifted his head and frowned as the gong sounded its single brassy note. "So it is, by God. However, there's nothing illegal about banging a gong. It might be completely unrelated to the dacoits." He looked at Andrew. "You haven't told me your reason for travelling to Mandalay, Baird."

"It's a personal matter, sir." Andrew had decided not to mention Bo Thura or Mary MacConnacher. He did not want his family history broadcast, nor did he want anybody to know the purpose of his mission until he had spoken to Bo Thura.

"Ah," Goudie was too much of a gentleman to pry. He smiled as a musket banged, followed by the sharper report of a rifle. "It sounds like my lads have contacted the dacoits."

Andrew instinctively slid behind one of the smouldering houses as a bullet zipped past, to thud into the ground. More musketry followed, with spurts of smoke in the surrounding forest and fountains of dust rising around the major.

The corporal returned with his patrol, his helmet awry and sweat streaking his face. He snapped orders that saw his men take cover, facing outward. "There must be a hundred of them, sir. They fired too soon, so I ordered the boys to fire a volley and retired on the village."

"Quite right, Corporal!" Goudie approved. He raised his voice. "Form up on the village, lads! Police as well!" He glanced at Jamieson. "We have an unknown number of dacoits along the riverbank, Jamieson, and the deep-water channel runs close to the bank for the next few miles. I'd advise you to remain where you are until we clear the dacoits."

Jamieson nodded. "Yes, sir." He glanced at Andrew. "The channel doesn't only pass close inshore here, Captain Baird; there's also a stronger than usual four-knot current. *Little Salamander* would only make a couple of knots at best, less than walking speed."

"We'd be a sitting target for the dacoits," Sinclair added. "Best wait until the swaddies have chased them away."[1]

"Captain?" The officer looked at Andrew.

"Captain Andrew Baird of the Natal Dragoons," Andrew explained.

"Natal Dragoons?" the officer repeated. "What the devil is a colonial African cavalryman doing up the Irrawaddy River? Never mind; you'd best keep your head down, Baird."

"I can help defeat these dacoits," Andrew decided. "I must get to Mandalay as quickly as possible. What's your plan?"

"Have you seen any action, Captain?" Goudie asked.

"Yes, sir. Three campaigns, including the Zulus and the Boers," Andrew replied.

"Were you at Rorke's Drift?"

"No, sir. Khambula, Isandhlwana and Ulundi," Andrew replied.

"Isandhlwana?" Goudie repeated. "You survived that?"

Andrew nodded. He had noticed that people

---

1. Swaddies- soldiers. A slang term usually pronounced as squaddies in the 20th and 21st centuries.

looked at him strangely when he mentioned surviving Isandhlwana as if he had no right to be alive.

Maybe they are right. Far too many good men died that day.

"In that case, Captain Baird, a few dacoits shouldn't present a problem," Goudie said. "Take two sections of Fusiliers and a police platoon to hold the outer perimeter."

"Yes, sir," Andrew replied.

I started my career as a colonial policeman. My world has moved full circle.

Andrew counted the British soldiers and Sikh policemen as they formed up in the village. Twenty-two Royal Scots Fusiliers and twenty Sikhs.

The Sikhs looked like a stalwart bunch, tall men with red turbans and neat beards. The havildar in charge spoke English and eyed Andrew suspiciously, wondering what right a civilian had to give him orders.

"I am Captain Andrew Baird of the Natal Dragoons," Andrew introduced himself. "I want you in extended order around the edge of the village. Keep under cover, or the enemy will use you as targets."

The havildar frowned. "We are not cowards to hide from dacoits and badmashes," he said.[2]

"No, you are Sikh policemen," Andrew remem-

---

2. Badmash – rogue, thief, robber. Havildar: the equivalent of a sergeant.

bered his father's constant praise of the Sikhs. "You are too valuable to be killed by some dacoit's bullet." He saw the havildar's brown eyes widen as he digested his words.

"Yes, Sahib," the havildar replied, telling his men what Andrew had said.

The Sikhs found shelter, peering through the smoke into the surrounding forest. The Fusiliers were already in position, aiming their Martinis at the forest fringe. On the flank, the corporal's section was engaged in sporadic fighting, with the heavy crack of their rifles contrasting with the duller thud of muzzle-loading muskets and an occasional Dacoit's shout.

In the intervals between the gunfire, Andrew heard the regular beat of the gong. Invisible and unhurried, the brassy notes acted as a surreal backdrop to the skirmish.

"It's unusual for dacoits to face up to armed police, let alone the Army," Goudie said. "They're getting very bold. I'd say somebody up there is backing them." He jerked a thumb to the north.

"Somebody?" Andrew repeated. "Do you suspect King Thibaw?"

"A man who murdered all his relatives to secure his succession to the throne is capable of anything," Goudie said. "Can you hold the fort, Baird, while I lead a fighting patrol along the riverbank?"

"Yes, sir," Andrew said, looking along his defensive line. The men were steady, Fusiliers and Sikhs side by side, waiting and occasionally firing.

"What's your name, Havildar?" Andrew asked.

"Sukhbir Singh, sahib," the Havildar sounded surprised at the question.

"Well, Sukhbir, I want you to choose five of your best men and form a support unit ready to reinforce wherever you are required."

"Yes, sahib."

"I don't know how dacoits fight," Andrew confessed, "but we have a thinly protected firing line, and if they rush us and break through, you'll be our last line of defence."

"Yes, sahib." Sukhbir seemed pleased at the responsibility, as Andrew suspected he would.

Goudie led from the front, passing through Corporal Rowan's section and pressing on. The Fusiliers held their Martinis with the casual familiarity of veterans. A few looked at home in the forest, while most were clumsy, making too much noise for Andrew's liking.

With proper training, these Fusiliers could be good soldiers. Lift your feet, lads, and watch for dry twigs.

The sporadic firing ended, with the waiting British and Sikhs watching the forest.

"Is that something over there, on the right?" a Glasgow voice asked.

"Aye, it's a bloody tree, Wullie. And there's another on the left. Close your mouth and keep your finger on the trigger."

Andrew smiled, happy to hear the Royal Scots Fusiliers had the same dark humour as the other British regiments with whom he had served.

The Sikhs were silent, holding their Sniders, hoping to see the dacoits. Andrew could sense their eagerness.

The Sikhs are desperate to fight. They want to prove themselves, like the knights in King Arthur's Round Table. He grinned at the thought of Sir Lancelot wearing a turban, wondering what Mariana would think of that and if he was slightly mad.

I must be mad; no sane man would become a soldier.

The monkeys were back, chattering in the trees, and Andrew realised he could still hear the gong.

It's never been silent since we left Thayetmyo. What the devil is that all about?

"Sahib," Sukhbir Singh stepped to his side. "The badmashes are out there." He pointed with his bearded chin. "I can feel them."

Andrew looked beyond the small fields to the forest surrounding the village's small fields, trying to penetrate the trees with his eyes. He saw nothing but green vegetation until something moved.

Human or animal?

Damn it, I've fought Zulus, Boers and Galekas; surely I can see a handful of damned badmashes in a few trees.

Andrew slowly raised his revolver, wishing he had a rifle. With its rapid fire, a revolver was fine for close-quarter work but had no penetration at any range over thirty yards. He watched the movement in the trees, mentally calculating speed, size, and distance.

If a dacoit is aiming at me now, he has all the advantages. Is that damned gong still sounding? Yes, it is.

Andrew sensed Sukhbir Singh tensing at his side and saw two police aiming at the same part of the forest.

"Wait," he said softly.

Are these Burmans going to attack us? Or are they laying an ambush for Major Goudie's patrol when it returns? If they catch Goudie in the open fields, they could inflict considerable casualties.

"Who is the best shot of your men, Havildar?" Andrew asked.

"Ajit Singh, sahib," Sukhbir replied.

"Very well. I want him to target that man in the trees and fire a single shot."

Sukhbir nodded and passed on Andrew's message.

Andrew saw the smallest policeman take careful aim into the forest and fire. The Snider cracked, smoke spurted, and Andrew saw leaves jerk among the trees. He heard a startled cry and a commotion behind the forest fringe.

Well done, Ajit. Now we know they are dacoits.

"On my word, fire a volley," Andrew ordered,

"but not parallel to the riverbank in case Major Goudie is leading the patrol back." He waited until Sukhbir passed on his message to the Sikhs and then did the same to the Fusiliers.

"We're ready, sir," an auburn-haired, steady-eyed corporal replied.

"What's your name, Corporal?"

"McGhee, sir," the corporal replied.

"On my word, McGhee."

Andrew gave his men a few more seconds.

"Fire!"

The Fusiliers fired together, as expected, and loaded without orders, waiting expectantly. Although the Sikhs were police rather than soldiers and were spread all around the perimeter of the village, the volley crashed out with near-military precision. Andrew saw leaves and twigs fly as the bullets crashed home and heard a long shriek as one found its mark.

"Another volley," Andrew ordered. "Fire!"

The Sikhs had also reloaded and fired another volley but without any sound from the dacoits.

They've either withdrawn or taken deep cover. Let's see if we can winkle them out.

"Cease fire!" Andrew ordered. "Corporal McGhee! Take a section into the trees, only a hundred yards, see what's there and return. Keep your men together, and don't leave any behind."

God knows what the dacoits would do to any British prisoners.

"Yes, sir!" McGhee led his men in open order, jinking and weaving across the fields in case the dacoits were waiting in ambush. Andrew heard them crashing around with hoarse shouts as they hunted through the thick bush.

I wish you were better trained in forest fighting, lads.

After ten minutes, Andrew heard a single shot, a coarse laugh, and McGhee returned with the patrol. They crossed the fields at a trot, with two men as rearguard, circling to scan the forest as they moved.

Corporal McGhee approached Andrew, saluted, and made his report.

"We found one dead dacoit, sir, and one shot through the stomach. The wounded man made a lunge at Private Halloran with his knife, and Halloran shot him."

"Very good, Corporal. Return to your post."

"Yes, sir," McGhee replied. "Come on, lads!"

Sukhbir watched the soldiers with what Andrew suspected was jealousy that his men were not involved.

You're policemen, Havildar, not soldiers.

Andrew toured the perimeter, trying to ignore the insects that tormented him and the insistent, regular beat of the gong.

"All right, lads?"

"All right, sir. All Sir Garnet."[3]

Andrew nodded. "Carry on, Fusiliers."

When Andrew returned to his central position, a volley sounded from along the riverbank, followed by a scatter of shots. Musket fire was mixed with the ear-splitting crack of Martinis, proving that both British and dacoits were firing. Andrew saw the Sikhs look towards the sound, with some men grinning and others lifting their Sniders as if to help.

These lads are natural soldiers.

The firing rose in intensity, then died away to an irregular spatter, followed by another two volleys in proximity. Andrew heard a cheer and then a few shots and then silence.

Major Goudie has met the dacoits.

Andrew listened; even the monkeys were silent, with only the rush and gurgle of the river as a backdrop and that incessant, frustrating, slow-banging gong.

"Shall I take a patrol along, sir?" McGhee asked. "The boys are wondering what's the to-do."

"No," Andrew shook his head. "You might be needed here if the dacoits double back."

"Yes, sir," McGhee replied.

---

3. All Sir Garnet: a British Army phrase of the late Nineteenth Century, meaning everything was all right. It was a reference to General Sir Garnet Wolseley, who was reputed to be Britain's best general of the period.

Major Goudie was the first to return to the village with his men marching at his back. One Fusilier was limping, with blood on his thigh, and the others were in high spirits despite the sweat that soaked their uniforms and the insects clouding around their heads.

"Did you see that dacoit jump when I shot him? The bullet lifted him clean off his feet."

"You shot him, be buggered man! That was my shot. Right in the chest."

"If you line two up together, one bullet does for both."

"We heard shooting," Goudie said to Andrew.

"We chased off a group of dacoits," Andrew replied, "and Corporal McGhee took a patrol into the forest."

"We met your dacoits," Goudie said. "They ambushed us, and we retaliated and charged them with the bayonet."

That would be the cheer we heard.

"Did you catch many?" Andrew asked.

"Hunting dacoits is like catching smoke with a fishing net," Goudie said. "One minute they're there, and the next they're elsewhere. Occasionally, we get hold of one, but when we do, we can be sure it's only some benighted villager looking for a few handfuls of rice and not one of the professional robbers."

"Is it safe for us to continue?" Andrew asked.

Goudie nodded. "I'd say so," he said. "I doubt

they linger along this stretch of the river. We inflicted a few casualties and scared them away for now, at least until Thibaw sends them back."

"Were they Thibaw's men?" Andrew asked.

"Probably," Goudie replied. "He sends them into British Burma to rob, murder, rape and generally commit mayhem. We shoot a few, capture others, and our judges release them on some pretext or other, and the whole thing starts again." He sighed. "I'd like to have captured the leader of that band, Baird. I glimpsed him through the trees, an ugly-looking devil with a gold-hilted dha. I'll keep my eyes open for him in the future."

"Yes, sir," Andrew added the information to his store. *I wonder if that was Bo Thura?*

"You'd better be on your way if you intend to reach Mandalay," Goudie said with a tired smile. "Thank you for your help."

"It was a pleasure, sir," Andrew said.

CHAPTER 7

LOWER BURMA, SEPTEMBER 1884

"Andrew?" Mariana stirred in her bed.

I heard somebody moving; I am sure I did.

Rising quickly, Mariana reached for the small revolver Andrew had given her on the voyage to India.

"You know how to fire a rifle," Andrew had said. "Can you fire a pistol?"

When Mariana replied in the negative, Andrew demonstrated the basics and made her practise every day, firing from the passenger deck at objects he threw in the sea. Mariana's first few efforts had been poor, with the bullets raising splashes yards from the target, but she had improved with practice and became an adequate pistol shot.

Now, Mariana blessed these forced sessions and held the revolver, peering into the dark. For one terrifying moment, her treacherous mind dragged her back to Inglenook, with the raiders breaking in and Elaine fighting and then screaming.

No, Mariana told herself. *That's past.* She took a deep breath, stepped away from the bed and strode to the window, revolver in hand. She dragged back the curtains, saw moonlight above the Golden Pagoda, and checked that the room was empty.

I am imagining things. Andrew's hardly been away, and my mind is playing tricks on me.

The sound of male laughter came to her, and she recognised Jennings' voice.

Don't go far, Mr Jennings. Stay close until Andrew returns. Mariana replaced the revolver under her pillow and lay on the bed, knowing she would not sleep. Memories of Inglenook returned, with every sound reminding her of the night the renegades came and that black hole in her memory, hinting at forgotten horrors.

"HAVE YOU FINISHED SOLDIERING FOR THE DAY?" Jamieson spoke around a large Burmese cigar.

"I have," Andrew replied.

"We'll get going then," Jamieson said. "We'll get a

few miles upriver before night and sleep on board tonight, mid-river."

Andrew nodded and stepped on board the launch. Sinclair had returned to *Little Salamander* to keep steam up, so they were back in the deep-water channel within ten minutes. The Fusiliers and police watched them leave without emotion.

"There's that gong," Jamieson said as they eased away from the still-smoking village.

The brassy clang followed them, a single stroke every fifteen seconds, sounding above the rush of the river and the engine's reassuring chug.

"It's following us," Andrew said, peering into the forest without seeing anybody. He took charge of the Snider and watched the riverbank as *Little Salamander* steamed only twenty yards from the trees.

"Maybe," Jamieson clamped his cigar between his teeth and concentrated on his steering, with his smoke adding to the smuts from the funnel. "Whoever's banging the gong can't be dangerous, though. If they meant us any harm, they'd have shot us when we were ashore."

Although Andrew nodded, he was relieved when the deep-water channel veered away from the bank to mid-channel, and they were further from potential danger. Even out here, with birds singing and the river much broader, he could still hear the sonorous beat of the gong.

"How far is the frontier?" Andrew asked. He

heard the Burmese fireman shovelling coal down below.

"Not far," Jamieson replied. "There's a tricky bit of navigation ahead first, and then you'll see the Burman frontier posts."

Little Salamander steamed on, threading between a group of islands and sandbanks as the river broadened. Jamieson sent one of the crew into the bow to cast the lead and report the depth of water.

"The channels alter here," Jamieson explained. "They could be shallow one trip and deep the next. We must be careful and read the river."

This stretch of water would be a good place for an ambush, Andrew thought, watching the islands with his rifle ready. A flotilla of fishing boats hugged the western bank, with men watching the steam launch chug slowly past.

"General rule," Jamieson spoke around his cigar, expelling spurts of smoke with every word. "The broader the river, the shallower the water and the more likely large vessels will run aground. The narrower the river, the faster the current and more difficult to push against." He removed his cigar to glance at Andrew. "The faster the current, the slower the ship travels and, therefore, the easier target for dacoits hiding in the forest."

When they passed the islands, Andrew unloaded the Snider and replaced it on its brackets in the wheelhouse. The deep-water channel was more central here as the river alternated between broad and narrow, with some gentle curves. He looked up as they rounded a bend, and a white fort glowered down at them.

"What's that place?" Andrew asked.

"We've just passed the frontier," Jamieson said. "That fort is Kulogon or Kuliyang, especially erected by Thibaw's pet Italian engineer. Take your pick of the name; the defensive work on the opposite bank is Minhla. These are King Thibaw's guardian posts."

Andrew lifted his binoculars and studied both fortifications with a soldier's eye. "If Thibaw puts in a couple of strong garrisons and adds some artillery, these redoubts could be tough to take." He grunted. "A couple of hundred Boer riflemen could hold them against anything except an ironclad ship and heavy artillery."

Jamieson nodded. "Maybe so," he said. "As far as I am aware, Thibaw doesn't have any Boer riflemen, although, as I mentioned, a couple of Italian engineers work for him. Nor do we have an ironclad ship or heavy artillery in Burma."

Andrew lowered his binoculars. "I hope we never need them."

"We might if we ever war with the Lords of the White Elephant, the King of all Umbrella Bearing Chiefs, the Lord of Earth and Air or whatever Thibaw calls himself these days."

"Will that happen?" Andrew asked.

"You've only been in Burma a few days," Jamieson said. "Yet you have already been involved with the dacoits. How much longer will Britain stand for a semi-barbarian king who deliberately sends bands of badmashes[1] into our territory?"

"That's the price we pay on every Imperial frontier," Andrew replied. "The Cape Colony, Natal, Egypt, Northwest India. We butt against the semi-civilised or uncivilised wherever we are."

"Why did we invade Zululand?" Jamieson asked. "To protect our frontier farms from such incursions. Why did we have so many wars along the Cape Colony border or the Northwest Frontier? The same reason: we wish to protect the people in lands we administer from the half-civilised folk next door." He issued a smart order that saw *Little Salamander* alter course to avoid a floating log. "War with the King of Ava is coming, mark my words. He's a nasty little piece, and his mother-in-law and that devil Maung Thandar, one of his ministers, have him under their grubby thumbs. The only way we can have peace is to have an open war and occupy the whole damned country."

"Or leave it," Andrew said. *I've seen enough of war.*

Jamieson nodded. "Or leave it to its own devices. And what would happen then?"

"I really don't know," Andrew said.

---

1. Badmash: thief, robber, criminal.

"Either the French would move in, and they're already knocking at the side door over in Tonkin, or the Chinese would invade, or Thibaw would continue to send his dacoits." Jamieson drew deeply on his cigar. "He could do that until we decide the game's not worth the candle, as we did in the American colonies. If we pulled out of Burma, we'd lose a hell of a lot of trade, and our entire eastern frontier would be aflame with dacoits. Burma itself would be a nightmare for the people, with perpetual civil war and cruelty."

"Is that what would happen?" Andrew asked.

"I believe so," Jamieson said. "If we leave Burma, we'd have let the Burmese people, the folk we've sworn to protect and govern, very badly down by handing them to a monster."

"Is it that bad?" Andrew asked.

"It's that bad." Jamieson shook his head. "Gladstone has a point. Once we've started on this Imperial lark, we just get deeper and deeper embroiled in other people's troubles that we have to sort out. Take it from me, Baird; empire building is a mug's game, best avoided."

"I'll be sure to tell Her Majesty and Salisbury [2] that when next I meet them," Andrew said.

---

2. Robert Gascoyne-Cecil, 3rd Marquess of Salisbury, was the leader of the Conservative party and became Prime Minister in 1886.

Jamieson smiled. "You're right, Captain Baird; people like you and I don't have much say in this world. We must just make the best of whatever hand the good Lord sees fit to deal us."

"We all have to do that, Captain Jamieson," Andrew said. He looked north, deeper into Thibaw's Kingdom of Ava, and wondered what lay ahead.

"YOU LOOK STUNNING TODAY," JENNINGS SAID AS Mariana stood in the hotel's foyer after breakfast.

"Thank you," Mariana replied. "I thought you didn't stay in the hotel."

"I breakfast here sometimes," Jennings said. "I like the conversation, and my humble house can become lonely with only the servants for company. Have you recovered from yesterday's scare?"

"Quite recovered, thank you," Mariana replied.

"That is good," Jennings said. "What are your plans for today?"

"I don't have a plan," Mariana said. "I was going to look at Rangoon, maybe go inside the pagoda if the monks don't object."

"I have some free time from my work," Jennings said. "It might be better if a man accompanied you." He smiled. "I know I cannot match the gallant Captain Baird, but it can be daunting for an Englishwoman alone in a strange city. Rangoon is not some quiet English market town, you see, or London, with a policeman at every street corner."

Mariana laughed. "I am quite used to strange places," she said. "I grew up in Natal, on the Zululand border, so I am not at all daunted by non-English people. Indeed," she widened her eyes. "Andrew and I have recently been to Scotland."

Jennings laughed, shaking his head. "Scotland! How exotic! That was daring of you moving amongst these primitive people."

Mariana smiled. "I can be a daring woman," she replied. "Sometimes I even talk to strange men in hotels."

"That is daring," Jennings agreed with a smile. "This strange man suggests he takes you to see the Golden Pagoda. It's quite an interesting place, Miss Maxwell."

"I am sure it is, Mr Jennings," Mariana said. "And you would be scintillating company. However, I will not accompany you today."

"As you wish, Miss Maxwell," Jennings bowed. "I wish you a very good day."

"Thank you, Mr Jennings," Mariana said. "I wish the same for you."

I don't think it is respectable to have another man accompany me so soon after Andrew has gone to Mandalay.

After a brief farewell to Wells, Mariana left the hotel and headed for the Golden Pagoda. She moved slowly, allowing herself time to absorb Rangoon's atmosphere. The streets were busy with traders, with an occasional farmer with his squeaking bullock cart, the ubiquitous array of laughing children, European, Burmese, and Chinese merchants, and dignified women.

The men were sturdy, mostly barefoot, often wearing the same simple longyi as the women, and seemed content to move without associating with the Europeans. Mariana noticed that women managed retail businesses with a freedom denied in most other countries. The trading women wore graceful clothes, and nearly all, prosperous or poor, wore large, hooped earrings, with some carrying cheroots in large holes in their ear lobes.

I won't be adopting many Burmese fashions, Mariana thought. *The dresses are too revealing, the way they cling to the women's bodies, the condition of their ear lobes is disgusting, and I don't like to see women smoking cheroots. I can't see myself smoking a cheroot as I walk around Berwick with gold-hooped earrings bouncing on my shoulders.*

Mariana stifled her laugh and realised that three Burmese men were watching her. She smiled at them without response and walked away, not picking any direction, yet hoping to reach the pagoda.

After a few moments, Mariana heard a high-pitched giggle behind her and looked over her shoulder. The three men were twenty yards away and following her.

Mariana quickened her pace, not yet alarmed but prepared to run. The street seemed to stretch forever, with the houses on either side becoming more ramshackle every ten steps. Men sat in the shade, smoking or gambling, watching her without interest.

I'm heading in the wrong direction. I want to return to the town centre.

Mariana turned around and saw the three Burmese only ten yards away, grinning. They looked dangerous, one with a long knife at his side and all three bare-chested and showing tattoos on their equally bare thighs.

What do they want with me? They would not dare follow if Andrew was here.

Mariana increased her speed again until she was nearly running, with the sound of her feet echoing from the buildings on either side of the street.

A crowd gathered on the street at Mariana's right, men and women who watched her and spoke together. A pack of dogs began to bark, showing their teeth, and a gaggle of children pointed to her and laughed, with one small boy jumping up and down.

What's so amusing about me? Is it laugh at the funny foreigner time?

The three men were closer now, ten yards away, with the central man holding the hilt of his knife. Mariana took a deep breath, wondering if she could outrun them or stand and fight. She knew she could not overpower three men but hoped the noise she made would attract some help.

Do they intend to rob me? Or worse?

I am not scared. Why am I not scared? What would Tennyson say?

"Though we are not now that strength which in old days moved earth and heaven, that which we are, we are; one equal temper of heroic heart."

I am not of heroic heart.

Standing with her back to the nearest building, Mariana faced the three men and raised her voice. "What do you want?"

They barely glanced at her as they walked past, laughing at some private joke.

Mariana let out her breath slowly as the children began to play a game, and one of the women smiled at her.

"Are you lost, Miss Maxwell?" Jennings strode towards her, smiling and swinging his Malacca walking cane.

"Not any longer, Mr Jennings," Mariana did not hide her relief. "For I am sure you will show me the way back to the hotel."

The pagoda will wait. I've had sufficient adventuring for one day.

"That will be my pleasure, Miss Maxwell." Jennings touched a hand to his hat. "It's easy to take a wrong turning in a strange city. You're only a short walk away." He stepped to Mariana's side. "I know

Rangoon fairly well, as I have business with the Burmese, as well as the Europeans."

Mariana felt herself relaxing in Jennings' company. "You are a busy man, Mr Jennings."

"One should always keep oneself busy," Jennings replied seriously. "Do what one has to do with a full heart; that's my motto." He smiled across to her, revealing even white teeth behind his well-trimmed moustache. "You're an adventurous lady walking alone in a strange city. I do like a lady with spunk, I must say."

"Thank you, sir," Mariana bobbed in a curtsey. The street seemed less dark and not at all dangerous as Jennings smiled at her and tapped his cane on the ground.

"Now, let's get you back to your hotel. This way," Jennings turned up a side street and, within five minutes, showed her Wells Hotel. "There you are, Miss Maxwell. I'd advise you not to wander too much in Burma, though, not with the dacoits going around."

"Are they dangerous?"

"I've never heard of them attacking a British woman, but there aren't many for them to attack." Jennings hesitated for a moment. "If you do choose to wander, please don't hesitate to tell me. I'd be delighted, more than delighted, to escort you. I am sure Captain Baird would not mind. He'd prefer to know you are safe with me than alone in Rangoon."

"Thank you, Mr Jennings," Mariana replied politely. "I will remember your kind offer." She smiled, pushing back a loose rogue strand of hair. "I was glad to see you in that street."

"I was glad to see you, too, Miss Maxwell," Jennings touched his cane to the brim of his hat. "Now, I must be off. Business, you understand."

"Of course." Mariana lifted the hem of her skirt and hurried to the hotel. When she turned at the door, Jennings was still watching. He lifted his cane in farewell, turned and strode away, with Mariana watching his tall, elegant figure in the light suit until he vanished around a corner.

She was smiling when she walked into the hotel and nearly bounced up to her room.

If I am a part of all I have met, as Tennyson says, then I must be a part of Mr Jennings. What a strange thought. How fortunate that he was there to look after me. Mariana closed the door, stepped to the long mirror, and looked at her reflection. She straightened her hair. *That's twice Mr Jennings has been on hand. He's like a guardian angel.*

I must get some clothes more suitable for Rangoon.

CHAPTER 8

KINGDOM OF AVA, UPPER BURMA,
SEPTEMBER 1884

"What in God's name is that?" Andrew pointed to the riverbank.

A row of strange wooden frame-works lined the west bank of the river, each bearing the naked body of a man spreadeagled on top. Two men were still alive, groaning and writhing in agony as they slowly suffocated. The other eight were mercifully dead, leaning against their bonds as birds and flies feasted on their tortured flesh.

"Dacoits," Jamieson said casually. "King Thibaw, his first minister Kinwun Mingyi or Maung Thandar captured them and had them executed by crucifixion." He spat into the river. "We all know that he sends dacoits over the frontier to harass British Burma, but occasionally, he stirs his Army to catch them. When they operate on his side of the frontier, of course."

Andrew saw the suffering in the nearest victim's eyes. "Dear God in heaven," he breathed. "What sort of place is this?"

"It's Upper Burma," Jamieson said quietly. "The Kingdom of Ava. We carry passengers along the Irrawaddy and further afield for the right price, but apart from that, we don't have much to do with Thibaw's subjects or His Majesty himself." He gestured to the agonised men on the crosses. "You can see why."

Andrew nodded as *Little Salamander* eased past, with her wash creating waves that broke against the torture frameworks. "I can see why," he agreed soberly, wondering again what sort of reception Bo Thura would give him. "Can't we release these poor fellows?"

Jamieson shook his head. "How would you like some foreigner to release a condemned British man from the gallows? Or release a murderer from jail?"

Andrew considered for a moment. "No," he said. "I wouldn't."

"Nor would the Burmans like us to interfere with their justice techniques. We may disapprove, but it's their system." Jamieson drew on his cigar. "I've heard that Thibaw likes to tie his errant subjects to an elephant's foot and let them trample them to death. I don't know if that's true, but it seems more merciful than that monstrosity," he nodded towards the crucified men.

The gong continued its regular beat, as it had ever since *Little Salamander* had left Thayetmyo. Andrew had grown used to the sound, accepting it as part of the journey. Although he lifted his field glasses occasionally, scanning the forest hoping to find the man, or men, who beat the gong, he was unsuccessful.

"How far to Mandalay?" Andrew asked as they steamed past open paddy fields and small, prosperous villages.

"Not far now," Jamieson replied. He spun the wheel, holding the spokes with three fingers. "Mandalay is not a bad town, as long as you forget any British notions of how a town should look. It's cleaner than most in the east, but there again, the Burmans are a clean people."

Andrew nodded. "I have noticed that," he said.

"Thirty years ago, when I first came here," Jamieson said, "Mandalay did not exist. Nearly everything you'll see has been built since then, which shows how industrious the Burmans can be when they put their minds to it or when somebody stands behind them with a big stick."

"I think most people are like that," Andrew murmured. "Not just the Burmans."

Jamieson laughed. "There's a lot of truth in that," he said. "Don't expect another London or even Rangoon. The Burmans change their capital like we change our clothes. It's been at Ava two or three times, Amarapura at least twice and Mongyaw a couple of times, but Thibaw seems to like Mandalay, so there it stands."

Andrew looked up as he heard human voices ahead. Three boats were racing towards them, each high-prowed and packed with bare-chested men who paddled as if their lives depended on it. Jamieson held his arm as he reached for the revolver inside his jacket.

"It's all right, Captain Baird," Jamieson said. "They're racing each other. Boat racing and gambling are Burman obsessions, like cricket and horse racing in England."

Andrew released the handle of his revolver. He watched the boats surge towards them, turn at a distinctive tree, and race back, nearly neck and neck, with bare-chested paddlers grunting with every stroke.

"They're fast," Andrew said. "And agile on the water."

"In the first and second wars we had with Burma," Jamieson said. "The Burmans used their warboats. I don't think they have any now."

"That's reassuring," Andrew watched the boats

disappear around a bend in the river. "They would have been formidable adversaries."

With the three racing boats out of sight, *Little Salamander* slowed down.

The gong sounded again, and its regular beat was even more sinister.

"There is the landing area for Mandalay," Jamieson said, allowing *Little Salamander* just sufficient steam to remain static on the river.

"Where's the town?" Andrew asked.

"Mandalay's a couple of miles inland," Jamieson replied.

Andrew nodded, took out his map and worked out the geography. He had travelled around four hundred and fifty miles from Rangoon, with the Irrawaddy running nearly north to south for most of the journey. For the last few miles, the river had run westward, and at the bend below Mandalay sat the terminus for the Irrawaddy Flotilla Company vessels. A dozen small craft sat alongside a Flotilla ship, with a group of naked laughing boys cavorting in the river.

"We'll tie up beside the Flotilla's terminus," Jamieson said. "What do you wish to do now?"

"I have to meet somebody in Mandalay," Andrew said.

"Mandalay has a large European community," Sinclair emerged from the minuscule engine room, wiping his hands on the ubiquitous oily rag. "Have you made arrangements to stay the night?"

"Not yet," Andrew said. He had slept rough on many occasions on campaign and was sure he could find somewhere in Mandalay's environs.

"Ma Gun runs a clean house," Sinclair said. "She's a decent woman with a modicum of English, although her establishment hasn't got the most pleasant of outlooks. Tell her that Robert Sinclair sent you."

"Thank you," Andrew replied. He looked up at the Flotilla paddle steamer *Panthay* beside them, dwarfing the tiny *Little Salamander*.

"Four guineas, Captain, I believe," Jamieson reminded, holding out his hand. "In case you don't come back."

"The fee was three guineas," Andrew corrected, handing over the money. "If you stay here overnight in case I want to return, I'll add another ten shillings plus the same fee to return to Rangoon."

Jamieson smoothed a hand over his jaw. "Make it an extra fifteen shillings, and it's a deal."

Andrew knew his man. "Call it twelve and six," he said, and they shook hands.

As Andrew left *Little Salamander*, a smaller, lighter draught Flotilla vessel left the terminus, heading north.

"She's steaming to Bhamo," Jamieson noticed Andrew's interest. "That's the head of navigation on the Irrawaddy and the last town before Yunnan in China. It's a troublesome spot, with the Burmans and Chinese not on friendly terms."

Andrew nodded. "I doubt I'll ever visit." He climbed the sandy bank on which the terminal was situated.

Andrew was unsure what to expect. The ground was level, with a broad road to the terminus and a group of chattering women carrying large earthen pots to fill at the river. Another woman stood with two ponies for hire.

Andrew thought of the two-mile journey ahead in the heat and quickly arranged to hire a pony.

"Shan ponies," the woman explained with a smile.

"Very good," Andrew recognised the quality of the horses.

After so long on foot and water, Andrew was pleased to ride again, yet within a few moments, he knew his pony was only partially broken. It was a high-spirited animal that needed all his skill to control, but once he had proved he was the master, it relaxed into a pleasant, if not speedy, walk. After a few moments, the track rose alongside a bund that kept the cultivated countryside safe when the Irrawaddy flooded. The pony negotiated the rise without difficulty, and Andrew came to a broader road than most in Britain, with houses on either side.

The houses were built of bamboo and matting, with poor-looking people watching the traffic passing by. Andrew guided his pony past a constant trickle of pigs and bullock carts, hordes of children, and tail-wagging dogs, with scores of people walking purposefully to or from Mandalay.

Andrew stopped when he neared the town. A wide moat encircled the city, with the road running straight over a sturdy bridge.

He heard the single clatter of the gong and glanced over his shoulder. A hundred yards down the road, a slender man held a brass gong in his left hand and struck it with a stick. When he caught Andrew watching him, he turned and ran, leaving the road to disappear in the houses lining the road.

I saw that man in Thayetmyo. Has he kept pace with us all the way?

Knowing he could not catch the man among the confusion of houses, Andrew turned his Shan pony and headed towards Mandalay.

A twenty-six-foot-high brick wall enclosed the town, with battlements at the top and a dozen gates allowing access. Above each entrance, a tall, pyramidal teak tower added dignity, while smaller watch-towers thrust out at various places around the walls.

What lies inside these walls? Andrew wondered. *And how will Bo Thura contact me? How will I let him know I have arrived? There are too many questions here.*

A group of soldiers stood or crouched beside the

gate, watching the travellers. Two stared at Andrew and looked away without comment. Once through the gate, Andrew stepped onto a macadamised, hundred-foot-wide road, that arrowed through the town. He realised there was a network of roads from each gateway, with the houses ranged alongside. Most of the houses were of a familiar Burmese pattern: bamboo built, raised on bamboo piles, and thatched with leaves. A few houses were stone-built, with Chinese owners.

The gong began again.

Why the devil is that man following me? Andrew stopped beside an open space where a group of women traders had set up a bazaar for brightly coloured waistcloths and turbans. He could hear the gong sounding and slipped among the stalls. He suddenly ducked down behind a stall, surprising the Hindu owner.

Crouched on the ground, with a curious dog sniffing at him, Andrew listened for the gong and grunted in satisfaction. The sound had ended.

Whoever that man is, he's following me and bangs his gong when he knows where I am.

Andrew remained low, with the dog slowly wagging its tail and the stall keeper staring at him in stupefaction. He lay on the ground and watched as the gong-man peered around the bazaar and ran away, evidently desperate to find his quarry. Andrew allowed him a few minutes, rose, winked at the stall keeper, and slid away from the bazaar. A Burmese woman in a figure-hugging cobalt-blue longyi, a *htamein*, stepped back quickly when Andrew passed, and then he was back on a main street.

Dogs and pigs roamed freely among the fifty or sixty thousand inhabitants, and although they growled and bickered constantly, they also rid the streets of rubbish and discarded food.

Andrew wandered, trying to work out Mandalay's geography. In common with all eastern cities, Mandalay had its quota of bazaars, where people could purchase all the necessities of life and many of the luxuries. Andrew smiled to think of Mariana let loose in the Silk Bazaar as he looked around. Bo Thura's message was to arrive at Mandalay and wait to be contacted without any details.

Was that gong man Bo Thura's messenger? If so, he could have contacted me at any time.

Andrew heard the brassy clatter of the gong behind him. *You found me, then.* He turned around and saw only a bustling street. He sighed and decided to walk to the palace complex, wondering if he had wasted his time and money coming to Burma.

How about Mary MacConnacher? Somebody undoubtedly kidnapped her. Is somebody playing an elaborate hoax on me? If so, why?

Dominating the city, Thibaw's palace was the largest structure in Mandalay. It was situated in the centre, with all the other buildings radiating in a status-dominated organisation. Andrew thought the palace was among the most interesting buildings he had seen. Built of teak, it had richly carved upturned eaves, complete with gilding and vermilion. The outer walls were twenty feet high, red and crenellated, supported by earth embankments seventy feet wide at the base and tapering upwards.

Around the walls spread the moat, two hundred feet wide, filled with sparkling water and decorated with floating lotus plants. The royal barge floated on the water, looking like something from the Middle Ages.

Well, Bo Thura, here I am. Contact me.

Andrew stepped aside as a party of Burmese soldiers filed past. Stocky, unsmiling men in light jackets, they mostly carried old-fashioned muzzle-loading muskets and long, slightly curved dhas. They had broad-brimmed brass hats on their heads, which Andrew thought looked very uncomfortable, although the decorative griffins in front were attractive. Some wore red coats with green facings, similar to the old British redcoats; others were bare-chested. Unlike British soldiers, Thibaw's men did not wear trousers, with bare legs and feet.

Andrew watched the soldiers for a few moments, wondered how they would stand against British regulars, and saw a woman walking towards him.

That woman was at the silk bazaar.

"I know all the Europeans in Mandalay by sight,"

the slender Burmese woman in the blue longyi stepped up to Andrew. "You are new here."

"I am," Andrew admitted. "You speak good English."

"Thank you." She was in her late twenties, Andrew estimated, with a smiling face and a presence that stirred something inside him. "Are you interested in the palace?"

"I know nothing about it," Andrew admitted. He glanced around, searching for the man with the gong or anybody who might be from Bo Thura. *How does one recognise a dacoit?* People moved around, busy with their affairs, and although a few glanced at him as an interesting foreigner, they quickly moved away.

"The king's palace and gardens are within those walls," the woman spoke with near reverence. "As are the treasury, the royal courts, the mint, and the royal arsenal."

"That's impressive," Andrew said. The woman smelled fresh, scented lightly of flowers.

"Yes," the woman seemed pleased with Andrew's reaction. "We carried it from Amarapura."

Andrew shook his head. "I'm sorry, I don't understand. What do you mean, you carried it?"

"The former king thought that Amarapura was too restricted for a king of his stature, the Descendant of the Sun, so he moved here and built Mandalay," the woman explained. "He had his palace dismantled and carried here, piece by piece, and rebuilt."

Andrew looked at her. "I didn't know that was possible," he said as his respect for the Burmese people increased.

Who is this woman? She is beautiful, but that's not why I feel this immediate attraction.

Andrew heard the gong again, the single, regular stroke, slow and sonorous. *These people are different from us, but they are highly organised and very clever.*

"The king lives in the centre of his capital," the woman said, "with his chief officials around him in these houses." She indicated the larger buildings immediately outside the palace walls. "The next level of society lives beyond that," the woman waved a hand behind her. "The lesser officials, Army officers, and such like, while the merchants and common people live on the outskirts but are still within the city walls."

Andrew nodded. "Mandalay is very well organised," he said.

Keep talking. Ask her a question; get to know this woman. I must get to know her. Andrew smiled, looking the woman up and down from the top of her immaculately styled head to the painted toes of her bare feet. Her earrings were gold, nearly touching her shoulders, and Andrew knew she was aware of his interest.

"Do you like our pagodas?" the woman asked.

"I have admired Burma's pagodas ever since I arrived," Andrew said truthfully. "Could you tell me more about them?" He allowed his eyes to examine her face with her fine eyes and high cheekbones, that intelligent, nearly mocking twist to her lips and the slightly outthrust, defiant chin. *Who are you? What is your name? Can I ask her name in this country, or is that against their traditions? I wish I knew more.*

"That is the king's pagoda," the woman pointed to an impressive building towering above a surrounding wall. "What is your name, sir?"

"I am Andrew Baird," Andrew said, smiling. "And you are?"

"A messenger," the woman said, dropping her smile.

"A messenger? From whom?"

Who are you? Tell me your name!

The gong had stopped. Andrew could only hear the murmur of voices and the movement of bare or sandalled feet on the ground. He saw the slender man standing nearby with the gong in his hand. A second man joined him, short and stocky; he had a livid white scar running diagonally across his face and a long *dha* at his belt.

Andrew repeated his question.

"From whom are you a messenger?"

In response, the woman withdrew a piece of paper from inside her longyi and pressed it into Andrew's hand. She held Andrew's gaze for a long moment and winked surprisingly. "You'll have to read it," she advised.

"What's this?" Andrew glanced at the note, and when he looked up, the woman was gone. "What the devil? Come back!"

A few people glanced at him when he shouted, but he could not see the woman. The stocky, scarred man stood in his path, with one hand holding the hilt of his dha.

"I want to talk to you!" Andrew tried to push past the stocky man, who proved immovable as granite. The slender man still held the gong, watching Andrew as if unsure whether to fight or run.

A child pointed to Andrew and giggled until his mother scolded him into silence and threw an apologetic smile towards Andrew. The crowd seemed to thicken, with a couple of the king's soldiers threading through the civilians behind a group of yellow-clothed monks.

A man with a gold-hilted *dha* led the king's soldiers, and Andrew remembered Goudie mentioning such a man. The stocky man and the gong carrier drifted casually away as the soldiers marched past with a curious, high-stepping gait.

Andrew reread the note. It had two words, written in English and Burmese. *Yin Pauk.*

Yin Pauk? What the devil does that mean? Andrew stepped into the crowd, searching for the woman without success. *I'll ask Jamieson and Sinclair. I must see that woman again; is that her name? Or is it a place where I must meet Bo Thura?*

Sinclair was working on *Little Salamander's* engine when Andrew appeared. "Evening, Captain," he said. "Is your business concluded, and you all set to return?"

"I am not sure," Andrew said. He showed Sinclair the paper. "Does that name mean anything to you?"

Sinclair barely glanced at the paper. "Yin Pauk is a bit of a village about halfway between here and Bhamo," Sinclair replied at once. "It's well off the beaten track, on the border with the Shan and Kachin people and not too far from the Chinese frontier."

"Is it inside Burma?" The different names meant little to Andrew. He had only studied the map as far as Mandalay.

"Officially, yes. King Thibaw is the monarch," Sinclair said, "although his authority is a bit limited, especially since the Chinese are threatening Bhamo. Why do you ask?" He cleaned his hands on an oily rag, half-smiling as if he already knew Andrew's answer.

"I have to go there," Andrew decided what the short note meant.

Sinclair put his rag down. "How do you intend to do that?" He glanced at *Little Salamander*.

"Is Yin Pauk accessible by water?"

Sinclair nodded. "It is, but it's not on the Irrawaddy," he said. "It's on a tributary river."

"If it's on a river, could *Little Salamander* get there?"

Sinclair stood up and threw the rag to his fireman. "That depends on Captain Jamieson," he said. "You'll have to ask him."

"Ask me what?" Jamieson walked the fifteen paces from the bow.

"Could you take me to Yin Pauk?" Andrew asked.

Jamieson considered for a moment. "For a price," he replied. "A high price. Yin Pauk is a dacoit's stronghold."

"How high?" Andrew knew that Jamieson held all the aces.

"Eight guineas."

"That's a lot of money," Andrew said.

"No negotiations," Jamieson grinned. "Or you can try to hire a native boat in Mandalay."

"Eight guineas will nearly clean me out," Andrew said.

"You want me to take you to territory that the Shans, Karens and Burmans all claim, with the Chinese waiting in the background," Jamieson said. "It's a playground for the dacoits with some of the densest forest in one of the remotest parts of Burma."

"Eight guineas it is," Andrew knew he would not trust any Mandalay boatman to take him. "When can we leave?"

"Tomorrow," Jamieson told him. "Be here before dawn, and we'll catch the best of the daylight." He nodded to the town. "Be careful if you go back into Mandalay; there's trouble brewing."

"I'll be careful," Andrew said. "I saw a few of the king's soldiers in the city."

"Best keep out of their way," Sinclair advised. "They can be very charming or utterly ruthless." He shouted something to his fireman. "We'll have *Little Salamander* coaled up and ready to steam."

CHAPTER 9

KINGDOM OF AVA, SEPTEMBER 1884

Andrew estimated there were about a hundred Europeans in Mandalay, mostly traders but with others who looked decidedly shifty. The merchants greeted people with false bonhomie as they sought sales, while the others looked sideways at everybody as though assessing them as rivals or enemies.

Who are these fellows? Politicians? Ambassadors? Lawyers?

Although most of Mandalay's European residents were British, Andrew also heard French and Italian spoken in the streets. He remembered Jamieson mentioning that Thibaw had Italian engineers working for him.

"You're a stranger here," an overdressed and perspiring man said.

"I am," Andrew agreed. *This fellow is a merchant and prosperous by his appearance.*

"Where are you staying?" The man smiled and held out his hand. "Harding. Charles Harding, of Harding and Dowding."

"Andrew Baird." They shook hands. "And I am looking for accommodation for the night. I heard that Ma Gun's place is the best."

"Ma Gun is the most decent place to stay," Harding told him. "Come with me, and I'll take you there."

Andrew touched the revolver inside his tunic, wondering if he could trust this unknown man in a strange city. "Thank you, Harding," he decided.

Ma Gun's was a two-storey, timber-built house with a shaded veranda and a genial Burmese hostess.

Ma Gun greeted them with a broad smile. "Welcome, gentlemen. Now, would anybody like tea? Palm-toddy? Samshu perhaps, or Eagle Brandy?"

"Robert Sinclair recommended you, Mrs Gun," Andrew said.

"Robert! How is he?" Ma Gun asked, smiling.

"He's doing well," Andrew replied.

"You can have Robert's old room," Ma Gun said, ushering Andrew to a small upstairs room with a window offering a view of an ominously large building with high walls. Harding followed into the room, treading heavily on the teak floor.

Andrew nodded out of the window when Ma Gun left. "What's that building, Harding? It looks like a barrack block."

Harding grinned. "That's the jail, Baird. I hope you don't mind criminal neighbours."

"As long as I am outside and they're inside," Andrew replied.

Harding laughed. "Let's hope King Thibaw doesn't discover your past misdeeds."

"I'll keep them secret," Andrew promised. "Good night, Harding." He unpacked the case he had carried from *Little Salamander*, placed his revolver under the pillow and closed the matting blind. Mosquitoes whined around the room, and a line of red ants scurried across the floor. Andrew sighed, lay on the surprisingly comfortable bed, adjusted the mosquito net, and hoped for an undisturbed night.

Images from the past few days jumbled through his head, from the crucified dacoits to the skirmish around the village, the sound of *Little Salamander's* engine and the scent of that intriguing Burmese woman who had passed him the message. *I'll never see her again*, he thought. The gong ran through his memory, and he groaned, unsure if it was his imagination or reality. Andrew sat up, blinking. The gong sounded throughout the night, clanging every minute, sonorous, monotonous. He pulled the single threadbare blanket over his head, trying to deaden the noise.

That gong must mean something. I'll ask around to-morrow unless I leave the hotel tonight, find the blasted thing, and throw it in the Irrawaddy beside its skinny little owner. Wait, now. What's that noise?

The new sound was unmistakable, the regular tread of soldiers marching in step. A man, either an officer or NCO, shouted a command, and the soldiers increased their pace with the sound of bare feet slapping on the ground like hail on a November window.

Sinclair said there was trouble brewing.

Andrew reached for the revolver under his pillow and sat up, realising he could hear the gong even through the marching feet.

Something's happening out there. I'd recognise a military tread anywhere.

Struggling out of bed, Andrew dragged back the mosquito netting, wafted away a couple of whining mosquitoes, pulled on his trousers and jacket and jerked open the door.

"Is that you, Baird?" Harding emerged from the next room with a dressing gown flapping loosely over an embroidered nightshirt. He blinked at Andrew and fastened the cord of his dressing gown. "You're carrying a gun," he said.

"It's me," Andrew replied, sliding his boots onto

his feet. "What's the to-do?" He smelled alcohol on Harding's breath.

"Thibaw has ordered the execution of some infamous dacoits, and the Army is toddling along to do the deed."

"Oh, I see." Having witnessed some of the dacoits' work, Andrew was ambivalent about their fate. "Well, it's nothing to do with us, Harding."

"Perhaps not," Harding agreed, still eyeing Andrew's revolver. "What-ho! Something else is happening out there!"

Andrew was first to the window and peered outside. He saw the soldiers running towards the jail and a group of men facing them at the gate. Some of the men held improvised weapons, lengths of wood, broken furniture, and a small knife.

"That doesn't look healthy," Harding said. "It looks like a jailbreak, by God."

"I'd try to escape if the king was going to crucify me," Andrew told him. "Here are more soldiers."

A company of Thibaw's soldiers appeared, with their light red jackets catching the rising sun and their muskets and rifles leaning against their shoulders. Seeing them arrive, the convicts attempted a desperate rush to break free.

The soldiers levelled their rifles and fired, with the sound of shots echoing from the high walls. Three of the escapees fell, one dead and the others writhing on the ground.

"No second chances there," Harding said. He seemed fascinated by the drama outside the jail.

"Better a quick death than crucifixion," Andrew replied. He watched the soldiers' movements, noting how the officers gave commands and how the men obeyed. *They are quick and responsive*, he thought. *These lads could give us trouble if we ever fight them.*

As the soldiers encircled the prisoners, firing at any who broke through the cordon, other prisoners pushed out of the jail. Some carried homemade weapons, lengths of wood or knives, and a few threw missiles towards the military.

"That's a bit of a mismatch," Andrew murmured.

Harding nodded, licking his lips.

An active man, obviously an officer, barked a command, and the soldiers knelt and fired a ragged volley that tore into the mass of escapees, hitting eight or nine. Another order saw the soldiers reload and present their rifles. Andrew noted that some carried modern weapons, French or British, while others had ancient muzzle-loading muskets.

"It's a massacre!" Harding called without tearing his attention from the scene.

"It is," Andrew agreed.

Realising the military was shooting anybody who tried to escape, the prisoners turned around and pushed back inside the jail, stamping over each other in their sudden desire for sanctuary. The soldiers fired again, with bullets thumping into unresisting bodies, causing blood to spray above the crowd and splatter the prison walls. When the officer snapped another order, the soldiers ceased firing. A stray shaft of sunlight glittered from the gold hilt on the officer's *dha*.

You again! Andrew thought. *You pop up wherever there is trouble.*

"This is terrible. I've seen enough now," Harding said as the officer stepped among the dead and wounded with a small group of men around him. He gave another brisk order, and his men began to shoot the wounded. After a few moments, only dead men and a few dead women sprawled on the ground.

"There is no mercy in Mandalay," Harding said. Despite his protestations of disgust, he remained at the window.

"Remember the Gordon Riots in London," Andrew reminded. "There was no mercy then, either. Or at Peterloo."[1]

Harding grunted and continued to stare at the drama outside.

With the prisoners trapped inside the jail, an of-

---

1. The Gordon Riots of 1780 were a series of anti-Catholic riots in London. After days of trouble, the government called in the Army. Estimates of the dead vary between three hundred and seven hundred. The Peterloo Massacre of 1819 occurred when a body of cavalry attacked a rally for electoral reform at St Peter's Field in Manchester. The cavalry killed eighteen people and injured between 400 and 700.

ficial emerged from the royal palace and spoke to the officer commanding the troops.

"Who is that?" Andrew asked.

"I think that's Maung Thandar," Harding said. "He's one of Thibaw's ministers and a bad man to cross."

Andrew rummaged in his baggage, found his field glasses, and focused on the king's minister. He shivered as he saw the man's face.

If ever there was a study of pure evil, that's it standing there.

Maung Thandar spoke quietly to the officer and stepped back, smiling. The officer snapped an order, and a section of soldiers ran to the far side of the jail.

"What's he up to?" Harding asked, trying to stretch his neck to peer around the jail.

"Nothing pleasant, I'll be bound," Andrew replied. He lowered his field glasses as Maung Thandar withdrew another few steps. A woman joined him, with soldiers and interested civilians stepping out of her way in total respect.

"Good God! That's Hsinbyaumashin," Harding said. "That's the queen's mother."

"What's she doing here?" Andrew asked.

"Causing trouble," Harding replied. "I reckon she's the cause of half the palace murders and the instigator of the other half."

"I'll keep out of her way," Andrew promised. He

lifted his head. "Smoke," he said. "And fire." He swivelled around to view the far end of the jail. "The Army has set fire to the jail."

"That must be what Thandar ordered," Harding sounded excited. "What is he trying to do?"

"He's forcing out the prisoners," Andrew said quietly. "They can either remain inside the jail and burn or leave and face the soldiers." He watched, aware of the futility of intervention, as the flames took hold of the building. The screaming began a few minutes later, and a horde of desperate people, men, women, and children burst out of the jail. They ran towards the waiting soldiers, who fired constantly, using their *dhas* on anybody who survived the bullets. The officer watched without apparent emotion, unlike Hsinbyaumashin, who nodded and smiled as the slaughter continued.

"Oh, good God in heaven," Harding said.

Andrew, war-hardened to horror, watched as prisoners, some on fire, ran out of the jail to be butchered, as the king's minister and mother-in-law watched.

"Time to leave," Andrew said. "Come on, Harding. We're getting out of Mandalay before this thing spreads." *I must reach Yin Pauk to rescue young Mary. I can't stay here.*

"Where will we go?" Harding asked.

"To the river. There's a boat there that will take us away."

Grabbing their baggage, Andrew and Harding left the hotel. The crackle of flames sounded behind the musketry and shouting of the soldiers. One sturdy soldier pointed his musket at Andrew, changed his mind, and ran towards the jail.

"Which way to the river?" Andrew asked, looking around him.

"This way!" Harding chose a road. "No! Wait!"

A section of soldiers appeared on the street. One shot a passing woman and laughed as his companion hacked off her head. The others looked around, with one man pointing towards Andrew and Harding.

"Try this way," Andrew suggested, choosing a street at random. Harding followed, glancing over his shoulder as he heard shouting behind them. A woman began to scream.

"More soldiers!" Harding warned.

"They've got the blood lust," Andrew said. He heard a loud noise ahead and saw another body of soldiers running, yelling, and shooting at anybody they saw. One man carried a woman's head by her hair, with blood trailing onto the street. "Back to the hotel!"

CHAPTER 10

MANDALAY, BURMA, SEPTEMBER 1884

"Is it safe there?" Harding asked.

"God knows," Andrew replied, "but safer than on the streets unless the soldiers set fire to the hotel." He saw the colour drain from Harding's face and shook his head. "We'll be safer inside," he said.

They hammered on the locked door, shouted who they were and dived inside when Ma Gun opened up.

"Come in, gentlemen," Ma Gun said, apparently unconcerned at the mayhem around her house. "Would you like tea? Palm-toddy? Samshu perhaps, or Eagle Brandy?"

"No, thank you, Ma Gun," Harding replied. "It's

a bit early for that."

"Lock and bar the door," Andrew ordered. "Lock all the windows, pile furniture behind them, and have water ready in case of fire." He looked around at the guests: six frightened and confused European men, with Ma Gun smiling and apparently unconcerned. "If you have any weapons, I'd suggest you fetch them now."

"They won't attack us, though," one man said. "I'm English."

"I doubt they care what we are now their blood is up," Andrew replied. "In fact, they might consider foreigners as fair game."

The man frowned and smoothed a hand across his moustache. "But we're not foreign! We're English! Didn't you hear me?"

"I heard you. Do you have a revolver?"

"No." The man glared at Andrew. "I am Marmaduke Patchley of the Surrey Patchleys."

"Do you have any sort of weapon, Mr Patchley?" Andrew held the man's gaze.

"No."

Most of the men had left to strengthen their rooms or fetch whatever they had. They gathered inside the front door ten minutes later, brandishing a variety of revolvers, shotguns, and hunting rifles. One man carried a large Adams revolver.

"Good," Andrew said. "We don't have enough people to guard every room, so we'll barricade the upper floor and guard the ground level. Ma Gun and men without weapons can hold water in case of fire and look after any wounded. That means you, Mr Patchley."

"Tell them we're English, and they'll leave us alone," Patchley insisted.

"That won't work," Andrew told him tersely as Ma Gun offered everybody a selection of drinks.

"Who are you to tell us what to do?" Patchley asked.

"Captain Andrew Baird, Natal Dragoons," Andrew replied. He raised his voice. "Does anybody here have any military experience?"

"I was in the county militia once," a balding middle-aged man said. "I took part in a couple of field exercises."

"Good. Take charge of the back of the building and the left side. I'll take care of the front and right. Watch for incendiaries, men who want to burn the place down." Andrew glanced at Harding, who looked surprised at Andrew taking charge. "Mr Harding, go upstairs and keep an eye open for possible threats. You are our standing picket. Check to ensure the windows are secure."

"Yes, Captain Baird," Harding thumped upstairs.

With the upper storey as safe as possible, Andrew toured the ground floor, piling furniture behind the front and back doors and unguarded windows, working out fields of fire and listening to the increasing noise outside. He heard shooting, maniacal laughter, and the screams of terrified people, together with the constant crackle of flames from the blazing jail.

"Whatever is happening out there is not good," a man said, holding his rifle like a talisman.

Andrew nodded. "We can't do anything about it," he said. "All we can do is look after ourselves, keep out of the way and hope nobody attacks us."

"Trouble!" Harding called from above. "A mob of soldiers is approaching the house! Could you come up, Captain Baird?"

"Coming!" Andrew ran upstairs and joined Harding at the window.

Around a hundred soldiers marched down the smoke-filled street, singing and laughing. They balanced their rifles over their shoulders, and a man in front held a long bamboo pole with a human head thrust on the top. He laughed as blood dribbled the length of the pole and onto his hand.

Harding looked away. "Are they coming here?"

"It looks that way," Andrew said. "Stand by to repel boarders."

"Standing by," Harding forced a twisted smile. He held up his borrowed rifle as if for inspection.

Andrew took the rifle from him, checked it was loaded, slipped the safety catch on, and returned it. "Aim low," he said, "and don't jerk the trigger. Aim here," he patted his belly, "the broadest part of the body."

"Yes, Captain," Harding replied.

"You'll be fine," Andrew encouraged him.

The mob straggled closer, chanting loudly and bouncing the disembodied head up and down. More blood dribbled down the bamboo onto the holder's arm. He laughed again and lifted the head higher so that the man's head stared directly at the hotel through sightless eyes. The tongue protruded slightly, lolling from broken lips. In the centre of the men, three soldiers carried burning brands with the flames spitting and blue smoke coiling upwards.

"Keep a watch on them," Andrew ordered Harding. "For God's sake, don't fire unless they attack us first. We don't want to start a war."

"I won't," Harding said. He moved back slightly, enabling him to see outside without anybody noticing him.

"Good man," Andrew said and ran back downstairs.

"They're coming closer!" A sandy-haired merchant thumbed back the hammers on his shotgun.

Andrew pushed the barrels away. "They're no threat to us yet," he said. "They might only walk past. Keep your nerve."

Patchley peered out of the window. "Do you see what they have on that stake?" His voice rose, high-pitched.

"I see it," Andrew said. "Don't look if it bothers you." He felt the tension in the hotel as men glanced outside at the chanting mob parading the human head. "Keep calm, gentlemen and ladies," Andrew said. "They're not threatening us."

"I've got a charge of twelve-bore for the first man who comes too close," the sandy-haired merchant said.

"Don't fire unless they attack us," Andrew ordered. "We are in their city and their country. We may disapprove of their customs, but we've no right to interfere."

Father always insisted we should not interfere with anybody's religion, customs, or women. He emphasised that such interference was a sure way to create trouble. Damn! I am using his advice again.

One of the Burmese soldiers stepped closer to the hotel. He spoke to the man at his side, and both approached the front door with rifles slung over their shoulders and long *dhas* at their belts.

"They're coming closer!" the sandy-haired merchant levelled his shotgun.

"They're doing us no harm," Andrew said. "Keep your finger off that trigger!"

"One more step, and I'll shoot!" the merchant pulled the shotgun to his shoulder.

Andrew pushed him away. "You'll start a war!" He grabbed the shotgun and replaced the hammers. "I told you to wait for my order, damn it!"

"Tell them we're not foreigners! Tell them we're English!" Patchley yelled.

The two king's soldiers stopped five yards short of the front door and shouted something.

"What do they want?" Andrew asked Ma Gun, who remained in the centre of the room, smiling.

"They want to know if we're hiding any criminals in here," Ma Gun replied. "They say there's been a jailbreak."

"Tell them we know about the jailbreak, and we're keeping the door locked to ensure no dacoits come inside," Andrew said. He felt the comforting weight of his revolver but wished he had trained men with him rather than nervous merchants.

Ma Gun shouted what Andrew had told her. He watched the two soldiers hesitate. One unslung his rifle and slid a cartridge into the breech.

"I told you! I warned you we should shoot them!" the sandy-haired merchant said.

"We're English!" Patchley yelled. "English!"

"Shut up!" Andrew hissed. He watched the two soldiers talking outside the front door. The main body of soldiers halted and were watching, occasionally shouting to their colleagues.

If they decide to attack, I'll shoot the first two. After that, anything could happen.

Andrew held his revolver in a surprisingly steady hand. He could nearly taste the tension in the room. A man coughed behind him, and another gave a nervous giggle. The sandy-haired merchant regained his shotgun and thumbed back the hammers.

The next two minutes are crucial.

When the leading soldier shouted something, Andrew looked at Ma Gun.

"He said we had better send out any criminals, or they'll burn us down," Ma Gun translated, still smiling.

"Are you feeling courageous?" Andrew asked.

"I am a Buddhist," Ma Gun replied. "I have nothing to fear."

"That's a good answer," Andrew approved. "You and I will open the front door and assure these men we are not harbouring any escaped prisoners." He felt the horror within the hotel. "I'll look after you, Ma Gun."

Ma Gun smiled and began to move aside the furniture that barricaded the door.

"If you open the door, they'll all rush in!" the sandy-haired merchant said.

"I doubt it. They want a quick kill, not a fight against revolvers," Andrew held up his pistol, "and shotguns. Once they see we're ready to defend the place, they'll sheer off, sure as eggs."

"You'd better be right!"

Pulling back the last of the furniture from the front door, Andrew and Ma Gun stepped outside. The two soldiers were ten yards away, resting on their rifles with their colleagues thirty yards further back.

The two soldiers spoke together, addressing Ma Gun. She replied immediately, glancing at Andrew.

"They're asking who you are," she explained.

"Tell them I am Captain Andrew Baird of the Natal Dragoons," Andrew said.

"I did," Ma Gun said with her ready smile. "They want to know why you are here."

"I am meeting a personal friend," Andrew said.

The soldiers did not look interested. They asked another question, with one stepping closer. Andrew laid his revolver across his front, ensuring the royal soldiers saw he was armed.

"They're asking if we're hiding any escaped prisoners."

Andrew lifted the revolver. "Tell them we have no escaped prisoners, and I will shoot anybody who comes into the hotel without your permission." He smiled as Ma Gun repeated his words.

The two soldiers glanced at each other. One stepped towards Andrew until somebody shouted, and he looked over his shoulder.

The officer with the gold-hilted dha stood beside Maung Thandar at the rear of the troops. Maung Thandar spoke to the officer, who snarled another order, and the man carrying the disembodied head stopped. He ran to the front of the hotel and rammed the bamboo stake into the ground, with the head facing the hotel. The officer snapped something, and the soldiers marched on with Maung Thandar and the officer at the rear.

Maung Thandar examined Andrew as he passed, then turned his head and strode, long-legged, to join the soldiers. The officer lingered a few moments longer, examining Andrew up and down before marching away.

He'll know me next time.

"What now?" Harding asked when Andrew returned and locked the door.

"Now we sit it out until things quieten down," Andrew said, "and then we leave."

Ma Gun's smile returned when Andrew closed the door. "Good," she said. "Now, would anybody like tea? Palm-toddy? Samshu perhaps, or Eagle Brandy?"

Andrew nodded. "Ma Gun, you are a treasure. I'd love some tea. No, make that palm-toddy."

Ma Gun smiled as she poured Andrew a drink. "You are welcome, Captain Baird."

The day passed slowly, with a slight scare, when a handful of the king's soldiers passed the hotel. None of them looked, and the sandy-haired merchant lowered his shotgun with a look of regret.

"Maybe next time," Andrew sympathised.

"I rather enjoyed all the excitement," the merchant said. "I should have been a soldier."

They spent the night in the hotel, listening with

gradually decreasing worry, and Andrew left before a glorious dawn burst over Mandalay. Keeping his revolver handy, he hurried through deserted streets, ignoring the occasional crumpled corpse and passed through an open gate where guards dozed carelessly.

Jamieson nodded when Andrew arrived. "You survived, then, Captain Baird. I'm glad we're heading upstream to Yin Pauk." He lit a large cigar and puffed aromatic blue smoke into the humid air. "Indeed, I doubt we'll be heading downstream for a while," he said. "Look down the river."

Andrew glanced past the Irrawaddy Flotilla terminus. Soldiers marched along the riverbank and manned small boats on the water, stopping all traffic from moving south. "Upstream it is then," he said, fingering the piece of paper the woman had given him. "Maung Thandar and Thibaw's mother-in-law have concreted our decision."

Jamieson removed his cigar. "Aye, maybe so, Captain Baird, but I'll still charge you full fare for the journey. I have fuel to pay for, and we're heading into dangerous waters."

Andrew smiled. "I would not expect anything else," he said.

He looked up as the gong began its sonorous beat. *I hope that the Burmese woman is in Yin Pauk. I must meet her again, whoever she is.*

"Are you ready, Captain?" Jamieson asked.

"I am," Andrew said. He had a last look at the

landing stage and the road to Mandalay, where he had met the woman in the blue figure-hugging longyi.

"Cast off!" Jamieson shouted, repeating his words in Burmese and *Little Salamander* eased out against the current.

Ma Gun's words followed him. "Now, would anybody like tea? Palm-toddy? Samshu perhaps, or Eagle Brandy?"

CHAPTER 11

LOWER BURMA AND THE KINGDOM OF
AVA, SEPTEMBER 1884

"We could go out on the river," Jennings
said. "You and me."

"That would be nice," Mariana
agreed. After growing up in the open country of Natal, she found the crowded streets of Rangoon con-
fining. "Where would we go?"

They stood beside the quay, where the great
paddle steamers of the Irrawaddy Flotilla lay, and
ships came in from half the world. Mariana watched
each vessel, hoping Andrew would alight from one,
although she knew it was far too early for his return.
She thought of her little chart where she marked off

each day, with only half a week crossed out and the rest seeming to stretch forever.

"Just a little pleasure sail," Jennings said. "Nowhere in particular. Maybe watch a boat race; the Burmans are great racers and gamblers."

"That would be fun," Mariana replied. She tore her mind from thoughts of Andrew, knowing she only hurt herself. "You're fun, aren't you?"

"Thank you. So are you," Jennings said. "Life is about living, Miss Maxwell. My philosophy is to get as much enjoyment as possible."

"Oh," Mariana smiled at him. "I think Andrew's life is about duty more than enjoyment, although he does know Tennyson's poetry."

Jennings met the smile. "Tennyson, eh? The Light Brigade man. How about this one:

"If I had a flower for every time I thought of you,

I could walk through my garden forever."

"I like that one," Jennings said. "It suits you rather well, Miss Maxwell."

"Oh, do you think so?" Mariana replied. She altered the angle of her parasol to protect her face from the sun.

"Undoubtedly," Jennings replied. "How about this Tennyson quote: 'Tis better to have loved and lost than never to have loved at all.' That's also true."

Mariana waved away a questing insect. "I can't

imagine a life without love in it," she said. "Tennyson is a very clever man."

"He understands human nature," Jennings agreed. "Now, let's find ourselves some transport and get afloat." He escorted her to the river's edge and searched for a suitable boat. "When you are back in Britain, and I remain here, sweltering under the Burman sun, I will sigh in happy memory of how your presence lightened the dull truth of my existence."

Mariana laughed. "Oh, Mr Jennings, you do talk nonsense. You'll forget me the minute I turn my back."

"And what a lovely back it is to turn," Jennings said. "No, Miss Maxwell," he lowered his voice. "I will never forget you. I think you are a special kind of girl, or lady rather, the kind of lady only the most fortunate of men meet, and then only once in a lifetime."

Mariana smiled at him. "I am not special." She handed a small coin to a persistent beggar and watched him run off, whooping in joy. "These poor people have nothing at all."

"That boy probably makes more in begging than most dock labourers do by the sweat of their brows," Jennings said.

Mariana pointed with her parasol. "Is that not a boat there? The man seems to know you."

"I can't think why," Jennings said. "I've never

seen him before in my life. Now you wait here a moment, my dear, and I'll make the arrangements." He hurried ahead, lifting his hand to hold the boatman's attention.

Mariana watched them talk for a few moments while another of Tennyson's quotes rang in her ears. "Who are wise in love, love most, say least." She smiled, resolved to speak little when they were on the water, and allow Jennings to lead the conversation. *I believe that men like to be the dominant talkers,* she told herself. *I'll be quiet as a mouse or a demure lady and listen to Mr Jennings' words. After all, he is the most entertaining company.*

Jennings returned within five minutes, smiling as he extended a hand. "There we are, you see? I have arranged terms with the boatman, who has agreed to take us on a little trip on the Irrawaddy."

"Well done, Mr Jennings," Mariana replied, keeping pace with him along the quay to a small flight of wooden steps leading downward.

The boat had an upsweeping prow and stern, with three boatmen, the middle-aged man Jennings spoke to and a couple of supple youths in their late teens. Jennings descended the three steps to the boat first, turned, and held out a helping hand.

"Come along, Miss Maxwell."

Mariana took Jennings' hand and stepped into the boat, gasping slightly when it rocked. The middle-aged boatman shook his head, smiling as the youths grinned. One shifted from side to side, making the boat move violently.

Just like youths would do back home, Mariana thought. *People are not much different wherever one travels.*

The middle-aged boatman growled something and gave the nearest youth a cuff across the head.

That's a father and his sons, Mariana realised.

"It's all right, Miss Maxwell. The boat is stable," Jennings assured her. "You are perfectly safe with me. I won't let you fall in the river."

"I am glad to hear it, Mr Jennings," Mariana replied, slightly embarrassed by her recent display. She sat carefully, placing her parasol at her side.

The boat had two leather-padded passenger seats. Jennings helped Mariana sit and nodded to the father, who spoke to his sons and pushed off.

"Where are you taking me, Mr Jennings?" Mariana asked, holding her hat in place with her left hand as a gust of wind threatened to lift it from her head.

Jennings watched the boatmen take them past the Irrawaddy Flotilla steamer. "We'll have a little tour of the ships first, then maybe, if you are agreeable, paddle downstream to a little island I know. It's an idyllic spot with a most sublime beach where dear Adelie and I used to spend many a happy hour."

"Dear Adelie?" Mariana asked.

"My wife," Jennings said. "Or rather, my late wife."

"Oh, my dear Mr Jennings, I did not know," Mariana leaned forward to pat his arm. "I am terribly sorry to hear that. It must have been awful for you. When did you lose her?"

Jennings held the back of her hand. "Thank you, Miss Maxwell. It was two years ago now. The least said, the better, eh?" He spoke to the chief boatman, and they paddled around the ships, with Jennings telling Mariana their origin and cargo.

"She is *Calcutta Maid*, with rice for Sydney. That vessel is a teak carrier bound for London and that one, *Lord of the East*, has machinery parts from Glasgow. Am I boring you, Miss Maxwell?"

"Not in the slightest," Mariana said.

Jennings sat back. "As you see, Rangoon is a thriving port, Miss Maxwell, one of the finest in Southeast Asia."

"I see," Mariana tried to hide her disinterest.

"You are bored," Jennings said. "This subject does not interest you."

"It does not," Mariana agreed. "I am sorry, Mr Jennings."

"Then we shall discuss something else," Jennings decided with a quick smile. "Adelie's island is a fair distance off, or we can watch a boat race."

"The boat race," Mariana decided immediately.

"The island was special to Adelie and you. I shouldn't disturb that memory."

It's best not to intrude where Mr Jennings has memories. That would not be fair.

"The boat race it is," Jennings said and spoke to the head boatman, who grinned, altered course, and steered them across the river. Mariana watched a sublime three-masted clipper ease in under the care of a Rangoon pilot, and then they were paddling up the far bank to a busy village.

"This place has a regular boat race with its neighbour," Jennings explained. "It's not quite as prestigious as the Oxford and Cambridge race but equally important to the people here. They gamble huge sums of money on it."

In a flash of insight, Mariana asked, "Have you gambled on the outcome of this race, Mr Jennings?"

"I have," Jennings admitted cheerfully. "One cannot live out East without adopting some local habits. It helps one fit in." He murmured something in Burmese, and the boatmen stopped. They sat in the middle of the river with the water gurgling on either side and the two young boatmen paddling occasionally to maintain their position.

A long, galley-type boat emerged from each village, both gilded and brightly painted, one in red and the other in yellow and gold. High-prowed and slender, they looked fast as they cut gracefully through the water. Crews of eager men in brief waistcloths wielded long paddles and shouted what Mariana took to be cheerful insults at their rivals.

"My money is on the boat with the red paint-work," Jennings said as their boatmen joined in the yelling.

"Then I will also cheer it on," Mariana said. "My father used to attend horse races. He always put a few pounds on his favourite."

"A man after my own heart," Jennings said. "If my boat wins, we'll crack open a bottle of champagne."

"I've never drunk champagne," Mariana admitted.

"Then you have never fully lived," Jennings told her solemnly. "I tell you what, Miss Maxwell, if my boat wins, I'll introduce you to my house, and we'll drink my success in a glass of champagne." He smiled at her. "I bought half a dozen bottles just for you. That is, if you trust me, of course."

"Of course I trust you!" Mariana pointed to the village. "Look! The boats are lining up!"

The boats manoeuvred side-by-side, with the paddlers glowering at each other and a man in each stern banging a large brass gong.

"That's our favourite," Mariana said, pointing to the red boat. "Come on, the red boat!"

"That's the fellow," Jennings agreed. He raised his voice in a shout, yelling something in Burmese that made the older boatman laugh.

"Faster, the red boat!" Mariana encouraged again.

For a moment, the excitement of competition took control, and she forgot her loneliness without Andrew.

Mariana did not see who gave the order, but all the paddlers began to work furiously, thrashing the water into white fury. The men in the sterns kept the time, smashing their mallets against the gongs as the paddlers grunted or chanted.

"This is exciting," Mariana said, but Jennings was not listening; he stood with his legs balanced against the seat, waving his arms and shouting.

The two boats raced side-by-side as they passed Jennings's vessel, and then the red boat inched into the lead. Mariana cheered, standing up to show her support. As she did so, she knocked her parasol over the side, and the swift current quickly whisked it away.

"Oh, dear!" Mariana made a despairing clutch, nearly overbalanced, and righted herself with difficulty as the middle-aged boatman steadied her with a hard hand.

Jennings spoke to the chief boatman, who indicated the taller of his two sons. The youth stood up, glanced at Mariana, stripped off his waistcloth, poised naked for a second and jumped overboard.

"Oh, it's all right!" Mariana said, watching the youth's supple body as he kicked away from the boat and into the current. He reached the parasol in a few seconds, twisted in the water, and returned, hoisting himself onboard and handing the parasol to Mariana.

He grinned at her, dripping water and obviously pleased with himself.

"Thank you," Mariana was treated to a vibrant, naked young man standing a foot in front of her. She placed the parasol at her side and realised Jennings was watching her closely.

"Tell him to put his clothes back on," Mariana said quietly. "I grew up on the Zululand border where seeing naked Zulus was normal. You can neither shock nor impress me with a human body, Mr Jennings."

"That was not my intention, Miss Maxwell," Jennings said.

"Once this race is finished," Mariana said, "I think you had better take me back to Rangoon."

They all turned to see the red boat win by a clear margin. "Congratulations, Mr Jennings," Mariana said, but the magic of the day was gone. She could see the triumph in Jennings's face, yet she realised he was also disappointed, although she was unsure why.

ALL THE EXCITEMENT IN MANDALAY HAD PUSHED the Burmese woman from Andrew's mind, but now he was safely aboard *Little Salamander*, her image returned. He found himself smiling at the memory. There had been something very satisfying about her presence as if he had known her all his life. He sat on deck, watching the riverbank drift by and wondered who she was.

Have you forgotten Mariana already? Andrew rebuked himself before answering his question. *Mariana turned me down, remember? I am not obliged to stay loyal to a woman who rejected me.*

He sat under the canvas canopy, watching the river drift by and the ever-changing scenery on the bank, with villages and paddy fields, patches of forest and an occasional man sitting on an elephant as they piled teak logs.

The gong has stopped. Andrew straightened up. *Have they lost me?*

Little Salamander pushed upriver, with Jamieson frequently glancing behind him as if expecting the king's soldiers to follow his launch.

"Is there anybody there?" Andrew asked.

"No. I'd be happier going downstream," Jamieson admitted. "If there is turmoil in Mandalay, God only knows what's happening in the rest of Upper Burma."

"The king's soldiers were a bit busy downstream," Andrew reminded him. He paused for a moment, wondering how much information he should release. "By going upriver, you're helping to save a young girl's life."

"Who?" Jamieson asked.

"Young Mary MacConnacher," Andrew said and waited for the inevitable questions.

Jamieson did not ask anything. Decades in Burma had taught him not to pry. He grunted and spat into the river. "She'll be long dead by now," he said. "Or worse."

"Worse?"

"Her kidnappers may have sold her into slavery in China, Tonkin or somewhere else up that way." Jamieson nodded north. "The East can hold you in thrall, or it can repulse you. There is amazing beauty here and horrors the like you cannot conceive."

"Maybe I don't want to conceive them," Andrew said. He thought of a young child in the hands of dacoits and shivered. "Get me to Yin Pauk," he said quietly, touching the butt of his revolver.

"That's what you are paying me for," Jamieson agreed. He eyed Andrew up and down, opened his mouth to ask a question and clamped it shut again. Andrew let him wonder.

Little Salamander passed a village, with her wash gently rocking half a dozen fishing boats. The villagers watched them without interest and returned to their work. The wake subsided, *Little Salamander* moved on, and the villagers forgot her.

We are transitory here, Andrew thought. *We may change the face of the cities, but we are irrelevant in the countryside; these people live their lives as they have for a thousand years.*

"We'll leave the Irrawaddy tomorrow," Jamieson said. "You'll have to reconcile yourself to sleeping in your cabin for a couple of nights."

"Thank you, Captain," Andrew said.

THE FOREST SEEMED TO CLOSE IN ON ANDREW AS *Little Salamander* left the Irrawaddy and chugged slowly up a narrow tributary. He heard the cry of bright birds and swatted vainly at the mosquitoes that clouded around his head.

"How far is this place?" Andrew asked. "We've been away for days."

"Not far, now," Jamieson said. "A few miles up this river, then we branch off again, and after that, it's only a few miles more."

Andrew curbed his impatience. His map did not mention the village of Yin Pauk, and he was entirely in Jamieson's hands. He thought of young Mary MacConnacher languishing in the hands of some savage dacoit.

The poor girl must be suffering agonies. God knows what horrors they are putting her through. He shivered, refusing to contemplate the possibilities, and wondered anew what sort of person Bo Thura was.

The river narrowed further, with an occasional village on the banks, frail bamboo huts built on stilts with near-naked men sitting smoking in the sun or venturing onto the water in their boats. Andrew saw a man staring at them, then lifting a stick to hammer on a brass gong. The sound reverberated along the river, to be repeated by unknown and unseen hands within the dense green curtain of the forest.

They've found me again.

"They're sending a message that we're coming," Andrew said. He unfastened his holster to get easier access to his revolver.

"I'd say so," Jamieson agreed. He gave a sharp order to Sinclair, and *Little Salamander* slowed, with the brown water surging on either side of the blunt bow.

"Why are we slowing down?" Andrew asked.

"Shallows ahead," Jamieson told him. "When we have heavy rain here, the river changes course, throwing up sandbanks where the previous week we had sufficient depth for a vessel of twice our draft. We must move carefully on this river, even more than on the Irrawaddy."

Andrew nodded. He did not want to run aground with strange messages sounding in the deep forest. *Little Salamander* slowed and Jamieson sent the deckhand forward to peer into the water.

"I don't know this tributary well," Jamieson explained. "But that lad does. He'll act as river pilot while I steer."

Andrew nodded, listening to the gongs sounding on both banks and the incessant chatter of birds.

Jamieson obeyed the pilot's orders, guiding *Little Salamander* past some dangerous sandbanks just underneath the surface. The pilot shouted something, and Jamieson translated for Andrew.

"Only a quarter of a mile of these, and then we're in clear water," Jamieson said.

The gongs continued to sound, echoing from the trees and competing with the birdcall, although the insects were unaffected.

The steamer eased around a bend into a stretch of water clear of sandbanks, where tall trees overhung the river. One tree had fallen into the water and remained there, thick with vegetation as the river churned creamy-white all around. A boy crouched on the trunk, watching *Little Salamander.* He did not respond when Andrew shouted a greeting.

Jamieson steered *Little Salamander* around the obstacle and smiled as the river widened. Andrew could see no sandbanks ahead, only another fallen tree extending into the water.

"That's better," Jamieson said and ordered increased speed.

Andrew looked up as the gongs suddenly stopped. Only birds and insects broke the silence, with the rhythmic grumble of the screw so constant that Andrew barely noticed it. "Something's happening," he said. He looked astern and saw half a dozen men on the fallen log, all carrying firearms.

The Burmese pilot looked alarmed, glancing from side to side as if expecting the trees to come alive. He shouted something, and the fireman emerged onto the deck.

Trained by serving through three campaigns, Andrew was first to notice the flicker of movement ahead. "Slow the boat," he said.

"Why?"

"Something's wrong," Andrew said. "Your crew knows. Slow the blasted boat!"

"Half speed," Jamieson said.

"That tree is moving!" Andrew said.

Jamieson turned the wheel, heading for the right bank to create some space and then heading hard to port to move *Little Salamander* in a U-turn.

Andrew watched as the tree pushed into the river, gradually shedding its greenery until he saw it was a paddle-powered Burmese warboat.

"What's happening?" Sinclair emerged from the engine room and saw the warboat paddling towards them. He reached inside the wheelhouse for the Snider rifle that hung on brackets above the door.

"There's no point in that, Sinclair," Andrew said. "Look behind you."

Three smaller boats paddled out from the river-bank, each with half a dozen armed men sitting inside, while the men on the fallen tree aimed their rifles at *Little Salamander*.

CHAPTER 12

KINGDOM OF AVA, OCTOBER 1884

"It's an ambush," Andrew said.

"Dacoits," Jamieson said. "We're dead men unless they're only after plunder."

"Your crew seem to agree," Andrew said as both Burmese crew members jumped overboard and swam towards the shore.

"Do we fight or surrender?" Sinclair loaded his Snider with practised hands.

Andrew realised that any man who chose to work in the Burmese backwater must have steady nerves. He tapped his revolver.

"I rather think they knew we were coming," Andrew said. "I suspect they want me rather than you."

"You?"

"I suspect so," Andrew said. "Remember that gong that followed us to Mandalay? It sounded outside Ma Gun's place when I stayed there. I think somebody was letting me know they were watching me."

"Why?" Sinclair checked the sights of his Snider. "We'll stand by you, Captain Baird."

"Thank you, Mr Sinclair." Andrew calculated the odds. With around thirty men in the warboat and another fifteen astern, resistance would end in all their deaths. *If that is Bo Thura, he only wants me, not Jamieson or Sinclair.*

"Put your rifle away, Mr Sinclair. One rifle won't be much use against so many."

"I'm damned if I'll surrender without a fight!" Sinclair growled as Jamieson lifted a boathook and stood in truculent defiance.

The warboat paddled swiftly towards them while the three smaller boats formed a line downstream, blocking the steamer's escape. Andrew fastened the button of his holster and stepped amidships to be clearly seen. He felt his heart beating faster, wondering what the next few moments would bring.

I came out here to meet a dacoit and now is my opportunity. I hope Mariana is all right in Rangoon.

"They're a wild-looking bunch," Andrew said as the warboat drew alongside and a dozen of her crew boarded the steamer. Most wore a simple waist cloth or something similar, with a long *dha* in their hands.

A few dacoits carried firearms, and one held what looked like a large hatchet. All were tattooed, some from head to foot and others only from the waist down.

Andrew controlled the increasing hammer of his heart as he stepped forward. "My name is Captain Andrew Baird."

Should I have told them my rank? It may make things worse.

While the bulk of the dacoits stared at Andrew in incomprehension, one man stepped forward as the rest made space for him. He was short, stocky, and broad-shouldered, with a scar running diagonally across his face.

I met you in Mandalay, my scarred friend.

"Baird," the man grunted. "Windrush." He lifted his *dha* and ran a thumb along the blade.

Andrew felt the tension rise among the dacoits.

If I give the wrong answer here, these lads will skewer me, like as not.

"Captain Andrew Baird," he jabbed a finger at his chest, hoping his voice did not betray his nervousness. "My father is General Jack Windrush."

Andrew heard the water rushing past and the whisper of wind in the trees. The dacoits were utterly quiet as they listened to the conversation.

How the devil can I communicate with this brute? His English is as basic as my Burmese. Is this fellow Bo Thura?

The scarred man jabbed a finger on Andrew's

chest. "Windrush?" He peered closer, his mouth slightly open and his eyes basilisk hard.

"Baird," Andrew repeated, much to the amusement of the other dacoits. A slender, heavily tattooed man leaning against the rail said something that made them roar with laughter. Andrew jabbed his finger again, "Andrew Baird!"

The scarred man turned to face his compatriots as though exasperated at Andrew's responses. He said something that made the dacoits laugh again, and the man leaning against the rail pushed himself forward, ruffled the scarred man's hair and shoved him to join the rest.

I hope to God these are the right dacoits and not a rival gang. I'll try again.

"My name is Captain Andrew Baird. Bo Thura sent for me. Do any of you know where Bo Thura is?" He spoke slowly and clearly, hoping somebody had a smattering of English. He pointed a finger at the scarred man. "Are you Bo Thura? Bo Thura?"

The man from the rail took another step forward. Even more heavily tattooed than his compatriots, the man wore only a waist cloth with a silver-hilted *dha* suspended from a simple leather belt. He looked to be about fifty, with the force of his personality shining through.

"I know Bo Thura," the tattooed man spoke in perfect English. "I asked you to come here, Cousin. I am Bo Thura."

Andrew was unsure whether to bow or hold out his hand, for despite his appearance, Bo Thura had the accent and bearing of a British gentleman. His smile was also familiar, although Andrew could not think from where. "Why?" Andrew asked and added. "How is Mary MacConnacher?"

"Bearing up," Bo Thura said, looking Andrew up and down. "His smile broadened. I haven't killed her, if that's what you're worried about, Cousin, but nor do I have her with me."

"Where is she?" Andrew tried to ignore the dozen dacoits who swarmed on board the steamer and began to lift everything portable while Jamieson and Sinclair tried to defend their vessel. "Could you stop your men stealing, Bo Thura? You asked me to come here. This man had the kindness to give me a ride, so you are in his debt."

Bo Thura didn't ask me to Burma to murder me, so I should be safe. I am not sure about Jamieson and Sinclair.

Bo Thura snapped something, and most of the dacoits returned to their warboat, although they did not return the stolen items. The scarred man remained. He held his *dha*, stood in the bows, and watched Andrew suspiciously.

"My men like to loot," Bo Thura explained. "That's why they became dacoits."

"British soldiers have also been known to loot," Andrew said. "I don't want my colleague harmed."

"He won't be," Bo Thura said. He snapped an order, and the scarred man and three others moved towards Andrew with *dhas* in their hands. "As long as you come with me."

"Are you kidnapping me as you did with Mary MacConnacher?" Andrew remained still.

"You are my honoured guest, Cousin Andrew," Bo Thura replied with that familiar wry smile. "Don't you want to meet your family?"

I didn't come all this way to baulk at the last minute. "Take me to young Mary," he said, stepping onto the Burmese warboat.

Bo Thura followed, with the scarred man last to leave *Little Salamander.*

"The handsome gentleman is Aung Thiha," Bo Thura explained. "He is my personal bodyguard."

Andrew nodded. "He looks a handy chap to have at one's side," he said.

"You'll get to appreciate his fine qualities," Bo Thura replied. "Find a space in the boat."

On a word from Bo Thura, the dacoits lifted their paddles and swept away, leaving the steamer abandoned in the middle of the river. Jamieson and Sinclair were unharmed and staring after them. The dacoits on the riverbank had vanished.

"Where are we going?" Andrew asked.

"To the border," Bo Thura replied as the paddlers shoved hard and the warboat sped upriver at an impressive speed, emphasising every stroke of the paddles with a grunt. The smell of male sweat was powerful in the boat. "Bhamo."

"How far is that?" Andrew asked. He saw a human head near the bow, rolling from side to side, and wondered who the unfortunate owner might have been.

"Two days," Bo Thura said. "If we are lucky. Settle back, cousin."

"Is young Mary in Bhamo?"

Bo Thura gave that wry smile that Andrew found so strangely familiar. "You'll see." He tilted his head to one side. "Tell me, Cousin Andrew, why you changed your name from Windrush to Baird. Are you ashamed of your father? I met him once, you know, when he was a raw lieutenant, and I was a boy."

"No," Andrew replied. "I am not ashamed of my father. I wanted to try and make my way without his influence."

"Ah," Bo Thura nodded. "Pride rather than shame. Why pick Baird?"

"Baird was my grandfather's name on my mother's side."

Bo Thura nodded. "You must tell me about your mother and that side of our family."

"I will," Andrew promised. "Once I am sure Mary MacConnacher is safe."

"She is safe," Bo Thura assured him. He raised his voice. "San Kyi!" A man rose from the paddlers' ranks, stepped to the stern, and began to beat time on a large brass gong.

"That fellow's followed me from British Burma," he said.

"San Kyi was keeping his eye on you," Bo Thura said. He relapsed into silence, looking sideways at Andrew as if unsure they were related.

I have mingled with frontiersmen, Zulus, and Boers, and now I am in the company of Burmese dacoits. Yet I only want a quiet life in the countryside. I hope I can get young Mary back safely and return home.

Andrew knew that the smaller, lighter ships of the Irrawaddy Flotilla steamed as far as Bhamo, but he was unsure what to expect so near to the Chinese frontier. He slept on board the warboat, huddled uncomfortably on a wooden seat, and watched the wooded hill country ease past.

"Nearly there, Cousin," Bo Thura encouraged.

"What's this all about, Bo Thura?" Andrew asked. "Why kidnap a child only to release her?"

Bo Thura smiled. "I will explain everything in time," he said.

Bo Thura eased the warboat to a berth on the riverbank as Andrew watched a small Irrawaddy Flotilla vessel steam downstream. They left the warboat and walked casually into Bhamo.

Andrew found Bhamo a compact town within a timber stockade, a defended gateway, and a mixed population of Shans, Chinese, and some Burmese officials, with the Burmese in the minority. Although there were only a few hundred houses, Bhamo was a bustling town with an excited atmosphere that reminded Andrew of the settlements on the Natal and Cape Colony frontier. The people were busy, agile and curious about the European stranger. Near the town centre, a large building stood secure behind formidable walls. Andrew knew Bhamo's Governor would live inside the luxurious palace.

Andrew sensed the tension in the town as if everybody expected something to happen, but nobody knew what.

"Welcome to Bhamo," Bo Thura said. "The departure point for caravans to Talifoo in Yunnan, if you are interested. It's a very convenient place, Cousin. If Maung Thandar sends a force against me, I slip into Chinese Yunnan. If the Chinese take a dislike, I move deeper into Burma, and if both want me, I can slide into Shan country."

Andrew remembered Maung Thandar during the killings in Mandalay. "Thandar is a violent man," he said. "Would he send men against you?"

"He may do," Bo Thura replied without giving details.

"And if the British want you for raiding in Lower Burma?"

Bo Thura smiled. "I am at the furthest point from British territory," he said. "No British expedition could reach this far without Thibaw's permission, and he won't give that."

"No, I don't suppose he would," Andrew agreed.

The houses were a mixture of Burmese and Chinese, mostly neat and clean, with a different feel to southern Burma. Bo Thura ushered Andrew into a small house, where two elderly women shifted aside to make room. Aung Thiha and San Kyi followed as Bo Thura sat on a low stool and invited Andrew to join him.

"As we're on the frontier, everything has two names. The local tribe between the Irrawaddy and Salween Rivers is the Kakhyen to the Burmans and Yeuh-jin to the Chinese; the British call them the Karen. Naturally, the tribesmen don't recognise either name and call themselves the Singphoos, which simply means human beings or just men."

"All things to all people," Andrew said.

"I rather like them, Cousin," Bo Thura said. "They are thieves and robbers; when thievery fails, they take to barter and trade." He smiled again, with bright humour in his eyes. "Rather like the English, really, a nation of pirates turned to trade. General Albert Fytche thought them 'dirty, unkempt barbarians armed with bows and arrows, lawless to the last degree,' and who are we to agree with a British general?"

"Fytche was the Chief Commissioner of Burma, wasn't he?" Andrew asked.

"He is also Lord Tennyson's cousin," Bo Thura said. He shook his head. "But times are changing. Being a Windrush, I can smell the wind."

Andrew started; his father had used the same expression and had the same wry humour around his mouth.

"What does the wind scent tell you?" Andrew asked.

"The wind tells me that my position is insecure," Bo Thura said. "The British are becoming unhappy with Thibaw, and the Chinese will soon move south to this town."

"Will they?" Andrew asked.

"Undoubtedly," Bo Thura told him. "And when that happens, my position here will deteriorate from insecure to untenable, and I will have to seek sanctuary with my father's people." That wry smile returned. "That's where you come in, Captain David Andrew Windrush, who now calls himself Andrew Baird."

Andrew met the smile with one of his own. "I won't come in anywhere until I know Mary Mac-Connacher is safe. Where is she?"

He felt the sudden tension in the room and leaned back, with his revolver a comforting pressure under his tunic.

"I'll ask again, Bo Thura. Where is Mary Mac-Connacher?"

CHAPTER 13

RANGOON AND BHAMO, OCTOBER 1884

"Do you like horses?" Jennings asked as they sat in the lounge of Well's Britannia Hotel.

Mariana put down her pen and closed her journal. "Everybody likes horses," she replied.

"Good," Jennings said. "If you come with me, I'll show you the finest horses in Burma, if not in all Southeast Asia."

Mariana glanced at her journal. She had hoped to finish the page. "Is it far?"

Jennings shook his head. "Not far at all."

Mariana nodded. "Let me put my journal away and freshen up, and I'll join you down here in ten minutes."

"All right," Jennings agreed. "Half an hour it is." He met her smile with a knowing grin, for he prided himself on understanding women.

Jennings' stables were on the outskirts of Rangoon, a quarter of a mile from the British Army Cantonments. A staff of half a dozen young Burmese women and men smiled as Jennings appeared.

"That's an impressive building," Mariana said. "Do you own it?"

"I and some others," Jennings said. "We have formed a syndicate to improve the breeding stock of horses in Rangoon and start a Turf Club here. [1] Do you know anything about horses?" He looked at Mariana sideways, finger-grooming his moustache.

"A little bit," Mariana admitted. "I grew up on a farm in Natal, remember? My father had two daughters and no sons, so he taught us how to ride, farm, and shoot."

"You'll know a good horse when you see one, then," Jennings observed.

"I should," Mariana replied. "My father bred them. Show me your horses, sir."

"This way, Miss Maxwell," Jennings opened the tall stable door and ushered Mariana inside.

Mariana breathed deeply of the familiar scent. "Horses are always such homely animals," she said.

---

1. Rangoon Turf Club was founded in 1887.

"Horses and cattle belong with people, while sheep and goats should be in the wilds."

Jennings fondled the nearest horse's ear. "Do you like my babies?"

Mariana walked the length of the stables, where ten horses extended their necks to nuzzle her as she passed. She stopped at each one, stroking their glossy hides and talking softly.

"They look like thoroughbreds," Mariana said.

"That's what they are," Jennings replied proudly. "These are the best horses from the best breeding stock in Southeast Asia. As I said, we plan to open a racecourse in Rangoon soon, this year, next year or shortly afterwards, and I intend to win every single race." He smiled across to Mariana. "I've invested nearly everything I own in this operation."

Mariana walked back along the stable, speaking to each horse in turn, fondling their ears and running her hands down their necks and flanks.

"These are adorable animals," she said. "Do you ride often?"

"Every opportunity I get," Jennings replied. "Rangoon is a bit limited normally, but things are looking up. I have my eyes on a tasty little filly to add to my collection."

"These beauties are mainly stallions," Mariana pointed out. "You could perhaps do with a couple of mares to balance things."

"Mares are always welcome in my stable," Jennings said. He caressed a powerful black. "When we establish the Rangoon Turf Club with regular races, you will be an honoured guest and Queen of the Course on Lady's Day."

"Like at Ascot during the Royal Meeting?" Mariana asked.

"Exactly like that," Jennings enthused. "Perhaps the queen, or rather the Empress, will grace us with her presence."

"I am sure Her Majesty would be proud to include Rangoon in her next visit," Mariana said.

They lingered in the stables, with Jennings extolling the qualities of each horse and Mariana listening. Her father had been a keen horseman, as had all the pioneer farmers in Natal, but out of necessity rather than desire for glory or profit. Maxwell's horses were noted for stamina and strength rather than for speed. After an hour in the cool stables, Mariana was reluctant to leave for the humid heat outside.

"You have lovely horses," she said. She thought of Lancelot, Andrew's Kabul pony, and wondered how he would compare with Jennings' pedigree bloodstock.

"Thank you," Jennings replied. "Will you come to my house for dinner, Miss Maxwell?"

Mariana hesitated. "That is a very kind invitation, Mr Jennings, and I am tempted."

"Does that mean no?" Jennings asked.

"I am afraid so, Mr Jennings," Mariana replied. "It means not on this occasion."

"I thought you enjoyed my company," Civilian exaggerated a pout.

"I do enjoy your company," Mariana told him. "But a lone woman meeting a man during the day is acceptable, but meeting a man in the evening?" She smiled. "People would talk. However innocent your intentions, and I am sure you are as innocent as a newborn lamb, people would still gossip."

"Which people?" Jennings asked. "Rangoon society is cliquish and close-knit, but any gossip will be confined to this little backwater of a town. Nobody either knows or cares what happens here."

"Andrew might," Mariana said quietly.

Jennings stepped back. "Andrew might," he repeated, "but Captain Baird will have no cause to be alarmed, Miss Maxwell."

"Thank you, Mr Jennings," Mariana said. "Perhaps next time."

"WOULD YOU LIKE A SMOKE, COUSIN?" BO THURA asked.

"I'd prefer to ensure young Mary is safe," Andrew replied.

"Smoking is a pastime in Burma," Bo Thura seemed in no hurry to move. "Everybody in the country, from Thibaw to the poorest farmer, smokes. Unless you understand our customs, you'll never understand the country."

I have no desire to understand the country.

"Will you smoke with me, Cousin?"

Bo Thura's mocking tone irritated Andrew. "Indeed, Cousin," he replied. "Tell me how you make these cigars of yours." He felt the atmosphere in the house alter as if he had taken a step towards acceptance.

"Aung Thiha will demonstrate," Bo Thura said.

Aung Thiha produced half a dozen large coarse leaves and filled them with a handful of woodchips.

"That's the start," Bo Thura said.

Aung Thiha added some raw sugar and a small amount of tobacco. He smiled at Andrew, rolled the leaf around the mixture, lit it, took a couple of puffs and handed it over.

"Thank you," Andrew said. The cigar was nearly five inches long. Aware that everyone was watching, he steeled himself and inhaled, held the smoke in his lungs and slowly exhaled.

They expected me to fall about, choking and coughing. That was their test. They won't realise that public schoolboys used to find quiet places and smoke everything from tarry ropes to crushed nettles.

"Not bad," Andrew said, passing the cigar to Bo Thura. "I've smoked a lot worse. Now, where is little

Mary? Or will I catch the next steamer to Rangoon?"

Bo Thura grinned and stood up. "Follow me, Cousin. Now you've mastered the art of smoking a cheroot, we'll have to tattoo you!"

Andrew rose. "I can't see the Army allowing an officer to have tattoos." *What would Mariana think if I returned to Rangoon covered in Burmese tattoos? Or the good folk of Berwick?*

Bo Thura led them from the small house, with Aung Thiha walking between him and Andrew. People in the streets paid little attention as Bo Thura threaded through an area of poor-looking housing.

"Little Mary is in there," Bo Thura pointed to a bamboo hut like most of the others in the village. He stepped aside and smiled again.

Andrew took a deep breath, took hold of the handle of his revolver, and stepped inside the house, wondering what horrors he would find.

The house was cool and dim, with light easing through the windows and a pleasant scent of cooking and aromatic cigar smoke. Andrew heard a child laugh and a woman's low voice, followed by another laugh.

Three women looked around when Andrew entered. All had long Burmese cigars in their mouths while two children sat between them. One was a little Burmese boy; the other was undoubtedly European, a small girl with ginger hair who smoked her cheroot as adeptly as any Burmese.

The Burmese woman Andrew had met in Mandalay sat on the right, watching Andrew through musing, cynical eyes.

Andrew was unsure if he wanted to look at the little girl or the Burmese woman.

Rescue the girl! Rescue Mary and return to Rangoon.

"Mary?" Andrew asked. He felt his heartbeat increase and tried to ignore the woman.

The ginger-haired girl removed the cigar from her mouth and favoured Andrew with a broad smile. "I'm Mary," she said and spoke to her neighbours in fluent Burmese. The women laughed and looked at Andrew.

"You look surprised," Bo Thura said. "What did you expect?"

"I am not sure what I expected," Andrew admitted. "How have they treated you, Mary?"

"This is Than Than Aye, and this is Myat Phaya," Mary introduced the women. "Who are you?"

Than Than Aye. That's the Burmese woman's name.

"I am Andrew Baird," Andrew said. "I've come to take you home."

"I am home," Mary told him seriously. "I don't want to go back to that other place."

Bo Thura laughed. "Now you've seen young Mary, Cousin Andrew, and know she is safe and well cared for, we can talk."

"I'll come too," Than Than Aye said. She stood gracefully and walked beside them, with her hips an inch from Andrew's and her sandalwood perfume heady in his nostrils.

I must get to know this woman. Than Than Aye; that's an intriguing name.

How about Mariana?

Mariana turned me down.

Than Than Aye edged closer, with her hips lightly touching his. Andrew started, knew she was taunting him and abruptly looked away.

"You look nervous, Andrew Baird," Than Than Aye said softly. "Does a woman's company concern you?"

"I am not nervous," Andrew denied, shifting further away.

Than Than Aye laughed, "You may be the best soldier in the British Army, Captain Baird, but you have much to learn about women. We understand you." She looked at him through the corners of her eyes, smiling.

"I've come here for Mary," Andrew said.

"And you'll leave with her, Captain," Bo Thura promised. "Once we have reached an agreement."

Mary jumped up when Aung Thiha entered the room. "Aung!" She shouted, stretching out her arms. "*Kyawal! Kyawal!*"

Aung Thiha's scarred face puckered into a grin. He

lifted Mary, swung her in the air and placed her across his back. Stooping to all fours, he thundered around the house with Mary on his back, shouting, *"Kyawal!"*

"Kyawal means buffalo," Than Than Aye explained. "As you see, we are treating the little girl abominably!"

"So, I see," Andrew agreed, trying not to smile at the spectacle of the scarred warrior acting as a buffalo for the laughing child.

Bo Thura touched Andrew's arm. "You have seen Mary, Cousin. It's time we talked business. Come to my house. This way."

Bo Thura's house was slightly larger than the others in the village, neat and clean. A woman smiled at Andrew as he arrived, offered him a cigar, and sat in a corner of the spacious room.

"I thought the house we visited was yours," Andrew said.

"That was Aung Thiha's house," Bo Thura said, smiling. "Sit down, Cousin."

Andrew sat on one of the backless stools and studied the house. He saw a faded red coat hanging in the corner of the room and wondered if his Great Uncle George had owned it.

"Yes," Bo Thura answered his unspoken question. "That uniform belonged to my father. Sit down, Cousin."

Bo Thura laughed at the expression on Andrew's

face. "What did you expect, Cousin Andrew? Human heads on stakes? A cannibal feast?"

"Perhaps one of these," Andrew said. "You've gone to a lot of trouble with kidnapping that young girl and bringing me halfway across the world. Why did you want to see me?"

"I didn't want to see you," Bo Thura replied. "You are only a lowly colonial captain with no influence. I wanted to see your father, the general, the famous Fighting Jack Windrush, but as he's not available, you will be a perhaps adequate replacement."

"Thank you," Andrew replied ironically. "A replacement for what purpose? Why have you brought me thousands of miles across the world?"

"I need your help to get me safely into British Burma without your military hunting me down." Bo Thura laughed, with his eyes sparkling. "I am sure I could evade your clumsy khaki columns, but I don't want to. I want to settle in a quiet village without armed sentries and a bodyguard watching over me."

"You could still do that in Upper Burma," Andrew pointed out.

Bo Thura shook his head. "Unfortunately, Cousin, I can't. I have fallen out of favour with the authorities here, and do you know what they do to dacoits they capture?"

"They crucify them," Andrew answered brutally.

Bo Thura nodded. "Exactly so. It's rather a painful way to die."

Andrew remembered the crucified men he had seen. "I imagine so," he replied. "What did you do to annoy the king?"

"It wasn't the king," Bo Thura shook his head. "He's a weak sort of fellow, completely under the thumb of his mother-in-law and that savage Maung Thandar."

Andrew hid his surprise. "If not the king, then who have you annoyed?"

"Maung Thandar," Bo Thura said. "You may have heard of him?"

"I have heard of him," Andrew confirmed. *Maung Thandar was the evil-looking man involved in the massacre at Mandalay jail.*

"He is the devil," Bo Thura lit a cheroot and leaned back, holding Andrew's gaze. "He controls the dacoity, issuing licences and taking a percentage of all the dacoits gain. He sends bands into British Burma to disrupt your economy and weaken your prestige."

All the rumours are correct, except Maung Thandar takes a cut of the profits. "Does he, now?" Andrew expressed surprise. "I'll pass that information on when I return to Rangoon with Mary. Why did you kidnap her?"

"As bait," Bo Thura admitted. "I knew the

British would not allow a little girl to be kidnapped, and I sent a note asking for your father."

"I see," Andrew said. "How did you cross Maung Thandar?"

"I refused to pay his tribute," Bo Thura said.

"That would annoy him," Andrew agreed.

Typical bloody-minded Windrush. This fellow may look like a Burmese dacoit, but the Windrush blood runs true. I should have known when I saw that wry smile: Father has the same look.

"Why don't you just cross the border into British Burma?"

"I have a certain reputation," Bo Thura said. "If the British caught me, they'd either hang or shoot me. Both are preferable to crucifixion, but I'd prefer to live a little longer."

"I can imagine," Andrew said dryly. "What do you want me to do?"

Bo Thura drew on his cigar. "It's quite simple, Cousin. I want you to return to Rangoon with little Mary, tell the Chief Commissioner that the reformed Bo Thura rescued her from a band of evil dacoits, and I wish to come into British Burma under your protection. Put in a good word for me."

"As you said yourself, Bo Thura," Andrew reminded, "I am only a lowly colonial captain. I have no influence."

"Use your father's name," Bo Thura said. "Everybody knows Fighting Jack Windrush."

Andrew pondered for a moment. "That might work," he admitted. *All my adult life, I have tried to break free from my father's influence and make my own way in life. Now, a distant relative from a far-off country is asking me to revoke my values to help him.*

Is the result worth the price?

Could I leave young Mary MacConnacher here with these people?

"I can talk for you, Bo Thura," Andrew did not give a direct answer, "but what can you offer the British in return? Returning Mary and telling the Chief Commissioner you will no longer rob and steal in British territory may not be enough for him to welcome you with open arms."

"I can offer more than that," Bo Thura said.

He's playing his hand one card at a time. "Tell me more," Andrew said. "I am not yet convinced I want to help you."

Bo Thura smiled again. "Even though we are related, and I could kill you at a whim?"

"That is not in question," Andrew said. "You are a powerful man with an array of dacoits at your back while I am a lone stranger. My life is in your hands."

"It is," Bo Thura agreed. He pondered for a moment. "You will be aware that the French are in Tonkin, just over the border."

Andrew nodded, sensing that Bo Thura was about to impart important information. "Our newspapers are full of the French activities in Tonkin."

Bo Thura drew on his cigar again, allowing the smoke to trickle from his nostrils before he resumed his conversation. "Were you aware the French have designs for Upper Burma?"

Andrew took a deep breath. "I did not know that," he said. "Are you sure?"

"I am sure," Bo Thura said, smiling. He waited for a moment. "Would that information prove useful to the Chief Commissioner?"

Andrew considered before replying. "It might be," he said. "Of course, he would need proof. The word of a known dacoit would not be sufficient."

"I have proof," Bo Thura said.

Andrew held Bo Thura's gaze. "What sort of proof?"

"I have a document that shows the French involvement and what they intend to do in Thibaw's kingdom, written in Burmese and French."

"Good God!" Andrew stood up and paced the length of the airy room. "Have you read it?"

"I have," Bo Thura said.

"What does it say? Give me the details so I can inform the Chief Commissioner."

Bo Thura smiled. "If I tell you too much, Cousin, I have given away my trump before the cards are even dealt."

Andrew thought of the consequences of the French moving into Thibaw's kingdom of Ava, controlling the upper reaches of the Irrawaddy. With the British and French sharing a common frontier in an already volatile region, disputes were inevitable, especially if the French tried to prove their strength.

"The French in Upper Burma would cause all sorts of problems," Andrew said. "We put the French noses out of joint a few years ago when we gained control of the Suez Canal and Egypt. Now, they are moving into our spheres of interest in Asia. Tit for tat, and they know we are already wary of trouble with Russia over Afghanistan."

Bo Thura leaned back, smiling. "Can Great Britain afford a dispute with two major powers, Russia and France, simultaneously?"

"Let's hope it never happens," Andrew said.

How does a dacoit in the Burmese backwaters know so much about European politics?

"Little Mary MacConnacher is my opening gambit, Cousin Andrew, and the French document is my trump. Do you believe Sir Charles Crossthwaite, the Chief Commissioner, may grant me a pardon and permission to live in British Burma?"

Andrew nodded slowly, with his mind exploring the ramifications of a French presence in Mandalay. "I believe he may," he said, "if I can get the information to him before he learns from other channels."

He realised Than Than Aye had been listening to their conversation, scrutinising him through her fine eyes.

"Good," Than Than Aye said. "That's one thing

decided." She put a small hand on Andrew's arm. "It's my turn now, Andrew."

Andrew started, saw Bo Thura's amused smile, and followed Than Than Aye out the door.

"Now, Miss Maxwell," Jennings said. "I have invited you to my house on two occasions, and each time, you have made an excuse to refuse my hospitality. Now, I am formally requesting that you join me for dinner this evening."

"Not this evening," Mariana said. "Another time, perhaps."

They sat in the foyer of Wells Britannia Hotel, with the fan slowly revolving above and a pleasant hum of activity all around.

"Your Captain Andrew seems to have got himself lost," Jennings said. "He has left you alone for far too long."

"Something must have delayed him," Mariana said. She thought of the three weeks she had marked in her journal. She had marked off each carefully inscribed day, completed another three weeks and was already on the next. Her marks filled the lined page, and only she knew the stains came from her tears.

"That is correct," Jennings said. "Something or somebody." He smiled at his attempted humour.

"Perhaps Captain Andrew has found himself an attractive Burmese lady."

"Andrew would not do that," Mariana said stoutly. She lifted her chin. "Andrew is a man of his word."

I rejected him in Edinburgh. Oh, why did I do that? Maybe he will never come back.

"Of course not," Jennings agreed. "I spoke in jest or perhaps in worry because the good Captain Andrew is so late."

These Burmese ladies are attractive. One captured Sergeant Wells, and Andrew's great Uncle George married another. Mariana shuddered. *Andrew's father, General Windrush, married an Indian woman; maybe it's a family trait. I wish we had never come East.*

"Are you all right, Miss Maxwell?" Jennings asked. "You look very pale suddenly. Sit down, please, and I'll fetch a glass of water." He raised his voice, calling for a waiter.

"I am all right," Mariana said as a waiter appeared with a glass of tepid water. She saw Wells watching from the corner of the room and mustered a smile.

"I've upset you, haven't I?" Jennings asked. "Unforgivable, and you such a lovely lady. I cannot apologise enough."

"There is no need to apologise, Mr Jennings," Mariana said. "Please excuse me." She rose, turned away and hurried upstairs to her room.

CHAPTER 14

BHAMO, KINGDOM OF AVA, DECEMBER
1884

"I like you, Andrew Baird," Than Than Aye said as they left the house. "And I know you like me." She led him to an open area, where women gossiped and children played.

"I do," Andrew agreed.

Than Than Aye laughed openly. "How much do you like me, Andrew Baird?"

I feel as if I've known you all my life, Andrew thought. "Why do you ask?"

Than Than Aye bumped her hip against Andrew's thigh. "In what way do you like me, Andrew Baird?"

Andrew thought of Mariana, but that feeling of

having known Than Than Aye all his life returned. "You are a very attractive woman, Than Than Aye."

Than Than Aye laughed and bumped her hip against him again. "Do you think of me as a woman? Or as something else?"

"As a woman," Andrew replied immediately.

Than Than Aye's laugh was louder than ever. "You can't do that, Andrew. We share the same blood."

"What?" Andrew stared as Than Than Aye stepped back, with her eyes bright. "Say that again."

"You heard me the first time," Than Than Aye said. "I am Bo Thura's daughter, your cousin."

"Oh, dear Lord in Heaven!" Andrew shook his head. "I am sorry, Than Than Aye. I had no idea!" He stepped away as Than Than Aye continued to laugh.

"We can still be friends," Than Than Aye told him seriously. "But not the way you hoped. I told you I understand you, but you have much to learn about women."

When Andrew looked at her again, he realised that all desire had vanished. He saw her as a friend or a relative, but nothing else.

"Dear Lord in Heaven," Andrew repeated as Than Than Aye scrutinised him.

"Now you understand," Than Than Aye said. "You recognised something in me. It was blood. Blood calls to blood, Cousin."

Andrew grasped at that fragile straw. "I see," he said.

"Good," Than Than Aye nodded. "Now we can be friends. You'll want to take little Mary back to her mother." She grasped Andrew's arm in a sisterly fashion. "Bo Thura will need to hear."

"WE'LL LEAVE FOR RANGOON TOMORROW," Andrew said as they sat in Bo Thura's pleasant house. He held the Irrawaddy Flotilla timetable in his hand and consulted the lists. "The Flotilla steamer *Kaw Byoo*, under Captain Terndrup, will arrive in the morning, and she'll take me to Mandalay. From there, I'll catch the Flotilla steamer for Rangoon."

Bo Thura nodded. "You will take Mary with you," he said.

"I will," Andrew said. "That is why I came here." He looked out of the open door as the light faded. It already seemed normal to sit in a bamboo and teak house near the Irrawaddy River. When he returned to Berwick, he knew this episode would appear as a dream, as if he had never heard the tinkle of temple bells or smelled the sweet spices of Than Than Aye's cooking.

"Don't forget to ask the Chief Commissioner about me," Bo Thura gave his wry smile.

"I will tell him you rescued Mary from a band of very unpleasant dacoits and want nothing more than to return her to her mother," Andrew said solemnly. "I will praise you to the high heavens and remind Sir Charles that you also found details of the French plans to increase their influence in Thibaw's kingdom."

"Good," Bo Thura sat in the corner of the room. He drew on his cigar and passed it to Than Than Aye.

"I cannot guarantee Sir Charles' reaction," Andrew said. "I can only do my best." He accepted the cigar from Than Than Aye, drew deeply and passed it on to Bo Thura.

"Mary will be nervous about leaving us," Than Than Aye said. "I'll come with you to keep her calm."

"Will you be safe in Rangoon?" Andrew asked.

"Do you think the British will recognise who I am?" Than Than Aye asked. "To them, I'll just be another Burmese woman." She glanced at Andrew. "I'm better looking than most, though," she said and laughed.

Everyone looked up as Aung Thiha entered the room and whispered something to Bo Thura, who glanced at Andrew and shook his head.

"What's the to-do?" Andrew asked when Aung Thiha left as gracefully as a cat. "What's happening?"

"The Chinese are happening," Bo Thura replied. "Come with me."

"The Chinese?"

"I'll get the little one," Than Than Aye said and hurried away.

"This way, Cousin," Bo Thura guided Andrew through Bhamo. Groups of men and women gathered at doorways and in the streets, talking, smoking, and often laughing. They spoke casually to Bo Thura as to a long-standing acquaintance and stared curiously at Andrew.

Europeans must be a novelty here despite the Irrawaddy Flotilla's steamers.

"Look over there," Bo Thura said quietly, "but don't stare. One is never sure how the Chinese may react."

Andrew saw a small group of men drifting through the north gate, talking to each other while looking around them. Like many men at this frontier, they carried arms, either long, slightly curved swords or long muskets.

"They look a handy bunch of fellows," Andrew said. "Are they the Chinese you mentioned?"

"They are Chinese, from Yunnan province," Bo Thura agreed. "They've been sliding into Bhamo all night in twos, threes and small parties."

"I see," Andrew said.

Bo Thura watched the incomers for a few moments. "They are irregular Chinese military by the way they stand. I'd say there's trouble in the wind, Cousin. You're wise to get out of Bhamo tomorrow. I might take my people out as well."

Andrew glanced at him. "Are the Chinese any threat to you?"

Bo Thura attempted to look innocent. "There is one Yunnan official who thinks he has a grudge."

"What happened?" Andrew asked.

"He lost a prize horse once and blamed me for taking it," Bo Thura said.

"Did you take it?" Andrew asked directly.

"Yes," Bo Thura replied. "I didn't think he'd make such a fuss about it. He's threatened to execute me in various unpleasant ways unless I replace his horse."

"Maybe you'd best avoid him, then," Andrew advised. He watched as another group of men eased inside Bhamo. Their long, colourful jackets and tight headgear told him they were neither Burmese nor Chinese.

"Kachyeus," Bo Thura said quietly. "You'd call them Kachins. Sometimes, they ally themselves with the Chinese; sometimes, they act alone. They are wild tribesmen from the hills, often fighting with the Burmese, who claim their lands."

"What do they want here?" Andrew asked.

"Maybe to trade," Bo Thura said. "Maybe to rob, and maybe they are watching to see what happens, as we are."

Andrew glanced over his shoulder at the Governor's palace, thrusting above the mass of houses. "Should we warn the Governor?"

Bo Thura did not hesitate. "No. He would not trust the word of a British man and could arrest me. We'll sit tight tonight, and you'll leave on the steamer tomorrow."

"Does everyone want to arrest you, Bo Thura?" Andrew asked.

"Not everyone," Bo Thura replied. "But you can understand why I seek sanctuary in British Burma."

"I won't forget to tell Sir Charles," Andrew promised. He nodded as another group of Chinese slipped through the gate and moved purposefully into the town. "I think we should return to your house," he said. "We've left the women alone there."

Bo Thura locked his doors and windows and set two watchmen for the night, with Aung Thiha patrolling the streets.

"Keep Mary safe," Andrew ordered.

"I have her," Than Than Aye replied reassuringly.

Andrew slept uneasily with his pistol beside his bed. He remembered his recent experience in Mandalay and wakened every few moments, listening for the sound of gunfire or a shouting mob.

The trouble began before dawn. Bo Thura was already awake, and Than Than Aye had Mary dressed and fed. Andrew heard the deep notes of a gong, a single shot, and the rising cries of a crowd.

Here we go. Andrew had slept half-dressed and only had to slip on his tunic and boots before leaving the small cubicle where he slept.

"Trouble," Bo Thura reported with a calm smile. "San Kyi tells me there are about six hundred Chinese and Kachins inside Bhamo. That's about five hundred more than I'd like."

Andrew heard the gong again, with the sound bringing back memories of his voyage from Thayetmyo.

The shooting increased, accompanied by wild cries and screaming.

"Upper Burma is a wild place," Andrew said as Bo Thura sent his men to watch the windows.

"King Thibaw does not keep an orderly kingdom," Bo Thura said calmly.

Andrew glanced over his shoulder, where Than Than Aye was washing Mary's hair in a basin of warm water. Both sang a song in Burmese.

That child will find it hard to reassimilate into British culture. She is as well cared for with the dacoits as she would be back home. If I can even catch the Flotilla ship with this blasted trouble.

"Open the door," Andrew ordered. "I'm going to see what's happening."

"You're a fool if you do," Bo Thura told him.

"I can't make a decision without intelligence," Andrew replied. "Open the blasted door!"

Chinese and Kachins seemed to be everywhere,

running through the streets in chaotic groups, firing at random, chasing women and slowly moving towards the Governor's palace where the small Burmese garrison lived.[1]

It's Mandalay all over again.

Andrew slid into the shelter of a bamboo and matting house as a party of Chinese marched past. They headed directly for the eastern gate, casually shot the gatekeeper, and dragged the heavy teak doors open. A host of men, irregular Chinese soldiers and Burmese villagers poured inside and ran to the Chinese quarter. They shouted as they ran, with some brandishing weapons.

The Chinese are well organised; they've planned this operation in advance.

As the Chinese approached the palace, the gates banged open, and a lone horseman burst out. He was splendidly dressed and sleek with good living.

That's the Governor, Andrew realised.

The Governor's horse reared and whinnied at the sight of the crowd, nearly throwing the rider. He controlled the animal with difficulty, waving his left hand, and galloped away towards the Irrawaddy. A platoon of palace guards followed and fired a single

---

1. The Chinese attack on Bhamo in December 1884 seems to have taken the Burmese by surprise. Hundreds of Chinese irregulars infiltrated the town and took control within a few hours, although sporadic fighting lasted a couple of days.

ragged volley at the invaders before joining him in flight.

So much for Thibaw's soldiers, Andrew thought as the Chinese ran through the open gates into the palace and made free of the arsenal. About half the Burmese soldiers threw away their hats, ripped off their jackets and began to loot the town, breaking into houses and carrying away everything they fancied.

I've seen enough. Time to get back to Bo Thura's house. There won't be any Flotilla steamers in Bhamo today.

"Well?" Bo Thura waited behind the door with a rifle in his hand.

"Chinese and Kachins everywhere," Andrew reported. "The Governor and his guards have run, and half the garrison have joined the Chinese in stripping the place bare."

"As I thought," Bo Thura said. "We'll stay here until the dust settles." He smiled. "You'll just have to accept my hospitality." His smile faded. "Keep your revolver handy."

Andrew glanced at Mary, who was sitting quietly beside Than Than Aye, quite content to watch proceedings and share a cheroot. "The sooner I get her back to her parents, the better."

Bo Thura frowned. "Why? They'll probably pack her off to some maiden aunt in England, who'll restrict everything she does, or worse, her parents will send her to some terrible school with cold baths every morning. She'll be happier with us."

Andrew had a sudden memory of his school days in England. "That's probably true," he said. "All the same, she belongs with her parents." He looked around as a fresh burst of gunfire sounded.

"Shut and barricade the door," Bo Thura ordered.

They heard the fighting intensify and then fade away to sporadic shooting and an occasional burst of shouting and screaming. Bo Thura kept his doors locked, and his men took turns on guard. On one occasion, a group of Burmese soldiers approached until Bo Thura fired a warning shot in the air. He shouted to them, then translated for Andrew. "I told them that I'll blow the head off the first man to touch my property."

Andrew nodded. "I'll take the second man," he said, showing his revolver.

Bo Thura's laugh could have been a copy of Andrew's father. "That's the way, Cousin."

The soldiers replied with loud shouts, brandishing their weapons. One saw Andrew, recognised he was European, drew his *dha* and gestured to his throat.

"That man says he'll cut off your head," Bo Thura told Andrew.

"I'll shoot him first," Andrew said. He wondered how long these soldiers would stand before a Zulu charge. He held the knifeman's gaze, aimed his revolver and smiled.

"I know you will," Bo Thura said quietly.

The soldiers melted away as the sun rose, bringing oppressive heat to the barricaded house. Smoke from burning houses clouded the street, settling as a blue-grey layer close to the ground. It was noon before the soldiers returned, with a stout, swaggering man leading a yelling mob.

"They mean business this time," Andrew said.

"You can also read the wind," Bo Thura looked at him sideways.

"So, it seems," Andrew agreed. He checked his revolver was fully loaded, winked at Mary, and returned his full attention to the soldiers outside.

The mob's noise increased as they gathered their courage before attacking. Andrew saw firelight reflecting from their weapons and thought of the similar situation in Ma Gun's house in Mandalay. He glanced back, where Mary and Than Than Aye shared a small cheroot. Mary waved to him.

How ironic, to come to rescue the child just as trouble erupts.

"How many are there?" Bo Thura asked.

"Forty? Fifty?" Andrew hazarded. "It's hard to tell with the smoke drifting over them."

Bo Thura grinned, lifting a Martini-Henry from a dark corner of the room. "We'll see how they like this," he said.

"Where did you get that?" Andrew recognised the markings on the rifle. "That's a War Office issue!"

Bo Thura's grin widened. "I took it from one of your soldiers," he said. "He looked the other way at the wrong time."

"You're a rogue, Bo Thura," Andrew lifted his revolver as the soldiers moved closer. One fired a musket, with the bullet smacking into the wall without penetrating the teak.

"You know the locals, Bo Thura. Is it better to return fire or sit tight?"

"Return fire, Cousin Andrew," Bo Thura replied.

CHAPTER 15

BHAMO, KINGDOM OF AVA, DECEMBER
1884

Andrew fired on Bo Thura's word, with his bullet catching the soldier on the right leg. He fell without a sound, dropping his musket.

The other soldiers howled with anger and charged forward, waving their *dhas* or wildly firing their rifles. Andrew shot one, saw Bo Thura hit another, and they ceased fire as a second group appeared on the flank of the soldiers.

"That's Aung Thiha," Bo Thura said proudly. "He never lets me down."

Andrew saw the stocky man slice at a soldier with his *dha*, cutting the man's arm clean off, then thrust the point into another soldier's throat. Aung Thiha was laughing, enjoying the battle as he ran into the thickest of the soldiers. They scattered before him, with Andrew and Bo Thura firing at any who came close to the house.

"Your Aung Thiha is some fighter," Andrew said as the soldiers fled, and Aung Thiha shouted after them in triumph.

"He is," Bo Thura agreed proudly. "He'll remain outside until the danger is past."

If the Burmese Army has many like Aung Thiha, we'll be hard-pressed to defeat them.

They remained in Bo Thura's house all day, listening to the shouts, screams, and occasional shots from the streets outside. Twice more, parties of soldiers passed the house, one Burmese and one Chinese. Neither lingered, and Andrew began to relax. He hoped that Mariana was all right, thanked God that the Wellses were there to keep an eye on her, and wished he was back in Berwick.

I've been away from Mariana far longer than I expected. He had the crazy idea of introducing his new relatives to his father, wondered how they would get along and shook his head. *The strain must be affecting me if I am thinking like that. Let's hope the Irrawaddy Flotilla steamer arrives soon, and we can start the journey back to Rangoon. I can't allow Mary to remain in this dangerous environment.*

The night was tense, with Andrew expecting the

rogue Burmese soldiers to return. He slept sitting upright in a chair with his revolver in his lap with the safety catch on. Twice, he woke to see Than Than Aye holding Mary. Each time, she smiled across at him.

That's my cousin. How could I have thought anything else?

The morning brought a sharp shower of rain that cooled the town but ended after half an hour, leaving water weeping from the roofs but nobody in the streets. Within ten minutes, the rainwater began to evaporate, creating a fine mist over the houses.

"The Flotilla steamer is overdue," Andrew said. "We'll see if she arrives and if we can get on board. I'll have another look around the town today."

Bo Thura looked up from his bowl of rice. "Why?"

"I want to see if it's safe to take Mary through the streets. I don't want to chance stray gunmen and mob rule."

"I'll come with you," Bo Thura decided.

They left the house half an hour later, wary of any sound as they threaded the streets towards the river. Andrew held his revolver, Bo Thura his rifle, and they moved from shadow to shadow without seeing a living human. Half a dozen bodies lay on the ground, men, women, and children, while packs of dogs and pigs roamed free.

"There's a ship in the river," Andrew said hopefully as they stopped at the wide-open town gate.

"That's a Burmese steamer," Bo Thura told him. "One of Thibaw's gunboats. Pass me your field glasses."

Andrew passed them over.

"The Governor's on board," Bo Thura said. "He's on the bridge, talking to the captain and drinking something."

A lone dog barked, joined by others in a cacophony of noise that echoed over the deserted streets.

Andrew retrieved his field glasses. "I see him. He doesn't seem concerned at the loss of his town and the death of his people." He peered down the river. "I can't see *Kaw Byoo* yet."

"She'll be here," Bo Thura said. "Captain Terndrup is a reliable man." He grinned. "I know the Flotilla steamer captains by name and reputation. In my occupation, such information is useful. Return to the house now before a Chinese patrol finds us."

Bo Thura was correct. Andrew saw *Kaw Byoo's* smoke in the middle of the morning, and she arrived in the early afternoon.

"Come on!" Andrew said. "Bring Mary, Than Than Aye. You'd better come too, Bo Thura. If we can get you on the steamer, you can be close to the border with British Burma when the Chief Commissioner grants you a pardon."

"If he grants me a pardon," Bo Thura said.

"He will," Andrew said.

"You have more faith in the British sense of fair play than I have," Bo Thura gave his wry smile.

"Come on, Cousins!" Andrew ordered. "We have an agreement!"

They left Bo Thura's house when they saw the smoke and hurried towards the riverbank, joining an increasing crowd of people anxious to escape Bhamo. Than Than Aye held Mary's hand, lifting her when the crowd grew denser.

Captain Terndrup approached the quay cautiously, pulled alongside and tied up as a nervous crowd of refugees waited to board. One of *Kaw Byoo's* crew stood on the upper deck with a Snider, watching the town through nervous eyes.

The second the crew put out the gangplank, the refugees rushed forward, clamouring to board, but Captain Terndrup stopped them by brandishing his revolver. He gave a sharp order, and the armed crewman fired a shot into the air.

"Ticket holders first!" Captain Terndrup shouted. "Show your tickets to the crew or stay on shore!"

"There might not be room for us," Andrew looked at the swelling crowd of anxious people trying to escape from the carnage in Bhamo.

"We can use my boat," Bo Thura said, avoiding the captain's gaze. "I'll take you as far as Mandalay."

"No, we can't," Andrew pointed to the quay, where Bo Thura's boat lay a smouldering wreck beside half a dozen others, ruined by Burmese or Chinese soldiers.

Bo Thura shrugged philosophically. "I'll get another," he said.

"I'm sure you will," Andrew said, "but that doesn't help young Mary or your cause with the Chief Commissioner."

As *Kaw Byoo's* crew checked the refugees' documentation, Captain Terndrup took a small boat over to the Burmese vessel. Watching through his field glasses, Andrew saw him speaking to the Governor. After a few moments of heated debate, Terndrup returned to his ship. He spoke to *Kaw Byoo's* officers first, climbed to her upper deck, and lifted a metal speaking trumpet.

"Silence!" Terndrup shouted and had one of his Burmese crew translate his words to the anxious refugees. "The Burmese Governor of Bhamo has granted me permission to take a party ashore and gather up all the European civilians who wish to leave. I will guarantee a place on the ship to any armed men who accompany me."

Andrew turned to Bo Thura, who shook his head and withdrew into the crowd.

"Bo Thura!" Andrew stretched out a hand.

"Let him go," Than Than Aye said quickly. "Captain Terndrup knows who he is."

Andrew nodded and pushed Than Than Aye and Mary towards the captain. "I'll come if you take this woman and child to safety."

Captain Terndrup frowned. "That is not what I said."

"This lady helped me rescue the little girl from her kidnappers," Andrew explained, finding it a strain to shout above the crowd's clamour. "I am Captain Andrew Baird of the Natal Dragoons."

"A soldier?" Terndrup replied. "I need all the experienced men I can get." He glanced at Than Than Aye and Mary. "Agreed, Captain Baird. Bring them on board."

Andrew expected the protests from the Europeans when Than Than Aye stepped forward. "But she's a Burman!" a red-faced merchant said. "The captain said he'd rescue the Europeans. I'm English, damn it!"

Terndrup ignored the howls as Andrew escorted Than Than Aye through the crowd and onto the gangplank.

"Don't stay on deck," Andrew hissed in Than Than Aye's ear. "Get inside where nobody can see you and keep safe. I'll find you later." He gave her a gentle push. "Go on! Ignore the shine." [1] He stepped to the captain's side.

"Mr Higgins!" Captain Terndrup shouted to the

---

1. Ignore the shine: ignore the noise.

mate. "You take charge of the ship. Don't let anybody board until we return. Captain Baird, you are with me."

"Yes, sir," Andrew agreed.

Two more volunteers joined Terndrup's eight-strong force that trotted into Bhamo, with the Chinese and Burmese soldiers watching from a distance.

"We have a few American missionaries to rescue first," Captain Terndrup said. "Then I believe some Europeans have gathered in one house near the town centre." He looked around as a crowd of Burmese followed the landing party, with some howling abuse and others throwing stones and handfuls of mud.

"They don't seem to like us very much," Terndrup told Andrew.

"They were slaughtering each other and robbing the town blind yesterday," Andrew told him. "They don't like anybody very much."

A force of wild-looking irregular soldiers stood before the American missionary church, with a smartly dressed official in charge.

"Captain Terndrup?" the official stepped forward as the landing party halted, unsure what to expect.

"I am Terndrup," the captain stepped forward, with Andrew keeping his revolver ready.

"The Reverend Soltan is waiting for you with his people," the official said. "I am Kiugkwek-li, in command of the Chinese in Bhamo."

Terndrup bowed politely, then held out his hand. "Thank you for meeting me, Kiugkwek-li."

The two men examined each other with evident mutual respect.

"If there is anything I can do for you, Kiugkwek-li," Terndrup said. "I will be happy to oblige."

The Chinese official, tall, refined and elegant, nodded. "If you come across a Burmese dacoit called Bo Thura on your ship," he said. "Hold him for me."

"I'll do that," Terndrup nodded grimly. "Bo Thura. I know the name."

Kiugkwek-li is the Chinese official who has fallen out with Bo Thura. Is this attack part of Chinese policy? Or is it a personal hunt for my cousin? Either way, it's no wonder Bo Thura did not try to board Kaw Byoo.

The Americans came out slowly and noisily: a small group of missionaries, their wives, and a larger number of Karen followers and Christian converts.

The Reverend Soltan, a grave, dignified man with a long face and spectacles, bowed to Kiugkwek-li and formally thanked him for his assistance.

They spoke briefly as the Chinese soldiers helped the missionaries from the building, and then Kiugkwek-li spoke again to Captain Terndrup.

"We cannot endure Burmese oppression of our people any longer, Captain," Kiugkwek-li said. "When you return to Bhamo, China will be in charge. We will keep the country as far south as

Mandalay and leave the British to hold the remainder."

"I look forward to seeing you again, sir," Captain Terndrup replied without committing himself to any political opinion.

"We will rid the area of the robbers and thieves," Kiugkwek-li said. "Especially the one known as Bo Thura!" He looked around as if expecting Bo Thura to spring from behind a building.

With the Americans safely beside Captain Terndrup, Kiugkwek-li's soldiers provided an escort to the second group of European refugees.

"Out you come!" Andrew shouted. "These Chinese lads are helping!"

The Europeans stared out fearfully, realised it was safe and emerged in a flood, some carrying cases and a few with Burmese or Karen servants laden with their possessions.

"The ship is waiting," Captain Terndrup said. "Form up in an orderly fashion!"

The civilians made a noisy mob, jostling for position as they followed Captain Terndrup. Some eyed the Chinese with disfavour, and a couple demanded priority treatment as they claimed to be important people.

"Get in line there!" Andrew snarled. "We are all in the same position."

When the Chinese escort left, the Burmese pressed closer, a mixture of soldiers and civilians taunting the European refugees. Andrew pushed one wiry youth back when he grabbed a woman's bags.

"Sir," Andrew approached Terndrup. "I think the armed men should be around the civilians to keep the rabble at bay."

"Do that, Captain Baird," Terndrup said. "I'll put you in charge of the escort."

Andrew nodded and snapped orders to the armed men.

"Two on each side, two in front and two in the rear! Keep a space between our people and the mob. Don't shoot anybody, and don't start trouble, but use a firm hand to show we mean business."

With the howling crowd in front and pressing on the sides, progress to the ship was slow.

"Push them aside!" Andrew hurried to the front of the European column when a surge of Burmese soldiers threatened them. He raised his voice to a roar. "Move aside there! Make way!" He pushed a snarling man out of the way, ducked as somebody swung a stick at him, felled the attacker with a right hook and gestured for the column to move forward.

"They're chanting 'kill the foreigners,'" a frightened merchant said. "They're baying for our blood."

"They can bay all they like," Andrew said, shoving a loud-voiced man aside. "They weren't so brave when the Chinese invaded." He raised his voice. "Push on, Captain Terndrup!"

Andrew circled the refugees, helping the inexperienced civilians and sailors with their unaccustomed duty. He grunted as a stone smashed into his head, opening a cut, looked for the thrower and saw only a mass of shouting faces.

"Get away!" Andrew grabbed a roaring Burmese by the arm and dragged him away. He kicked savagely at a gesticulating man who had grabbed a Karen woman by the hair and punched another in the face. "Keep moving, Captain!"

Andrew felt blood flowing down his face; he blocked a youth's flying kick and lifted one of the escort, whom three men had knocked down.

This escape is getting ugly. I hope there's not much further to the quay.

The crowd grew denser as more Burmans realised the Chinese escort had left, with rushes at the refugees and more missiles flying. Stones bounced off the road in front, women hurried their children away from the mob, and men tried to protect their wives.

"Push through!" Andrew said, encouraging the escort. He saw one of the sailors stagger as a stone cracked against his head and searched for the stone thrower without success. He knew that such people usually hid at the back of the mob, using others as shelter.

"You cowardly bastard!" Andrew roared, knowing his words were useless against the noise of the mob.

"Here's the quay!" a man shouted.

The mate had held *Kaw Byoo* secure and now ordered the crew to clear the gangplank. The crew pushed down, some with long staves, as they pushed the waiting crowd back.

"Make way! Make way, damn you!" The crew, British and Burmese, struggled against the press of civilians as missiles flew to clatter against *Kaw Byoo's* hull and bounce from her deck. Some hit the sailors or landed amidst the refugee column.

Captain Terndrup stood aside and ushered the refugees on board, with the crowd on the quay pressing forward to escape from Bhamo.

Andrew stood on the opposite side of the narrow gangplank to the captain, ensuring nobody fell into the water. He saw Than Than Aye on the ship, looking strained as she held Mary tight by the hand and watched the crowd clamour to get aboard.

"Get inside!" Andrew roared. "Than Than Aye! Get away from the deck! It's unsafe." He did not know if Than Than Aye heard him as the last refugees swarmed up the gangplank.

"That's them all on!" Terndrup shouted. "Is steam up, Mr Higgins?"

"All ready, sir!" the mate replied.

"Then let the others on board and stand by to depart!" Terndrup ordered. "Captain Baird! Get the escort on board as quickly as possible."

"Yes, sir!" Andrew said no more as his men hurried onto the ship. The first of the crowd followed, kicking, punching, and pushing each other in their panic to escape Bhamo.

"Form an orderly queue!" Andrew shouted. He saw one overweight man shove a slender woman aside and thrust forward, with a young lad crawling between others' legs and snaking on board. The slender woman fell into the water between *Kaw Byoo* and the shore. A man with two screaming children tried to rush the gangplank until a group of active young men elbowed them aside.

Terndrup looked up as gunshots sounded from the town.

"Get the last of these people on board!"

"We can't take any more!" Higgins replied. "We're already overcrowded."

"All right! Cast off aft! Cast off forward! Let's get away from here!"

Andrew saw one woman make a despairing leap from the quay to reach *Kaw Byoo* but fall short and land in the water. She began to swim to the ship until one of the sailors threw her a line. When she grabbed hold, the seamen pulled her in.

"There you are, darling, safe as the Bank of England, now!"

Andrew heard the shooting increase as he approached Than Than Aye and Mary.

That's the first part over, but now we must pass through Upper Burma.

He patted the French documents in his inside pocket and wondered what Sir Charles Crossthwaite would say.

CHAPTER 16

IRRAWADDY RIVER, KINGDOM OF AVA, DECEMBER 1884

Andrew heard the first shots only an hour after *Kaw Byoo* left Bhamo. An unseen rifleman fired from the forest, with one bullet hissing over the steamer and the second boring a hole in the hull. One of the passengers screamed, and there was a minor stampede to get inside the frail protection of the interior.

"Is this normal?" Andrew asked Captain Terndrup.

The captain had not flinched. "It happens," he said. "Sometimes they shoot at us, sometimes they leave us alone." He shrugged. "They've never stopped us yet."

Andrew remembered his father's tales about tribesmen sniping at convoys passing through the Khyber Pass and wondered at the mentality of the snipers.

Perhaps they just don't like the British in their country, or are just natural predators.

Even with the current on their side, *Kaw Byoo* seemed to take an age to travel downriver. The steamer was overcrowded, with no space on board to stretch out. Food was limited, and the smell of human sweat and fear was overpowering.

After two days, another unidentified man shot at *Kaw Byoo.* Andrew saw him run along the riverbank, trying to keep pace with the steamer.

"Give me that Snider," Andrew asked. He took a packet of ammunition from behind the wheel, rammed in a cartridge and ran on deck. The shooter was a hundred yards in front of the steamer, using a tree bough as a rifle rest.

"Shoot him!" the overweight merchant shouted. "Kill him!"

Andrew aimed, took first pressure on the trigger, allowed for the speed of *Kaw Byoo* and fired an instant before the attacker. He saw his shot hit the ground an inch in front of the marksman and raise a fountain of dirt.

"You missed!" the overweight man accused bitterly.

"I know," Andrew said. "Look at the lad. He can't

be more than fourteen years old." He felt Than Than Aye watching him, reloaded the Snider, and watched the marksman run across a flooded paddy field, leaving his musket behind. *Kaw Byoo* chugged on, keeping to the deep-water channel as Andrew appointed himself sentry.

"You could have killed that boy," Than Than Aye said.

"He was only a boy," Andrew replied. "A youth testing his masculinity. I gave him a fright, and no harm done."

Than Than Aye touched his arm, nodded thoughtfully and walked away.

ANDREW KEPT THAN THAN AYE AND MARY OUT of sight when they berthed at Mandalay. "I don't know who might recognise you," he said.

"I'll keep out of the way," Than Than Aye promised.

Andrew watched as most of the Burmese and Karen refugees left the ship. As the crew loaded coal and supplies from the terminal's ample supplies, a few Europeans boarded. Three of the new arrivals noticed Than Than Aye with Mary and asked a hundred questions that Andrew was not keen to answer.

"Is that your child?" A bumptious man nudged

Andrew and pointed to Mary. "I said, is that your child?"

"I'm looking after her," Andrew replied.

"You aren't doing a very good job, are you?" the man laughed at his pretended humour. "She looks rather, well, rather like a Burman, doesn't she? Tanned and ragged. You're not going native, are you?"

When Andrew gave a non-committal reply and turned away, the man shook his head and addressed his fellow Europeans.

"That fellow's a damned jungle wallah. That woman he's with is probably his mistress and the child; Good God! The child will be their offspring, like as not."

"That type gives us all a bad name," another man said. "It shouldn't be allowed."

When Andrew turned angrily Than Than Aye put a small hand on his arm. "Do they matter, Andrew?"

Andrew took a deep breath. "No," he said.

"Do their opinions matter?"

"No," Andrew replied.

Than Than Aye smiled. "They are small people with inflated opinions and, as such, are best ignored."

Andrew nodded. "You're a clever woman, Than Than Aye."

"I am not very clever," Than Than Aye replied.

"I just understand people. There won't be any trouble if we keep out of their way."

"That's good advice," Andrew replied. "It will be a long journey to Rangoon."

"Every minute survived is a minute less," Than Than Aye said, smiling.

ANDREW STEPPED FROM *KAW BROO* AT RANGOON with Than Than Aye at his side and Mary in his arms. He looked around, feeling strange in this urban environment, with European traders around him and English spoken as often as Burmese. The noise and bustle were slightly intimidating after his time in Upper Burma.

"I've never been to Rangoon before," Than Than Aye kept close to Andrew, staring around her. "I've never seen so many Europeans in one place."

"You're part European yourself," Andrew reminded her. "You have as much right here as they have. Probably more, as you're three-quarters Burmese in Burma and you're quarter British in a British possession." He grinned at her. "You belong to both worlds. Stay close to me, Than Than Aye."

"Where are you going?" Than Than Aye asked, holding his arm.

"We're going to hand Mary over to her mother," Andrew said.

"Shouldn't you give her to the authorities? Maybe to Sir Charles Crossthwaite?"

"Probably," Andrew said, "but if I know anything about officials, they'd make Mary's mother jump through hoops to get her back. They'd ignore Bo Thura's supposed part and claim all the credit for themselves. On the other hand, if Mary's mother has her child, she'll never let her go, and the Press will write columns about it. They love such a story."

"Is it good that the Press should write a story about Mary?" Than Than Aye pressed closer to Andrew as a dark blue Brougham carriage whirred past with two matching grey horses pulling hard. The man inside looked vaguely familiar as he stared out of the window at them.

"A newspaper column will give Bo Thura maximum publicity, so his name is known as the man who rescued Mary from the evil dacoits," Andrew explained. "Indeed, let's stop at the *Times of India's* offices and pass the word." He held Than Than Aye's arm reassuringly. "It's all right. Let me do the talking."

The clerk at the *Times* office looked up without interest as Andrew entered. "Yes?" he said with a look of disdain. Andrew realised the clerk would see him as a travel-stained, unkempt man with a Burmese woman and a rough-looking red-haired child.

The clerk spoke quickly. "Is it an advertisement

you want to place? If you're seeking employment, you've come to the wrong place. We've no vacancies, and the coolies get all the labouring jobs anyway."

"Who is your chief reporter?" Andrew asked.

"Charles Mulhanney," the clerk replied. "Why? Do you want to report a missing bar of soap?" He smirked at his attempted humour.

"No," Andrew told him. "I want to report a found child. Tell him that Mary MacConnacher will soon be back with her mother, thanks to the help of a Burman called Bo Thura." Andrew leaned across the polished desk, took hold of the clerk's collar, and pulled him closer. "Will you pass that information on?"

"Yes, sir!" the clerk said, nodding violently.

"Good man," Andrew said, replacing him on his feet. Ignoring the clerk's astonishment, Andrew turned on his heel and stalked away with Than Than Aye at his side.

"He wasn't a pleasant man," Than Than Aye said, looking at Andrew with amused eyes.

"Men with a little authority often like to abuse what they think is their power," Andrew said. He led them towards the British Cantonment, shielding Mary from the worst of the noise and ignoring the curious glances of passers-by. With his ragged clothes and days-old beard, he knew he must look like the wild man of the woods, while Than Than Aye wore the clothes of an up-country villager rather than the more sophisticated clothing of the town.

The sentry at the cantonment gate stared as Andrew approached. "Who the hell are you, then, chum?"

"Captain Andrew Baird of the Natal Dragoons," Andrew said, "Stand aside and let me pass."

"Pull the other one, mate; it plays *My Grandfather's Clock*," the sentry held his Martini-Henry across his chest. "Off you go, now, and take your little winker with you."[1]

Andrew kept his patience, feeling Mary stirring in his arms. "Tell your sergeant I have arrived," Andrew said, putting an edge in his voice. "And be quick about it!"

The sentry stiffened, recognising the voice of authority. "Yes, sir." He stepped back and raised his voice. "Sergeant!"

"What's the to-do?" The sergeant was in his late thirties with a world-weary look in his eyes. He looked at Andrew. "Who are you?"

"Captain Andrew Baird of the Natal Dragoons, and this child," Andrew held up Mary, "is Mary Mac-Connacher."

The sergeant stared at Andrew, then at Mary and

---

1. Winker: a bright-eyed young woman, sometimes by association a prostitute, mistress or lover.

back at Andrew. "Good God in Heaven, sir. How did you manage to rescue her?"

"I didn't," Andrew said. "A Burmese gentleman named Bo Thura rescued her and contacted me. May we come in?"

"Yes, sir," the sergeant said. "Sanderson, tell Major Goudie what's happening. Come in, sir, and the lady, too."

The news had spread before Andrew reached the Royal Scots Fusiliers' quarters, and he saw a black-haired woman running across the maidan with her clothes loose around her and her bare feet flapping on the ground.

"My baby! Mary! My Mary!"

Mrs MacConnacher nearly threw herself at Andrew in her eagerness to regain her child, with scores of soldiers in all states of dress and undress hurrying across the maidan to witness the reunion.

"Oh, sir! How can I thank you?" Mrs Mac-Connacher asked, holding Mary tightly as tears flooded from her eyes. "Oh, Mary, what have they done to you?"

The familiar sight of Major Goudie stalked across to Andrew. "It's yourself, Captain Baird! Well done, sir, well done indeed! Let me shake your hand." He looked Andrew up and down.

"Captain Baird! Well, bless my soul! Well, Captain, whatever else you do in your life, you have performed a noble deed by rescuing this child from the grasp of the barbarians. Whatever else you might achieve in your career, you will never be forgotten, sir. Mark my words."

Andrew saw a smartly dressed civilian approaching and guessed it was the reporter from the *Times of India*. He waited until the reporter was within earshot.

"I did nothing," Andrew said. "All credit must go to Bo Thura, the Burmese gentleman who rescued the child and notified me."

"What was that name again?" the reporter asked. "Bo Thura? How do you spell that?"

"How the devil should I know how he spells his blasted name?" Andrew asked testily. "Spell it any way you like? You reporters usually do, anyway."

Than Than Aye stretched out a hand to Mary as Mrs MacConnacher took her confused and crying daughter away.

"No more *kyawal* for her," Andrew said quietly, remembering Aung Thiha laughing as he acted like a buffalo and carried Mary on his back. "Mary will never forget you," he said.

"Nor will I forget her," Than Than Aye said. "You'd better return to Mariana, Andrew, or she'll think you have forgotten her."

Andrew nodded. "Thank you," he said as Than Than Aye smiled, turned, and walked gracefully away, swinging her hips to tease him. He saw the blue Brougham coach again, with the curtains inside the windows twitching as if the occupant was watching him.

MARIANA STARED AS SHE OPENED HER DOOR, AND Andrew smiled at her. "I thought the Burmans had killed you," she said quietly. "I've had no news for ever so long."

"It was a bit hectic," Andrew slumped onto a chair. "And the telegraphic and postal system in Upper Burma leaves a lot to be desired."

Mariana nodded. "You look awful," she said.

"You don't," Andrew replied. He grinned. "I've been looking forward to this minute for a long time. Let me look at you."

Mariana stood within the door, with a beam of sunlight from the window highlighting her hair. Her eyes were busy on Andrew, and concern shadowed her pleasure. "Where have you been, Andrew? It's been months."

"It feels like years," Andrew told her.

Mariana took the sun well despite the bonnets that hung from pegs on the wall. An elegant blue dress hugged her curves as it extended to the ground. Andrew thought of another woman in a blue longyi and shivered. *How could I ever have looked at anybody else?*

"We can't have you walking around like that,"

Mariana said firmly. "Look at you! Even the cat wouldn't drag you in!"

Than Than Aye would say something like that. Mariana is growing more like Than Than Aye all the time.

Andrew caught himself in the oval mirror on the wall. He had lost about a stone, his cheekbones prominent above an unshaven face, while his eyes seemed huge and staring. His clothes were rumpled, faded, and roughly patched. "Give me a minute, and I'll tidy myself up," Andrew said.

"You'll do more than tidy yourself up," Mariana said. "It's a bath for you, Andrew, before anything else, and we'll get rid of these clothes! Have you been rolling in mud?"

"It's been an interesting time," Andrew replied. He looked Mariana up and down, enjoying her company, and reminded himself of her movements, manner of speech, and even the hidden smile in her eyes. "I've missed you."

Mariana started. "I've missed you, too," she said.

"We have much to catch up on," Andrew told her.

"I heard you brought little Mary MacConnacher home," Mariana said. "How was she?"

"She was fine," Andrew said. "As long as her mother doesn't mind her smoking cigars." He laughed at Mariana's expression. "I'll explain later."

"Why not explain now?" Mariana asked.

"I can't stay long," Andrew said. "Sir Charles Crossthwaite wants to see me."

"The Chief Commissioner?" Mariana looked impressed. "You'd better get ready, Andrew." She stepped closer. "Try not to be long."

"I'll try my best," Andrew promised.

"Sir!" Andrew stood at attention. Even after Mariana's ministrations, he knew he looked shabby, with his Natal Dragoons uniform smelling of mothballs and unfamiliar in Rangoon, while he was underweight and drawn with hardship.

The Chief Commissioner's office was resplendent with polished teak and brass. His desk was tidy, and a map of Lower Burma dominated one wall.

"Captain Baird," Sir Charles eyed Andrew up and down. "You've been through the mill, I hear."

"It's been interesting, sir," Andrew agreed.

Sir Charles nodded. "You helped the Royal Scots Fusiliers repel a dacoit attack on a Burmese village."

"I played a small part, sir. Major Goudie was in command."

"And you were at the massacres in Mandalay."

"Yes, sir," Andrew said.

"And saw the Chinese invasion of Bhamo."

"I did, sir," Andrew said. "The Chinese were no threat to us, sir. They treated us well."

"Indeed," Sir Charles indicated that Andrew should sit down. "Yet you still managed to bring young Mary MacConnacher home."

"Than Than Aye helped, sir, and Bo Thura had her safe and well." Andrew did not mention that Bo Thura had kidnapped Mary. "Indeed, Bo Thura brought my attention to her plight."

"Why did this dacoit contact you, Baird? He could have handed the child to any British post."

Andrew had anticipated the question. "We have a slight family connection, sir. My father met Bo Thura's father in the last Burmese War, back in Fifty-two."

"Your father being Major-General Windrush," Sir Charles said.

"That's correct, sir," Andrew agreed.

When the Governor nodded, Andrew wondered how much he already knew or guessed.

"Very good," Sir Charles said. "However, this information far surpasses all the rest." He lifted the document that Andrew had carried back from Bhamo. "Do you know the contents, Baird?"

"No, sir. It was sealed when Bo Thura handed it to me, and I didn't break the seal."

Sir Charles grunted. "Very commendable. If it's genuine, and I have no reason to doubt its accuracy, this document is a copy of a secret treaty between King Thibaw and France. It gives railway concessions in Upper Burma to France with interest on profits going to Thibaw." Sir Charles looked up. "The Kingdom of Ava is quite cash-strapped, despite Thibaw taxing the gambling dens he encouraged."

"I noticed gambling dens in most of the towns in Upper Burma, sir," Andrew agreed.

"Yes." The Chief Commissioner returned his attention to the document. "This agreement allows France to establish a bank in Mandalay, with France securing the finances by controlling all the customs receipts on the Irrawaddy River." He looked at Andrew. "As we control most of the commercial river traffic, Baird, the French will be raking in tax money from us."

"Yes, sir." Andrew could understand how that would rankle among the British commercial world. "The Irrawaddy Flotilla Company or the Bombay and Burmah Trading Corporation would not appreciate paying money to French tax collectors."

"Indeed," the Governor said. "The French would also gain the revenue from the tea trade and the Burmese ruby mines."

Andrew took a deep breath. "It seems the French would control Upper Burma in all but name. I wonder what Thibaw gets out of this arrangement?"

Sir Charles gave a faint smile. "I have not finished yet. You may not have heard the latest while you were gallivanting around Upper Burma, rescuing children and battling stray dacoits."

"What has happened, sir?" Andrew asked.

"Thibaw's officials claim that the Bombay and Burmah Trading Company have been underreporting the volume of teak it fells and exports and has not been paying its employees."

Andrew remembered the men and elephants working the teak forests. "Are the allegations true, sir?"

"No!" Sir Charles snapped. "The Burman officials are corrupt."

"What was the result, sir?"

"The Burmans are demanding the company pays twenty-three lakhs of rupees to Thibaw, under pain of forfeiture of their forests."[2]

"I see," Andrew said.

"I suspect that some French company will move into Bombay and Burma's place the day they leave," the Governor said. He leaned back in his padded leather chair, put the document on his desk and pressed his hands together. "You have provided me with some interesting information, Captain."

"Yes, sir," Andrew said. "It was all from Bo Thura, sir. I was merely the carrier."

"Quite," Sir Charles replied. "I have heard a ru-

---

2. A lakh is a hundred thousand, so twenty-three lakhs is two million, three hundred thousand.

mour, a shave as you military people call it, that the French consul in Rangoon boasts the British need French permission even to enter Mandalay."

Andrew shook his head. "That's inaccurate, sir. I would estimate that three-quarters of the Europeans in Mandalay are British."

Sir Charles nodded again. "I'd rather believe that than the word of some Frenchman. Remind me, Baird; who is this fellow who found this document?"

"A man named Bo Thura, sir. The same gentleman who showed me where Mary was."

"What did he want in return?"

"A free pardon for past misdeeds and permission to live in British Burma," Andrew said. "He asked me to request a written pardon and a safe conduct from you before he arrives."

The Chief Commissioner pressed his fingers harder together. "Why doesn't he just cross the frontier, Captain?"

"He's afraid the British will hold his past misdeeds against him, sir," Andrew replied. "He has been a dacoit in the past but is now a reformed character."

"I'll look into it," Sir Charles promised. "If this fellow is wanted for a serious crime, such as murder or rape, any pardon is out of the question."

Andrew touched the French document. "Even though he found us evidence of this treaty, sir? And helped restore Mary to her family?"

"As I said, Captain Baird, I will investigate it. The fate of one dacoit, reformed or not, pales into insignificance beside our international obligations and difficulties. I'll contact the Secretary of State for India with details of this treaty and release the main facts to the press." He grinned. "That should alarm the French."

"Yes, sir. And Bo Thura?"

"I told you I'd investigate his case. When I've made my decision, I'll let you know. Good day, sir."

"Good day, sir," Andrew replied.

He breathed deeply when he left the government building, for dealing with officialdom always drained him. The bustle of Rangoon's streets was almost a relief.

"Andrew?" Mariana hurried to meet him. "How did it go?"

"How is it always with government officials?" Andrew said. "One-sided and vague. We'll have to wait and see."

Mariana opened her parasol to shade her face from the sun. "It's good to have you back," she said. "Now you can tell me your adventures."

"And you can tell me yours," Andrew said. He ignored the dark blue Brougham that whirred past.

CHAPTER 17

RANGOON, LOWER BURMA, 1885

When the press published what they knew of the treaty between France and Upper Burma, the British merchants in Rangoon were outraged, which, Andrew suspected, was what Sir Charles had intended.

"Allow the French to inspect our ships on the Irrawaddy?" Jennings said as he read the *Times of India* before dinner. "I'll be damned if that's going to happen. By God, we'll fight them."

"Fight who?" Andrew sat in the hotel's foyer, sipping his whisky and water and watching the world go by.

"We'll fight the French, by God," Jennings said. "And King Thibaw."

Andrew watched Mariana descend the stairs. He thought she looked immensely graceful. *Mariana has matured into an exceptionally beautiful lady. She was right to turn down my marriage proposition. She can do far better than me.*

"What are you two discussing so passionately?" Mariana asked, smiling at both as they stood for her.

"International relations," Andrew told her. "We're putting the world to rights."

Jennings was two steps ahead and pulled out a chair.

Mariana slid gracefully into the chair, politely thanked Jennings and looked around the foyer. "It's busy in here this evening."

"This French nonsense has brought people together," Jennings said. "There might be war, and that could be bad for business."

"Jennings has been telling me he's going to take the Queen's Shilling, or the Empress's Shilling now, and chase the French out of Thibaw's kingdom." Andrew enjoyed Jennings' reaction.[1]

"I am not joining the army," Jennings denied immediately. "I meant Britain might fight the French, not me personally."

"Ah," Andrew said. "My apologies, Jennings. I must have misunderstood."

---

1. In 1877, the British Prime Minister, Benjamin Disraeli, proclaimed Queen Victoria as Empress of India.

"I'm sure you would be a fine soldier, Mr Jennings," Mariana said. "You're tall, strong and commanding." She smiled, brushing back an imaginary loose strand of hair. "I think you'd look very dashing in a scarlet dress uniform."

Andrew looked from Mariana to Jennings and back. *What's this? Has my Mariana found another sweetheart?* Andrew lifted his glass and examined Jennings over the rim. *He is presentable, I'll grant you, if not quite to my taste. I would count my fingers after I shook his hand, but women have different ideas than men.*

Mariana caught Andrew's gaze. "Mr Jennings has been looking after me," Mariana said.

"That's good," Andrew replied with what he hoped was a smile. "Did you need looking after?"

Mariana coloured. "I was a bit lonely," she said. "You were away longer than I expected."

"I was away longer than I expected, too," Andrew replied.

"I counted the three weeks you said," Mariana said, "and then three more weeks, and another three until I quite filled my journal with little numbers and crosses."

"I am sure the good Captain was doing his duty, Miss Maxwell," Jennings said. "The *Times of India* mentioned some of your exploits, Captain Baird. You did excellent work when you rescued that little girl."

"Thank you," Andrew said. He looked up when

the door banged open, and a harassed-looking lieutenant entered.

"I am looking for Captain Baird," the lieutenant announced. "Captain Andrew Baird of the Natal Dragoons."

"That's me," Andrew admitted, raising a hand.

The lieutenant approached, standing to attention a yard from the table. "The Chief Commissioner sends his compliments, sir, and would like a word with you whenever it is convenient."

Andrew glanced at the suddenly silent Mariana. "Now would be a good time," he said. "Will you be all right alone for a time, Mariana?"

"I'll be fine, Captain Baird," Mariana replied formally and forced a smile. "Mr Jennings will keep me company again. Your duty must come first."

"Sir Charles will want to tell me he's pardoned Bo Thura," Andrew said.

"Duty must always come first," Jennings echoed as Andrew followed the lieutenant out of the room.

SIR CHARLES NODDED TO ANDREW FROM BEHIND his desk. "Sit down, Captain Baird."

Andrew sat, listening to the fan creaking above his head. He glanced over the desk, hoping to see a Commissioner's Pardon.

Sir Charles looked up from an open file. "You have seen active service in Africa, I believe."

"Yes, sir, against the Galekas, Zulus and Boers."

Sir Charles nodded. "And you know something of Burma."

"Not much, sir."

"You've visited Mandalay and as far north as Bhamo, which is a damned sight more than most have done. Is that not correct?"

"Yes, sir."

Sir Charles held Andrew's gaze. "Good. We are perilously short of experienced officers here, and those blasted dacoits are causing no end of trouble."

Andrew guessed what was coming. "I only came here to rescue Mary MacConnacher, sir. As soon as you grant Bo Thura a pardon, I will let him know and get back home."

Sir Charles fixed a cold eye on Andrew. "I may grant Bo Thura a pardon, Baird. That depends on his behaviour. In the meantime, I am going to send you to the Royal Scots Fusiliers."

Andrew understood the unspoken threat. If he turned down the appointment, the Governor would not grant Bo Thura's pardon. "Yes, sir."

Sir Charles continued, "The Scots Fusiliers headquarters company is based in Rangoon Cantonments, and they have detachments all along the frontier, trying to prevent the dacoits from infiltrating from Upper Burma. They circulate their rifle companies, leaving one in Rangoon to aid the police."

"I see, sir," Andrew said.

"The colonel of the Royal Scots Fusiliers and I want you to take command of a mobile patrol of Burmese Police and Fusiliers and guard the outskirts of Rangoon from dacoits."

"Yes, sir," Andrew replied.

"Your experience fighting in South Africa will come in handy, Captain. You'll have a free hand to organise your men and a roving commission, which suits you colonial soldiers." Sir Charles smiled encouragingly.

When will I get home? I've had enough of Burma.

"You'll be keen to get started, Captain," Sir Charles said. "I hope you have success against the dacoits."

"I'll try my best, sir," Andrew promised. "And please don't forget Bo Thura's rescue of Mary Mac-Connacher."

"Good day to you, Captain Baird," Sir Charles replied.

"Good day, sir," Andrew left the building and saw Than Than Aye standing on the opposite side of the street.

JENNINGS SMILED AT MARIANA ACROSS THE RIM OF his glass. "Captain Andrew is no sooner back than he's away again, hobnobbing with the Chief Commissioner, no less." He sighed. "Maybe he's too good for the likes of us."

"Andrew is not that way inclined," Mariana replied.

Jennings laughed. "I didn't for a second think he was. All in jest, my dear Miss Maxwell. All in jest." He poured them both more wine. "I see your Captain Andrew brought a little friend back from Upper Burma with him."

"Yes," Mariana said. "Young Mary Mac-Connacher. He rescued her from the dacoits. All the papers are full of it." She sipped at her wine. "But you know that already."

"Not young Mary; I know all about her." Jennings shook his head. "The other one."

"Which other one?" Mariana asked.

"Didn't you know?" Jennings raised his eyebrows. "I thought he would have told you. When Captain Andrew returned from the Kingdom of Ava, he brought a woman with him. I happened to pass them when I was in my carriage."

"What woman?" Mariana asked with her heart thundering inside her chest.

"Surely he's introduced her to you?" Jennings shook his head. "Some oversight, then. He's probably been too busy with all his official business." He smiled. "You know how these soldiers are. Everything is duty, duty, duty, and the rest of the world gets pushed aside. He'll be with her now, like as not, or as soon as the Chief Commissioner finishes with him."

"Oh," Mariana stood up. "I must see this mysterious woman."

Jennings stood politely. "I doubt you have anything to worry about, Miss Maxwell. If you ask him, I am sure he will explain."

"Oh, it will be nothing," Mariana said, forcing a smile. "Even so, I must ask him about this lady he so conveniently forgot to mention."

"It's probably perfectly innocent," Jennings said.

"I am sure it is," Mariana replied. Lifting her skirt, she swept out of the hotel, leaving Jennings alone at the table. He smiled after her, sat down, and ordered another drink.

Mariana hurried from the hotel, ignoring the usual beggars as she paced to the Chief Commissioner's office, where Andrew had headed.

I don't believe Andrew has found another woman, but why shouldn't he? I turned him down. He has every right to find somebody else.

Mariana stopped as she saw Andrew a hundred yards ahead, talking with a woman. She was tall for a Burmese, slender and straight-backed, and her faded blue longyi fitted snugly to her body.

Oh, God, she's beautiful. Andrew!

Mariana watched as Andrew and the woman spoke together, seemingly lost in each other's company. The woman laughed and placed a proprietorial hand on Andrew's arm. Mariana could see her affection as she spoke.

She knows him well. They must have met in Mandalay. Was that why he was so long up there? Was he with that woman all this time?

Mariana slid into a doorway to watch, feeling her heart race. *Now, I am a Peeping Tom, spying on a man who has always done his very best for me.* She again remembered rejecting Andrew's marriage proposal in Edinburgh and wondered if that had chased him away forever.

Andrew! Why didn't you understand? It's not that I don't want you, and you know I love you. I am just not ready for marriage yet. Something is missing. I don't know if you want me for myself or if you want a substitute for my sister. And there is that shadow in my mind.

I don't know, Andrew!

Andrew spoke again, and the woman replied, apparently explaining something in great detail.

What is she telling him? I wish I could hear.

Mariana tried to ease closer, but a bullock cart passed, with the two animals clopping their hooves on the ground, and the ungreased wheels squeaking so loudly they blocked out every other sound. When the cart passed, Mariana looked for Andrew and saw him walking away with the woman at his side.

Damn and blast! Mariana used one of Andrew's favourite expressions when he was frustrated. *Double damn and blast. Now, I will never know. I can't tell him I was spying on him.*

Mariana felt sick as she watched Andrew and Than Than Aye walk away.

What should I do?

CHAPTER 18

RANGOON, LOWER BURMA, JANUARY 1885

Andrew looked over his men. He had one young lieutenant, a sergeant, two corporals, and a Sikh havildar. They commanded twenty Fusiliers and twenty police, equally divided between Sikhs and local Burmese. The Fusiliers looked like typical British infantry, mostly small-made men from the industrial slums of west central Scotland with a sprinkling of beefy countrymen of Ayrshire. He had hand-picked Corporals McGhee and Rowan, remembering them from the skirmish beside the Irrawaddy. Andrew knew he would get to know the rest over the next few weeks and months.

The Sikhs were brawny, bearded, and bold, eyeing him without expression, while the Burmese were stocky, agile, and alert. Andrew recognised Sukhbir Singh, the Sikh havildar.

"We'll make these men into an efficient force," Andrew told the lieutenant.

"Yes, sir," Lieutenant Morton agreed, with the sweat beading on his sunburned face.

"We've met before, Havildar," Andrew said to Sukhbir Singh.

"Yes, Sahib," Sukhbir Singh was a tall man with a neat beard and three medal ribbons.

"I want two groups of ten police and ten soldiers. Lieutenant Morton will take one group, and I'll take the other. You know the police best, Havildar, so organise them equally."

"Yes, Sahib."

"I'll address the men first," Andrew said.

"Yes, Sahib," Sukhbir Singh replied without any facial expression.

"The dacoits have been operating at will throughout British Burma," Andrew told them. "Our intelligence people believe they intend to strike at Rangoon soon." He waited until his words were translated. "I intend to ensure that does not happen."

After acting as a static garrison in Rangoon, the Fusiliers looked pleased at the prospect of action. The Sikhs grinned when the translator passed on the information, while the Burmese remained impassive. Andrew wondered how many understood what he said.

"We will operate at night," Andrew said. "That's when the dacoits terrorise the innocent villagers, so that is when we will hunt them down."

The men nodded again. They understood the idea, but Andrew wondered if they had the ability or training to work at night. He thought the dacoits would run rings around both British and Sikhs, while Andrew wondered if the Burmans had the motivation to be a useful force.

"We'll start training tonight," Andrew said. "The Burmese police will instruct us in the local terrain, and we'll work in the dark."

As Andrew had expected, the Burmese were better at night than the Fusiliers or the Sikhs. Most of the British stumbled, spoke loudly, and got lost; the Sikhs advanced at speed in the wrong direction, and the Burmese watched with cynical amusement.

That first night, the dacoits attacked an outlying village, killed one woman, and robbed the rest. A scared civilian told of a man with a green-tasselled yellow umbrella supervising the attack.

The following day, Andrew took his men on a route march around the area, ensuring they had a basic grasp of the local geography. He made them study maps, had the NCOs work out the fastest routes between villages, and pinpointed the most suitable places for standing patrols and pickets.

After a few hours' sleep, he trained his men again that night.

"Lift your feet high when walking; you have less chance of scuffing loose stones and breaking twigs. Watch your colleagues all the time and stop every few moments; darkness and silence are your friends."

The men listened. Andrew dismissed the least competent, drafted in others, and continued with his training.

On that second night, the dacoits penetrated the suburbs of Rangoon, robbed two shops, and set a house ablaze. Again, a witness mentioned the yellow umbrella with the green tassels.

On the third day, Andrew concentrated on his men's marksmanship and stamina. He knew he had limited time in which to work and pushed them hard. Two more men fell out, and he returned them to their regiment and brought in two keen youngsters. That night, he split his men in two. He commanded one group and Lieutenant Morton the other, and they patrolled the countryside around Rangoon.

Andrew's patrol saw the glow of another fire, arriving too late to catch the dacoits, although one of his Sikhs fired at what he claimed was a running man. The resulting venison was a welcome addition to their rations.

"What do you think, Morton?" Andrew asked.

"The men are clumsy but keen," Morton was a steady-eyed youngster. "They won't let you down."

"That's my opinion," Andrew said. "Here's what we'll do." He outlined his plans to the lieutenant, working with a large-scale plan of the area.

If only civilians understood how essential organising is for even the most minor military operation, they might have a higher opinion of the military.

"When do we start, sir?" Morton asked.

"Tonight," Andrew said. "The men will have to learn as they work. The dacoits are becoming too cocky."

Morton nodded grimly. "Yes, sir. I'll make the arrangements."

"Tell the men to watch for a dacoit with a yellow umbrella with green tassels," Andrew said. "He might be organising these attacks."

"I will, sir," Morton said.

When Andrew alerted the Rangoon police to his intentions and mentioned the umbrella, the inspector drew in his breath.

"A yellow umbrella with green tassels!" he said. "That's Buda Sein! He's probably the worst of them all and far more important than a mere dacoit. According to our sources, he's Maung Thandar's companion, maybe his relation."

Andrew grunted. "We'll see if we can curb his attacks."

The inspector looked worn and old. "I wish somebody could stop them. I am sick of ravaged villages and murdered people who depend on us for protection yet are too scared of the dacoits to help us help them."

Andrew shook his hand. "We'll do our best," he promised.

The inspector grunted. "We think the dacoits will stir up trouble inside Rangoon, Captain Baird. Could you base your men in the city, please?"

Andrew nodded, wondering if the last few nights of training were wasted. "I'll do that."

Andrew stationed his men in Rangoon's northern suburbs, the area most vulnerable to dacoit attack. He placed them in pickets of four men, with six-man mobile patrols operating between each picket.

"If the men on patrol hear or see anything suspicious, move immediately to that area," Andrew said. "If you see dacoits, attack immediately. Try to drive them to one of the static pickets so we trap them between two fires."

The men nodded. Nights with little sleep had tired them, but all were veterans of Burma and knew how difficult it was to catch the dacoits. Andrew knew they preferred actively hunting the enemy rather than waiting to react.

"We might just come across ordinary thieves, sir," Lieutenant Morton said.

"Call on them to surrender," Andrew advised. "If they don't, then assume they are dacoits."

"Yes, sir," Morton said, passing on Andrew's instructions. The men, British, Burmese, and Sikh, nodded, happy that Andrew had allowed them limited freedom.

Rangoon's streets were quiet at night, with fewer pedestrians than Andrew had expected. He placed his static pickets at strategic spots and organised patrols between them, varying their routes to ensure the dacoits did not know where the soldiers would be next.

"Don't be predictable," Andrew warned. "Keep the dacoits guessing."

On the first night of Andrew's patrolling regime, the dacoits set fire to two houses and robbed another. Andrew increased the range of his patrols to cover a larger area. The second night, the dacoits looted half a street, leaving Andrew feeling frustrated.

"Somebody will know what's happening," Morton said as they sat in their makeshift barracks in the northern suburbs. "They won't tell us anything, though, or they'll give us misinformation."

Andrew considered for a moment. "That could be useful," he said. "Let's ask around, Morton. Here's what I suggest." He unfolded new ideas.

"Do you think they will work?" Morton asked.

"I don't know," Andrew replied. "We are using

their strengths against them: lies, deceit, and mistrust."

Morton shrugged. "It's worth a shot, sir."

Andrew and Morton tried bribery the following day, offering a handful of rupees to anybody who told them where the dacoits might strike next. A Burmese policeman acted as interpreter.

"This man says the dacoits will rob in the east, sahib," the interpreter said.

"He thinks the dacoits are going to attack the south," the interpreter told Andrew.

"The east of the city," the interpreter said.

When Andrew and Morton compared notes, their information was similar.

"It looks like the dacoits will target the east or the south," Morton said. "What now?"

"Now, we play them at their own game," Andrew said grimly. "Either the locals fear the dacoits, or they're in cahoots with them. I don't trust them to tell us the truth."

"Nor do I, sir," Morton agreed.

"If they have given us false information, we will use that against them."

"How?" Morton asked.

"None of our informants mentioned the west of the city," Andrew leaned back in his creaking chair. "In fact, they were careful to point us anywhere except the west."

Morton agreed.

"That suggests the dacoits are going to strike in the west," Andrew said and grinned. "We have four hours before dark. I want you to gather as much straw and old rags as possible."

Morton stared at him. "Sir?"

"Straw, old rags, and old uniforms," Andrew ordered. "Send out the men on foraging expeditions and bring everything back here."

"Yes, sir," Morton looked confused as Andrew grinned at him.

"Off you go, Morton. As quick as you can."

When the men trickled in with their bundles of rags, uniforms, and straw, Andrew had them make dummies. Muttering in discontent, the men stuffed the old uniforms with rags and straw until Andrew was satisfied the result looked vaguely like a human.

Ajit Singh, the Sikh marksman, proved himself an artist, adding watermelons for heads and drawing features on their faces.

"Well done, Ajit," Andrew said. "Well done, men." He grinned at them, with the Sikhs and Burmese responding with smiles and the Fusiliers stony-faced.

When the evening drew near, Andrew marched his men to the east side of Rangoon. He placed half his men in two large houses, making it obvious they were there.

"Make a noise, men," Andrew ordered. "Laugh, swagger and mention dacoits."

The men obeyed, watching their strange officer through suspicious eyes.

When night fell, Andrew silently withdrew the pickets, leaving dummies in their place.

"Who thought of that idea?" Morton asked.

"It is a trick we used when we fought the Boers," Andrew said. "We'll see if it's as effective against the dacoits." He marched his men quietly to the west of the city, placed them in pickets of five men and waited.

"Keep hidden," Andrew ordered his men. "Don't move unless you see the dacoits or if I give the order. Lieutenant Morton, take a section, circle to the rear of the area and wait. With luck, we'll flush out some dacoits."

If I am correct, we'll have struck the first blow at Buba Sein's dacoits. If I am wrong, the men will think I am a fool, and more civilians will suffer.

Very few people walked the night-dark streets of Rangoon as if they expected something to happen. Andrew watched a pair of police walk past, talking quietly and waited with his men behind him.

Andrew checked his watch. It was two in the morning, four hours until dawn.

"Smoke, sir!" Corporal McGhee said. "I can smell smoke!"

"Well done, McGhee!" Andrew said. "Check your rifles are loaded, boys; loosen your bayonets in their scabbards." He heard a wild scream. "Move in!" he said.

Thirty police and Fusiliers doubled towards the fire, with Andrew at their head. He felt the suppressed excitement of his men. Hunting dacoits was frustrating, with contacts few and the police and Army usually arriving too late to do more than count the cost. One successful brush would lift the military and police's spirits.

The flames glowed yellow in the night sky, a beacon directing Andrew to the dacoits.

"Morton, take your men around the rear and head off any who try to run. The rest, extended order, and watch for civilians! Corporal McGhee, take the left flank."

They hit the streets in a long line, with Sikhs and Fusiliers carrying bayoneted rifles as they ran towards the flames. The Burmese police carried carbines and moved silently. Andrew saw a group of men around a wailing woman, swore and lifted his revolver.

"Leave that woman alone!" he roared, knowing the dacoits would not understand the words.

When one of the Burmese police shouted an order, the closest two dacoits looked around, their eyes gleaming in the firelight. One lifted a *dha* as if to challenge Andrew, noticed the rapidly advancing soldiers and ran. The second was slower, and a Sikh shot him as he hesitated. The sound of the rifle alerted the others, and half a dozen men erupted from two houses, most burdened with the loot they had stolen.

One dacoit shouted something, crouched to face the soldiers, realised he was outflanked and ran.

"After them, boys!" Corporal Rowan ordered. One Fusilier dropped to his knees and fired a snap-shot; the others chased the dacoits, their bayonets glittering.

More dacoits appeared; one fired at Andrew, dropped his flintlock musket and screamed as a Fusilier spitted him with his bayonet.

"Got you, you thieving bastard!"

Fleet-footed, many of the dacoits escaped, only to run against Lieutenant Morton's section. Andrew heard the scatter of shots and shouts, Morton's sharp commands and somebody laughing.

That's a Sikh laugh: Sukhbir Singh.

"Round up the prisoners," Andrew said. "We'll hand them into the nearest police station." The op-eration, hours in planning, was over in minutes.

He looked at the three dead dacoits on the ground. "Lieutenant Morton, look after the prison-ers. The rest, try and put out the flames and look after the civilians."

Andrew felt suddenly drained. Compared to the major battles in which he had been involved, the skirmish had been simple, yet he was glad it was over.

❄

WITH THE DACOITS DISCOURAGED FROM RAIDING Rangoon, an increased force of sixty men under his command and free rein to roam anywhere within five miles of Rangoon, Andrew felt his spirits lift. Rangoon, like every crowded city, depressed him with its narrow streets and lack of space.

The countryside was more open than Andrew expected, with fertile fields, small prosperous villages and small areas of forest. He led his men from village to village, with his Burmese police talking to the villagers and asking about possible sightings of dacoits. The replies were all the same.

"They haven't seen any dacoits, sir," the police reported.

After two days of uneventful patrolling, Andrew thought the area was safe. "It looks as if our patrols have done the work," he said.

"Maybe," Lieutenant Morton replied.

"You sound doubtful," Andrew said.

"I've been in Burma longer than you, sir," Morton reminded him. "My experience with dacoits is that they'll be wherever they are not expected."

"We'll have one more local sweep," Andrew decided, "and then we'll move to a wider circuit."

He led his men in extended order across the fertile countryside, checking each house and village for strangers.

"Sir!" Corporal Rowan shouted as they skirted a paddy field outside a village. "There's somebody on the ground here. I think she's dead."

Andrew hurried over. The woman was about forty, stark naked and fastened to a bamboo structure above the embers of a fire.

"The bastards have roasted her, sir," Rowan said, staring at the corpse.

"They have," Andrew said, calling for two Burmese police officers. "Go into the village and find out what happened," he ordered.

As the police approached, a score of men erupted from the far side and ran. One delayed for a moment to fire a single shot at the British patrol and then joined his companions.

Got you!

"Sikhs and Fusiliers! Extended order!" Andrew shouted. "Get after these men! Lieutenant Morton, secure the village!"

Andrew ran forward with the Fusiliers and Sikhs on either side. "Keep in sight of each other," Andrew ordered. "Be careful of an ambush."

The fleeing men ran into the nearest copse. A moment later, a spatter of musketry sounded.

"Fusiliers! Get in there!" Andrew roared. "Sikhs! Get around the rear of the trees and keep the dacoits inside!"

Andrew knew the dangers of moving into close country in pursuit of desperate men, but the sight of the tortured woman had angered him as much as the Fusiliers. He thrust into the trees with a Fusilier on either side.

"If you see anything moving, use your bayonet," Andrew ordered. "Don't shoot in case you hit one of the Sikhs."

They moved forward slowly, with the Fusiliers stabbing viciously at every bush or patch of undergrowth.

One man yelled and leapt backwards when he saw a snake, and then they saw movement ahead. The Fusiliers bounded forward, bayonets ready, to stop when they realised they had met the Sikhs.

"Where are the dacoits?" a Fusilier asked, raising his rifle.

"They've melted away," Sukhbir Singh replied. "They always melt away."

Andrew nodded.

If we had cavalry or even mounted infantry, we could have caught them before they entered the trees. We must adapt and improve.

CHAPTER 19

RANGOON FEBRUARY AND MARCH 1885

F inding sufficient mounts for his mounted infantry was difficult in Rangoon, but Andrew used every bit of persuasion he knew, added a few empty threats, and mustered a score of horses. True, most had seen better days, and some were more fit for putting out to pasture than chasing dacoits, but they all had four legs, a back, and a head.

They'll do, Andrew told himself. *They'll have to do.*

A check of his men found ten Sikhs who were experienced horsemen and three Fusiliers with a country background. The Burmese were experts on the river but had no knowledge of horsemanship and showed no inclination to learn.

"I need another seven mounted infantrymen," Andrew said. "If I don't find any Fusiliers, I'll recruit civilians!"

The men looked at one another, and eventually, two stepped forward. Andrew nodded to his senior NCO. "Sergeant Jardine! Find me five volunteers."

"Yes, sir!" Jardine said and rapped out five names. "You men are now mounted infantry. If you scare the horses, I'll have you. If you fall off, I expect you to land at attention. If you break your fool necks, I expect you to find a replacement to take your place."

"Thank you, Sergeant," Andrew said.

"That's all right, sir!" Jardine replied.

For the next week, Andrew split his force in two. While Morton commanded the usual patrols, he taught his mounted infantry the rudiments of drill and riding. Andrew had ridden horses since he could walk, as had some Sikhs, while most of the Fusiliers were town-bred, without equine knowledge.

"Your horse will sense your fear," Andrew told them. "Your horse will know you lack experience and confidence. Your horse will try to be your master. It is up to you to prove him wrong."

The more nervous of the mounted infantrymen eyed their mounts with trepidation. The horses returned the glances with what Andrew thought was amusement.

"Your first lesson is to take care of your horse," Andrew said. "You will feed and water him before you feed yourself. You will keep his stables clean and groom him before you have breakfast. You will treat him like your brother and get to know him as your best friend."

The men listened, some smiling nervously and others without expression.

"When we ride out, the experienced men will lead, and the others will follow," Andrew said and split his class in half. While he taught the better men the tricks he had learned fighting the Zulus and Boers, the rest struggled to remain in the saddles.

They'll improve, Andrew thought. *I hope they will improve quickly.*

"We ride to battle and dismount to fight," Andrew said. "We should have short-barrelled carbines but must make do with Sniders and Martinis."

Andrew trained them to remain in their saddles and follow simple bugle calls and hand signals. He also taught them to ride in formation and how to extend to ride line abreast to cover more ground.

"I should have months to train you," Andrew said. "I don't know how much time the dacoits will allow us, but we will train day and night until they return."

He pushed them hard, used the Sikhs as examples, praised them when needed and shouted when they hesitated. After a week, the men had lost their fear of the horses. After a month, some were becoming reasonably competent riders. Andrew forced them out when the monsoon rains lashed the ground, and they rode with heads bowed and horses splashing through the mud. He borrowed a civilian vet to inspect his horses, sent the bill to the Chief Commissioner and ignored the unpleasant reply.

The northeast monsoon season ended at the end of February, and the dry season opened with brilliant sunshine and heat that seemed to bounce off the ground. Andrew ensured the men watered their horses before they filled their water bottles and continued to drive them hard. He set section against section, Sikh against Fusilier, experimented with mixed Fusilier and Sikh sections, and returned to single units. The men sulked, grumbled, and slowly grew in confidence and ability.

As March eased away, Andrew could watch his creation ride past in columns of two and feel some justified satisfaction close to pride. He returned to their makeshift headquarters, promising to return to Wells' Britannia Hotel that evening for a rare visit to Mariana.

"Sir!" Sergeant Jardine trotted up on his Shan pony. "The dacoits are back!"

Mariana quoted Tennyson to herself as she walked to the commercial heart of Rangoon.

"Tears, idle tears, I know not what they
   mean,
Tears from the depths of some divine despair
Rise in the heart, and gather to the eyes,
In looking on the happy autumn fields,
And thinking of the days that are no more."

Mariana stopped at the imposing stone building that rose three storeys from the street and displayed its coat of arms of a ship in full sail above a St George's Cross. Mariana checked the firm's name, *Jennings and Stanley,* muttered to herself, stepped inside the grand front door and rang the little brass bell for service. She controlled her nerves by smiling and speaking more loudly than usual.

"I want to see Mr Jennings," Mariana said as a clerk hurried to the front desk but slowed when he saw a woman standing alone.

"Do you?" The clerk was Burmese, wearing European clothing and the smug expression of a minor official with power over all who entered his domain. He looked Mariana up and down. "What is your name, please?"

"Miss Maxwell," Mariana said coldly. "Miss Mariana Maxwell."

"Miss Mariana Maxwell," the clerk repeated the name slowly. "Wait here, please." With a last look at Mariana, he left his position and disappeared through a door at the back.

Mariana glanced around the reception area. The floor was polished teak, with panelled walls and an ornate ceiling with the expected fan. A flight of stairs curved upward, past the firm's coat of arms and pictures of ships and the Golden Pagoda.

Have I done the right thing coming here? Mariana suddenly felt like a frontier farmer's daughter, out of place in this establishment of mercantile trade and wealth.

"Miss Maxwell!" Jennings burst through the door behind the counter and strode forward, dismissed the clerk with a curt word and held out his hand. "How good to see you again. But you look troubled. Is anything the matter?"

"Indeed not, Mr Jennings," Mariana realised the clerk was listening and lowered her voice. "I wish to talk to you."

Jennings glanced at the clerk, told him sharply to be about his business and ushered Mariana to the stairs. "I have an office upstairs, Miss Maxwell. We will be more private there."

The office was teak panelled, with a carved teak desk, two deep leather armchairs and a full-length mirror. Filing cabinets and a glass-fronted, walnut drinks cabinet lined one wall, with windows overlooking the harbour on the other. A large telescope stood on a swivel beside the windows.

"I like to keep an eye on the harbour," Jennings explained. "I want to know when my merchandise is arriving and departing. Sit down, Miss Maxwell, and tell me what troubles you."

Mariana folded her skirt beneath her as she sat, with the armchair soft and yielding around her.

Jennings took his place on the second armchair, facing Mariana across two yards of polished teak floor. "I sense you want to talk, Miss Maxwell, so I won't delay matters." He raised his eyebrows, smiled, and settled back in his chair.

"Mr Jennings." Mariana hesitated for a moment. "You have twice offered to show me your house. I know this is very forward of me, but if you were to ask me a third time, I would agree."

"Then that is settled," Jennings said. He lowered his voice. "Miss Maxwell,"

"Mariana," Mariana corrected. "Please call me Mariana."

If Andrew chooses to neglect me and is probably with that Burmese woman, I am entitled to be friendly with Mr Jennings.

Jennings bowed from his chair. "That is kind of you. I am Stephen, as you know."

"Stephen," Mariana said. "I like that name."

Jennings stood, keeping his gaze on Mariana. "Miss Maxwell, Mariana, will you do me the honour of joining me for dinner in my house?"

"I would be delighted, Stephen," Mariana replied, with her heartbeat increasing. "When?"

Am I betraying Andrew? No, he has left me, and this is a simple dinner between friends, nothing else.

Stephen considered for a moment. "Shall we say tomorrow evening at six? That will give the servants time to prepare something special for you."

"I don't need anything special," Mariana said. "Please don't go to any trouble."

Jennings shook his head. "I want something special for a very special lady," he countered.

About to deny she was special, Mariana thought of Andrew with the Burmese woman. *After all the years he has known me, he finds another woman. Maybe this Burmese woman is not his first. Perhaps he knew a whole string of women in Africa and Britain.*

"Thank you, Stephen. I will come at six, prompt." Mariana lifted her head.

"I'll send a carriage for you," Jennings promised. He lowered his voice. "May I be permitted to make a confession?"

"Of course," Mariana said, prepared to forgive him anything.

"When I first saw you," Stephen spoke quietly. "I thought you were just one of the fishing fleet, but as I got to know you, I realised you were something special." He looked away, lowering his voice. "You are like no woman I have ever met before."[1]

---

1. The Fishing Fleet: single women who travelled to India to find a husband. Those who failed were known as 'returned empties.'

Mariana bobbed in a little curtsy without leaving her seat. "Thank you, Stephen. That was lovely of you."

What would Tennyson say? He said: "Come friends, it's not too late to seek a newer world." Mariana smiled despite the nervous hammer of her heart. *I am seeking a newer world with a man who has never been anything but kind to me. Stephen has paid me every attention and looked after me while Andrew was away courting that Burmese woman and pretending to be a soldier while the country is at peace.*

"Now," Jennings stepped to the drinks cabinet. "I know the sun is hardly over the yardarm, but neither of us is a sailor, so we don't have to follow that archaic custom. A brandy and water, Mariana?"

"THEY'RE BACK?" ANDREW ASKED.

"Yes, sir," Sergeant Jardine said, standing at attention at Andrew's side. "One of the standing patrols has reported that a gang of dacoits is raiding five miles north of Rangoon."

"Thank you, Sergeant," Andrew said. "Now we will see how good the mounted infantry is." *I won't be seeing Mariana tonight, then.*

"Parade dismissed! Fill up your water bottles and report back in ten minutes with fifty rounds of ammunition. We're dacoit hunting!"

Andrew had prepared for such an event. He had put Sukhbir Singh in charge of the Sikhs and Lieutenant Morton with the Fusiliers' infantry. Sergeant Jardine gave Andrew the details, and he folded a map, stuffed it in his saddlebag and grabbed more ammunition for his revolver.

"Morton, take the infantry at the double and support the horsemen."

"Yes, sir," Morton said.

"Your job is to guard the villages."

"Yes, sir," Morton ran to organise his foot soldiers.

"The rest of you, mount and ride!" Andrew addressed the assembled mounted infantry. He told them their destination and grinned. "Right, lads! It's time to put all that training to the test. Follow me!"

After months of patrolling, Andrew knew the land well and rode directly to the affected area. He saw the rising smoke a mile away and gave quick orders to his men. "Sukhbir Singh! Take your men and head them off. Your job and mine is to pursue the dacoits. Lieutenant Morton and his men will guard the villages."

"Yes, Sahib," Sukhbir grinned and saluted, with his men eager to meet the dacoits.

"The rest, follow me." Andrew glanced over his shoulder. Nobody had fallen off his horse, and the Fusiliers had kept in formation. He knew the Sikhs were better horsemen than the Fusiliers and allowed

Sukhbir his head while Morton's section would guard the civilians.

Men and women working in the fields looked up as the mounted infantry passed, with a bullock cart pulling to the side to allow them passage.

"Keep the pace up!" Andrew ordered. He knew the men suffered in the heat and had prepared them by allowing looser clothing and trying to find shade whenever possible. He heard the regular crunch of hooves on the ground and felt a glow of satisfaction that he was commanding regular soldiers again in a worthwhile campaign.

We are protecting civilians against very unpleasant people. This is why I signed up, not for glory but to make a difference, to do good.

After twenty minutes, the Fusiliers heard a crackle of musketry ahead and involuntarily increased their speed.

"Push on, lads!" Andrew ordered. He could see movement ahead, the blur of galloping horsemen accompanied by hoarse shouts and sporadic firing. Andrew saw a village on the right, with smoke rising from a burning building and Sukhbir's Sikhs riding around an area of long grass.

"Fusiliers!" Andrew barked. "Move towards the grass, trot!" He had deliberately kept his instructions simple, without the complicated manoeuvres that fully trained cavalry would perform. He watched his men ride forward, keeping in approximate formation as they approached the long grass.

"Dismount!" Andrew ordered. "Form a firing line. At the double!"

The Fusiliers dismounted, with every fourth man taking control of the horses' reins while the rest ran forward to take their positions. Most of the men immediately understood what was happening, while others looked confused but obeyed orders.

"The Sikhs have flushed out the enemy," Andrew explained. "The dacoits are running for the grass to hide. Havildar Sukhbir Singh's men will drive them this way, and we will stop them."

After weeks of chasing the elusive dacoits with little result, followed by hard months of training, the Fusiliers were pleased to see them in the open.

Andrew heard the shouts of the Sikhs as they hounded the dacoits.

"Lie down!" Andrew ordered his Fusiliers. "We want to surprise the enemy."

The men obeyed, with their khaki uniforms merging with the sun-dried grass. Andrew crouched, revolver in hand, as he watched the scene unfold.

The mounted Sikhs stretched in a continuous line across the maidan. They shot at any dacoit who doubled back, herding the majority towards the supposed shelter of the grassland. Andrew heard the men plainly: the high-pitched shouts of the Burmese and the deeper voices of the Sikhs.

The first dacoit plunged into the long grass, with his companions following. With the grass obscuring his vision, Andrew could not make out details.

"Ready, lads! Make sure you're loaded," Andrew called. He felt his men's tension as they rubbed sweating palms on their legs or shook the perspiration from their eyebrows.

The dacoits were running desperately, maybe forty or fifty of them, half-naked men with firearms and *dhas*, hoping to hide in the grass as the Sikhs pursued in high excitement.

Andrew timed his orders, waiting until the dacoits were only a hundred and fifty yards away, sufficient distance for two volleys. "Ready! Aim low! Don't hit the horsemen; they're on our side!"

"I dinnae think Sergeant Jardine is on our side!" an anonymous voice called.

Andrew began the countdown. "Three, two, one. Fire!"

The Fusiliers fired with an unaimed volley that sliced into the grassland. Andrew did not know how many dacoits they hit. The shots surprised the mounted Sikhs nearly as much as the enemy, and Andrew ordered a second volley before uttering the order, "Fix bayonets! Bayonets... Fix!"

He heard the ominous snick as the Fusiliers attached the eighteen-inch-long bayonets to the barrels of their Martini-Henry's.

"Corporal McGhee, keep your section here to

stop any dacoits who evade us. The rest, in open order, advance!"

With the mounted infantry behind them and the Fusiliers in front, the dacoits had nowhere to run. Some threw up their hands in surrender, others tried to fight, and a few threw themselves on the ground, hoping to look dead or invisible in the long grass. Remembering the tortured or murdered villagers and the pillaged villages, the British and Sikhs had little mercy. They shot or bayonetted until Andrew and Sergeant Jardine called for restraint. One man faced Andrew squarely, holding a long *dha* in defiance, only turning to run at the last minute.

Andrew saw the man was broad-chested, with a tattoo across his face and a gold hilt on his *dha*.

"Catch that man!" Andrew ordered, but by the time the nearest horseman could turn, the dacoit had disappeared.

Damn it! He looked like the leader of the whole bunch! He might have been Buda Sein.

The British and Sikhs rounded up five living dacoits as prisoners, and Andrew ordered a count of the dead.

"Have the prisoners dig one large grave," he said. "We'll bury them here."

The dacoits were a sorry-looking bunch. They mostly wore minimal clothing, with bare feet and rudimentary weapons. Most possessed a *dha*, and some had only short knives or heavy staves.

"Sahib!" Sukhbir Singh called out, raising a hand to Andrew. "Look at this, sahib."

Andrew marched over. "What have you found, Havildar?"

Sukhbir rolled over the nearest dead dacoit and pointed to his neck. "There, sahib."

Andrew saw the dragon tattooed on the nape. "It's a dragon, Sukhbir."

"Yes, Sahib. Only the king's soldiers have a dragon tattooed there," Sukhbir said. "This man is no ordinary loose wallah. He is one of the king's soldiers."[2]

Is this an isolated case of one of Thibaw's soldiers joining a dacoit raid? Or has the king sent his men to cause havoc in British Burma?

"Check the others," Andrew ordered. "See if there are any more soldiers."

Three of the dead had a dragon tattoo on their necks.

I'll have to report these tattoos to Sir Charles.

"Check the prisoners," Andrew said.

One man tried to run when the Sikhs and Fusiliers began to ask questions, but the Sikhs were ready, and a mounted man caught him by his hair and dragged him back.

"Check them for dragon tattoos and ask who led

---

2. Loosewallah – bandit, thief.

them," Andrew said. "One of our Burmese policemen can translate."

Only the prisoner who tried to escape had a dragon tattoo.

"You'd best go for a walk, sir," Sergeant Jardine said. "I'll ask the fellow who tried to escape."

"No ugly business," Andrew said.

"No, sir," Jardine replied.

Andrew knew it was sometimes better to leave experienced men like Sergeant Jardine to perform necessary but unpleasant tasks.

After checking his men, Andrew returned to Sergeant Jardine, who saluted.

"Their leader is a fellow named Buda Sein, sir," Jardine said. "The dacoit was a stubborn fellow, but Sukhbir and I persuaded him to tell us."

Andrew saw the dacoit looking battered, bloody but alive. He remembered the woman the dacoits had roasted to death and quelled his conscience. "Thank you, Sergeant. We'll take the prisoners to the jail in Rangoon." He thought of the man with the golden-hilted *dha* and wished he had caught him.

That man, Buda Sein, is trouble. He'll return, and we'll be ready for him.

CHAPTER 20

RANGOON, APRIL TO AUGUST 1885

M ariana looked at herself in the mirror, patted her hair in place, and adjusted her earrings. She had never worn earrings before coming to Burma and would never adopt the Burmese habit of boring holes in her ears to hold cheroots. However, Mariana rather liked the idea of gold hoops that caught the light when she moved her head. She tilted her head again, watching her reflection and smiling.

What would the good people of Berwick think if they saw me like this? They'd be scandalised. Good God! Some domestic servants even hang men and women's washing on different clothes lines.

Mariana touched the gold rings, smiling.

Anyway, Stephen gave me these gold earrings so I will wear them for his sake.

Mariana sighed and looked down on herself. The dark dress contrasted nicely with her blonde hair, while the earrings connected the two. Mariana smiled at her reflection, seeing her grey eyes crinkling at the corners. She leaned closer to the mirror. *Are those lines around my eyes? Oh, Lord, I hope not; I must be getting old before my time. I am twenty-four and still unmarried. Maybe I'll end up an old maid.*

She thought again of Andrew's proposal in Edinburgh and shook her head. *If I had agreed, I'd be married to a man I rarely see. Where is he now? Is he playing at soldiers or with his Burmese woman?*

Mariana started at the tap on her door. *Andrew!* "Who is it?"

"The maid, Miss Maxwell," a light voice replied.

"Come in," Mariana called.

The maid was small in stature, efficient and friendly. "A carriage has arrived for you, Miss Maxwell."

"Thank you," Mariana replied, standing up. "How do I look?"

The maid stepped back. "Like Supayalat," she said solemnly. "Thibaw's queen. The gentleman is fortunate."

"Thank you," Mariana said, smiling. Taking a deep breath, she left her room and hurried down the stairs, passing the old Burmese woman at the foot of the pillar.

The carriage was more luxurious than anything she had ever seen, a tall wheeled blue Brougham with a matched pair of greys and a dignified coachman wearing a long blue coat and a top hat. A servant opened the door for Mariana, saw her comfortably inside and quietly closed the door. As the servant joined the coachman in front, the Brougham eased away, with the sound of hooves and whirr of well-greased wheels strangely soothing.

I am going to a gentleman's house, alone and unescorted. Mariana watched the streets pass by without interest. *I hope I am doing the right thing.*

The journey to Jennings' house on Rangoon's outskirts took a full twenty minutes, and when the Brougham came to a smooth halt, the servant dismounted to open the door for Mariana. She took a deep breath, smiled politely, and descended.

"Welcome to my humble abode, Miss Maxwell," Jennings greeted Mariana as she left the carriage. Dressed in an evening suit and tails, he bowed deeply and offered his arm.

"Thank you, Mr Jennings," Mariana replied. "I am Mariana, remember?"

"And I am Stephen. Come this way, Mariana."

The house was two-storeyed and L-shaped within immaculately groomed grounds. Stephen had arranged for the servants to stand in a double row outside the columned front door. They bowed as Stephen and Mariana passed.

"How lovely," Mariana curtseyed in return, which made Stephen smile.

The interior of the house matched the exterior with a combination of local and European furniture. Massive teak pillars held the upper floors in place, while the main reception room had a large brass Buddha on a plinth, with a six-foot-tall palm tree in an elaborate brass pot on either side.

"I've never seen anything like this before," Mariana said.

I could not imagine this in Berwick or Natal.

"Do you like it?" Stephen snapped a finger, and a graceful servant took Mariana's light coat.

"I do like it," Mariana said. "Have you converted to Buddhism, Stephen?"

"Heavens, no," Jennings smiled at the idea. "But while in Rome, you know. Anyway, it helps my Burmese visitors relax when they see I don't reject their philosophy. It is a philosophy, you know, and not a religion."

"I was not aware of that," Mariana said as Jennings paused to allow her to admire the room.

"The Buddhists don't worship the man, only the perfection he achieved," Jennings told her.

Andrew already told me that.

"I see," Mariana said, starting as somebody rang

a gong, with the sound reverberating around the house.

"I am sorry," Jennings touched her arm. "I should have warned you about the gong." He smiled disarmingly. "Dinner is ready. I don't believe in waiting when one is hungry. Are you hungry, Mariana?"

"I have starved myself since breakfast," Mariana admitted. "It would be less than polite not to bring an appetite with me."

Jennings laughed. "Well said, Mariana. I do like a lady with an appetite." He stopped as a servant opened the door for them. "Do you prefer British, European or Burmese fare?" He held up a sealed envelope. "I have written your reply here."

"British," Mariana replied without hesitation.

"Open it," Jennings handed over the envelope. The slip of paper inside read "British."

"How clever you are," Mariana said, smiling. She stepped through the door into the hallway.

"I think I know you well," Jennings told her. He gave her his arm. "Shall we go into the dining room?"

Mariana smiled, with her head whirling at the attention and the novelty of the situation. "Yes, please," she said, walking at Jennings' side.

The circular table was smaller than Mariana had expected and much more intimate, with only two places set opposite each other. A single candle burned in the centre, with the light reflecting from an array of plates and glasses that Mariana found daunting. After Andrew's austere lifestyle and the reality of life on the Natal frontier, Mariana was nearly overwhelmed by such luxury.

"You look surprised, Mariana," Jennings said.

"A little," Mariana admitted. "It's lovely. It's all lovely."

Behind the table, large windows allowed a view of the garden, where coloured lanterns hung from trees to give an almost surreal and calming effect.

"I am glad you approve," Jennings said. "Are you all right with soup to begin with? Or would you prefer something else?" He smiled. "I can cater to whatever taste you prefer, Mariana."

"Soup is fine, thank you," Mariana saw that Jennings was trying his best to make her feel comfortable.

The servants moved smoothly throughout the seven-course meal, which included soup, freshly caught fish, a rather tough chicken, and some vegetables Mariana did not recognise but which Jennings explained to her with humorous asides.

They finished with fruit and laughter as Jennings entertained Mariana with a fund of humorous anecdotes about his life in Burma.

"And now wine, dear Mariana," Jennings said. He signalled to a servant. "Champagne!"

Mariana watched as the servant opened the bottle with a loud pop that made her start.

"Oh!"

"It's all right, Mariana. It's meant to do that," Jennings explained.

With the large window behind her, Mariana lifted the glass tentatively, watching the bubbles rise to the surface and explode.

"Drink," Stephen encouraged. "I bought half a dozen bottles of champagne in honour of your visit. Champagne is far too exclusive for me to drink alone."

"Thank you," Mariana said and sipped delicately. "It's very bubbly."

"Some people call champagne bubbly," Jennings said.

Mariana giggled. "It tickles my nose."

"Enjoy the sensation," Jennings watched her over the rim of his glass. "Here's a toast to us," he said. "May we have a long and happy friendship."

Mariana lifted her glass. "To us," she agreed and giggled again.

After they finished the champagne, Jennings threw the empty bottle to a servant, who caught it with practised hands.

"Where are my manners!" Jennings said. "I do apologise, Mariana. I have been so intent on introducing you to the pleasure of champagne that I neglected to show you the rest of the house."

"Oh, I don't mind," Mariana said. She smiled, seeing Jennings as a slightly blurred figure on the opposite side of the table.

"Would you like to see the rest of my house?" Jennings asked.

"I'd love to," Mariana said.

The upstairs rooms were as luxurious as those on the ground floor. Each had large windows facing the garden, while the neighbouring house was in darkness.

"How many bedrooms do you have?" Mariana asked, holding onto Jennings for support.

"One main bedroom and four guest bedrooms," Jennings replied.

"How lovely," Mariana said. She swallowed hard. "Could I go home now, please? I don't feel very well."

AFTER THEIR INITIAL SUCCESS AGAINST THE dacoits, Baird's Mounted Infantry patrolled the ground north of Rangoon. Andrew called on every village and town to reassure the population that the British were there to protect them. The villagers greeted him politely and resumed their daily life.

When Sir Charles Crosthwaite saw Andrew's accomplishments, he increased his force to two hundred men, a mixture of mounted men and infantry.

"I only intended you to be here temporarily, Baird," Sir Charles told him. "But I want you to remain until the present crisis with King Thibaw is resolved."

"Have you thought further about Bo Thura's pardon, sir?" Andrew asked.

"I am gathering information, Baird. This Bo Thura has been a pain in our neck for some time."

"Yes, sir," Andrew said.

"Many people would not wish Bo Thura to be secure within British territory," Sir Charles said. "I have yet to make up my mind. In the meantime, keep hunting your dacoits."

"I will, sir," Andrew promised.

The mills of Sir Charles grind slowly when he wants me to clear Rangoon of dacoits. I hope Mariana is all right. I am neglecting the poor girl terribly.

MARIANA STOOD IN JENNINGS' OFFICE WITH HER hands folded before her, feeling like a schoolgirl standing before the headmistress.

"You look very contrite, Mariana," Jennings said. "Whatever is the matter?"

"I do apologise for my behaviour in your house," Mariana said. "I am most thoroughly ashamed of myself."

"For what?" Jennings asked, smiling. "Sit down, Mariana. For goodness' sake, sit down."

"I fear I had too much to drink," Mariana remained standing.

"That was my fault entirely," Jennings said. "I should have known you were unused to champagne. Can you forgive me?"

"Only if you forgive me," Mariana replied. The conversation had gone better than she expected.

"Then we are both forgiven," Jennings said. His smile broadened. "You were quite charming in that condition."

"Some men would have taken advantage of me," Mariana said. "You were a perfect gentleman and took me back to the hotel."

Jennings smoothed a finger over his moustache. "You must know by now that I respect you, Mariana. I would never dishonour you. Sit down, do."

Mariana sat down, smoothing her skirt beneath her. "Thank you, Stephen. I am so glad you understand."

Jennings chuckled. "You are worth understanding. Shall we try again?"

ANDREW ENHANCED HIS TACTICS WITH STRONG pickets of police backed by infantry in the villages and mounted patrols to discourage the dacoits. His theory was simple: the infantry held the dacoits with rifle fire, and the noise would attract the nearest mounted men, who would hunt the fugitives. If the mounted men came across a party of dacoits, they drove them towards the nearest village, where the picket waited with their rifles.

Remembering the success of his deception with the dummies, Andrew had his men make another twenty, asked Ajit Singh to create their faces, clothed them in worn khaki and positioned them within the standing pickets.

"If the dacoits see these dummies," he explained. "They might think we are stronger than we are and leave us in peace."

Lieutenant Morton laughed. "Yes, sir. We've strengthened our force with men we don't have to feed or pay. Best not tell Gladstone, or he'll replace us all with dummies."

"Using dummy soldiers is not a new trick," Andrew said. "When we expected Bonaparte to invade Britain, we built the Royal Military Canal in Kent and manned it with wooden soldiers."

"Were they any good?"

"I never heard of them getting drunk," Andrew replied solemnly.

In addition to placing dummies with the standing pickets, Andrew augmented the mounted patrols with straw-filled and watermelon-headed uniforms. He did not know if his ideas fooled the dacoits, but the Sikhs found them amusing and gave names to their latest recruits.

Andrew supervised as his Sikhs and Fusiliers tied the dummies to their horses. Skilled with his hands, Fusilier Jordan carved fine wooden rifles for the latest recruits.

"There we are, sir. That should fool Johnny Dacoit." Jordan stepped back, smiling at his handiwork.

"I think so," Andrew agreed. "They'll think we have improved our armament and doubled the size of our force."

If I can clear these dacoits away, maybe Sir Charles will grant Bo Thura his pardon, and Mariana and I can get home. Why am I so concerned about a Burmese dacoit? Is it because he's family? Is blood thicker than water? I can't think of any other reason.

CHAPTER 21

RANGOON, AUGUST TO NOVEMBER 1885

Andrew watched his Mounted Infantry ride past. The Sikhs were naturals, riding like centaurs, as easy in the saddle as on foot. Despite all of Andrew's work, the Fusiliers were not as good. With a few exceptions, they looked what they were: infantrymen on horseback.

"I'll improve you," Andrew promised and continued to train them. He spent every spare moment with his men, working them until they were sick of the sight, smell, and sound of horses.

He spread his Burmese police and Sikhs around the villages and asked his Burmese to infiltrate the villages and ask questions.

"The local people will not talk to us," Andrew

said, "but they might talk to you. Good intelligence is half the battle. If we know what the enemy is doing, we have a massive advantage, so ask questions. I want this Buda Sein in jail."

The Burmese police spread across the villages, some in uniform and most in plain clothes. As they asked their questions, Andrew continued to train his Mounted Infantry. In the evenings, he read over the notes the police gathered, and twice, he met Mariana for a few tense hours.

"Can't you tear yourself away from your duty for a few days, Andrew?" Mariana asked.

"I can't," Andrew told her. "People's lives are at stake."

"Well, is there a room in the barracks for me?"

Andrew thought of a lone woman sharing the barracks with his Mounted Infantry and police. "That would not be a good idea," he said.

Mariana did not hide her disappointment. "I hardly ever see you," she said.

"It won't be much longer," Andrew told her. "Then we'll be heading back home."

Andrew tried to see Mariana at least once a week but felt they were drifting apart. He wrote her letters, left them in her room and returned to duty feeling sick and depressed; the only cure was to lose himself in his duty.

Duty is what Windrushes do. We live for our duty, God help us.

After two months, Andrew thought his Fusiliers were reasonably competent Mounted Infantry. He could watch them with satisfaction and planned to spend more time with Mariana when the Burmese police handed him two reports. He read them and called for Lieutenant Morton.

"The police say the villagers in Pat Lan have stopped talking to them, Morton, and the nearby settlements are nervous."

"What does that mean, sir?" Morton asked.

"I think Buda Sein is using Pat Lan as his base," Andrew decided. "If not him, then somebody else. Either way, we'll visit Pat Lan with the mounted infantry."

"The Sikhs might feel left out," Morton said.

"The Sikhs will continue to patrol," Andrew told him. "I want to test the Fusiliers."

If they are successful, I can inform Sir Charles that his Mounted Infantrymen are fully trained, and he no longer needs me. I'll pick up Bo Thura's pardon and Mariana and we'll catch the next ship home.

WITH THE MOUNTED INFANTRY AT HIS BACK, Andrew rode over the darkened countryside north of Rangoon. He hoped his deduction was correct, or this entire expedition was a waste of time.

Andrew stopped on a slight ridge a mile from Pat

Lan, with the sun hinting at its morning appearance. He glanced behind him, counting his men. They were all present.

Good: nobody has dropped out.

Andrew gathered the Mounted Infantry around him.

"That village is Pat Lan, and I suspect that Buda Sein is in there," Andrew said. "You all know that Buda Sein is the instigator of many dacoit attacks on and around Rangoon, which means if we arrest him, we'll strike a major blow at the dacoits."

The Fusiliers nodded, grunted, or murmured assent.

Andrew continued. "We will surround the place and arrest all the men inside. If anybody resists, shoot them, and watch for a man with a yellow umbrella and green tassels." He lowered his voice. "That is Buda Sein."

The Fusiliers looked pleased, nodding, adjusting their equipment and checking their rifles.

"Corporal Rowan, take the right flank. Sergeant Jardine, go round the rear and ensure nobody escapes. Corporal McGhee, take the left flank. I'll give you ten minutes and boot in the front door with my section." He waited until the men murmured their understanding before he continued. "I expect resistance, men, so be prepared to fight."

Andrew expected the grins; after months in their company, he knew his Royal Scots Fusiliers. He checked his watch. "Try not to be seen, men. I'll be moving in in twenty minutes; that will be ten past six. Go!"

He watched the Fusiliers disappear, noting the improvement in their riding. They were still not as good as his Sikhs but far better than they had been. After five minutes, the sections divided, vanishing in the gloom.

Andrew checked the time, watching the minute hand jerk forward. *How strange that such a small thing as a watch regulates our lives. We live by the clock as it ticks away our allotted span, three score years and ten, divided into these minuscule fragments of time.*

"Right, men!" Andrew raised a hand. "Follow me!"

Andrew's section stayed a few paces behind him as he moved forward. He wished he had Lancelot, his Kabul pony that had never let him down, but this Shan mount was an adequate replacement. Andrew had named it Shansi, a meaningless name that seemed to suit it, and he fondled the pony's ears in sudden affection.

Andrew kept his men under control, glanced at his watch, ensured his NCOs were in position and halted a hundred yards outside the village. He heard voices from the outlying houses, heard a growling man quieting a barking dog; a baby began to wail, a woman laughed, and somebody sounded a gong.

The brassy clamour wakened old memories as Andrew raised his voice.

"They've seen us!" Andrew shouted. "Forward, lads! Forward the Royal Scots Fusiliers!" He kicked in his heels. "Extended order! Round up all the men! Don't hurt any women or children."

Andrew knew he did not have to add his final order to the Fusiliers, but it was always best to re-mind them. In the heat of action, when men were in danger, they could fire without checking their target.

He heard his NCOs shouting, one after another, and ordered every second man to dismount to con-trol the civilians and prisoners as he entered the vil-lage. He expected the arguments, the anger, and the frustrated disquiet from frightened wives and moth-ers. Andrew knew that these reactions were normal when soldiers dealt with civilians. Burma was no dif-ferent from Ireland, Africa, India, or the Scottish Hebrides.

Someone fired a musket, the muzzle flare coming from the rear of the village. Andrew heard the echo of the shot and, a moment later, the reply from half a dozen Martini-Henrys.

That's my boys. Don't allow any dacoits to escape.

Andrew's section was busy, working in pairs as they kicked open doors and hauled out any men they found. Most were villagers, confused, angry, scared, but not dangerous. Women, wives, sisters, or mothers clung to their men, screaming and sobbing in fear.

Other men were truculent or looking for an escape.

"Keep the men secure," Andrew said to Corporal Rowan. "If a wife or mother claims anybody, release him. Hold the others and look for the green umbrella." He repeated the orders to Corporal McGhee.

The Fusiliers nodded, holding their rifles with grim professionalism. After months of frustrating training, hunting dacoits, and witnessing their handiwork, they had no intentions of allowing any to escape.

The firing at the rear of the village broke out again, with British volleys following scattered dacoit musketry.

"You're in charge, Corporal," Andrew said, mounting his horse. Kicking in his spurs, he rode towards the firing, pulling the rifle from its bucket holster.

Sergeant Jardine had stopped a breakout at the rear of the village, with his men in extended order and every fourth man holding the horses. The increasing light revealed a row of determined men in faded khaki with sun helmets on their heads and Martini-Henry rifles in steady hands.

A score of dacoits huddled behind the houses while two desperate men held a woman in front of them as a human shield. Andrew stretched forward, holding his rifle at arm's length. He nudged the nearest dacoit in the back of the head with the muzzle of the Martini.

"Release her!" Although Andrew doubted if the dacoit understood his words, the threat was plain. The man stepped back in fear, shouting to his companion. The second dacoit pulled his captive closer to him, snarling at Andrew. The woman screamed, struggling to free herself, with clawed hands raking the dacoit's face.

As the dacoit reared back, Andrew altered the angle of his rifle and fired. The bullet smashed into the dacoit's temple and exited at the back of his head, taking half his brain in a welter of blood and splintered bone. His hostage screamed again and ran, with the first dacoit watching his friend's death curiously, yet without visible emotion.

A young Fusilier ran up, immediately understood what had happened and jammed his Martini into the surviving dacoit's chest.

"Hands up, chum!" The Fusilier was about twenty, with an angelic face except for eyes that had already seen the worst of the world. When the dacoit hesitated, the Fusilier jerked up his rifle barrel, catching him under the chin and forcing his lower teeth into his upper lip. "Hands up, you bastard, or I'll blow your bloody head off!"

This time, the dacoit's hands shot into the air as blood dribbled from his mouth. "Now get back there!" The Fusilier glanced at Andrew. "I've got him, sir."

"So I see," Andrew reloaded his rifle. "Put him with the other prisoners, Fusilier."

"Yes, sir. Come on, you!" The Fusilier jabbed his rifle into the dacoit's bare back.

The firing at the rear of the village had ended, and Andrew pushed on, peering through drifting gunsmoke.

"Sergeant Jardine!"

"All secure, sir," Jardine replied quietly.

"Did you find Buda Sein?" Andrew dismounted to talk to Jardine.

"Not a shadow of him, sir," Jardine replied. "Unless he's pretending to be one of the ordinary dacoits."

Andrew saw a flurry of activity on his left. A Fusilier yelled, aimed, and fired as two dacoits burst from the back of a house and ran, jinking and weaving, into the surrounding fields. The first carried something in his right hand.

"That's a folded umbrella!" Sergeant Jardine shouted.

"Get these men!" Andrew jumped on his horse as the two men splashed through a paddy field, with the Fusiliers firing after them. The second man staggered as a bullet smashed into his shoulder. He turned around, his long hair loose over his shoulders as he shouted defiance. Another bullet knocked him face down into the mud, where he struggled for a minute, raised a hand, and lay still.

The first dacoit was further away, with his yellow umbrella distinct against the green forest behind. Andrew pushed Shansi beyond the village and into the paddy field until the mud became too deep, and the horse began to struggle.

"That's far enough, Shansi," Andrew murmured. "That's far enough." He heard the sergeant call "cease fire," heard a single shot, saw the umbrella twitch as a bullet hit it, and then the yellow vanished.

He's gone. Buda Sein has escaped again. Damn and blast the man!

"Gather the prisoners together, Sergeant, and we'll sort the wheat from the chaff. The good people of Burma will be pleased to hear we've removed another dangerous dacoit gang from the countryside."

"I'm sure they will, sir," Sergeant Jardine said.

Andrew stared into the forest, certain that Buda Sein was watching him from the shelter of the trees.

We'll meet again, Buda Sein!

AFTER ANOTHER MONTH AND A COUPLE MORE successes that saw half a dozen dead dacoits and twelve disconsolate prisoners, the dacoits' attack on Rangoon's environs faded away.

"You did well, Baird," the Chief Commissioner said from behind his desk. "Now, I will advise the military to adopt your techniques of a combination of standing pickets and flying columns to keep the dacoit menace down all across Lower Burma."

"Thank you, sir," Andrew replied.

"Not that they will listen," Sir Charles said gloomily. "Senior military officers live in the past. If it was good enough for Wellington, they say, it's good enough for me."

"I can't imagine the Army forming a square in the middle of Burma," Andrew said.

"Don't give them ideas, Baird. Wellington cut his teeth in India, remember? He was a sepoy general before he fought in Spain." Sir Charles stood up. "I take it you have heard the news about the impending war?"

"I have been a little busy lately," Andrew said. "I know we sent an ultimatum to King Thibaw."

Sir Charles nodded. He stepped to the window and stood in silhouette with his hands behind his back. "We've had about enough of King Thibaw, his dacoits, his threats against British subjects, and his machinations with the French."

"Yes, sir," Andrew agreed. "If you'll remember, Bo Thura was first to alert you to the French negotiations in the Kingdom of Ava." *That was a hint about his long overdue pardon, sir.*

Sir Charles grunted. "Put him aside for now,

Baird. We have larger issues on hand than the future of one blasted criminal."

"I see, sir," Andrew said.

"As you said, we have sent an ultimatum to the Kingdom of Ava," Sir Charles said, "and I will remind you why."

Andrew remained standing while Sir Charles stood at the window. "Recently, the French sent a new consul, Monsieur Haas, to Mandalay. He became very close to King Thibaw and negotiated the terms of the Ava-French treaty. They agreed to establish a French bank in Burma and a railway from Mandalay to the border with our territories. The French would have a major role in businesses presently controlled by the Burmese government."

"I see, sir."

Sir Charles grunted. "With French troops in Tonkin, it's only a small step for them to enter Mandalay, and with a direct railway to our border, any minor dispute could have unpleasant consequences."

"Yes, sir," Andrew agreed.

"Obviously, we don't want the French to have influence on our border, so we asked them to remove Monsieur Haas, which they did." Sir Charles nodded. "That was a satisfactory outcome, but Thibaw continues to give us trouble."

"I am aware of the dacoit incursions, sir," Andrew reminded.

"The Burmans have also imposed a fine on the

Bombay Burmah Trading Corporation, as you know," Sir Charles continued. "We disputed Ava's supposed claims about under-reporting the amount of teak the company extracts and the spurious accusations of non-payment for the employees. When the Kingdom of Ava sent its officials to seize some of the company's timber, we demanded they accept an arbitrator to settle the disagreement."

"Did they agree, sir?"

Sir Charles remained in silhouette. "We told them we would appoint the arbitrator. They refused."

"Perhaps they doubted the neutrality of an arbitrator we chose, sir," Andrew narrowed his eyes against the glare from the window, trying to see the Chief Commissioner's expression.

"We're British, damn it," Sir Charles snapped. "We play by the rules. When they refused, we decided we had enough of their nonsense, and on the 22nd of October, we sent them an ultimatum."

Sir Charles stepped away from the window and paced the room before returning to his desk. "We demanded that they accept a British resident in Mandalay; that should forestall any more trouble from Monsieur Haas and his countrymen. We told them to suspend any legal action against the Bombay and Burmah Company until our resident arrives in Mandalay and that we should control the Kingdom of Ava's foreign relations. Lastly, they should grant us commercial facilities to develop trade with northern Burma and China."

Andrew considered the British demands. "I doubt any self-respecting ruler would accept these terms, sir. It removes virtually all independence from the country."

"How many villages have Thibaw's dacoits burned?" Sir Charles countered. "What will stop him from convening with the French or fining more British companies? We need a firm hand to deal with such people."

Andrew remembered the tortured women and ravaged villages. "I see, sir."

"King Thibaw's reply was not positive," Sir Charles said. "It was inadequate and said he would consult France, Germany, and Italy." The Chief Commissioner shook his head. "The cheek of the man!"

"What happens now, sir?"

"It will be war, Captain Baird, and then we'll be rid of the dacoit menace and have peace to develop trade and prosperity for the people of Burma."

"Yes, sir," Andrew said. Since his arrival in Rangoon, he had known that war with Thibaw's kingdom was possible but had hoped to return home before hostilities began.

"You'll wonder why I am telling you all this, Captain Baird," Sir Charles said. "As a keen young officer, you'll be desperate to play your part." He smiled. "I believe your nickname in the Zulu War was 'Up-and-at-'em,' and now is your chance to enhance your reputation further. When this war starts, which will be soon, I want you in the leading ship. You know the river and have proved you can master the Burmans in battle."

"I only fought dacoits, sir," Andrew reminded, but Sir Charles brushed away his objections.

"Nonsense! You soldiers! You praise yourselves too highly, or you hide beneath a modesty blanket. Now get yourself ready, Baird. Count your bullets, sharpen your sword, gird up your loins or whatever you soldiers do before battle."

"Yes, sir," Andrew was slightly dazed.

"See that girl of yours, eh? Miss Maxwell, isn't it?" Sir Charles was suddenly jovial. "Off you go, Baird. You're dismissed."

CHAPTER 22

RANGOON, NOVEMBER 1885

Andrew left the government office with his head spinning and his hopes of returning home dashed.

What will Mariana say to another indefinite period in Rangoon? Maybe I should move us out of Wells' Britannia and rent a bungalow? Hopefully, it's a short war.

When Andrew visited the British Cantonments, the talk in the Fusiliers' Officers' Mess was all about the impending war.

"I heard their Queen Mother declared the Burmans would resist to the last," a jovial major proclaimed.

"That should prolong the war, then," Major Goudie said. "Rather than two days, it will take a week." He saw Andrew and welcomed him with a handshake and a whisky and water. "You've been doing great things with the Mounted Infantry, I hear, Baird. What do you think about this war, then? Is it time to sort out old Thibaw?"

"Maybe so, sir," Andrew replied.

"There's no maybe about it, Baird. Thibaw's been sending his blasted bandits against us for months now. It's time we retaliated."

The Fusiliers' officers gave Andrew more details. "According to bazaar shaves, the Burmans are strengthening the palace fortifications and razing the houses near the ramparts to give their guns a clear field of fire."

"Thibaw's chief minister, Kinwin Mingyee or whatever he's called," a tall captain said. "He seems sensible. He told Thibaw to agree to our terms. Thibaw replied that if Mingyee was afraid of us, he should become a Buddhist monk!"

"From what little I've heard of Mingyee," Andrew said, "he's a dangerous man. I doubt he's our friend. He's more likely befriending who he thinks will be the winner."

Major Goudie gave an approving nod. "I think the same," he agreed.

"How about the civilians in Mandalay?" Andrew asked.

"We sent a steamer, *Dowoon*, upriver to evacuate them," Goudie said. "The Burmans detained it at

Mandalay." He shrugged. "We don't know any more at present."

Andrew grunted. He had been so busy with the Mounted Infantry he had ignored the larger picture. He heard the officers talk about the Rangoon Port Trust lending the Army six barges to use as floating batteries, with the Royal Artillery fitting two sixty-pound howitzers to each. The Army would requisition Irrawaddy Flotilla steamers and mount twenty-five-pounder guns for a Naval Brigade to batter past the frontier forts.

"Upper Burma is a wilderness," one young lieutenant said. "We'll have to travel by river."

Andrew listened without adding many comments.

"The Burmese think Thibaw is omnipotent," the same subaltern said with the certainty of youth. "They can't conceive of disobeying him, even though they hate him." He glanced at Andrew. "What do you think, Captain Baird?"

"I think most Burmans only want to get on with their lives without being pestered by kings, dacoits or British soldiers." Andrew finished his whisky and stood up. "As do I. If you will excuse me, gentlemen, I must leave you."

How the devil can I tell Mariana that we can't leave Rangoon yet?

"No!" Mariana stared at Andrew across the width of her room. "You're doing what?"

"I'm going to war," Andrew told her. "We're going to war with Thibaw, and I'm wanted."

"Why?" Mariana asked. "Don't they have enough soldiers? Why must you fight all their battles for them?"

"It's my duty," Andrew replied.

"Your duty?" Mariana tried to control her temper. She lowered her voice to a whisper. "Go and do your blessed duty, Captain Andrew Baird. Go on!" She pointed to the door. "Go!"

Andrew opened his mouth to speak, realised he had nothing to say, turned and left the room. "Damn and blast," he said when he entered his quarters and stood with his back to the door. "Damn and blast it all to hell and gone."

Andrew paced the room for a few moments, realised he needed more space and left the hotel to walk Rangoon's streets, now busy with an influx of British and Indian soldiers and officers. He strode to the docks, watching the accumulation of shipping carrying men and munitions for the forthcoming campaign.

Poor old Thibaw doesn't know what a hornet's nest he has stirred up by getting into bed with the French and fining a British company. He watched a platoon of sepoys [1] march past, admired their bearing, and stopped when Than Than Aye stepped in front of him.

"Hello, Than Than Aye," Andrew said. "How good to see you again."

"Cousin Andrew," Than Than Aye took his arm. "Bo Thura asked me to find you. With this war coming, Maung Thandar has called up his followers to hunt my father down, and Bo Thura wants to know if Sir Charles has granted his pardon yet."

"Not yet," Andrew shook his head.

"When?" Than Than Aye asked.

"I don't know," Andrew replied.

"When it comes," Than Than Aye said, "will you bring it in person? Bo Thura doesn't trust anybody else."

"I'll try," Andrew replied.

How would Mariana react to yet another delay?

Than Than Aye read his expression, "You'll try, but Mariana would object. That's it, isn't it?"

"She's not at her best," Andrew agreed. "She's gone off me, I think."

Than Than Aye smiled, "Remember what I said, Andrew. Women need time."

"She's had years," Andrew replied.

"Wasn't she sick for most of these years?"

"Yes," Andrew admitted.

---

1. Indian soldiers.

"And you said she was recovering after her illness."

"Yes," Andrew repeated.

"And she's known you as a mentor and friend," Than Than Aye said. "Now, you expect her to alter her view of you to a lover and husband." She smiled. "Give her time. She had a terrible experience a few years ago; then you took her to war. Not long after, you shifted her to a different country, in a different continent, and now to a third continent with a completely different culture. That's a lot for somebody to assimilate, let alone expecting her to marry her guardian angel."

"I'm hardly Mariana's guardian angel," Andrew said.

Than Than Aye touched his arm, "You are in her eyes, Andrew, if all you've told me is true. I know her culture and mine are very different, but women are women in any society. Give her time and learn patience."

Andrew smiled and moved away as a heavy bullock cart pulled past. "I'll take your advice, Than Than Aye."

"Next time you see the Chief Commissioner, Andrew, could you remind him about Bo Thura's pardon?"

"I always remind him," Andrew said.

Than Than Aye looked away, "Then remind him

again, please. Tell him that Bo Thura will help all he can when the British invade."

"I will tell him," Andrew said. "I hope it helps."

"So do I," Than Than Aye replied. "I'll keep you in touch, Cousin. When the British invasion begins, my father will help."

"I can't guarantee Sir Charles will reciprocate," Andrew said.

Than Than Aye nodded, "If the British win, they will surely get rid of Maung Thandar and Buda Sein," she said. She smiled as she stepped back. "Don't give up on Mariana. Not yet."

Andrew nodded. "I won't. Thank you, Than Than Aye." He watched as a detachment of Madras Pioneers marched past, then turned to speak to Than Than Aye, but she was gone. He sighed and continued his walk.

"MARIANA," JENNINGS SAID QUIETLY AS THEY SAT opposite each other in the hotel dining room. "May I ask you a personal question?"

"You may," Mariana replied and quickly added, "as long as it's not too personal."

"If you think I am being too forward," Jennings said, "tell me to keep quiet or slap my face. I will understand."

Mariana smiled, shaking her head. "I don't think

I'll ever slap your face," she said. "Go on. Fire away. I'm ready." She sat erect in her chair. "I've braced myself for whatever you say."

Jennings laughed. "I know you and Captain Andrew have separate rooms in Wells' Hotel and live in the same house in Britain."

"The same house but separate rooms," Mariana forestalled Jennings' question. "We have separate rooms." She lifted her chin slightly. "And it has always been separate rooms, Stephen, and separate beds."

Jennings touched her arm. "I did not mean to imply any impropriety," he said.

Mariana relaxed. "You are an interesting man, Stephen. You are a very polite gentleman, yet you ask the most astounding questions."

"You are an example of the most amazing self-control," Jennings told her. "I know you have feelings for Captain Andrew, yet you remain, forgive me, pure."

Mariana looked away. "Captain Baird has been a good friend of mine for many years," she said. "Nothing else."

Jennings bowed from his seat. "Forgive my frankness on such a delicate subject," he said. "I had no right to ask." He lowered his voice. "With Captain Andrew's interest in his Burmese friend, I should have already known."

"I am not some delicate rose from a closeted

background," Mariana kept her voice cool. "Coming from a Natal farm, I am fully aware of the facts of life. However, Stephen, I think we should discuss other matters."

HEAVILY MOUSTACHED AND STEADY-EYED, General Sir Harry Prendergast was an Indian-born veteran of half a dozen campaigns who wore his medal ribbons with pride. Andrew saw the crimson ribbon of the Victoria Cross and knew he was facing an exceptionally brave man.

"Captain Baird," Prendergast said. "I am gathering as much information as possible about the Burmans before I lead the Queen's Army against them."

"Yes, sir." Andrew stood at attention on the opposite side of Prendergast's desk. The fan above creaked slightly as it rotated, with the draught rustling the maps on the wall.

"Thibaw and his officials have called up all their men to contest our advance," Prendergast said. "You've seen them in action, Baird. What was your impression?"

"I only saw them marching and attacking convicts and civilians," Andrew replied. "I'd say they were a tough-looking bunch but ill-armed. They carried a mixture of ancient muzzle-loading muskets and some modern rifles."

Prendergast nodded and scribbled a short note on a pad before him. He used only his right hand, with a wound during the Indian Mutiny disabling his left arm.

"Morale? Skills?"

Andrew considered for a moment, "I'd say their morale is high when they have a purpose. They carry their rations with them, so they can travel fast, without needing a commissariat, and dig trenches as protection from musketry or artillery."

"Are they all professional soldiers?"

"I don't believe so, sir. The King's Guards are full-time. One can identify them by a dragon tattoo on the nape of the neck." Andrew dredged his memory. "I don't believe Burma has a large standing army, but every man will be expected to fight during a war. Thibaw has an armoury in Mandalay, and the nation will provide food. I don't believe the king pays them."

Prendergast wrote more notes. "Artillery?"

"I didn't see any, sir, but I believe they have some," Andrew replied. "I know they have two or three Italian engineers modernising their forts, so I presume they will also have added artillery."

"That equates with my other sources," Prendergast said, spreading a map on the table. "You've sailed this route, Baird, so you can correct my mistakes."

"I'll do my best," Andrew promised, "though I am sure the captains of the Irrawaddy Flotilla steamers would be more useful."

Prendergast turned his steady eyes on Andrew. "They know the river, Baird. They can't give details of the defences like a military man can." He returned his attention to the map. "Thibaw has two groups of forts that could prove difficult for our advance up the Irrawaddy. Both lie between the frontier of British Burma and Mandalay. The first is here, about sixty miles from the border." He stabbed his finger down. "The Minhla group." He looked up at Andrew. "Would you agree, Baird?"

"I would, sir," Andrew said.

"Tell me your observations." Those steady eyes fixed on Andrew again.

"I saw two forts there, one on either bank of the river. The Minhla fort on the west side is old and looked neglected. I think recent floods have damaged it. On the eastern side is Kolegone, or Kuligon or Kuliyang; take your pick of the name. The Italian mercenaries supervised as the Burmese built it."

"Strength?"

"Kolegone is brick-built," Andrew said. "And situated on a slight eminence. I don't know how many guns it has, but a decent gunner could command the river for a couple of miles at least. The Italians are fine engineers, sir."

Prendergast grunted. "We think Kolegone has ten guns, but of small calibre. It has a large garrison of the king's troops, with Kinwin Mingyi's son-in-law in charge, which may or may not be advantageous to the Burmans. That depends on how loyal they are to Mingyi. What is your opinion, Captain Baird?"

"The position is strong, sir, but I cannot speak for the garrison. If I were to take it, I'd land a force lower down the Irrawaddy and take it from the rear, as most of the guns will face the river."

Prendergast lifted his chin. "Such a move would necessitate a long march through wooded country, Baird, which is ideal for ambushes."

"Yes, sir, but if the landing force put out flanking parties, they could cope."

Prendergast grunted again and ran his finger further up the map, following the course of the Irrawaddy. "The second group is here, the Ava or Singon group, although only God knows what the Burmese call it. These forts are only a few miles below Mandalay."

"Yes, sir," Andrew agreed.

"There are three forts, with what we call Ava or Singon fort, marginally to the west of Ava, the ancient capital on the left or west bank. On the right or eastern bank and nearly directly opposite is the

Sogaing Fort, while slightly further upriver, on a small island near Ava, is Shabyadon Fort." He glanced at Andrew. "Any comments, Baird?"

"I passed them last year," Andrew said. "They are brick or masonry built, but I'd not call them strong, and I didn't notice any guns. The Burmese may have added artillery since I was there, of course. I think our men can take them without too much difficulty."

Prendergast scribbled Andrew's observations on his pad. "Thank you, Baird. That will be all for now. We are advancing up the Irrawaddy to defeat Thibaw, and when the fleet is assembled, you will be in the leading vessel."

"Yes, sir," Andrew replied.

Prendergast grinned. "Another chance to add to your laurels, eh, Captain? Your knowledge will come in useful, no doubt."

"I hope so, sir," Andrew said.

MARIANA ANSWERED HER DOOR TO ANDREW'S gentle tap. She greeted him with a smile, stepped aside and allowed him to enter.

"What did the general say?" Mariana asked.

"He said I'm returning to war," Andrew told her. He expected hot words, but instead, Mariana sighed and produced a foolscap-sized leather notebook.

"I'll keep a record of the days in here," she said.

"That's a lovely book," Andrew said. "Better than your last one."

"Yes. Stephen got me this one. Wasn't that nice of him?"

"Very nice."

Stephen. Not Mr Jennings.

"He even had it embossed with my name," Mariana said. She showed Andrew the gold lettering on the front of the book with *Mariana Maxwell* in copperplate writing.

"That was kind of him," Andrew said. "You must be very attached to Mr Jennings."

"We are good friends, Andrew," Mariana said and sighed again. "When you were out, Andrew, an army officer left a note for you." She handed it over and waited for him to open the envelope and read its contents. "What does it say?"

"It says I have to report on board the motor launch *Katherine* the day after tomorrow," Andrew said. "I am sorry, Mariana. I am leaving you alone again to go to war."

"I'll be all right," Mariana said bravely. *I won't be alone, Andrew. Stephen will look after me.*

CHAPTER 23

IRRAWADDY RIVER, NOVEMBER 1885

"You must be Captain Andrew Baird," the officer was young, freckled, and energetic. "I'm Midshipman Cosmo Birnie and the captain ordered me to look after you."

They shook hands on the quayside, where the morning sun cut through a faint mist and an array of shipping was berthed alongside or anchored in the river.

"You've to come with me to *Kathleen*," Birnie said. He looked Andrew up and down, marvelled at the campaign medals on his chest, and led the way with a rolling gait that did not disguise his long, determined stride. While Andrew wore a khaki uniform and a sun helmet, Birnie had a blue Royal Navy jacket above white trousers and a blue cap at a rakish angle on his head.

"Is that all your dunnage?" Birnie nodded at Andrew's single bag, "Or is there more to come?"

"That's it all," Andrew said.

"Good show. We don't have much space on *Kathleen*."

"Which ship is *Kathleen*?" Andrew looked at the assembled vessels, from the two-decked Irrawaddy Flotilla paddle steamers to the ocean-going steamships and three-masted clippers. He smiled when he saw Jamieson steering *Little Salamander* between two larger vessels with the cigar in his mouth, making nearly as many fumes as his vessel's smokestack.

"That's her there," Birnie pointed to a tiny steam launch with a canopy stretching her full length and a hands-breadth above the tallest crew member. "We're a gunboat with two guns, a Nordenfeldt and a shallow draught for the river. We have an eighteen-man crew and one passenger, which is you." He grinned at Andrew. "Come along, old fellow, I mean, please step this way, sir!" He led them into a small dinghy, where two bearded seamen rowed them to the steam launch.

"Welcome aboard, Captain Baird," a long-jawed officer said, "cast off forward, cast off aft!"

Andrew had no longer stepped on board than

Kathleen was on the move, with smoke issuing from her single funnel amidships.

"That's Lieutenant Frederick Trench in command," Birnie said in a hushed tone as he ushered Andrew to the stuffy below decks. "He's the senior lieutenant on HMS *Turquoise.* We're all from *Turquoise,* you see, and the captain—you have to call Trench captain because he's in charge—was a bit miffed having to come back to Rangoon to pick you up."

Andrew shared a cabin with Birnie, the most junior officer on board. Both had to stoop to fit in the cabin, and Andrew's bag fitted under the only bed.

"I'll sling a hammock," Birnie said cheerfully. "Do you know what's happened here?"

"No," Andrew admitted. He liked this grinning youth.

"Not many soldiers know much about the Senior Service," Birnie said. "When we heard that we might have to fight Thibaw, the Royal Navy only had a single vessel in Rangoon: HMS *Woodlark,* a gun vessel with Captain Clutterbuck in command. We in *Turquoise* were in Trincomalee, and Captain Woodward was sent to Rangoon, so we toddled over at full speed."

Andrew imagined the ship steaming across the Indian Ocean, with the crew eager to arrive in Burma before the hostilities started.

"Then Sir Charlie something-or-other got involved and ordered the Indian Marine, that's India's navy, to get the paddle steamer *Irrawaddy* and two screw steam launches ready for war. That's *Kathleen* and our sister ship *Settang*, in case you hadn't guessed. The guns and men come from HMS *Woodlark*, and Captain Clutterbuck is in overall command of the naval side of operations."

Andrew glanced out of the porthole and saw *Kathleen* was pushing hard up the river.

"*Irrawaddy* has two twenty-pounder breech-loaders and two nine-pounder muzzle-loaders. We were all sent up to Thayetmyo, on the frontier with Upper Burma, and then Cap'n Trench was ordered to come and pick you up." Birnie grinned. "That's you up to date, sir."

"Call me Baird," Andrew said, "and I'll call you Birnie."

"Baird and Birnie it is," Birnie said. "I'd better get back on deck in case the old man needs me." He scrambled up the miniature companionway to the deck above, leaving Andrew to look around the cabin.

"Is Captain Andrew away again?" Jennings asked, sitting opposite Mariana in the dining room.

"He is," Mariana replied, sipping a cup of luke-warm coffee.

Jennings shook his head. "How long for this time, Mariana?"

Mariana shrugged. "Until the war is over, I expect."

Jennings nodded. "I presume he had to do his duty, but it's hard on you, Mariana."

"I'll be all right," Mariana said.

"Remember, I am here if you want to talk to somebody," Jennings said.

Mariana looked up. "Thank you," she said. "I won't forget."

"You are always welcome in my house," Jennings told her, smiling. "We won't bother with the champagne next time."

Mariana managed to smile. "That would be best," she said.

Jennings patted her hand. "I'm sure the war will be over soon. Until then, don't hesitate to visit my office or house."

"Thank you," Mariana watched Jennings saunter from the hotel and suddenly felt very lonely.

IRRAWADDY RIVER, 12ᵀᴴ NOVEMBER 1885

"There's trouble ahead!" Birnie reported cheerfully.

"What's happening?" Andrew emerged from

below decks to see *Kathleen* hove to in mid-channel with a vulture circling overhead.

"Your spy has informed Captain Raikes, the deputy commissioner, that Thibaw has sent a seven-gun steamer downriver from Mandalay."

"My spy?" Andrew asked.

"Yes indeed," Birnie tilted back his cap to scratch his head. "Apparently, he sent a note with your name on it."

Bo Thura has kept his word. I hope Sir Charles does likewise.

Birnie unfolded a chart of the river. "According to your friendly little spy, the Burman steamer intends to fortify Toungwia Island and land reinforcements at Singboungweh."

The names meant nothing to Andrew until Birnie pointed them out on the map. For all his excitability, Birnie's hand was steady as he traced the enemy steamer's course along the bends of the Irrawaddy.

"Thibaw's steamer will leave Mandalay on the 13th," Birnie said. "Or so your spy claims." He looked up, smiling. "Is that why you're with us, Baird? To keep communication with a Burman spy?"

"Maybe," Andrew evaded a direct reply as he studied the map. "Why choose Singboungweh?" he asked. "The river is fairly broad there. Our ships can just go to the far side."

Birnie laughed. "There speaks a land-based soldier," he said. "The river may be broad, but it's also shallow." He pointed to some figures written on the river. "These figures show the depth of water when the river was last surveyed. You'll see that they are in low single figures except for here," Birnie indicated a stretch close to Singboungweh. "This is the deep-water channel where our ships must sail, and artillery at Singboungweh will cover it."

Andrew nodded. "I understand," he said. *I had forgotten about the deep-water channel during my months fighting Buda Sein's dacoits.*

Birnie grinned. "We can't allow the enemy to reinforce his garrisons, can we? So Colonel Raikes asked Colonel Sladen for permission to steam up river and sort King Thibaw's ship out."

Andrew learned that Colonel Sladen was the field force's Chief Political Officer. Sladen spoke to General Prendergast, who granted permission for the gunboat *Irrawaddy* and *Kathleen* to steam upriver to confront Thibaw's vessel.

The much larger vessel *Irrawaddy* joined *Kathleen* when she steamed northwards out of Thayetmyo. The sun rose in glorious orange and red at their backs, and birds called from the trees. Andrew checked his watch. It was six in the morning of November 14th, 1885, and they were going to war.

They steamed gently upstream, the water chortling under their counters and the villages along the riverside already awake. Men in fishing boats eyed them curiously as women worked the paddy fields, children pointed and played, and the patient water buffalo plodded in their daily routine.

"It's all very peaceful," Andrew said.

"On the surface," Birnie replied, scanning the river with a long brass telescope. He pushed his cap further back on his head and jerked a thumb towards the riverbank. "God knows what's happening in there."

At eight that morning, the steamers crossed the frontier into Upper Burma. Andrew felt the atmosphere on *Kathleen* alter, as Lieutenant Trench ordered the men to the guns and posted a lookout aloft. Within five minutes, they passed a village, with half a dozen boats pulled up on the muddy bank but not a single villager in sight.

Kathleen edged closer to the bank, with Birnie examining the village through his telescope.

"Maybe they're scared of us, or perhaps Thibaw has ordered them to evacuate," Birnie said.

"Either way, it could be ominous," Andrew said.

Irrawaddy and *Kathleen* chugged on, with *Irrawaddy's* paddles churning the water to a cream-brown froth and the crew watching the riverbanks, alert for danger. They passed the village of Tagoumaw and trained their weapons on the Burmese soldiers who stared at them.

"Is that Thibaw's men?" Birnie asked.

"With the light jackets and the brass helmets?" Andrew said. "That's the king's soldiers."

"Remain at battle stations," Lieutenant Trench ordered, "but don't fire unless they do."

We don't want to be blamed for starting this war, and we won't be the aggressors if Thibaw's men fire the first shot.

The steamers passed Tagoumaw, with the Burmese soldiers watching without expression. *Irrawaddy's* wash caused large waves to break along the shore, sending the small fishing boats dancing as birds screeched and monkeys chattered above.

"We're deep in Thibaw's territory now," Andrew said. "Nearly two hours past the frontier."

"Steamer ahead, sir!" the lookout shouted. "I don't recognise her!"

"All hands, get ready!" Lieutenant Trench shouted, although, in such a small vessel as *Kathleen,* he could have passed the message without raising his voice. Andrew saw a stir in *Irrawaddy* as men rushed to the guns. He felt a renewed tremor of anticipation run through the launch.

"There she is!" Birnie said.

The Burmese steamer looked like an old Irrawaddy Flotilla vessel, slightly dilapidated but armed with artillery. She sailed close to the right bank, towing a flat, with both the steamer and flat dark with soldiers.

"Stand by your guns!" Lieutenant Trench ordered.

"Excuse me, Baird," Birnie said and took the three steps to the forward gun. The seamen waited, watching the Burmese steamer.

"Fire a warning shot!" Trench ordered. "Don't hit her!"

The gun crew had been waiting for the order, and the twenty-pounder banged out with a jet of smoke. *Kathleen* shuddered, and Andrew watched as the shot landed fifty yards away from the Burmese vessel, throwing a column of dirty brown water high into the air.

"They're still moving, by God!" Trench shouted. "They're getting up steam!"

Irrawaddy and *Kathleen* moved closer, with the respective commanders watching the river for shoals.

"*Irrawaddy* is sailing rather close to the right bank," Andrew said.

"She's keeping to the deep-water channel," Birnie replied. "Right at the bend of the river."

"Look ashore," Andrew said. "Burmese soldiers. And artillery inside that earthwork!"

"That's a new fortification, by George," Birnie said. "It's not marked on the chart!"

"The Burmans have been busy," Andrew agreed.

As the British vessels eased closer to the bank, the

Burmese opened fire with small arms and artillery. Bullets whined around *Kathleen,* with some rebounding from the metal plates protecting the forward gun. A shell exploded nearby, sending a tall column of brown water fifteen feet into the air. When the water subsided, dead fish floated on the river's surface.

"Return fire!" Trench ordered cheerfully. "Thibaw's men have fired the first shots!"

Andrew saw the men on *Irrawaddy* also aiming and firing at the Burmese on land and afloat. With some Burmese behind the earthwork and others hidden in thick jungle, the British could hardly see their land-based attackers.

"They've got tents as well," Birnie said. "How civilised of them."

Irrawaddy was firing her Nordenfeldt multi-barrelled organ gun, with the heavy bullets ripping through the trees and raising spurts of mud and dust from the Burmese fortification. Andrew compared the weapon to the Gatling guns he had seen in Zululand, wondered at the innovations in military technology, and ducked as a bullet smashed against the rail he leaned on. He realised the Burmese were making good practice, with bullets whining and hissing around the launch and gunboat, splashing alongside the thin hulls and ricocheting from the upperworks.

"They're fighting well," Birnie said, grinning. He

had pushed his cap so far back on his head that Andrew wondered why it did not fall off.

The bluejackets fired, shouting encouragement as they eased around the bend. They aimed at the Burmese camp, the king's steamer, and the crowded flat. The twenty-pounder made good practice on the camp, landing a succession of shells on the earthworks and the tents. Through his binoculars, Andrew saw the Burmese defenders firing back, with smoke billowing around the surrounding trees.

With the bend negotiated, *Irrawaddy* and *Kathleen* reached a wider stretch of deep water, with bullets hammering off the upperworks. Simultaneously, the Burmese steamer cast off the flat, with men leaping from both vessels and swimming towards the shore.

"Warm work, Lieutenant Baird!" Birnie said, grinning.

"Warm enough," Andrew replied as the bluejackets fired their Nordenfeldt. An officer had issued Martinis to the men, who used them enthusiastically and with more skill than Andrew expected.

"*Irrawaddy* is signalling, sir!" A young rating approached Lieutenant Trench. "Board the enemy steamer and carry her to Thayetmyo!"

"A prize, by God!" Trench gave a string of orders that saw *Kathleen* surge towards the Burmese steamer, and the crew responded eagerly despite the bullets that whistled overhead and splashed alongside. "Mr Birnie! Issue cutlasses to the men!"

The bluejackets buckled on the short, lethal swords that their forefathers had carried during the French wars and which their distant ancestors had used in the days of Morgan and Woodes Rogers. They cheered as *Kathleen* approached the enemy.

"That's the way, lads!" Trench encouraged. He was first to board the Burmese steamer, just as the remainder of her crew jumped overboard.

"Take over the engines!" Trench ordered. "Captain Baird, could you take a party of riflemen and make these damned Burmans keep their heads down, please?"

Andrew obeyed, and three men, all whom Trench could spare from *Kathleen*'s minuscule crew, followed him to the rail.

With *Kathleen* and the captured steamer closer to the bank than *Irrawaddy*, the Burmese concentrated on the British launch with artillery, muskets, and rifles. Andrew's few men loaded and fired, worked the Martini's underlevers to eject the spent cartridges, loaded again, and exchanged dark humour as they eased past the shore.

"There are their leaders," Birnie said, with a hand on Andrew's arm. He extended his telescope, ignoring the bullets that whistled past and knocked splinters from *Kathleen*'s woodwork. "These Burman lads had better be careful Chips doesn't get hold of them. The carpenter won't be happy at all this work they're giving him."

"Yes, indeed," Andrew had seen the carpenter shouting at the men to take care of the deck planking. He would be incensed at the damage the Burmese bullets were doing to his woodwork. "Maybe we'd better find some cover from these marksmen."

Birnie laughed. "They're such bad shots that the safest place is directly in their line of fire. By God, Baird, I think that's Poung Woon with these lads!"

Andrew focused his binoculars, momentarily forgetting the danger. He recalled the images he had seen of the Burmese leadership. "By God, I believe you're right."

Birnie laughed. "If I remember correctly, Poung Woon promised to bring Thibaw the heads of General Prendergast and Colonel Sladen within a fortnight."

"He'll have to get a shift on, then," Andrew said. "The days are slipping away."

A burst of fire from *Irrawaddy* sent the Burmese deeper into the forest, and then *Kathleen* was past the most dangerous area. The trees screened the enemy as effectively as any camouflage.

"Did you see the fellow at Poung Woon's side?" Birnie asked as he snapped his telescope shut.

"Not properly," Andrew replied.

"Nor did I, but I thought it was Maung Thandar."

Andrew lifted his binoculars again, attempting to penetrate the dense forest. "Maung Thandar," he repeated. "He is the man who sends the dacoits into British Burma."

"Is that right?" Birnie replied. "I know he's one of Thibaw's ministers."

"He's a bad man," Andrew said.

"Back to Thayetmyo, men!" Trench shouted. "We've done our duty today."

Towing the flats and steaming with the current, *Kathleen* reached the relative sanctuary of the broader channel, but the Burmese followed, firing from the forest. Andrew occasionally glimpsed their light uniforms and yellow flashes from the muzzle flares.

"Aim at the smoke, boys!" Andrew shouted above the crackle of musketry and thumping of the engines. He saw one bullet strike the rail at his side, buckling the steel and leaving a thick blue-grey smear. The closest bluejacket laughed.

"Somebody will have to clean that up," he said, thumbed a cartridge into the breech of his rifle, aimed and fired. "That's for you, Thibaw, for damaging our new ship!"

The Burmese in the earthworks shifted their attention to *Irrawaddy*, with their artillery fire raising fountains of water that splashed her as she turned downstream. *Irrawaddy's* Nordenfeldts returned the fire, with her bullets landing more accurately than Andrew expected from a moving ship.

The Nordenfeldts don't have the power to destroy the fortification.

"*Irrawaddy's* not damaging the earthwork!" Birnie agreed with his observation. "Captain Clutterbuck will have to land and storm the place, sir!"

Andrew shook his head as his military caution took control. "We don't have enough men," he replied. "There might be two or three hundred Burmans dug in there."

Birnie grunted and supervised as his men fired and reloaded. "If you say so, sir."

"The Burmese flat's loose," Trench said. "No, by God, two flats are loose. Let's capture them as well."

CHAPTER 24

IRRAWADDY RIVER, NOVEMBER 1885

Andrew glanced at the seamen, who all seemed pleased about returning to more dangerous waters. He knew the Royal Navy's daredevil reputation and had met the seamen of the Naval Brigades in both the Zulu and the Boer Wars, but here, on their own element of water, they seemed to welcome trouble.

"Aye, aye, sir!" the men said immediately.

"Are you coming, Captain Baird?" Midshipman Birnie asked, grinning as he buckled on a cutlass. "You were known as Up-and-at-'em in Africa, were you not?"

Andrew realised his reputation was at stake. Surrounded by eager seamen with cutlasses and Marti-nis-Henry, he knew he had to agree.

"I hoped you would not leave me out," he said.

A petty officer with a neat red beard clapped him on the back. "That's the spirit, sir!"

When *Kathleen* drew alongside, Birnie led half the boarding party onto a small boat.

"In you come, sir!" the petty officer said, helping Andrew into the bouncing boat. "Sixpence for a tour of the bay, threepence to capture the Burmese flats!"

Birnie sang as they headed to the flats, which floated close inshore.

"Come on, *Kathleens!*"

The Burmese greeted their arrival with a storm of musketry that splashed around the boat and knocked splinters off the gunwale.

"They don't like us very much," Birnie said, holding his cap as the passage of a bullet knocked it askew. "Come on, lads, attach a line to the flat!"

The seamen jumped onto the nearest flat, with Andrew moving to the side and firing towards the Burmese. He did not expect to hit anybody but hoped his fire might deter a little.

"That's the way, lads! Back to the boat, lively now!"

Andrew remained where he was, firing and loading as the seamen fastened a line from the flat to their boat and rowed the short distance to *Kathleen*.

"Lash her to *Kathleen*, boys!" Birnie said. "You can leave her now, Captain Baird!"

As the flats had no independent means of propulsion, the seamen fastened them to *Kathleen*, ignoring the bullets that crashed on board, splintering the wood.

"Handsomely now, lads!" Birnie ordered. "No holidays here!"

The seamen obeyed, lashing the flats to the sides of the launch with a skill that Andrew could only admire. He continued to fire at the Burmese, aware of the futility of a single rifle but determined to do something to help.

"This flat's full of gunpowder, sir," the petty officer said. "Bags and bags of it!"

Andrew looked downward. "So it is." He realised he was standing on sacks of gunpowder. *If a Burmese thought to ignite the gunpowder, they'd blow us all up.*

"Queer sort of cargo, sir," the petty officer reported. "Gunpowder, sandbags and pointed stakes. Maybe they were going to build a palisade."

"Maybe so," Andrew said. "We'll work that out when we get to Thayetmyo." Despite his experiences in previous campaigns, he did not feel comfortable standing on hundreds of pounds of highly combustible gunpowder while scores of Burmese fired rifles at him. The petty officer grinned, showing tobacco-stained teeth.

"That's something to tell your grandchildren, sir.

The day you served with the Naval Brigade and sailed a cargo of gunpowder down the Irrawaddy River."

Andrew could not share the petty officer's humour. "We'd best dump the gunpowder," he said, placing his rifle at his feet.

Birnie straddled one of the sacks, ripped it open with his cutlass and lifted a handful of the contents. "Poor quality rubbish," he decided. "If it were reliable, I'd give it to the gunners, but this stuff is as likely to blow up in storage as propel a cannonball." He glanced at Andrew. "What do you suggest, Captain Baird?"

"Throw the whole damned lot overboard," Andrew said. "And as quick as possible!"

Birnie grinned. "That's the spirit, sir! Come on, lads, lighten the lighter, free the flat and dump the danger."

As *Kathleen* chugged downstream with smoke and smuts pouring from her funnel, the seamen lifted the bags and threw them into the river, delighting in the task.

"There goes another one!" a red-faced seaman roared. "Into the river with you!"

"Don't make any sparks, lads," the petty officer warned. "Or the powder will go up rather than down, and we'll all be shaking hands with Davy Jones or whoever the god of this blessed river may be."

The Burmese continued to fire on them from the riverbank, with *Kathleen* replying with rifles and her Nordenfeldt. As they moved downriver, fewer bullets hit the vessels, with only superficial damage and no casualties.

By the time they reached Thayetmyo, the flat was nearly a thousand pounds lighter, and the gunpowder bags littered the riverbed. Andrew breathed easier.

The garrison cheered as *Irrawaddy* and *Kathleen* steamed into Thayetmyo with the king's steamer and the two flats as prizes. Khaki-clad British soldiers and smiling sepoys rushed to see the Navy display their latest victory.

Officers and men joined together as somebody shouted for three cheers, and the men responded, laughing and pointing at the steamers.

"That's a jab in the eye for old Thibaw!" Birnie said. "We captured his steamer, singed his beard and returned without a single casualty."

Andrew saw *Irrawaddy's* carpenter shaking his head at the bullet holes in his ship and knew there would be hours' work ahead for the chippy and however many men he dragooned into service.

"The Navy did well," Andrew agreed. "Not bad for a campaign fought hundreds of miles away from the sea."

Birnie laughed. "The Army can't do without us now. Why, we had men fighting in Zululand, even."

"I remember," Andrew said quietly.

Captain Clutterbuck scrambled down from *Irrawaddy* and leapt onto the flats to examine the cargo.

"What have we here, gentlemen?"

"Logs and sandbags, sir," Birnie said. "We think the Burmese were going to strengthen their forts."

Clutterbuck examined the logs. "Maybe so," he mused. "And maybe not. Have you seen this, Trench?"

"No, sir," Trench joined them on the flat.

Clutterbuck descended to the shallow hold. "These logs are fastened to the bottom of the flat. Where were the explosives?"

"Dead centre, sir, and the full length of the ship."

Clutterbuck nodded, pulled himself to the deck and lit his pipe. "Do you know what I think? I think Thibaw was going to sink this vessel in the deepwater channel. The explosives were to sink the ship, and the sandbags held the logs in place. One of our vessels would come up, ram into the pointed logs and sink, effectively blocking the channel."

"Clever buggers, these Burmans," Trench said.

"They are," Clutterbuck agreed. "Unless the Italians came up with the idea." He stepped free of the flat and swung onto *Irrawaddy*. "Whoever it was, Italian or Burmese, we'll have to be aware of traps in future."

"Yes, sir," Trench replied.

Clutterbuck puffed out blue smoke. "We were fortunate that your friend warned us, Baird. I'd shake his hand if I ever met him."

"I'm sure he'd appreciate that, sir," Andrew said.

Bo Thura would much prefer the free pardon he is desperately trying to earn.

ANDREW STOOD ON THE QUAY AT THAYETMYO, watching as the fleet formed up for the invasion of Thibaw's Kingdom of Ava. He had been on three campaigns, but this was his first when the British Army travelled mainly by water. The ships mustered in a long line, with the stately double-deckers of the Irrawaddy Flotilla Company, the clumsy-looking flats, and the Royal Navy vessels with artillery and Nordenfeldts. Between them, a host of smaller craft hurried to and fro with messages, supplies and jaunty seamen. Andrew grinned as he saw Jamieson steering *Little Salamander*, cigar in mouth and looking as disreputable and solid as ever.

"I've never seen anything like this before," he said.

Birnie pulled on his cheroot, examined the glowing tip, and threw the stub into the river. It lay on the surface for a few seconds before submerging into the dark water. "I doubt anybody has," he said.

"We are witnessing history." Birnie grinned. "No, Captain Baird, we are making history. Isn't it fun?"

Andrew wondered if he had ever been as young and enthusiastic as Cosmo Birnie. "It's certainly interesting," he said.

Andrew studied the leading ship, the Indian Marine vessel *Irrawaddy*, with its twenty-five-pounder cannons and Nordenfeldts. It seemed a potent vessel to lead the British fleet upriver to Mandalay.

Immediately astern was the steam launch, *Kathleen*, with the busy bluejackets working at cables and cleaning the deck.

Trust the Navy to keep everything sparkling bright even as we go to war in a country of rivers and jungles.

Beyond *Kathleen*, the Irrawaddy Flotilla steamer *Thambyadine* carried Major General Prendergast and his HQ staff. Then came *Pulu* and *Palow*, both filled with Naval Brigade seamen. It seemed imperative that a contingent of seamen accompanied the British Army on its campaigns. Andrew remembered the seamen at Majuba, carrying cutlasses against the Boer rifles. Their uniquely nautical language coloured the air as their officers put them through cutlass drill, with their white uniforms bright in the sun.

Yunnan was next, accompanied by the barge *White Swan*, with the Cinque Ports battery of the Royal Artillery. Behind them were *Panthay* with

Major Smith's mule battery and *Shwaymyo* with the Madras sappers and the Bombay Mountain Battery.

The paddle steamers look rather sad, reduced to troop carriers, with a flat barge fastened to each side of the steamer. The sepoys look efficient, though.

The steamer *Burma* carried the Hampshire Regiment and General White's HQ. Andrew wondered how the redcoats, or khaki coats now, would enjoy having a general living in luxury on the steamer while they crowded onto the flats.

Chuitsabu followed with the First Madras Pioneers and Twelfth Madras Infantry. Andrew had never served with Indian sepoys before. He watched them through a veteran's critical eyes, hoping they were up to the same standard as the men with whom he had served in Africa. *If they are half as good as the Sikh policemen, we'll be all right.*

Ashley Aden carried the Twenty-third Madras Infantry, the Hazara Mountain Battery and telegraph stores. Again, Andrew surveyed them and nodded approvingly to see *Paulang*, a hospital ship, easing nearby. Having immediate medical care available would encourage the troops. Andrew remembered watching wounded men carried down from Laing's Nek during the Boer War and loaded on an unsprung wagon. *Paulang* would save that agony.

Other Irrawaddy Flotilla ships followed. *Attran* with more artillery, *Aloungpyah* with the 23rd Royal Welsh Fusiliers, *Thuriah* with the 11th Bengal infantry and some native labourers, *Talifu* with the mounted infantry and *Rangoon* with flats, acting as a reserve hospital ship. Astern, there was *Mendoon*, a brand-new vessel acting as reserve steamer with more labourers and a supply of coal for the steamers. Finally, *Kahyn* carried the commissariat and acted as the postal steamer.

Eighteen of the twenty Irrawaddy steamers had flats lashed alongside, more than tripling their carrying capacity.

Andrew viewed the fleet, smelled the smoke that drifted from their smokestacks in the humid, oppressive air, watched the mass of men, infantry, artillery, bluejackets, labourers, and river sailors, and wondered if Thibaw realised what he had stirred up.

Let's hope for a short and decisive campaign, a British victory and a pardon for Bo Thura so I can get home with Mariana.

CHAPTER 25

IRRAWADDY RIVER, NOVEMBER 1885

Andrew stood in the bow as half the British fleet remained at Thayetmyo, and *Kathleen* scouted ahead. He listened to the rhythmic beat of the paddles as *Irrawaddy* steamed alongside, with a dozen other vessels following in a two-mile-long line. Andrew glanced astern, saw the soldiers on the flats watching the riverbanks, and wondered what they were thinking.

At that point, the east bank of the Irrawaddy River had thickly forested hills over five hundred feet high. The hills rose parallel to the river, casting a dense shadow to create a dark and forbidding atmosphere, with even the birds quiet. Monkeys watched like silent sentinels from the trees. A single fallen log projected into the Irrawaddy at the angle where it turned towards the west, with the water frothing creamy brown over the top.

The ships pushed on towards Patanayo and Maloon without the Burmese offering any resistance.

"We're easing towards Mandalay," Birnie said.

"I wonder if Thibaw will just throw in the towel," Andrew said. "If we were facing the Zulus or the Boers, we'd have to fight for every bend of the river. So far, the Burmans have not even sniped at us. We'll see what happens when we come to the first of their forts."

When the ships rounded a sharp curve, the river straightened out, with around three miles of clear water ahead. The sun reflected from the waves, causing a dappling effect near the banks.

"Over there," Birnie gestured to the north, extending his long brass telescope. He grinned at Andrew over his shoulder. "Now the fun will really begin," he said.

Andrew lifted his binoculars. The fort of Kolegone dominated the hillside to the north, with the sun glinting from its stone walls. On the opposite bank, the older Minhla looked less formidable but still defiant.

"That could be dangerous," Andrew said.

If the Burmans have armed Kolegone with long-range

artillery, the guns could hit anything on the river and slow, or even stop the fleet's passage.

The ships eased to a halt, with the engines idling and smoke drifting over to both banks. General Prendergast called a conference of the officers on board *Thambyadine*, and Andrew hastened over in a small boat as the men watched, smoked, or played cards.

"We have two positions to carry, gentlemen," Prendergast said ponderously. "Minhla on one bank and Kolegone on the other. Of the two, I rate Kolegone as being the more dangerous." He looked around his officers. "We'll take Kolegone by a turning movement around the hills where it stands."

The officers nodded, with some viewing the hills through binoculars and others staring at a map of the Irrawaddy.

"That means a march through the jungle," the Liverpool Regiment's colonel said. "If King Thibaw has his army nearby, they could fall on the troops when they're among the trees."

"That's a possibility," Prendergast agreed. "I expect the Burmans to make a good defence. The position is strong, and they can do major damage to our ships from there. *Irrawaddy* will shell Kolegone to occupy the defenders as the Liverpool Regiment marches around the rear. The mule battery will accompany the infantry to give some fire from the rear of the position."

The officers nodded. The plan seemed sound.

"It's all up to the soldiers now," Birnie removed his cap to mop his steaming face. "I don't fancy marching through the forest with Thibaw's men on the prowl."

"They know what they're doing," Andrew said. He watched as the troops disembarked on the east side, looking pleased to have something to do free of the confines of the ships. Officers and NCOs barked orders as the men clattered across the gangplanks, their boots sounding hollow on the solid planking. They filed onto the riverbank, stamping their feet, talking, and exchanging jokes in the customary manner of British soldiers. Some stopped to stretch their legs; others peered into the trees while a few checked the locks of their rifles.

The officers gave brief orders. "Right, men. Column of fours, load your rifles and on we go. Lieutenant Philips, you have the skirmishers. Lieutenant Owen, you have the rearguard. At the double now!"

Andrew watched the Liverpool Regiment march away, with part of him wishing he was ashore with the infantry.

I don't feel in control of anything in a boat. The captain and seamen are in charge here, and I am merely a passenger.

"Even after we take Kolegone, there's plenty of river between here and Mandalay," Birnie sounded disappointed at the lack of Burmese resistance.

"We haven't won here yet," Andrew reminded him. He consulted his map and nodded to the opposite bank. "Don't forget Minhla village. There's another masonry redoubt there that General Prendergast will want to secure."

"There's a boat approaching!" the lookout shouted. "With a military officer on board."

The boat pulled alongside, and an officer of an Indian regiment bounded onto *Kathleen.*

"Are you Captain Andrew Baird?" the major asked.

"I am," Andrew admitted.

"Major Pollock of the Second Bengal Infantry," the major introduced himself. "Colonel Baker believes you are interested in seeing how the sepoys fought."

"Yes, sir," Andrew agreed. "I have never fought with Indian soldiers."

Major Pollock grinned. "Well, now's your opportunity, Captain. One of our lieutenants has come down with fever, so I am an officer short. Well volunteered."

"Thank you, sir," Andrew said. "I was feeling a bit of a bystander."

Andrew joined the sepoys, wondering how to give orders without understanding the soldiers' language. They returned his interest, staring at his unfamiliar uniform.

Colonel Baker was younger than Andrew expected, heavily sun-tanned and neatly bearded. He addressed his men, spoke to his officers and finally to Andrew.

"We're going to take that redoubt, Baird. It's around ninety yards long by fifty broad, and the longer side is parallel to the riverbank." Baker indicated their target. "I am the senior officer present and, therefore, in overall command of the landing party, and I expect you to lead from the front. If you lead, my Bengalis will follow. If you don't want to lead, you can remain behind." His smile faded as he glared into Andrew's eyes. "Don't let my lads down, Baird."

"I won't, sir," Andrew replied.

In addition to the Second Bengal Infantry, the Eleventh Bengal Infantry and Twelfth Madras Infantry landed on the west bank of the river. The steamers manoeuvred close to the riverbank, efficient sailors lowered the gangways, and the infantry filed ashore as orderly as if they were on a holiday excursion but with less fuss and noise. Andrew was one of the first to step onto the soft ground, expecting to hear the sharp crack of a Burmese rifle or see a screaming tattooed soldier swinging a *dha*. Only the heat and insects greeted him.

"Some place this," Petty Officer Durnford stamped his feet and touched the hilt of his cutlass. "Come on, boys, but be careful you don't drop that box!" Durnford commanded the small contingent of seamen, who carried explosives in case they had to blow open the gate of the fort.

As the sepoys filed ashore, their officers sent out pickets to watch for the enemy, and Major MacNeill of the headquarters staff spoke with Mr Phayre, a civil officer whose task was to ease relations with the Burmese.

"Head inland," Colonel Baker ordered, and the company officers gave orders that saw the sepoys moving into a thick jungle.

"Keep alert, men!" Andrew joined his regiment, with the sepoys eyeing him with as much curiosity as he had them.

They're wondering if I am good enough to be one of their officers, Andrew thought. *I can't blame them for that.*

The forest was so thick with undergrowth that the flank guards could only operate a few yards from the main body, and the advance guard was less than ten yards distant.

"We can't push through the jungle," Colonel Baker decided. "Stick to the path and watch for ambushes."

A single narrow track, overgrown in parts, penetrated the deep forest with sufficient space for men to walk two abreast at its widest. Andrew stepped ahead of his platoon of Bengalis, examining the trees on either side and expecting a volley of musketry at every step.

"Where the devil are the Burmese?" Pollock asked. "Don't they want to fight for their blessed country?"

"Maybe they don't want to fight for King Thibaw," Andrew replied.

The sepoys moved on, alert for danger, checking all around them, professional soldiers doing their job. They edged on for three nerve-wracking miles, with Andrew pushing in front to join the skirmishers of the Bengalis and the 12th Madras.

The volley came from the right as the skirmishers entered a small and welcome clearing. Andrew had time to see a village wilting under the sun when he heard the crackle of musketry and saw the smoke and muzzle flares. He felt the wind of a bullet's passage and saw a Madras sepoy gasp and crumple, holding his leg.

"Ambush! Find cover and return fire!" Andrew ordered, firing his revolver at the village, from where spurts of smoke showed the position of the attackers.

The Madras skirmishers were agile, kneeling or lying as they fired, with some moving towards the village. The Bengalis obeyed Andrew, dropping to the ground without fuss, firing, reloading, and firing again.

As his men engaged the enemy, Andrew studied the enemy's position. The king's soldiers had erected three defensive stockades within the village and placed six modern artillery pieces to fire down the only road.

Somebody knows his stuff. These stockades offer mutual protection, and the guns are well-positioned.

A large house stood within easy firing range of the village, presumably belonging to the local *woon*, the government's administrative officer.

That house would make an excellent defensive position.

A few hundred yards behind the village, three pagodas offered cover for scores of Burmese soldiers. Andrew grunted, checking his Bengalis. They were aiming and firing without any haste.

After a couple of volleys of musketry, the Burmese switched to their artillery, with solid shot bouncing down the road and crashing through the trees. One shot whistled above Andrew's head and smashed into a tree twenty yards behind him, bringing down a large bough.

"They're going to stand and fight," Colonel Baker said with satisfaction. "Keep firing, boys." He glanced around. "This damned jungle will make it hard to extend our men and keep contact." He grinned through his moustache. "Thank God we've got good quality infantry, Baird!"

The Burmese continued to fire, with a belt of smoke wreathing the village, speckled with spurts of orange and white muzzle flares.

"Dear God!" Lieutenant Sillery of the

12th Madras jerked upright and looked at the spreading stain on his tunic. He collapsed slowly, still staring at the enemy.

Baker lifted his voice. "Bring on the Second and Eleventh Bengal Infantry! I want them to support the skirmishers!"

The sepoys hurried forward, forming an extended line on the edge of the clearing.

"Fire on the village," Colonel Baker was in his element, striding from position to position without heeding the enemy's rifle bullets or artillery. "Keep their heads down," he ordered, "and move in slowly. Lieutenant Downes and Lieutenant Harris take two companies of the 11th Bengal, extend on the right, and take the village and stockades in flank. Captain Channer, take two companies of the Second Bengal and extend on the left. Let's squeeze these Burmans! Baird, you and I will push on in front."

"Yes, sir!" Andrew signalled to his men to follow. Thankfully, the havildar had a grasp of English and quickly translated Andrew's words to his men.

Major MacNeill led the 11th Bengal on the right, with Major Hill, Captain Peile and Lieutenant Drury in support. The Burmese remained under cover, firing at the advancing sepoys without giving ground. One bullet hit Lieutenant Drury, who fell, gasping and spitting out blood. Seeing their officer down, the sepoys gave a loud cry and surged forward, bayonets extended.

The Bengalis charged into the Burmese fire, desperate to drive the enemy from their defences. Major MacNeill grunted as a Burmese bullet slammed into him. He looked down at the red stain on his arm, said, "They're not stopping me," and continued to lead his men until another shot knocked him down. He rolled over, shook his head, rose and staggered on.

"Come on, men!" Andrew roared. He charged forward with Colonel Baker marginally in front and the sepoys behind him.

As the sepoys advanced, outflanking the stockades, the Burmese fire slackened, and they gradually withdrew from the village. Andrew saw a moving mass of men, some wearing the official light jackets and brass helmets but most without.

"Well done, my lads!" Baker shouted, reloading his revolver. "Come on, Baird! We'll make a sepoy officer of you yet, by God! If it was good enough for the Duke, it's good enough for anybody."

Andrew watched as the Burmese made a fighting withdrawal from the stockades to the pagodas, whose combinations of stone walls and intricate passages gave excellent cover.

"Come on, Bengalis!" Andrew shouted, running across the open ground with bullets zipping past him or burrowing into the dirt at his feet. The Burmese continued to fire, bringing down half a dozen of the advancing sepoys. Andrew was vaguely aware of Lieutenant Downes and Harris leading their men, advancing in short rushes rather than a single constant charge.

"These Burmese know how to fight," Baker said calmly. "They keep under cover and fire low."

"Unlike the Zulus," Andrew replied. "They always fired high, and so do most young British soldiers."

As the sepoys closed on the pagodas, the Burman defenders finally broke before the probing bayonets and ran towards the sanctuary of the forest.

"Shoot them!" Baker ordered. "Don't let them escape!"

The sepoys obeyed, aiming, firing, and reloading as fast as possible, hitting a score of the fleeing men before they reached the trees.

"That's cleared them out," Baker said with satisfaction. "It's a pity so many escaped, but it can't be helped. Well done, my lads. Get the *woon*'s house out of the way next, and then we'll deal with that damned redoubt."

Andrew nodded. The Bengalis were reloading, shouting abuse at the enemy, and behaving much like British infantry would in similar circumstances.

"Skirmishers!" Andrew shouted. "Advance a hundred yards on either side, and watch out for any Burmese counterattack!"

The Bengalis responded immediately, fanning

out with rifles ready, finding cover and waiting for the enemy.

"Come on, boys!" Andrew led his men to their next objective.

The *woon*'s palace was impressive compared to the villagers' wooden houses, but Thibaw's soldiers did not attempt to defend it. Baker's sepoys captured the palace without opposition, moving around the sumptuous building with ease. When Baker ordered it burned, the sepoys enjoyed lighting torches and putting the palace to the flames. Andrew watched as the smoke coiled upwards, glanced at the scatter of dead and wounded Burmese soldiers, and wondered at the wasteful futility of war.

They make a desert and call it peace, as Calgacus said. Are we any better than the Romans when they conquered much of the known world? Yes, we are: the Roman Empire was based on slavery, and we fight and abolish that horror wherever we can.[1]

"Right, gentlemen," Baker ordered. "Gather your

---

1. According to Tacitus, Calgacus, the leader of the Caledonians, made a rousing speech as he faced the Romans in what is now Scotland. Speaking of the Romans, he said: "These plunderers of the world, after exhausting the land by their devastations, are rifling the ocean: stimulated by avarice, if their
enemy be rich; by ambition, if poor; unsatiated by the East and by the West: the only people who behold wealth and indigence with equal avidity. To ravage, to slaughter, to usurp under false titles, they call empire; and where they make a desert, they call it peace."

sepoys together, and let's take the fort. We'll finish the day with another success."

Andrew checked his watch. It was one-forty in the afternoon. It had been a successful day so far, but perhaps the hardest part of the operation lay ahead.

"Wheel right," Baker ordered. "We'll march towards the river and take the redoubt from the rear." He grinned. "The defenders won't be able to retreat into the blasted jungle. It will be our bayonets or the Irrawaddy River for them."

Andrew joined his Bengalis, watching their satisfied faces. They had fought well in a difficult environment.

You'll do, lads, Andrew thought.

CHAPTER 26

IRRAWADDY RIVER, NOVEMBER 1885

The sepoys marched back into the forest, moving with a confident swing as Andrew ordered flankers on either side. His precautions proved unnecessary as they pushed through the trees without meeting any resistance. Once again, the forest closed in on Andrew, blocking out light and air, with insects buzzing around his head and the ground damp and slippery underfoot.

Moving with the skirmishers, Andrew was one of the first to see the Burmese redoubt. It stood at the edge of the clearing, rising abruptly against the hazy green backdrop of the forest with the flowing Irrawaddy in front.

"Stay under cover," Andrew whispered to his

havildar, gesturing with his hand so his orders were clear. Previous campaigns had taught him only to advance when he had thoroughly reconnoitred the enemy's position to assess their strengths and weaknesses. The Boers had a nasty habit of positioning themselves where the British least expected them, and Andrew anticipated the Burmese would be experts in their environment.

Andrew took out his binoculars, lay on the ground, hoping there were no snakes, and studied the redoubt. The walls were high, but a few blocks of masonry littered the ground in front, spoiling what could have been an effective killing ground for the defenders. A small house stood to the west of the building.

"What's that house?" Andrew asked the havildar.

"That's a priest's house, sahib," the havildar seemed pleased to be asked.

Andrew nodded and continued to study the defences.

There was a gate on the ground level, heavy teak and firmly closed with an array of defenders and a gingal – a large calibre smooth-bore musket mounted on a swivel – above. The sun glinted on the defenders' brass hats and the barrels of their rifles.

The Burmese would destroy any force attacking that gate, Andrew realised. He swept his binoculars around the walls and stopped. A rough ramp sloped up the height of the wall on the western face, evidently for the defenders to drag up artillery. The road was littered with shattered stones and pitted with holes, the effects of years of neglect, but Andrew thought the ramp offered the best access for a party of determined men.

We'll need covering fire to keep the defenders occupied and a rush by a storming party of volunteers, the forlorn hope, as the military used to call such men. How does the Indian Army organise such things?

Before Andrew reported his findings to Colonel Baker, it became evident that other officers did not share Andrew's cautious technique. Major Stead led his company of the Eleventh Bengal Infantry into the clearing with the men vivid against the dull greenery of the vegetation. The Burmese must have been waiting for their first sight of the sepoys and immediately opened fire.

The mixed rifles and muskets created a chaotic cacophony of noise, with bullets and balls churning up the ground.

"Keep down!" Andrew snarled to his men, "and return fire!"

The Bengalis responded eagerly, firing and reloading, some shouting and others in grim silence.

The Burmese fired from the redoubt's northwest corner, using a nine-pounder cannon and gingals that spread balls like a giant shotgun. The cannon shot ripped into the forest, wounding two of the sepoys.

"Fire at the walls," Andrew ordered. "Aim for that nine-pounder."

He did not know if his sepoys were good marksmen but guessed that being under fire would unsettle the Burmese gunners' aim. Andrew walked behind his men, encouraging them with his presence as he tried to ignore the bullets that whined around him.

Andrew swore when he saw Lieutenant Downes suddenly dash forward with seven of his men, yelling defiance as they crossed the clearing. Caught by surprise or sheltering from the musketry of Andrew's men, the defenders did not fire until Downes reached the cover of the masonry blocks. Once they realised what was happening, the Burmese tried to shoot downwards, but the massive stone blocks shielded Downes' men.

What the devil are these men doing? Eight men cannot capture an entire fort!

As Andrew pondered, another group of men rushed across the maidan, with Lieutenant Wilkinson of the 12th Madras Infantry leading three men to join Downes' party. The Burmese fired furiously, with bullets knocking chips from the stones without hitting a single sepoy.

Twelve men now, and more needed.

"Damn and blast it to hell and gone!" Andrew said. "Cover me!" Rising from cover, he weaved and jinked to the stone blocks, seeing the small spurts of dirt as Burmese bullets kicked up the ground around him. He heard himself laugh and wondered at his stupidity.

"Welcome, Captain Baird," Downes said with a casual smile. "Where do we go from here?"

"There's a ramp on the western wall," Andrew ducked as a large calibre gingal ball smashed into the block six inches from his face. He saw the blue smear the lead left on the masonry and wondered what sort of mess a ball of that calibre would make if it hit him.

"A ramp?" Downes said. "That will do." He nodded. "Here come reinforcements!"

They watched as Colonel Simpson and Lieutenant Hill were next to cross the maidan, leading a platoon of around twenty-five men of the 12th Madras Infantry. They ran to the priest's house, threw themselves down and opened a vigorous fire on the Burmese on the redoubt's walls.

"What sort of ramp?" Wilkinson asked, as casually as if he was discussing the weather.

"A rough one, probably to haul artillery up the walls," Andrew replied. "There is broken masonry at the foot that might provide some cover."

"I say we should rush into the fort," Wilkinson suggested.

"Exactly so," Andrew agreed. "As we've come this far."

They looked up as the sepoys increased their firing, and the Burmese replied. Simpson and Hill joined them among the scattered masonry blocks, running from the priest's house without losing a man.

"Captain Baird tells me there is a ramp up the western wall, sir," Atkinson reported. "We were thinking of storming the redoubt."

"That's my plan, too," Hill said. He smoothed a finger over his whiskers. "Wait until the Burmans fire their next volley and charge before they can reload."

The officers nodded and passed on the information to their men. The sepoys seemed keen to fight, fixing bayonets without orders and tensing for the rush.

Here we go again. Thank God we are facing Burmese soldiers and not the expert Boer marksmen.

The sepoys in the forest fired, the Burmans retaliated, and Colonel Hill shouted, "Now!"

"After me, boys!" Wilkinson said, repeated his words in Urdu and ran forward, with the sepoys and other officers following in a mad jumble. Andrew was in the middle with a havildar on his right and a grinning sepoy on his left. The latter was shouting madly, the words meaningless to Andrew but seeming to inspire the sepoys' colleagues.

Wilkinson and Downes led the charge up the ramp, with men staggering on the uneven surface, recovering, and running on. Wilkinson tripped on a piece of loose rock, and one of the Burmese defenders slashed his *dha* on the officer's head. Wilkinson fell, with the defender stabbing at his prone body.

Downes was next onto the wall. He shot the *dha*-wielding Burmese with his revolver, then hit another man wearing Thibaw's Army uniform. A third defender lifted his musket to attack, so Downes shot him in the chest, knocking him off the wall into the courtyard below.

Andrew glanced upward, saw the Burmese massing on the wall, aimed his revolver and shot one man, fired again, wounded a second and pushed forward. A surge of sepoys passed the officers to swarm inside the redoubt while Simpson and Hill ran forward. Andrew shot at a stocky Burmese, saw his bullet hit the man full in the face and spray blood, bone, and brains behind him, and ran along the fort's inner rampart.

The sepoys were fanning out, slaughtering anybody who stood in their way, using bullets, rifle butts or bayonets indiscriminately.

Andrew stood on a wide terrace thirty feet above the interior courtyard. The Burmese had six nine-pounder cannon and five gingals on the terrace, covering all four sides of the redoubt. Sepoys and Burmese battled on the flights of stone stairs that led to the open interior, with Wilkinson lying badly injured amongst Burmese casualties at the head of the ramp.

Two Burmese ran at Andrew, one with an ancient musket and the other with a *dha*. The musketeer knelt, aimed, and pressed the trigger, but his weapon misfired. The gunpowder in the pan exploded without igniting the charge in the barrel.

A flash in the pan, Andrew said to himself and shot the man. The Burmese with the *dha* ran on, yelling until a Madras sepoy spitted him with his bayonet.

"Shoot them!" Hill ordered as the Burmese crammed the stairs in their frantic effort to escape the sepoys' bayonets. The sepoys obeyed, firing into the mass as the officers emptied their revolvers, hastily reloaded, and fired again. In the courtyard, a press of panicking Burmese struggled to open the great teak gates and thrust outside, some running toward the river in the east and others westward, where the sepoys waited for them with controlled volleys.

"We've taken the redoubt!" Downes shouted. "Well done, boys!"

Outside the walls, the 2nd Bengal Infantry had emerged from the forest and formed in parade ground order. They fired volleys at the fleeing Burmese, killing many. The Burmese dropped their weapons, threw off their Army uniforms and fled, with the sepoys capturing hundreds.

Andrew saw more British officers moving inside the redoubt. While he had participated in the assault up the ramp, Colonel Sladen and a handful of officers had burst open the northeast gate, and others had led the sepoys over the walls with scaling ladders.

"That was intense while it lasted," Downes said. He looked over the wall. "And here comes Colonel White's brigade."

White had landed his brigade an hour after Baker's, together with a battery of screw guns that the men had struggled to push along the narrow path.

"We captured fifteen guns," Downes said, drawing on a Burmese cheroot, "and quite a collection of prisoners." He smiled. "King Thibaw won't be very happy that we defeated his soldiers, and our gunners won't be happy because the Burmese claim our artillery didn't kill a single man." His smile expanded into a grin. "Our sepoys proved themselves a match for anybody, once again."

As the British consolidated their position, General Prendergast issued orders to the Army banning looting or abusing the villagers. "We want to keep the people of Upper Burma calm. Let them know we have no quarrel with them, and all we want is peace for the country."

"Let's hope the general's proclamation works," Downes said. "The last thing we want is a guerrilla war in this damned jungle."

Andrew thought of the dacoits he had chased around Rangoon. "Amen to that," he agreed.

The fleet sailed up from Thayetmyo and anchored off Minhla, with smoke gently easing from their smokestacks. The soldiers sat or lay on the flats, scrutinising the forest and wondering what lay ahead. Andrew watched as a procession of small craft ferried the wounded sepoys and Burmese onto the hospital ships.

Jamieson was there with *Little Salamander*, puffing on a huge cigar and steering his vessel with unconscious skill.

Birnie drew on his cheroot. "I wonder how they would deal with our wounded prisoners," he said. "Probably behead them or crucify them." He shrugged. "Please, God, they never take me alive."

Andrew looked at the forest covering, thought of the crucified dacoits, and nodded. "I'd agree to that," he said.

AS THE BULK OF THE FLEET REMAINED AT ANCHOR at Thayetmyo, with the men playing cards or lounging under the sun, *Irrawaddy* and *Kathleen* pushed ahead with most of the naval brigade. Prendergast sent strong patrols ashore to search for the enemy.

"The sojer lads are busy, sir," the bearded petty officer said, coiling a line.

"They are," Andrew agreed, staring at the riverbank.

"I heard they're finding lots of wounded Burmans from the affair at Minhla," the sailor stopped his work, pushed back his hat, and grinned at Andrew.

"I heard the same," Andrew said. "The swaddies[1] are taking the wounded to the hospital ships."

"That's very Christian of them," the seaman said. "They'll probably recover and try to stab the orderlies in the back."

Andrew lifted his binoculars and concentrated on one patch of jungle. "I thought I saw something move there."

"Did you?" the sailor asked. "Best tell Lieutenant Trench then, chum."

"It might only be an animal," Andrew replied. He watched as *Kathleen* churned on with smoke from her funnel drifting behind her and her wake creamy white astern. Her wash eased over the river, causing the small boats outside a fishing village to bob and nod and the fishermen to look up, no doubt cursing these intruders who disturbed the fish.

"Yes, sir," the seaman studied the forest. "It

---

1. Swaddies – soldiers. Today, it is more often mispronounced as "squaddies."

might be an animal or some of these Burmese lads. Better sure than sorry, sir. I'll pass the word on."

Lieutenant Trench listened to the report, nodded, sent a man to watch the riverbank, and pushed on. As *Kathleen* moved slowly away from Minhla, engineers and artillerymen worked at the redoubt, making the fort that the sepoys had captured with such sacrifice into a British strongpoint.

"The Burmans may double back," Prendergast explained to his officers. "They can retake this fort, add artillery and block us from either returning to British Burma or sending up reinforcements."

Andrew watched the British work to repair and strengthen the walls and create earthworks for artillery outside the redoubt. Across the river, Prendergast had placed a company of the Liverpool Regiment and two companies of the Second Bengal in the Kolegone fort, with Mr Phayre as the civil officer to ease relations with the Burmese.

"The Burmans will find the Liverpudlians and Bengalis hard to shift," Downes had said. "But I don't fancy that as a garrison duty, stuck in the middle of nowhere with a hostile forest at the rear and a river in front."

Andrew nodded. "Any border post can be frustrating," he agreed. "Months and months of boredom yet always aware the enemy could be watching, waiting for a minute when you relax your guard, then strike and run."

Now, Andrew was back on *Kathleen,* with Midshipman Birnie joining him as they pushed upstream against the current.

"The Burmans had a battery of four guns below the fort," Birnie said, looking up occasionally to watch the riverbanks. "They nearly hit us yesterday with one shot." He grinned again. "Imagine the trouble they could have caused if they had served their guns properly." He nodded backwards towards the main fleet. "If a shell exploded on one of the flats, we could wave farewell to half a battalion of swaddies, sir."

"You're right." Andrew lowered his binoculars as he saw a water buffalo emerge from a series of fields. "If they had held the forts with any determination, they could have caused carnage. I think the speed of our advance surprised them."

"The forts should have commanded the river from Minhla to Patanayo," Birnie agreed. "I heard there were Europeans helping Thibaw's men."

"Three of them, apparently, although I didn't see them," Andrew agreed. "Italians working for Thibaw. They ran before we could catch them. They jumped into a royal steamer and fled upriver."

"They ran at Kolegone, too," Birnie said. "They were waiting for a frontal assault, and General Prendergast's turning movement took them by surprise. As soon as the Liverpool regiment fired their first volley, Thibaw's men bolted."

"We seem to be winning this war," Andrew said. "Let's hope for a quick victory that brings peace to Burma."

Peace for Burma, a pardon for Bo Thura and a voyage home for Mariana and me. Andrew swatted a mosquito. Corbiestane Tower seemed even more desirable from thousands of miles away. *I wish I were at Corbiestane right now, with Mariana at my side.*

RANGOON, NOVEMBER 1885

Mariana felt her heartbeat increase as she stepped into the dark blue Brougham. She felt the slight jerk as the driver started the coach and stared out the window at the now-familiar streets of Rangoon.

Stephen won't let me down, Mariana told herself. *Stephen would never leave me alone for such a long time.*

The journey to Jennings' house seemed shorter than she remembered. Soon, she was walking to the front door, with moths fluttering around the oil lamps and her footsteps echoing in the humid air. She lifted her fist to knock, and the door opened.

"My dear Mariana!" Jennings smiled at her across the threshold. "I am so glad you came. Come in, my dear, come in!"

The warmth of Jennings' welcome dispelled Mariana's doubts, and she straightened her back, smiling as she entered the house. Everything was familiar, from the furniture to Jennings' smile, the faces of the servants, and the scents of incense. Mariana felt herself relaxing, allowed Jennings to ease off her jacket, and accepted a small glass of sherry.

"We won't try the champagne," Jennings said with a smile.

"Thank you, Stephen," Mariana replied. "That's probably for the best."

"It's simple fare today," Jennings said. "I hope that is all right with you?"

"Perfectly," Mariana said. "I am here for the company, not the food, although both were excellent on my last visit."

Jennings smiled. "And I am happy to have your company, too," he replied.

They sat in the airy front room with the fan above and the last rays of the sun easing through the tall windows to cast shadows on the floor.

"Beware of the dinner gong," Jennings said. "It gave you quite a start the first time you heard it."

Mariana smiled at the memory. "I made a bit of an idiot of myself, Stephen. I won't do that again."

Jennings leaned forward and took her hand. "Any blame was mine, Mariana. In my eyes, you could never be an idiot."

"Thank you, Stephen," Mariana said and lifted a finger as the dinner gong sounded. "There! I didn't start at all."

"Neither you did," Jennings stood and extended a hand.

Mariana accepted the hand without demur, and they walked into the candlelit dining room.

"How romantic," Mariana said, allowing Jennings to usher her into her seat.

MINHLA 19TH NOVEMBER 1885

The flotilla remained at Minhla, the ships swinging at their anchors as the Irrawaddy River surged past. The soldiers sweltered in boredom on the flats or welcomed the occasional patrol through the forest, although Thibaw's men left them severely alone. All the steamers had arrived, with the barge *White Swan*, containing the heavy battery, last to negotiate the river.

"I heard a shave that Thibaw sent three thousand men to reinforce Minhla," Birnie spoke through a cloud of cigar smoke. He smiled. "They must have turned back when we took his precious forts. We killed about sixty of the Burmans here."

Andrew nodded. "I was there," he said quietly. "They held their ground well, considering the quality of the troops they faced."

"There's somebody on the riverbank," Birnie said. "He's watching us."

Andrew turned around. *Bo Thura! What the devil are you doing here?* "I see him," he said. "Can I borrow your little dinghy? I want to talk to that man."

CHAPTER 27

IRRAWADDY RIVER, NOVEMBER 1885

"Cousin Andrew!"

Andrew smiled as Bo Thura slipped from the forest to stand at his side. "I don't have a pardon for you yet." Andrew glanced at the anchored British fleet. "Some of these lads would shoot on sight."

"They'll only see me if I let them," Bo Thura said casually.

"What the devil are you doing here?" Andrew asked.

"I've come to warn you," Bo Thura told him. "Maung Thandar is setting a trap for General Prendergast and Colonel Sladen."

"Tell me more," Andrew said. Together, Prendergast and Sladen were the directing force behind the invasion. If Maung Thandar killed or captured them, he would cause irreparable damage to the British.

"General Prendergast and Colonel Sladen are sailing in the steamer *Irrawaddy*," Bo Thura said. "They're scouting the river to see what's ahead."

"How the devil do you know that?" Andrew asked.

Bo Thura gave the wry Windrush smile. "I know what's happening before the general does; if I know, you can be sure that Maung Thandar does too."

Andrew looked up as a flock of parrots exploded from the trees. They passed overhead with a flapping of wings and a flash of bright colours to disappear upstream. "Tell me more," he said.

"I'll have to show you," Bo Thura said. "Come with me."

Andrew looked at *Kathleen*, which was moored a hundred yards out in the river with four bluejackets on guard. Birnie was watching everything he did, and there was a gentle waft of smoke from her funnel. "How long will it take?"

"A couple of hours," Bo Thura said.

Andrew checked his watch. "I'd better let the ship know where I am."

Bo Thura led at a smart trot along a path Andrew barely saw. He followed a yard behind, feeling the sweat dripping from him in the forest's humidity and ducking under the occasional low branch. The river remained a constant on their left, with the water swirling and chuckling, dappled in the sunlight, and often hung with clouds of insects.

The Irrawaddy is the lifeblood of Burma, Andrew thought. *It is the highway and the main artery.*

After thirty hard minutes, Bo Thura stopped, squatting on the path. "We'll have to skirt around a village here," he explained, "and go around a couple of paddy fields. If anybody talks to us, let me do the speaking."

Andrew nodded. "I will," he said.

Bo Thura had a British Martini-Henry in his right hand and the ubiquitous *dha* at his waist. He moved at a fast trot, with his feet making little sound. They eased around the village, keeping to a fringe of trees, while villagers continued their lives unheeding the war flickering around them. The majority of farmers were concerned with crops and their families, not politics and bloodshed.

After an hour, Bo Thura stopped at a broad field where a man guided a pair of buffalo. "Keep down," he said. "That man is spying for Maung Thandar."

Andrew watched the farmer. "How can you tell?"

"I know him. He'll relay every detail of your fleet to another of his kind, and Maung Thandar will know what's happening before the ships round the next bend. We'll have to circle this place."

Andrew followed as Bo Thura took a wide detour inland, with the farmer apparently innocently guiding his buffalo with a clear view over the river.

This detour will delay us, Andrew thought. *My two hours are ticking away.*

Once past the fields, Bo Thura moved even faster, skimming over the ground with Andrew struggling to keep up. He dashed the sweat from his forehead, took a deep breath and pushed on.

After another sweltering ten minutes, Bo Thura lifted a hand and stepped into the forest cover. Andrew did likewise, avoiding a giant tarantula spider that scuttled over his boot. He crouched, keeping his revolver handy. Bo Thura lifted a hand for silence and merged into the undergrowth.

Andrew heard the soft sound of sandals slapping on the ground and watched as a patrol of King's soldiers filed past with their curious, high-kneed step. He waited two minutes and emerged, with Bo Thura appearing simultaneously.

"Maung Thandar must be nervous to send out a patrol," Bo Thura said.

They moved again, slower now, with Bo Thura cautiously approaching each bend in the path and listening for any sound. After another ten minutes, he stopped.

"We're getting close," he said quietly. "We'll move through the forest for the last quarter mile. Keep close and don't make any noise."

Andrew had learned how to move silently in the

frontier war against the Galekas, but Bo Thura walked like a ghost, making no sound as he drifted through the undergrowth. After a difficult period during which Andrew twice lost sight of him, they climbed a small, sparsely wooded rise. Bo Thura lifted his hand, and Andrew stopped.

The ridge overlooked a broad stretch of the river. Bo Thura slid to his stomach and crawled forward with Andrew at his side. They both stopped when they reached the edge of a fifty-foot-high cliff, and Bo Thura gestured downwards.

A group of Burman soldiers stood guard over a horde of near-naked Burmese labourers. The men were working on three flats, placing sandbags in the bottom and fixing pointed stakes at slight angles.

I've seen that sort of arrangement before, Andrew thought. *The Burmese will sink the flats in the deep-water channel through which the flotilla must sail and sink the leading ship, presumably the vessel with Prendergast and Sladen on board.*

Bo Thura touched Andrew's arm and raised his eyebrows in a silent question. When Andrew nodded, they crawled carefully backwards.

"You see?" Bo Thura asked when they reached the relative safety of the forest fringe.

"I see," Andrew said. "Do you know where the trap will be sprung?"

"No," Bo Thura shook his head. "I found the flats; I did not find the plans."

"I'll have to warn General Prendergast," Andrew said.

"You know the way back," Bo Thura replied.

"I do," Andrew replied.

"Don't forget to tell General Prendergast who gave you the information," Bo Thura said. "And pass that on to the Chief Commissioner. I need safety in British Burma."

"I won't forget," Andrew promised. "If I survive."

"Be careful to avoid Maung Thandar's spy," Bo Thura reminded and slid away.

Prendergast listened to Andrew's warning with a stern face. His fingers drummed on the desktop as his staff mustered around, wondering what right this intruder had to speak directly to the general.

"This dacoit fellow," Prendergast said. "Can he be trusted?"

"He gave you the intelligence about the king's steamer," Andrew reminded. He thought it best not to mention the documents about the secret French treaty.

"That intelligence was correct," Prendergast allowed. "Now, you know where the flats are situated, but not the site of the alleged trap. Is that correct?"

"I saw the flats, sir," Andrew said. "They could be anywhere on the river by now."

Prendergast leaned back in his chair. "Let us summarise. We know there might be an attempt to sink *Irrawaddy* while Sladen and I are on board. Any fool could work that out."

"Maybe, sir," Andrew said. "If we consult the map, we can work out the best spot for the Burmans to lay their trap. It must be somewhere the deep-water channel is narrow and maybe close to the shore."

"That could be anywhere on the blasted river," Prendergast said.

Andrew studied the map, tracing the river with his finger. "Yes, sir, but somewhere between here and Mandalay. May I borrow this map, sir? I want to consult with a pilot and see where the deep-water channel is."

Prendergast nodded. "Do that, Baird."

Jamieson looked surprised when Andrew appeared on *Little Salamander*.

"I thought the dacoits had murdered you," Jamieson said, puffing furiously at his cigar.

"Not yet," Andrew said. "I need your help again."

"Do you, now?" Jamieson's eyes narrowed. "I'm not taking you up any blasted river until we've beaten Thibaw," he said. "However much you offer me."

"I just want advice," Andrew told him.

"What sort of advice?" Jamieson asked.

"Professional advice," Andrew said and explained the situation. "Even you can't charge for that."

Jamieson grunted. "My time costs money," he said and sighed. "Unroll your chart then, Captain Baird, and let's have a look."

They squatted on the hot deck, and Jamieson pointed out the deep-water channel routes in the rainy and dry seasons.

"What's this here?" Andrew indicated an area where the river widened around half a dozen islands.

"There are channels between the islands," Jamieson said. "Surely you remember passing them on your pleasure cruise on *Little Salamander*?"

"No," Andrew shook his head.

"Typical bloody soldier," Jamieson sighed. "Some of the channels are deep and others shallow. This one," he pointed to a winding channel between two large islands, "is the most favoured, and this one," he moved his finger to the right, "is best avoided, but the channels can alter after a period of drought or heavy rain."

"Thank you," Andrew studied the chart. "If you were going to ambush a ship, Jamieson, which channel would you choose?"

Jamieson stabbed his stubby finger down. "That one, Baird, and I'll thank you for a golden boy for the information."

"A sovereign?" Andrew looked up in dismay. "You drive a hard bargain, Jamieson."

"I need to fund my luxurious lifestyle," Jamieson said. "Coal doesn't come cheap, you know, and all these blasted Army vessels are driving up prices." He held out a grubby hand in anticipation.

General Prendergast looked up when Andrew returned. "Well?"

"If I were going to attack your ship, sir," Andrew said, unrolling the map on Prendergast's desk and ignoring his staff. "I would do it there, in the channel between these islands." He indicated the spot. "The passage is very narrow so that the flats would fill the channel, and the current is fast, which would carry away any survivors."

Prendergast surveyed the chart, nodded, and looked up. "All right, Baird. You did a lot of irregular work in Africa. Let's see how good you are here. Take a platoon along the riverbank and capture or destroy these flats if they are still there."

"Yes, sir," Andrew replied. The prospect of an independent command away from the confines of superior officers was appealing. "Which regiment can I select from, sir?"

"Use the 23rd Foot, the Welsh Fusiliers," Prendergast replied.

"Thank you, sir."

"I'll contact their colonel and send *Kathleen* up-river if you need nautical support." Prendergast smiled. "The bluejackets tend to fret unless we give them something active to do."

The colonel of the Fusiliers was waiting when Andrew arrived. "I don't like my men being used on some harebrained escapade," he said. "Especially when a young officer from some obscure colonial horse regiment has a bee in his bonnet." He looked Andrew up and down, nodding at the medal ribbons on his breast. "You've been on campaign already, I see."

"Yes, sir, the Frontier War, Zululand and against the Boers."

"Well, that might count for something, I suppose. I am sending one of my officers to keep an eye on you, Baird."

"Thank you, sir," Andrew replied. He did not want a Fusilier officer watching everything he did, but one did not argue with a colonel.

"Follow me," the colonel said. He had selected forty volunteers, including a sergeant, a corporal, and a hard-faced lieutenant. They stood beside the river, dressed in faded and stained khaki, holding their Martinis at their sides and staring at this upstart young captain.

"Well, men," Andrew addressed them. "My name is Captain Andrew Baird, and we are going on an important mission."

The Fusiliers looked straight ahead without any change of expression. The sergeant looked around forty, with a breast full of medal ribbons and a face that looked like it could chop teak.

"The Burmans plan to ambush our ship *Irrawaddy* as it passes through a narrow channel, sink her, and murder the general. We are to prevent this from happening."

The lieutenant and some of the men began to look interested. The majority continued to stare directly ahead.

"Are there any questions?" Andrew knew it was highly unusual for an officer to allow his men to ask questions, but he had learned his trade with irregular horsemen, where discipline differed from regular British regiments. Some of the men looked surprised.

Lieutenant Toshack lifted his voice. "Yes, sir," he barked. "Where is this ambush?"

"We think it is about ten miles upriver," Andrew said. "Where the Irrawaddy broadens, and there are islands between the banks."

"Thank you, sir," the lieutenant replied, glancing over his men.

"We will leave an hour before dawn tomorrow," Andrew said. "I want everybody to carry seventy rounds of ammunition, sufficient rations to last a day and night, a full water bottle and a blanket."

The men nodded. The first battalion, Royal Welsh Fusiliers, was a veteran regiment that knew how to fight, although they had not seen much action since the Indian Mutiny. The men had been in India for five years and were thoroughly acclimatised to the heat.

"Dismissed," Andrew ordered and watched the men march away.

Here we go again. Tennyson's poetry flashed into Andrew's head.

"Half a league, half a league,
Half a league onward,
All in the valley of Death
Rode the six hundred."

Let's hope I'm not leading these men into the valley of Death.

CHAPTER 28

RANGOON AND THE IRRAWADDY RIVER,
NOVEMBER 1885

Jennings looked at Mariana across the width of the circular table. "Did you enjoy the meal, Mariana?"

"Very much so," Mariana replied.

"More wine?" Jennings signalled to a servant, who poured red wine into their crystal glasses. "Here's a toast to us." He lifted his glass high.

"To us," Mariana echoed. The wine was sweet and cool, welcoming after the meal.

"More?" Jennings suggested. "Or shall I play for you?" He indicated the piano in the adjoining room.

"Do you play the piano?" Mariana accepted more

wine. "You are a man of many talents, Stephen. I've always wanted to learn the piano."

"I can teach you," Jennings said. "Come on over."

"I'll be a hopeless duffer," Mariana told him.

"Nonsense," Jennings said. "I don't believe you'd be a duffer at anything." He extended his hand and guided Mariana to the piano. "Put your glass on top, beside mine." Sitting her on the stool, he ran a finger over the keyboard and held her hands. "Now, let's begin."

ANDREW INSPECTED THE MEN IN THE LIGHT OF A waning moon. They stood relaxed, seemingly unconcerned by the prospect of a long march and a possible skirmish at the end.

"They're a handy-looking bunch," Andrew told the lieutenant.

"They're Welsh Fusiliers," Toshack replied, as if that was answer enough.

"That explains it, then," Andrew said. He set the corporal in charge of the rearguard, with orders to ensure nobody was left behind, and led the way along the forest track Bo Thura had shown him the previous day.

Andrew moved at a steady pace, stopping every thirty minutes for a five-minute break to allow the men to drink from their water bottles as the NCOs checked nobody had dropped out. The weather was not overbearingly hot, but the patches of dense forest increased the humidity. Andrew pushed the men forward, hoping they were as fit and determined as the infantry he had worked with in Africa.

The Fusiliers responded well, ignoring the mosquitoes and watching the trees in case of ambush.

After an hour, Andrew halted them at the outskirts of a village, remembering Bo Thura's warning about Maung Thandar's spies.

Let him spy and make whatever report he chooses. I have a platoon of quality British infantry here; I'll put my money on them to defeat any number of Thibaw's soldiers.

"Lieutenant Toshack, put out two-man pickets in front, flank, and rear."

"Sir." Toshack gave crisp orders, and the men moved out. Their khaki uniforms were not as distinct as the old-fashioned scarlet but still stood out against the prevailing dull green.

Andrew allowed the men ten minutes, then moved on, pushing them hard. He skirted the village, ploughing through the shallow paddy fields without stopping. He watched the Fusiliers waving to the women working in the fields and the men lounging and smoking outside the houses.

These Fusiliers seem a decent bunch.

The sound of boots thumping on the narrow path was reassuring, with Welsh, Irish, and English accents muttering as the Fusiliers progressed. When the trees thinned and the view was open to the Irrawaddy, Andrew saw *Kathleen* steaming in the deep-water channel, seemingly serene. It was a reminder that British sea power could reach hundreds of miles inland, provided there was sufficient water to float.

"How far, sir?" Toshack asked.

"We're over halfway," Andrew said. He glanced at the Fusiliers. They were hot and sweaty but composed, moving well. Nobody had fallen out. "One more halt, and then we'll be close."

Andrew saw the movement at the edge of the next field, with Sergeant Coslett ordering two men to investigate. Andrew kept the platoon waiting until the patrol returned.

"Nothing, sir," a long-faced private reported. "If anybody was there, he bolted when he saw us coming."

"Keep an eye open," Andrew ordered. "The Burmese like to use ambushes."

"We'll watch for them, sir," Sergeant Coslett promised. "Come on, lads, back on the road."

They pushed on, tiring now as the miles slid away and the sun rose. The men were familiar with the forest sounds and sensations but wary of Burmese attack.

"Halt!" Andrew stopped them when they reached the foot of the ridge. "I'll go ahead and see what's happening."

"Best not go alone, sir," Toshack advised. "Shall I come with you?"

"No." Andrew shook his head. "Stay with the men. I'll take Sergeant Coslett. If the Burmans kill me, I'll depend on you to destroy the Burmese boats and get your men back safely."

"Yes, sir." Toshack accepted the possibility of Andrew's death as part of a soldier's duty.

"You're with me, Sergeant Coslett," Andrew said and led him up the ridge. He stopped at the cliff above the flats and crawled to the edge, relieved that the flats remained where he had seen them the previous day. "There they are, Sergeant."

"The Burmans are moving them, sir," Coslett said.

The three flats floated close inshore, with a large group of Burmese in the water working around them. The Burmese kept close inshore as they attached lines to the flats, preparatory to towing and pushing them upstream towards the islands.

"Why don't they use one of their steamers?" Coslett wondered.

"The smoke would alert *Kathleen*," Andrew replied. "She's only a couple of miles downstream. As it is, the river has cut into the bank, and the overhanging trees conceal them."

"Shall I get the men, sir?" Coslett asked.

"Yes." Andrew nodded. "Bring them up. I'll keep an eye on the flats."

He watched as Coslett hurried back along the path with his rifle at the trail. Andrew saw a group of king's soldiers surrounding a tall man and recognised Maung Thandar.

That man must be the most active opponent we have in this war.

Maung Thandar gave sharp orders that saw the labourers push and drag the flats through the water against the current. When one man stumbled, Maung Thandar snarled something, and one of the soldiers cracked the labourer over the head with the barrel of his rifle.

You're an unpleasant man, Maung Thandar.

Andrew contemplated firing at Maung Thandar until he realised the range was too long for an accurate shot and would only give away his presence without gaining any advantage. He crawled along the cliff's edge, keeping level with the Burmese and hoping nothing delayed the Fusiliers.

The islands were a mile ahead, with the Irrawaddy already beginning to widen. With Maung Thandar giving vocal encouragement and his soldiers using slaps, kicks, and jabs from their rifles, the Burman labourers were making good time pushing the flats.

If the Fusiliers don't hurry, we'll be too late. Once the Burmese sink these things in the deep-water channel, they'll be the very devil to lift. They'll delay the expedition and give Thibaw time to organise a stiffer resistance, which will cost lives.

Maung Thandar shouted again, and the labourers put even more effort into pushing the flats, easing them upstream four feet at a time.

Andrew swore. *Where is Sergeant Coslett with the Fusiliers?* He could see the islands ahead, with the deep-water channel evident and *Kathleen* nowhere in sight. A troop of monkeys chattered above, seeming to laugh at Andrew's predicament.

I'll have to slow the Burmans down, Andrew decided, drawing his revolver. *I'll get closer and shoot at Maung Thandar.*

He was aiming at Maung Thandar when he heard the hollow thump of boots behind him.

Thank God for small mercies!

"Sorry we took so long," Lieutenant Toshack said. "We found a man spying on us and had to dispose of him."

Andrew nodded. "Well done, Lieutenant."

"What's happening here, sir?"

"The Burmese are making good time with the flats," Andrew said. "Bring your men along the river-bank. Double!"

Andrew led the way, with the Fusiliers panting after him. When they came close to the Burmese, Andrew ordered them to silence, moved fifty yards away from the riverbank until they had passed the toiling Burmese, and returned to the river. The

Burmese were close to the shore and a hundred yards upstream. Andrew lined his men on the riverbank, lying down and silent.

"Mark your targets, fire a volley, and then it's every man for himself," Andrew ordered. The Fusiliers looked at one another, surprised at this latitude from an officer.

"On my word!" Andrew realised the Burmese had become aware of their presence and were looking up, with Maung Thandar's guard clustering closer to him. "Fire!"

The Fusiliers fired a smart volley that felled half a dozen labourers.

Maung Thandar probably dragooned these poor devils into working.

"Aim for the soldiers as well," Andrew ordered, firing his revolver as the Fusiliers aimed and fired at the labourers.

With luck, the labourers will scatter and escape, leaving Maung Thandar without a workforce.

When the firing began, many of the Burmese immediately fled, diving into the fast-flowing river to swim away. Some splashed downstream, away from the Fusiliers' murderous fire, and a few remained, trying to shelter behind the flats or under the overhang of the banks.

Andrew aimed for Maung Thandar, fired, and saw a soldier step in front of his target. The revolver bullet hit the soldier in the face, knocking his head back. When he fell, another took his place, and then a fast Burmese boat appeared from upstream with half a dozen men paddling furiously.

"Shoot the paddlers!" Andrew shouted. "Don't let that man escape!"

The Fusiliers altered their aim as Maung Thandar scrambled into the boat. Two of the Burmese soldiers lifted rifles to return the Fusiliers' fire, with their bullets rising high above the Welshmen's heads. Splashes around the boat showed where the Fusiliers' bullets landed, while two of the paddlers crumpled, and splinters flew from the boat's bulwarks.

Maung Thandar rolled into the bottom of the boat as the crew thrust their paddles into the water and raced away. The Fusiliers hit another man, who jerked upright and slumped over the bulwark. Andrew emptied his revolver at the small boat, swore as it sped away, leaving a trail of blood, and returned to the main focus of his mission.

"Down to the river, lads. Grab those flats!"

The Fusiliers scrambled down the muddy cliff, with some men sliding and falling, to splash into the water with loud curses. Dead and wounded Burmese floated inshore, with the current carrying some away and others remaining tangled in the overhanging undergrowth.

"Get the flats!" Andrew ordered. "Sergeant Coslett! Take a section and fire at that boat!" Free of human restraint, the flats were spinning down-stream, and Andrew realised the current might yet take them to the deep-water channel as a hazard to shipping.

Lieutenant Toshack led a section into the water and grabbed the most distant flat, dragging it close to the bank, where it acted as a barrier to the other two. The three clumsy craft rubbed and bumped together.

"Well done, Lieutenant!" Andrew shouted. He saw the men struggling with the weight and ordered the remainder of the platoon to help, jumping to add his strength to the Fusiliers'. Sergeant Coslett returned, shaking his head.

"Sorry, sir, the boat escaped. It crossed the river and disappeared up a tributary."

Andrew cursed silently. "It can't be helped. Give us a hand with these damned things." He saw *Kathleen* in the deep-water channel and waved to attract her attention, hoping the lookout could see him so close to the bank.

"Lieutenant Toshack! Destroy or sink these flats! Ensure Maung Thandar can't salvage them."

"Yes, sir!" Toshack answered.

Andrew watched a Burmese corpse bob past, trailing greasy blood over the water, and signalled to *Kathleen* again. "Can nobody in that damned ship see me?" Eventually, he unholstered his revolver and fired three shots in the air.

The revolver fire alerted *Kathleen,* and Lieutenant Trench launched a small boat, with two sailors pulling at the oars and Midshipman Birnie in the stern. Andrew waded waist-deep into the water to meet them and grabbed the stem. "Did you see that Burmese boat?"

"We saw a small boat," Birnie said.

"Thibaw's minister, Maung Thandar, is aboard her," Andrew said. "She escaped up a tributary. See if you can follow her and capture or kill Maung Thandar. He's the focal point for Thibaw's resistance."

"I'll pass the message on," Birnie said.

"Move!" Andrew ordered. "We'll deal with the flats." He turned away as the oarsmen pulled their boat back to *Kathleen.*

"Lieutenant Toshack," Andrew said. "If you were planning to sink a ship between two islands in a river, what else would you do?"

Toshack considered for a moment. "I'd ensure the British commanders were either dead or captured, sir."

"Exactly so," Andrew agreed. "You'd position a force of infantry and maybe a battery of artillery on the island. I'll deal with the flats; you take a section upstream and check the islands."

"Yes, sir," Toshack said. He shouted for a corporal and set off upstream at a fast march, with his men nearly jogging to keep pace with him.

"How are we doing, Sergeant?" Andrew asked.

"All right, sir," Coslett replied. "We were going to knock the bottom out of the boats and sink them, but one's half full of gunpowder." He grinned. "We're going to make a devil of a bang instead."

"That's the spirit!" Andrew approved. "Blow the things to Kingdom Come!"

Coslett laughed. "We will, sir. Best stand clear!"

"Get the men back, Coslett! And drag these wounded Burmese away. They can't hurt us now, and I'll not kill wounded men."

"Yes, sir." When Coslett barked orders, the Fusiliers hauled the Burmese casualties back from the river.

"Whenever you're ready, Sergeant," Andrew shouted.

The explosions ripped all three flats to shreds, spread splinters over a fifty-yard radius and knocked branches from the trees. The water erupted in a seventy-foot-high fountain that hovered and then collapsed, bringing mud and dead fish.

"That was some bang," Coslett looked pleased with himself as his men cheered. Andrew thought there was something very satisfying in destroying the enemy's weapons.

"You didn't leave much of the flats," Andrew approved. He saw the shattered remnants of the stakes and fragments of the flats carried away on the current.

"We didn't leave much of anything, sir," Coslett said.

As the echoes of the explosion died away, the Fusiliers heard firing from upstream. "Lieutenant Toshack's found some trouble," Andrew said. "Gather the men together, Sergeant, and we'll see what's happening up there."

"Yes, sir," Coslett said, shouting for his men.

The Fusiliers emerged from the trees, laughing at the destruction. "Form up in a column of four!" Andrew ordered. "Sergeant, take the rearguard. I'll take the advance guard, and every fourth man watch the flanks."

The shooting was louder now and more insistent, as if Toshack was involved with a large body of the enemy. Andrew led the platoon at the double with his revolver in his hand.

He rounded a bend in the path and stopped as he saw Toshack's section withdrawing towards him, firing ahead and into the forest. Andrew glanced at his men, deciding how best to form up to defend themselves on the narrow path.

"Three abreast on the path," he ordered. "Front rank kneeling, second standing and third in reserve. Open up to allow Lieutenant Toshack's section through."

Well-trained, the Fusiliers obeyed.

"When our lads have passed," Andrew continued, "the front rank will fire a volley and file back through the other two ranks. The front nine men will face along the track, and the rest will face the forest."

Toshack's section ran back, hurrying without panic.

"Get to the rear," Andrew ordered as they reached him. "Where's Lieutenant Toshack?"

"He's coming, sir," the corporal was bleeding from a wound on his shoulder.

Toshack was last to appear, firing his revolver down the path, where a host of Burmese soldiers advanced.

"Ready, lads," Andrew said. "Once the lieutenant is safe, fire three rounds rapid!"

The Fusiliers waited as Toshack strode up to them, opened ranks to let him pass, closed, and fired rolling volleys.

Andrew estimated about fifty of Thibaw's soldiers were on the path, with the sun glinting from their weapons. The Fusiliers' first bullets ripped into the leading men, knocking down two and hitting a man in the second rank. The Fusiliers reloaded and fired without orders, the heavy bullets smashing down two or more men as the Burmese closed. A spray of blood rose with pieces of a man's skull.

"Keep firing, men," Andrew ordered.

Seeing the carnage in front, the Burmese soldiers at the back hesitated. "Load!" Andrew ordered. He heard the jerking of the underlevers as the Fusiliers ejected the spent cartridges and pressed in the new.

"Come on, you bastards," a Fusilier growled, presenting his rifle to the enemy.

Andrew hoped the Martinis continued to operate, for they had an unpleasant reputation for overheating and jamming at inconvenient moments.

Another volley hammered the faltering Burmese. One man crumpled, and another fell backwards, spouting blood. The rest turned away.

"They're retiring, sir," a Fusilier reported just as firing broke out further forward in the column.

"They're in the forest!" Toshack shouted. "Volley fire, men! One rank at a time."

Andrew nodded. If all three ranks fired simultaneously, the Burmese could attack while the men reloaded. Firing one rank at a time reduced the volume of fire but retained most of the firepower if the enemy charged.

"Keep moving," Andrew ordered. "Withdraw along the path."

I've brought my men into a bad situation, with the forest on one side, the enemy behind us and no space to manoeuvre. We'll have to rely on discipline and musketry.

The Fusiliers withdrew slowly, with one section firing whenever they saw movement in the trees and the rearguard ready if the pursuing Burmese appeared on the path. Gunsmoke coiled around them, marking their progress as men fired, cursed, re-loaded, and moved on, staring into the shaded trees.

"Steady, men!" Andrew shouted. "Keep together!"

The first Fusilier fell ten minutes later. A dozen Burmese fired from the forest, with one bullet striking a Fusilier high in the shoulder. The man grunted, put a hand to the wound and swore softly. "The buggers shot me," he said in disbelief.

"Help that man!" Andrew ordered and increased the speed. They had a long march ahead with an un-known number of the enemy all around. He glanced at the river, hoping for support from *Kathleen* or *Ir-rawaddy*, but the water remained clear of traffic. A gong sounded somewhere, encouraging Thibaw's men.

"Movement!" Coslett shouted and ordered a sec-tion to fire, with the bullets slicing leaves from the trees and chipping the wood. The platoon moved in a cloud of gunsmoke, with men watching all around.

"We could do with naval support here," Toshack echoed Andrew's thoughts. "A pity *Kathleen* is hunting Maung Thandar on the other side of the Irrawaddy."

"We must make do with what we have," Andrew replied.

A second Fusilier fell as they passed through a clearing, and the Burmese fired from behind a hastily constructed timber and earth stockade. The man grunted and crumpled to the ground with two Burmese bullets in him. He died without knowing what had killed him.

Andrew saw the enemy's brass helmets glinting behind the stockade and snarled. "Sergeant Coslett, outflank them on the left with one section, fire and get in with the bayonet. Lieutenant Toshack, get the men down and fire on the enemy; I'll take Three Section on the right flank. On my word, Coslett."

As Toshack laid down covering fire, Coslett and Andrew advanced on either flank of the earthworks. The Burmese did not wait to receive the charge but withdrew quickly, with the Fusiliers in pursuit.

"Stand and fight, you bastards!" the Fusiliers shouted. "Come back and fight!"

"Don't chase them!" Andrew ordered. He grabbed an excited Fusilier's arm. "Get back, man! They'll be waiting for you in the trees." He saw one fleet-footed Fusilier catch a Burmese soldier. The Burmese turned, drew his *dha*, and the Fusilier thrust his bayonet hilt-deep into the man's stomach.

"And that's done for you, Johnny Thibaw!"

"Reform!" Coslett bellowed. "Don't linger in the open!"

"Open order," Andrew ordered. "Don't close up until we reach the forest. Move at the double." He shuffled the ranks, moving the rearguard further up the column and men from the centre to the rear.

"Push on!"

The Fusiliers obeyed, marching and firing, with two men supporting the wounded and Andrew in the rearguard. He heard firing ahead, glanced over his shoulder and saw Coslett in the centre of the column giving brisk orders.

"Don't waste ammunition, boys! Only fire when I say!"

Andrew nodded. He had not anticipated a fighting withdrawal along the forest track, expecting *Kathleen* to provide adequate support. The appearance of Maung Thandar had altered the raid's dynamics.

"Sir!" Toshack reported. "Thibaw's soldiers hold a village ahead." The lieutenant looked calm, although rivulets of sweat had streaked lighter patches down his smoke-blackened face.

Andrew remembered the village where Thibaw's spy had lived. "Take over the rearguard, Corporal!" he shouted and hurried to the head of the column.

The Burmese had dug low earthworks around the village, and men fired muskets at the Fusiliers. The sun glinted from brass helmets, and a gong sounded ominously in the background.

"They've trapped us," Toshack said. "With a fortified village ahead, skirmishers in the forest and men behind, they've sprung a neat little ambush."

"They have," Andrew agreed. He saw a yellow umbrella in the village and knew a high-ranking officer commanded the Burmese.

THE CHILL OF THE IRRAWADDY

I'd put good money that's Buda Sein.

CHAPTER 29

IRRAWADDY RIVER AND RANGOON,
NOVEMBER 1885

"Dig in," Andrew ordered. "Form a semi-circle and hold our ground."

The Fusiliers obeyed, pulling together and finding cover wherever they could.

The longer we are here, the more reinforcements the Burmans can gather. I might have prevented Thibaw from sinking a ship and killing General Prendergast, but he'll laud the defeat of a British platoon as a significant victory. By the time the foreign propagandists have finished, it will resound like Isandhlwana or Majuba.

"Don't waste ammunition," Sergeant Coslett advised. "Only fire when I say, or you are sure of your target."

Fortunately, recent rains had softened the ground as the Fusiliers used bayonets and hands to dig out shallow shelters in the ground, all the time enduring a constant harassing fire from the Burmese.

"It's lucky they're poor shots, sir," Coslett said.

"Let's hope we are better," Andrew replied, checking his ammunition. He had twenty-four cartridges left.

With the men lying down, replying whenever a Burmese soldier showed himself, Andrew pondered his best move.

"Lieutenant Toshack," he said. "We can't stay here indefinitely. When dark falls, we'll advance against the village."

"Yes, sir," Toshack ducked as a bullet whistled overhead. "What then, sir?"

"We'll play it by ear when we capture the place," Andrew said. "There will be food in the village at least; the men must be getting hungry."

"Yes, sir. I'll pass on the word," Toshack said.

Andrew crawled around the ragged perimeter, trying to ignore the shots that buzzed overhead.

"There's one!" Coslett traversed his rifle to the right and fired. "Got him, I think."

"Good shot, Sergeant!" Andrew did not see the result of Coslett's shot, but a word of encouragement was never wasted. He admired the Fusiliers' fire discipline, for a detachment of Johnny Raws would be blasting away at every movement in the trees, while these Welshmen only fired when they had a definite target.

"How long until dark, sir?" Toshack asked.

Andrew glanced at his watch and swore when he saw it had stopped. *Is it broken? Or did I forget to wind it?* "I'd estimate an hour, Lieutenant."

Toshack glanced at the village, where yellow-white muzzle flares showed where the Burmese were firing. "It's going to be a long hour."

With the Fusiliers lying behind cover, the Burmese shots passed mainly overhead, with the occasional bullet burrowing into the damp path.

"Aim at the smoke and flashes!" Andrew advised. He saw some of the men counting their cartridges. "Don't waste ammunition."

"Sir!" Coslett spun and fired, "Behind you!"

Andrew flinched as the bullet passed so close he felt the wind and heard a yell. He turned to see a score of Burmans rising, dripping from the river.

"Two and Three Sections!" Andrew yelled. "Guard the riverbank!"

Half the Fusiliers faced around to meet this new threat, with some firing and resorting to their rifle butts and a fortunate few having their bayonets fixed. Andrew shot the nearest attacker and then joined Two and Three Sections in a furious battle with bayonet, boot and rifle butt against the Burmese dhas.

As Andrew's men struggled with the riverside attackers, the Burmese in the trees increased their fire.

Andrew pushed a man aside, pressed the muzzle of his revolver against a bare Burmese chest and squeezed the trigger. He smelled scorched flesh, saw the man's mouth and eyes open wide as he toppled backwards and saw a Fusilier thrust a bayonet into another attacker. A Burmese stabbed a Fusilier in the back, another shouted something, and then the skirmish ended.

The surviving Burmese withdrew back into the dark river, leaving a scatter of bodies on the ground and blood on the rushing water.

"Roll call!" Andrew shouted, slipping behind a tree when a bullet whined dangerously close to his head.

Sergeant Coslett called the roll.

"Ryan is dead, sir, and Collins wounded."

Andrew swore. He was losing far too many men on this expedition. The daylight was quickly fading, with long shadows across the river and insects increasing their assaults on the Fusiliers.

I didn't think the Burmese would come by river. Buda Sein is an innovative man. Unless we move soon, he'll think of another strategy to surprise us, and next time, we might not be so fortunate.

"Let's take that village," Andrew ordered. "There's more cover there than here."

Toshack lifted a hand. "Listen, sir! Can you hear that? It's an engine!"

Andrew lifted his head. "Yes, by God! You're right! Is that one of ours? Or a king's steamer?" He listened for a moment. "I can't hear any paddles thumping."

"I'll have a look, sir," Toshack slid backwards into the river, ducked under the bank and swam a few strokes. He returned within five minutes, dripping wet but smiling.

"She's ours, sir! *Kathleen*!"

"She won't see us in the dark," Andrew said as the launch's engines increased in volume. He stood up, and half a dozen Burmese fired, forcing him back down again. "That's a bit of a problem."

"She's slowing down!" Toshack reported and swore. "She's training her guns on us."

"Get down, boys!" Andrew roared. "*Kathleen* is going to fire!"

The Fusiliers tried to dig themselves deeper into the path as *Kathleen* opened up, with her shells exploding around the village and the besieged British.

"She thinks we're Burmese," a Fusilier said.

"Do I look like a bloody Burman?" another Fusilier asked.

"No, you're far too ugly to be Burmese."

Andrew heard the simple black humour of British soldiers hiding their fear as *Kathleen's* guns raked the village and forest, bringing down branches and twigs, knocking chunks from the trees and raising splashes from the river and clods of earth from the path.

"We're on your side!" a Fusilier shouted.

In the forest, the Burmese fired at *Kathleen*, bringing more shots in retaliation.

I've never been under British fire before, Andrew thought. *That's another experience I could do without.*

When the Burmese fire slackened, *Kathleen* concentrated on the village, setting two houses on fire and hammering the fortifications.

"With luck, *Kathleen* will chase the Burmese away," Toshack said.

The firing eased and started again as the Burmese fired a small-calibre artillery piece at the launch.

"Can these men not take a hint?" a Fusilier shouted. "Can't they just bugger off like sensible fellows?"

With his head close to the ground, Andrew did not see the landing party until the seamen were ashore. He heard the voices first.

"McGraw! Take five men to port. Simonds, take five to starboard, and I'll go right up the throat. Come on, *Kathleens*!"

The seamen yelled as they charged forward, with light from the burning buildings reflecting from fixed bayonets and cutlass blades. Andrew heard a scattered crackle as the defenders fired a final few shots and hurriedly withdrew, leaving the bluejackets in command of the village.

"Right, Fusiliers," Andrew stood up. "Let's make our presence known!" He strode forward. "*Kathleens*! Why the devil were you firing at us?"

Midshipman Birnie stared at Andrew. "Where did you spring from? We thought you were dead!"

"Not yet," Andrew replied, "although you did your best to kill us. Could you take us home now? We've had enough of footslogging over Burma."

MARIANA LIFTED HER HAND FROM THE KEYBOARD. "That's all you're getting from me tonight, Stephen. I'm tired."

"You will be, Mariana. Shall I sing you a song?" Jennings asked.

"Yes, please, Stephen," Mariana slid from the piano stool to allow Stephen access. She could feel the friendly warmth of his body close to hers.

"I'll start with a nonsense song," Stephen said, immediately singing in a rich baritone.

"I've seen a deal of gaiety throughout my noisy life,

With all my grand accomplishments, I ne'er could get a wife."

Stephen laughed as he sang, watching Mariana's

reaction to his words. She smiled in response, drank more wine, and enjoyed his gaiety.

"For Champagne Charlie is my name,
Good for any game at night, my boys,
Champagne Charlie is my name."

Mariana shook her head. "I don't believe you are a Champagne Charlie," she said. "I think you are much more than that."

"Why, thank you, kind miss," Stephen said, bowing from the stool. "Here's an old one, and I am sure you'll know the chorus."

"I don't know many popular songs," Mariana did not object as Stephen pulled her closer.

"Mid pleasures and palaces though we may
    roam,
Be it ever so humble, there's no place like
    home!
A charm from the skies seems to hallow us
    there,
Which seek through the world is ne'er met
    elsewhere."

Stephen played the piano like a professional, with his hands dancing across the keys as he smiled at Mariana. "And now the chorus, Mariana, one, two, three..."

Mariana joined in, lifting her voice to words she recognised.

"Home! Home!
Sweet, sweet home!
There's no place like home!
There's no place like home!"

Singing together created a bond, and Mariana laughed as Jennings opened a new bottle of red wine.

"I hope you can think of this house as your home, Mariana," he said. "Rather than your stuffy little room in Wells's Britannia."

Mariana smiled as the wine and the music made her head spin. "I'd like that," she said.

"I hoped you would," Jennings said quietly. "Do you know a song called 'In the Gloaming'? It's quite melancholic."

Mariana shook her head. "I told you I don't know many popular songs."

"I'll sing you the last verse," Jennings said, topping her glass again. He lowered his voice, holding Mariana's gaze.

"In the gloaming, oh my darling,
When the lights are soft and low.
Will you think of me and love me,
As you did once long ago?"

Mariana nodded. "Yes," she whispered. "Yes, I will. I'll always remember this evening."

"Then this house and all inside it is yours, my dear," Stephen said. "Including me. Especially me."

Leaving the stool, he snaked an arm around Mariana's waist, pulled her closer, and kissed her. Mariana returned his kiss and did not object when he pulled her closer.

CHAPTER 30

IRRAWADDY RIVER, NOVEMBER 1885

Andrew put aside his official report and stared at the next sheet of blank paper on his writing pad. He always considered that writing reports was easy: all he had to do was state the facts and stick to a formula. Writing personal letters, on the other hand, entailed thought and effort.

Dear Mariana, he wrote, leaned back in the tiny cabin, and chewed the end of his pen. *What can I say to her? I doubt she'd be interested in news of the campaign.* He looked out of the porthole for inspiration, saw only the surging river, sighed, and returned to chewing the pen.

What do I want to say? I want her to reconsider her

refusal. How the devil do I phrase that?

He looked out of the porthole again and saw *Thambyadine*, the vessel that held General Prendergast, steering erratically past them.

Somebody will get it in the neck for that.

He saw the boat approaching *Kathleen* and, a few moments later, heard the tap on his cabin door.

"Sorry, Baird," Birnie said cheerfully. "That's a message from General Whatshisname asking if your report is ready yet."

"I'll be a couple of minutes," Andrew replied.

"Best make them very short minutes," Birnie said. "*Thambyadine's* boat is alongside to take you to the general."

Andrew sighed, glanced at his letter to Mariana, lifted his report, and followed Birnie onto the deck. "Take me to General Prendergast," he said, stepping into the small boat.

Prendergast nodded to Andrew. "I heard you had a little skirmish with the enemy, Baird."

"Yes, sir. The Welsh Fusiliers did splendidly, and the Navy chased away the enemy." Andrew produced his written report. "It's all in there, sir."

Prendergast glanced at the document and placed it on his desk. "Thank you, Captain. I'll read it later. I believe you were once recommended for the Victoria Cross."

"Yes, sir, in Zululand," Andrew said.

"By whom?"

"Redvers Buller, sir," Andrew said.

Prendergast finger-groomed his beard. "Ah, Redvers Buller, a rising star and one of the Wolseley Ring."

"I believe so, sir," Andrew agreed.

"Why was his recommendation not approved?" Prendergast asked.

"I never heard, sir," Andrew said.

They stood in the general's study in the stern of *Thambyadine* with the great paddles thumping through the river and the troops crowding the flats. Andrew saw the hospital ship nearby, with the awnings sheltering the sick.

Why has Thambyadine chosen a different route from the rest of the fleet?

Andrew stepped to the window and stared forward.

"Which channel are we taking, sir?"

"I leave that to the captain, Baird. He follows the pilot's instructions." Prendergast sounded amused. "You've blown up the trap, Captain, so why do you ask?"

"The flotilla has been steaming line astern since we left Rangoon, sir, but now *Thambyadine* is steering a different course to the rest," Andrew said. "Could I have your permission to speak to the captain?"

"By all means," Prendergast said. "I'll come with you." They left the cabin together, with the staff officers perplexed that a general should speak to a mere captain from a colonial regiment.

Thambyadine's captain looked surprised when Prendergast and Andrew arrived at his side. "What's the trouble, General?"

Andrew did not waste time on politeness. He pointed to the smiling Burmese pilot. "That's not the usual pilot," he said. "Where's the usual pilot?"

"He's got a touch of fever," the captain explained. "This fellow took his place."

"This fellow is piloting you into the shallows," Andrew said. Reaching forward, he grabbed the pilot's shoulder and hauled him back. "What's your game, chum?"

As the man wriggled free, Andrew saw the tattoo on the nape of his neck. "That's the mark of the king's soldiers, Captain. This man is a spy!"

The pilot slid away and ran for the rail, with Andrew following. "Stop that man!" He unfastened his holster and hauled out his revolver. As the man poised on the rail and jumped into the river, Andrew fired three shots, seeing the splashes where the bullets landed. Soldiers on the flats a hundred yards away stared at them, wondering what was happening.

"I think you got him," Prendergast said. "He hasn't surfaced."

"These fellows swim like Tweed salmon," Andrew pointed out. "He's like as not doubled back and swum to the other bank."

The captain grunted. "Slow to quarter speed. Steer us behind the leading ship, helmsman; we'll follow the leader until we can find a trustworthy pilot."

Andrew nodded to *Little Salamander.* "I would recommend the master of that launch, sir. Captain Jamieson is an ex-Royal Navy man who has been plying these waters since the 1850s."

The captain stiffened his back. "I am master of *Thambyadine*, Captain Baird. I will not take orders from some ex-able seaman in a launch."

"Yes, sir," Andrew stepped back. "If you gentlemen will excuse me, I'll return to *Kathleen.*"

I've done my bit here. The captain can choose his pilot.

MARIANA DRESSED SLOWLY, AWARE THAT STEPHEN was sitting up in bed, watching her. She was not sure how she felt. Empty, perhaps; certainly not how she thought she should feel. The memories returned, hammering at her mind, tearing at her with their horror.

"I'd better get back to the hotel," she said.

Jennings slid from the bed without hiding his nakedness. Mariana looked away, not wanting to see any more.

"I'll get the coach ready," Jennings said, patting her bottom as he passed.

Mariana pulled away. "Thank you." She dressed hurriedly, averting her eyes as Stephen leisurely pulled on his clothes.

"You can stay the night if you wish," Jennings said.

Mariana shook her head. "No. No, thank you. I'd better get back." She was suddenly desperate to return to the hotel, to have familiar things around her and analyse what had happened.

"I'll see you tomorrow," Jennings said.

Mariana nodded, only wanting to be alone with her revived memories. She fought the tears that welled at the back of her eyes.

Oh, God, did that happen? I knew I could never marry Andrew.

"What's that?" the lookout shouted. "There's something in the water ahead, sir."

"Quarter speed," Lieutenant Trench ordered. "I see it."

Kathleen eased forward, barely making way against the force of the current. "What the devil is that?"

"It's a human head, Captain," Andrew focussed his field glasses on the object. "It's a human head on a stake." He swept his gaze across the river. "There are more of them, sir."

Kathleen slowed as Lieutenant Trench saw a line of human heads across the river, each thrust on the end of a pointed stake.

"Who the hell are these people?" Birnie asked.

"I don't know the answer," Andrew replied.

"Remove them," Trench ordered. "Birnie, take a boat out and lift these heads. I don't know who the poor devils were, but they deserve better than this." He glanced behind him. "Whatever you do, don't let the Press get hold of this horror. Keep it within *Kathleen*, or the journalists will have everyone howling for Burmese blood. Any Burmese blood."

"I knew some of these men, sir," Andrew said as he studied the disembodied heads. "That gentleman is named Harding, and that fellow is Marmaduke Patchley." Andrew could hear Patchley's voice proclaiming his Englishness. "The other men, I don't know." Patchley and Harding were the only Europeans on the stakes. The others were indigenous Burmese, victims of a war they had never sought nor could ever profit from, whatever the outcome.

"Bury them all," Trench said. "Whoever they were."

Andrew returned to his cabin and remembered his barely started letter for Mariana. He thought of Harding's kindness, Patchley's ignorant arrogance, and the unknown Burmese whom somebody had killed to intimidate the invaders.

War is the greatest obscenity mankind has created. It spawns every kind of evil under the excuse of defending one state or ruler against another.

Andrew sighed and returned to his letter.

WHEN MARIANA REACHED THE LANDING HALFWAY down the hotel stairs, she saw the Burmese woman standing in the foyer. She felt her heartbeat increase.

What's she doing here? Has she come to gloat that she captured my man? What should I do?

Mariana looked around for support, but the foyer was deserted except for the receptionist. Even Myat Lay Phyu was absent. Mariana steeled herself, straightened her back and approached the woman.

"Miss Maxwell," Than Than Aye said, stepping forward.

"Yes," Mariana said coldly. She held Than Than Aye's gaze, hoping to intimidate her.

Than Than Aye did not lower her eyes. "We have things to talk about."

"I can't think of anything we have to say," Mariana would have swept past if Than Than Aye had not moved into her path.

"We have to talk about Captain Andrew Baird," Than Than Aye said.

Mariana stiffened. "What about Captain Baird?"

"We have to talk about him," Than Than Aye said. "Please sit down, Miss Maxwell."

About to refuse, Mariana saw that Myat Lay Phyu had returned to her customary place at the pillar. Myat Lay Phyu nodded once and indicated a chair.

"If we must," Mariana said. She sat down, smoothing her skirt under her and keeping her back straight. "Speak."

"You are wondering who I am," Than Than Aye said. "And you think I propose stealing Captain Baird away from you."

"Is that what I am thinking?" Mariana asked coldly. "I do not believe I have made you privy to my thoughts."

"Your actions make your thoughts clear," Than Than Aye said. "Let me say you have nothing to fear from me."

Mariana was about to leave when she saw Myat Lay Phyu shake her head. "What should I have to fear from you? I do not even know who you are."

"I am Than Than Aye, Bo Thura's daughter and Andrew's cousin," Than Than Aye said.

"Oh," Mariana tried to hide her surprise.

Than Than Aye smiled, "Andrew and I are related by blood," she emphasised. "That is all."

Mariana felt the colour flood her face. "Then you

are not," she searched for the word. "Intimate. You are not together."

"Not in the way you imagined," Than Than Aye said.

"Oh," Mariana said again. "I thought."

"You thought what Stephen Jennings led you to think," Than Than Aye said.

"Stephen is a good man," Mariana said, unsure of her words. "He cares for me."

"Come with me," Than Than Aye said, "and I will show you what your good friend Stephen Jennings is really like."

When Mariana looked up, Myat Lay Phyu nodded once, and Mariana wondered if there was anything that enigmatic woman did not understand.

Mariana and Than Than Aye left the hotel together, and Than Than Aye signalled for a pair of rickshaws. She gave rapid instructions to the runners, told Mariana to sit back and took her place as elegantly as any sovereign. The runners pulled their rickshaws effortlessly through the streets, avoiding the bullock carts until they pulled up close to Jennings' house.

"We'll walk the rest," Than Than Aye said. "Come along, Miss Maxwell."

Mariana followed as Than Than Aye stalked through the mansions that filled this quarter of Rangoon. They stopped opposite Jennings' house, with bright birds singing from the trees and a couple of carriages grumbling past.

"Why are we here?" Mariana asked.

"Wait, and you'll see," Than Than Aye said.

Mariana did not have long to wait. Within ten minutes, Jennings' Brougham coach rolled to his house, and the servant opened the door. Jennings stepped out with a European woman at his side. Mariana watched as Jennings offered the woman his arm.

"Oh!" Mariana said. "Perhaps that lady is Stephen's sister."

"That is a very thin straw to support her weight," Than Than Aye said. She led Mariana across the road. "He won't see you," Than Than Aye promised. "He's too engrossed in his new attraction, and she is too stupid to care. Now listen to their conversation."

Jennings was talking, holding the woman's hands. "When I first met you," he said. "I thought you were just one of the fishing fleet, but now I can tell that you are something special. You are like no woman I have ever met before."

"Oh, the cad!" Mariana said, surprised. "He said those exact words to me."

"And to every other girl he attempts to seduce, I expect," Than Than Aye said. "You were not his first."

Mariana nodded. She had too many emotions running through her to speak.

"Do you wish to see more?" Than Than Aye put a small hand on Mariana's sleeve.

Mariana clung to her slender hope. "Yes," she said and lifted her chin defiantly.

Than Than Aye touched her arm, "Then I'll show you," she said. "Come with me."

"Where are we going?"

"You'll see." Than Than Aye led Mariana round the back of the neighbouring house and spoke to one of the servants. Mariana could not understand the conversation but saw Than Than Aye press something in the servant's hand.

What's happening? I wish I knew what was happening.

"This way, Miss Maxwell," Than Than Aye said, beckoning her to the back door. "Inside!"

"Should we? What if the owner comes?"

"This is the servant's area. The owner is far too important to come here," Than Than Aye explained. "Come on, Miss Maxwell."

The door led to a wooden staircase, which Than Than Aye rapidly mounted, with Mariana following. They stopped on the upper floor and pushed into a sparsely furnished room with a window facing Jennings' house.

"This will do," Than Than Aye said. "Stand at the window, Miss Maxwell, and tell me what you see."

"Stephen's house," Mariana said. She looked

downward, where Stephen's large windows allowed her to see the dining room. The circular table was set as it had been for her initial visit, and Jennings sat opposite the woman who looked more composed than Mariana had felt in that situation.

"Who is she?" Mariana asked.

"His latest conquest," Than Than Aye replied. "Her name is Ellen Ambrose, the younger daughter of Edward Ambrose of Edward Ambrose and Company."

"How do you know that?" Mariana asked.

"I make it my business to know things," Than Than Aye replied.

"They're drinking my champagne!" Mariana said indignantly.

"Your champagne?" Than Than Aye asked.

Mariana nodded. "Yes. Stephen bought half a dozen bottles of champagne just for me."

Than Than Aye shook her head. "No, Mariana. Stephen is the biggest wine and spirit importer in Rangoon. Jennings and Stanley buy champagne by the dozens of crates."

"Oh." Mariana watched Ellen Ambrose finish her glass and accept another, with Stephen drinking half as much and pouring most of the contents of his glass into one of the plant pots beside the table. "I wondered how Stephen finished his glass so quickly."

"Do you want to see any more?" Than Than Aye asked.

"Yes," Mariana replied. She knew it would hurt her, but she had to discover the truth. She felt Than Than Aye standing behind her as she waited, guessing what would happen. After half an hour, Stephen stood and extended a hand.

Ellen Ambrose took his hand and followed him upstairs. Mariana watched as they entered Stephen's bedroom.

"Oh, Lord," Mariana said as Stephen expertly undressed Ellen Ambrose. "Was he ever married?"

"Not to my knowledge," Than Than Aye said.

"No special island trips with his wife, then," Mariana turned away as Stephen shrugged off his clothes.

"No, but he does own a small house on an island. His own little love nest," Than Than Aye said. "He likes the hunt, and when he has made the kill, the bedding, he loses interest and moves to his next prey. You were a difficult target, while Ellen Ambrose was an easy conquest."

"I think I have seen sufficient," Mariana said.

Than Than Aye glanced out of the window, "I don't think I want to see any more of Stephen Jennings either. I can see more than enough from this angle."

Mariana agreed. The rear view of Jennings as he seduced Ellen Ambrose was less than appealing.

"Take me back to the hotel, please," Mariana said.

She felt Than Than Aye's unspoken sympathy as they walked silently through the streets and to her usual seat in the foyer under the friendly shade of a potted palm. Myat Lay Phyu watched from beside the pillar, somehow reassuring in her silence.

"Are you all right?" Than Than Aye asked.

Mariana shook her head. "Oh, God," she put a hand to her mouth. "I've ruined everything," she whispered. "Poor Andrew."

Than Than Aye did not talk for a few moments, "That may be so," she said eventually. "That is something you must discuss with Captain Andrew."

"Oh, God," Mariana repeated.

"Stephen Jennings led you astray," Than Than Aye said, "but it is not too late to put things right."

"It is," Mariana said. "You don't understand, Than Than Aye. In our culture, a woman must be pure, untouched before her wedding day."

Mariana saw the faces leering down at her, gloating, blood-splashed, laughing, cruelly callous. She shook away the images, unable to accept them.

Than Than Aye put a hand on Mariana's sleeve. "I doubt Captain Andrew has been a monk these past few years," she said dryly. "He knows the way of the world and will understand when you explain things to him."

"I can't tell him!" Mariana shook her head. "He will hate me forever."

Than Than Aye smiled. "He will not. You must trust him, Mariana."

"How can he trust me?" Mariana asked miserably. "After what I have done."

"Did you trust Stephen?"

"Yes," Mariana replied.

"Why?"

"I thought he loved me."

"Andrew loves you," Than Than Aye reminded. "He'll trust you."

"I don't deserve his trust," Mariana said.

"Oh, stuff and nonsense!" Than Than Aye scolded. "You are a red-blooded woman, that's all. If you want Andrew back, you must claim him and ensure you keep him. Feeling sorry for yourself doesn't help, and neither does brooding over the past."

"You sound like my sister," Mariana told her ruefully.

Than Than Aye laughed. "Good! If I were your sister, I'd give you a slap. Now straighten your back, look the world in the eye and let your man chase you until you decide to catch him."

Mariana smiled at the idea of holding a large net to ensnare Andrew.

"That's better," Than Than Aye said. "Now, let's see what's best to do."

Mariana felt fresh hope as she looked at Than

Than Aye, with Myat Lay Phyu listening to every word. Myat Lay Phyu held Mariana's gaze and nodded approval.

There's more, Mariana reminded herself. *There's a lot more that I can't tell them and can never tell Andrew. He will never want me if I tell him everything.*

CHAPTER 31

IRRAWADDY RIVER, NOVEMBER 1885

Andrew stood in *Kathleen's* bows as she floated at anchor in front of the flotilla, with the Irrawaddy chuckling under her counter and birds singing above. He raised his binoculars to peer forward.

I am the foremost man in the leading vessel in the flotilla. That means that at this minute, on the 24th of November 1885, I am the most forward British soldier in Burma. How do I feel?

Empty.

I wish I had made peace with Mariana before we left Rangoon. Compared to that, Upper Burma is unimportant.

"Weigh anchors!" The call sounded from astern, bellowed by some brass-lunged naval officer.

"Weigh anchors! Quarter speed ahead!" Lieutenant Trench echoed the call, and *Kathleen's* hands rushed to obey.

Andrew constantly admired the efficiency of the flotilla and the associated Royal Navy ships as they pushed forward against the strong current. The vessels always seemed to maintain their position despite the skirmishes with the Burmese, the state of the channel or the sudden torrential rain.

Kathleen edged in front, marginally ahead of *Irrawaddy*, as Trench followed the deep-water channel, constantly consulting with the pilot.

They passed several small villages, each with a quota of fishing boats on the river. The inhabitants clustered at the water's edge to watch them pass, with one or two waving without a single hostile action.

"There's another village ahead," the lookout called. "It's larger than the last few."

"That should be Kaoung-Wah," Andrew consulted his map just as he heard the bang of artillery and saw a sudden column of water rise a hundred yards in front.

"Somebody doesn't like visitors!" a rating shouted.

Andrew raised his field glasses to trace the origin of the shot. "There's a stockade outside the village," he reported. "It looks like it's only timber and newly made."

"Hold your fire," Lieutenant Trench said as the seamen on the forward gun looked hopeful. A moment later, one of the gun barges beside *Ngawoon* opened fire, with shells exploding over and inside the stockade.

"Good shooting!" Andrew said. He saw the white smoke drift from above the now shattered timber.

"Signal from *Irrawaddy*, sir," an eager rating reported to Lieutenant Trench. "Proceed forward and see if the Burmans still occupy the stockade."

"On we go, men!" Trench shouted. "Half speed ahead and watch for any gunfire!"

Kathleen's crew were in high spirits as the launch powered forward, with the helmsman weaving slightly to disrupt any enemy gunner's aim.

"They're not firing!" the lookout shouted.

"I want a landing party to check what's happening!" In a vessel as small as *Kathleen*, there was no need even to shout, but Trench bellowed every word as if he were on the bridge of a battleship. "Six men! Captain Baird, will you lead it?"

Andrew knew Trench was master in the vessel. "Aye, aye, sir!" he replied, much to the ratings' amusement.

"We'll make a seaman out of the soldier yet," a rating observed.

"We'll have to go to sea for that," the bearded petty officer replied.

"A riverman, then."

The petty officer glanced at Andrew. "He's halfway there already."

When *Kathleen* pulled close inshore, Andrew jumped into the shallows and led his six volunteers up a steep incline to the stockade. "Extended order!" He shouted and remembered he commanded seamen and not trained soldiers. "That means spread out, lads!"

Andrew zig-zagged in front of the landing party, watching the timber stockade ahead for bobbing heads and the spurting, darting flames of musketry. Instead, he saw nothing. He reached the log wall with the landing party a few steps behind him. As Andrew looked up at the nine-foot high wall, one of the sailors threw himself up, with the others following, more dexterous than soldiers. Andrew swore and dragged himself over the pointed logs to find the interior bare and deserted, with a single dismounted gun.

The sailors drew their cutlasses and checked every corner.

"Nobody here, sir!" they reported. "The place is as empty as a public[1] house on a Sunday afternoon."

"Back to the ship," Andrew ordered. He reported his findings, and *Kathleen* was already heading north when a body of infantry and engineers landed to destroy the stockade. The explosion echoed

---

1. A Public – a public house, a pub.

across the Irrawaddy as wood splinters rose and descended into the river.

"That's another nail in Thibaw's teak coffin," Birnie said as *Kathleen* steamed on, battling against the current as they probed deeper into the Kingdom of Ava.

At quarter past four that day, the lookout shouted another warning. "Burman soldiers ahead!"

Andrew lifted his field glasses. He saw movement on the high ground behind the village of Mingyan, with the sun reflecting from the brass helmets of royal soldiers.

"I'd say at least two hundred infantrymen," Andrew reported. "With earthworks lower down, close to the river." He scanned the area. Around and behind the earthworks, fields of grain mingled among acres of long waving grass.

Earthworks are a sure indicator that the Burmese intend to place artillery here. Once again, General Prendergast's rapid advance has caught Thibaw by surprise.

When *Kathleen* passed the information on, Prendergast sent her ahead, together with *Irrawaddy* and *White Swan*. Andrew saw the Royal Artillerymen on *White Swan* preparing for action.

"General Prendergast has ordered us to engage the enemy," Birnie said. "I hope they make a proper fight of it this time and don't cut and run."

"You bloodthirsty thing," Andrew replied.

Birnie laughed and pointed astern. "Look! Here's *Yunan* and *Ataran* coming to join us!"

Yunan was a 396-ton paddle launch, while *Ataran* was a twin-screw 140-tonner, both belonging to the Irrawaddy Flotilla Company. When a gun barge also steamed up, the British opened fire on the Burmese positions.

Andrew saw the seamen were eager to fight, loading and firing with a speed that the Royal Artillery would envy. As the gunners fired, the ships steamed forward, inching slowly against the current.

"There's another earthwork!" Andrew saw the turned-up earth and flattened grass where men had dragged a wheeled gun to its position. The Burmese waited until the British vessels were close before firing, with shells whistling overhead or falling short to churn up the Irrawaddy water.

"They're game!" Birnie shouted as if he enjoyed being under fire.

"Alter your target to that fellow, gunners," Trench ordered. He gave more precise orders, and the naval gunners returned fire.

As well as artillery, the Burmese attacked with musketry, so rifle bullets buzzed and hummed like a host of hornets, rattling against the metalwork and splintering the woodwork of the British vessels.

"This is more like it!" Birnie shouted. "Well done, Thibaw! Fight on, Burmese soldiers!"

As the ships pushed upriver, they silenced battery after battery, blowing up the earthworks and sending the Burmese riflemen running into the tall grass for the Nordenfeldts to hammer.

"We're near the village now," Birnie shouted. "It's more like a town, though."

Andrew lifted his field glasses from the latest battery to study Mingyan. "They're going to make a stand there," he said. "They have proper earthworks and larger calibre artillery."

The Burmans opened fire as the British flotilla came near, with one shell exploding in the air near *Kathleen* and spreading splinters across the launch.

"Good shot!" Birnie shouted. "Come on now, *Kathleens*! Show them what the Navy can do."

The firing was evenly matched, with the Burmese having the advantage of a stable battery while the ships had larger calibre guns. A host of riflemen supported the Burmans' battery, with bullets whistling around the ships' gun crews as smoke formed a greasy white cloud that hugged the water.

"They're making a fight of it," Birnie said as he commanded the forward gun. "Good show."

Andrew borrowed a Martini-Henry and fired whenever he had a clear target, which was not often among the gunsmoke.

The bluejackets wiped sweat off their foreheads, gulped down a mouthful of water and worked on loading and firing. Clouds of dust and dirt concealed the Burmese earthworks, split only by the flares of the Burmese artillery.

Around six in the evening, the Burmese fire eased.

"We've broken them!" Birnie said. "They put up a decent show, though."

"Somebody's still resisting," Andrew said, as a solitary Burmese rifleman fired, with the bullet zipping across the surface of the river.

Night fell swiftly, with the Burmese firing an occasional shot and the British retaliating with short bursts from the Nordenfeldts, so the flash and flare of gunshots lit up the river, the village, and the surrounding fields.

Shortly before dawn, Andrew saw a company of infantry land beneath the earthwork and march over the churned-up ground. They blew up the guns without the Burmese resisting, scouted the area, and returned to the ships at noon. A platoon remained behind to prevent the Burmese from returning.

"That was a smart little action," Birnie said with satisfaction. "By Jove, if the Burmans fight like that at Mandalay, I'll have something to tell the grandchildren, won't I just?"

"Do you have grandchildren, Birnie?" Andrew asked.

"Steady on," Birnie replied. "I haven't found a wife yet."

Andrew smiled. "Good luck. I'm sure plenty of women would love a man like you."

That evening, the flotilla anchored off Yandabo, still with *Kathleen* in the van and the rest forming a long line of ships. Andrew noticed more sick men under the awnings as the mosquitoes began their evening assaults.

"Yandabo is where we signed the treaty that ended the First Burmese War," Birnie said. "That was back in 1826, nearly sixty years ago, and we're still fighting them. Hopefully, this campaign will end any further hostilities. I don't like fighting in forests. Give me a broad horizon any time."

Andrew nodded. "I prefer the open spaces, too."

Let's end this river war so I can return to Mariana. I wonder when she'll get my letter? I hope she writes back.

CHAPTER 32

IRRAWADDY RIVER, NOVEMBER 1885

Jennings saw the letter lying on its silver tray as he stood at reception. "Is that for Miss Maxwell?" he asked.

The receptionist smiled and bowed. "Yes," she said. "That's for Miss Maxwell."

"I'll take it to her," Jennings said.

"Yes, sir," the receptionist handed it over.

Jennings slid the letter inside his jacket. *I'll burn that later,* he thought.

THE EXPEDITIONARY FORCE ANCHORED OFF PAGAN without further opposition, despite rumours of a formidable Burmese Army gathering to defend the capital.

Elsewhere, dacoits were causing trouble around the frontier, with the British flying columns hunting them. The British plan was for the expeditionary force up the Irrawaddy to reach Mandalay simultaneously with a land-based Tounghoo brigade on the first of December.

"Catch them in a pincer movement, eh?" Birnie remarked.

"That's the plan," Andrew agreed.

Kathleen moved off again, probing cautiously northward with the river bisecting Thibaw's hostile territory.

"There's an object ahead, sir," the lookout reported. "I can't see what it is."

"Half speed ahead!" Trench ordered. "All hands stand by with grappling hooks and boathooks. Be careful of any tricks!"

Andrew moved to the starboard bow, holding an unfamiliar boathook, a long pole with a brass hook on the end, in his hands. "It's a large flat!" he shouted. "The Burmese might have filled her with explosives or some other devilment."

"Keep your gun trained on her, Birnie," Trench ordered. "There could be hundreds of Thibaw's soldiers waiting to board us!"

A lithe sailor scrambled to the highest point of the launch. "She's deserted and drifting, sir. Nobody on board that I can see."

"Grapple her!" Trench ordered, and expert hands threw grappling hooks over the surging water. The seamen fastened her to *Kathleen*'s stern and towed her away from the deep-water channel.

"Anchor her beside the bank," Trench ordered. "She's no danger to shipping there. Send a message to Captain Clutterbuck that the passage is clear."

An hour later, Andrew heard paddles thumping behind them as the British fleet moved again on their remorseless journey towards Mandalay.

"More boats, sir!" the lookout shouted as the Burmese pilot guided them along the deep-water channel.

"Birnie: take a boarding party and see what these boats are," Trench shouted.

"Aye, aye, sir!" Birnie called on six men who rowed towards the boats and inspected them individually. "Stones, sir! Each boat has a cargo of heavy stones but no crew."

"Thibaw was probably going to sink these in the channel," Trench said. "Cut them adrift, scupper them, and shove them in the shallows."

The sailors worked happily, pushing the boats clear of the fleet's passage and cheering when each one spun downstream, slowly sinking.

"That's another in the eye for Thibaw!"

"That's the way, Tom! Show the King of Ava what we think of him!"

"*Kathleen* forever!"

With the passage cleared, *Kathleen* led the flotilla upstream, with men waiting at the guns and a man in the bow, casting the lead in case the pilot proved unreliable. After Andrew's discovery of the king's soldier acting as a pilot on *Thambyadine*, the seamen were wary of the Burmese pilots.

At four in the afternoon, with the sun reflecting from the rippling water, the lookout shouted again.

"There's a rowing boat ahead, sir! A big one, flying a flag! With an armed steamer as an escort! It's not a British flag, sir."

Andrew lifted his field glasses and joined the officers with their telescopes.

"She looks like a galley," Birnie said. "A high-prowed rowing boat from the *Odyssey*."

"She's a state barge," Andrew stated. "I saw her in the moat at Mandalay."

Birnie whistled. "A state barge, is she? By Jove, that's a royal boat, I'll be bound. And she's wearing a white flag. Is it a flag of truce? Or is she surrendering?" He shifted his telescope. "It's that armed steamer that bothers me. Is she going to fight?"

"We'll see in a moment," Trench said. "Stand by the guns, men, and have a reception party ready in case it's the king himself." He closed his telescope with a snap. "Take us alongside, helmsman. Mr Birnie! Have a party ready with a line."

"Aye, aye, sir," Birnie replied.

"Which ship is General Prendergast on today?" Trench asked.

"*Thurreah*, sir," Birnie replied.

"We'll tow the state barge to *Thurreah* and let the general look after them. Baird, could you take Petty Officer McGraw and board the steamer? We'll have our guns trained on them in case anybody gives you any trouble."

"Aye, aye, sir," Andrew replied, knowing a soldier using nautical terminology always amused the sailors. McGraw was the sturdy, phlegmatic petty officer with the neat red beard.

"This way, sir," McGraw said, leading Andrew into a small boat. He tapped the cutlass at his belt and the Martini in his hand. "We might have to fight them, sir. Do you have a weapon?"

"I have a revolver," Andrew said.

It seemed foolhardy, boarding an enemy craft crowded with men with only a handful of bluejackets, but the seamen accepted the situation.

"We're British sailors," one man said with a gap-toothed grin. He pulled at his oars. "We're the Senior Service, old Britannia's first line of defence, the heirs of Nelson."

"We're the bloody Andrew," McGraw said. "Stop gabbing and get on with your duty, Brierly!"[1]

---

1. The Andrew: according to folklore, in the early 19th century, an impressment officer named Andrew Miller pressed so many

456

Andrew nodded as McGraw hooked onto the steamer and swung on board without waiting for Andrew, who followed a second later.

The Burmese crewmen stepped aside as Andrew sent McGraw to the wheelhouse to take charge of the boat. The other seamen commandeered the guns, moving the Burmese gently away without any resistance.

"It's all right, sir," McGraw said quietly. "We'll look after the ship. You look after the officers."

Andrew nodded. "That's what I'll do," he said, watching a party of bluejackets leap onto the royal barge with a line. "We're taking you in tow, lads," a grinning seaman told the confused Burmese seamen. "You're going to see our general."

The Burmese stepped back, allowing the bluejackets to tie up their craft.

"Take her easy," Trench ordered, and Kathleen eased back to the main fleet with her screw churning up the water. Andrew watched the two vessels, one an example of the most modern maritime technology and the other a boat whose design had probably not altered for a thousand years, and wondered at the juxtaposition of East and West.

Kathleen brought the barge to *Thurreah*, and a body of King Thibaw's officials boarded the British

---

seamen that some seamen claimed he owned the navy. Many seamen called the Navy "The Andrew" in Miller's honour.

ship, looking about them as the bluejackets mounted a guard of honour with Martini-Henry rifles and shining cutlasses.

As the general met the officials, Captain Clutterbuck sent a detachment of sailors to the Burmese steamer.

"We'll take over now, sir," the young midshipman in charge looked only slightly surprised to see Andrew on the steamer.

"Thank you," Andrew returned to *Kathleen* with his men. McGraw chewed a wad of tobacco as though capturing an enemy ship with a handful of men was an everyday occurrence.

In the Royal Navy, Andrew thought, *it might well be an everyday occurrence.*

Kathleen waited alongside *Thurreah* as the Burmese officials handed over a letter from Kinwin Mingyi, Thibaw's chief minister, to General Prendergast.

"Either Thibaw is surrendering, or he's threatening to invade Britain and kidnap the queen," Birnie said.

"Maybe it's a proposal of marriage," Andrew suggested. "Thibaw already has a couple of wives. Perhaps he wants to add Queen Victoria to his collection."

"Good Lord! Do you think so?" Lieutenant Trench shook his head. "One wife is quite enough for anybody. Look! Thibaw's officials are returning!"

The officers on *Kathleen* waited for news while the men polished the brasswork, exercised the guns and sweltered in the heat. After an hour, Trench sent Birnie to *Thurreah* to find out what was happening.

Birnie returned in twenty minutes, grinning as he bounced back on board. "Thibaw is looking for a truce, sir," he reported, "but General Prendergast said he'd only stop fighting if Thibaw surrendered himself, his army and Mandalay."

"That's pretty unequivocal," Andrew said.

"Compared to what Thibaw did to his rivals and relatives, we are very generous," Birnie said. "The general promised to respect the lives and property of the king and his family, on one condition."

"What's the condition?" Andrew asked.

"The Europeans in Mandalay should be unharmed," Birnie replied.

"Let's hope they are," Andrew said. Like all his generation, he had heard of the massacre of British civilians in Cawnpore during the Indian Mutiny and the terrible repercussions that followed.

"Signal from Captain Clutterbuck!" Trench said. "We're moving again!"

Once again, *Kathleen* and *Irrawaddy* eased forward with the British fleet following deeper into Upper Burma. That night, as the sun sank in glorious orange-red, the flotilla cast anchor only seven miles south of Ava, the old capital of Burma.

"It's been a busy day," Andrew said. "Let's hope for success tomorrow."

Tomorrow is the crucial day. Thibaw will either decide to fight or the war will be over.

MARIANA SAT ON HER BED WITH THE FAN SLOWLY rotating above her head and a bird calling outside.

What have I done? Have I awakened myself to a new life or completely ruined the old one? What would Elaine say?

Mariana lay back slowly with her hands folded behind her head.

I can't tell Andrew what happened. He'll be devastated after all he's done for me over the years. If I tell him and beg forgiveness, he'll always think he is my second choice, as I do with him and Elaine. Then there is the other thing: how can I face Andrew after that? I can't tell him. Oh, God, what a mess!

Mariana felt tears form in her eyes and thought of her past, from the happy days in Inglenook on the Natal-Zululand border to the terrible time when the renegades murdered her family and kidnapped her. Andrew had rescued her and had cared for her during the long years when she recovered from the trauma. Andrew had brought her into his life and proposed marriage when he considered her sufficiently fit.

Oh, God, what a fool I have been. Andrew!

It's too late now. I have ruined my life. Is there any point in carrying on? Should I end it now?

"I CAN SEE SOLDIERS ON AVA'S RAMPARTS," BIRNIE said, with his telescope pressed against his right eye.

Andrew nodded. "I see them," he said. "The sun reflects on their brass helmets."

"The Burmese have sunk a dozen boats and other assorted rubbish on the approaches to the fort," Birnie reported. "Their soldiers could make things difficult for us if they choose to oppose our landing. I would not enjoy being in a small stationary boat, under Burmese artillery and rifle fire."

Andrew nodded. "That would be unpleasant," he agreed.

Behind them, the British fleet lay at anchor in a long line of steamers and flats, with the khaki-clad troops stirring to the calls of various bugles.

"Sir!" Petty Officer McGraw approached Andrew. "You're wanted on the flagship, sir. General Prendergast has summoned all the British officers of the rank of captain and above."

"Thank you, McGraw," Andrew replied.

What's happening now?

With no room in his cabin, Prendergast addressed his officers on the deck, with the water lapping at the hull and a flight of parrots wheeling and screeching overhead.

"Mandalay is the capital and king's residence of Upper Burma," General Prendergast said, "but Ava is the heart and soul of the country. That's why Thibaw is called the King of Ava. By the look of the Burmese garrison, it looks as if we might have to storm the defences."

The officers nodded, with many glancing at the fort, assessing the difficulties and possible casualties.

"We'll start with a naval bombardment," Prendergast said. "With all the ships in the fleet present, that should be quite sufficient to soften them up. We'll clear the obstructions when the barrage keeps them occupied, land the troops, and follow with a direct assault before the defenders recover."

"Who will make the attack, sir?"

"We'll send... what the devil?" Prendergast looked up as a naval lieutenant appeared with a slip of paper.

"Sorry to interrupt, sir," the lieutenant said with a hurried salute. "There's a Burmese vessel approaching with a flag of truce."

"Another one?" Prendergast said. "Why don't they just invite themselves in for tea."

The lieutenant smiled. "Perhaps they will, sir. There's also a message addressed to you, sir."

"I see," Prendergast took the message, tore it open and read the contents. He looked up. "Gentlemen, it appears that we won't have to take Ava by assault after all. King Thibaw has decided to surrender."

Andrew joined in the general cheer and mutual handshaking, although he felt more relief than elation.

As soon as I am free from this campaign, I'll push Sir Charles for Bo Thura's pardon, bring him to safety and return to Mariana. Maybe this time, she will accept my proposal, or perhaps she wishes to make her way in the world without me.

Prendergast boarded a small boat for the steamer *Palow*, where Captain Woodward ruled supreme, and sailed to the fort. Andrew saw the king's soldiers remaining on the battlements and hoped the Burmese had not planned any trickery.

As the general entered the fort, the fleet sailed a short distance north and anchored opposite Ava. As one of the smaller vessels, *Kathleen* probed at the sunken boats and stakes to find the best channel ashore.

"Aye, aye," Birnie jerked a thumb downstream. "Here comes the admiral. The fighting must be over right enough for the bigwigs to arrive."

Andrew saw the Irrawaddy Company paddle steamer *Palu* sail up to the fleet and cast her anchor. Rear-Admiral Sir Frederick Richards, the Naval Commander-in-Chief, boarded a small boat to *Palow*, where Prendergast had returned.

"Things are happening," Birnie said.

"It seems we're not involved," Andrew replied.

Birnie smiled. "No; we're only good for the fighting and the dirty jobs. The admirals have the champagne and the glamour."

"They're welcome to it," Andrew watched through his field glasses as regimental officers marched smartly to their troops, who filed into small boats for the bluejackets to row them ashore. When the vessels manoeuvred to the riverbank, the troops filed over the gangplanks.

Andrew watched the Indian and British troops take over the fortifications of Ava, replacing the king's troops on the battlements and at the guns.

The war is over. It was hardly a war, a procession up-river with a few skirmishes and a few dozen casualties. Once the dust has settled, I'll be free from Army regulations again.

As Andrew fretted and hoped, General Prendergast sent a brigade to garrison Sagain Fort on the right bank of the river. The sepoys moved in, the Burmese filed out peacefully, and the British relaxed a little more.

"It's all going very well," Birnie offered Andrew a cheroot, shared a match and puffed smoke contentedly around *Kathleen*. "That must be one of the easiest wars we've ever won. Not like Majuba, Old Boy, or Isandhlwana."

"No," Andrew pulled his pipe from his pocket

and tamped tobacco into the bowl. "Quite the opposite. Let's hope we can defeat the dacoits as easily as we did Thibaw's army."

Birnie grunted. "That may be a false hope, Baird. We've only commandeered about two and a half thousand stand of small arms, and many of them were old Brown Bess-era muskets. I'd guess the Burmans have squirrelled the more modern weapons away."

"Time will tell," Andrew said. "What's the adage? In war, it is essential that men should know what they fight for and like what they know. Something like that. Perhaps the Burmese did not love Thibaw sufficiently to fight for him."

"Perhaps not," Birnie agreed. "My worry is they might not love us either, and we'll be stuck in a long-drawn-out, small-scale war in the forests."

"That's a chilling prospect," Andrew said. "At present, it's a bit of an anti-climax."

Please, God, let me be away before that happens. I know where Bo Thura hides; if I had that blasted pardon, I'd pick him up, make a quick dash to the Frontier, and all would be hale and hearty. That important word, if!

After a night anchored off Ava, the fleet steamed the short distance to the Mandalay landing stage. The ships anchored in the river at nine in the morning, with the officers ordering the men to look their smartest. At one that afternoon, the Naval Brigade

465

and some of the Army disembarked and marched to Mandalay City.

"You're not required, Baird," Birnie said with false envy. "You can remain here in comfort while the rest of us don our best bibs and tuckers and swelter under the sun."

"I'll come along too," Andrew said. "I can't abide doing nothing, and anyway, I'd like to see the end of this campaign. I was in Mandalay before it began, so I'll see the climax."

Birnie laughed. "I thought you'd have seen enough of Burma."

"It gets in your blood," Andrew told him.

What did my father say about India? You hate India for a month and then love it forever. Burma has the same effect, as Jennings told us.

Andrew pulled on his uniform for the formal takeover of Thibaw's capital, marching behind the Naval Brigade as they entered the capital. While the sailors commandeered the eastern entrance of Mandalay, the soldiers filed around the walls and took over the other three gates.

Andrew remained with the Naval Brigade, observing without participating. He saw Colonel Sladen, acting in his civilian capacity, meet with Thibaw in the palace.

"It's all over," Birnie said, standing at sweating attention. "Thibaw is formally surrendering."

"With the whole flotilla and our Army here, the poor devil has no choice," Andrew said.

"Poor devil?" Birnie raised his eyebrows. "Tell that to the hundreds of people he murdered to climb to power."

Andrew was a silent witness as the Army made its triumphal entry into Mandalay. The men wore their khaki uniforms, and for a moment, Andrew sighed for the splendour of scarlet uniforms.

"War's not the same without the scarlet and pipeclay," Birnie mirrored his thoughts. "It's all professional now, ugly, sordid, and brutal. There's no glamour anymore."

"It was always ugly and sordid," Andrew said. "Colourful uniforms and flapping colours only painted over the reality."

"I know. But I do feel we are missing something. I yearn for the old days," eighteen-year-old Birnie said.

"Maybe you're right," Andrew replied.

Do we all view the past with nostalgia because we were younger and fitter there, with optimistic dreams of a future that never quite materialised? I hoped for Mariana. God, I am getting maudlin; I am only twenty-six years old. It must be the enervating climate here.

Andrew shook away his fit of depression. *I can still have Mariana if I convince her my love is genuine.*

The following day, the 30th of November 1885, Andrew saw another steamer plough up the Irrawaddy to berth alongside the fleet.

"Here comes the king's taxi," Birnie said as they stood at *Kathleen's* rail.

Commander William Morrison had brought *Tigris* to carry the king and his entourage to Indian exile.

"It's sad in a way," Andrew said. "The end of a dynasty."

"He was a murdering tyrant," Birnie gave his opinion. "Burma will be more peaceful under our rule."

Andrew remembered the tales of slaughter and the crucified men. "There is no doubt about that," he agreed. "All the same, I'll go onshore and watch the king's final departure."

"You do that, old man," Birnie said. "I'll remain onboard and have the ratings polish the gun."

Andrew stood under bright sunlight to watch Thibaw's final departure from his capital. Most of the spectators were women, looking very graceful in their colourful clothes. A few wept, either in genuine grief or with emotion at the passing of an era.

The king's two buffalo carriages rumbled over the wooden drawbridge across the moat. One carriage held Thibaw and his queens Supayalat and Supayalay, and the other carried his mother-in-law and servants, who leaned out of the coach windows, holding umbrellas. They stared at the novel sight of two long lines of khaki-clad British and Indian soldiers, one on each side of the road.

Are the soldiers intended as a guard-of-honour for the king? Or are they to stop any trouble?

The buffalos that drew the carriages were white and splendidly groomed. They marched proudly with heads held high, as if aware they were part of history, for never again would a native king grace the capital of Burma. The carriage wheels crunched on the road, the soldiers stood at attention, and only a few people in the crowd cheered.

Andrew saw a small group of lesser servants straggling in the rear of the carriages, and then they disappeared around a bend of the road. The dust settled, NCOs gave sharp orders, and the British and Indian soldiers formed up and marched away. Unsure how he felt, Andrew returned to *Kathleen*.

"And that was that," Birnie said. "We came, we saw, we conquered, and nothing was ever the same again."

"For the better, I hope," Andrew replied.

"Oh, indeed, for the better, but won't we be for the worse as well? When we've conquered all these queer, fascinating little barbaric kingdoms, won't we be the losers as well as the victors? We'll have lost what makes the world different and colourful." Birnie looked at Andrew, finished his cheroot and threw the stub into the moat, where it hissed for a second and died. "Ours not to reason why and all that."

"Ours but to bleed and die," Andrew said.

"On with life, eh? And hope the Burmans are happy with that blood-stained despot out of the way." Birnie shrugged. "They won't be, of course, and they'll blame us for everything from poor crops to the dacoits. That's the price of Empire, old boy."

Andrew thought of the dead and wounded sepoys at Minhla and the suffering sick lying under the awnings of the hospital ship. "One of the prices anyway," he agreed.

CHAPTER 33

RANGOON AND UPPER BURMA,
DECEMBER 1885

Mariana entered the telegraph station in
Rangoon and caught the operator's attention.

"Yes, miss?" The operator was sallow-skinned,
with tired eyes and thinning hair. "What can I do
for you?"

"I wish to send a telegram," Mariana said. She
had never been in a telegraph office before and was
unsure what to do.

"You've come to the right place, miss," the operator said, handing over a small, preprinted pad and a
stubby pencil. "Just write the address and your mes-

sage, and remember you have to pay for every word, so the briefer the message, the less you pay."

Mariana wrote a longer message than she expected before handing the pad back. "I don't know the address," she admitted.

"Do you know the name?" the operator asked wearily.

"General Jack Windrush," Mariana said. "He commands the troops in Southwest England."

"Fighting Jack," the operator permitted himself a slight smile. "I'll have his telegraphic address." He glanced at Mariana with renewed interest. "I served with him in Afghanistan," he said. "I won't be a jiffy, miss."

ANDREW WATCHED FROM *KATHLEEN'S* DECK AS THE royal party left for the long voyage to Rangoon and eventual exile to India. Two armed vessels acted as escorts in case of any rescue attempt.

Midshipman Birnie ran to Andrew, with his cap nearly falling from his head.

"Baird, old fellow. I mean, Captain Baird, sir!"

"Yes, Cosmo?" Andrew used Birnie's Christian name to ease any formality.

"General Prendergast wants to see you, sir," Birnie said.

"Then see me he shall," Andrew replied. With

the king in captivity, he imagined the war was over, he would be back in Rangoon soon, and he would patch up any difficulties with Mariana. He assumed Prendergast would be releasing him from his official duties. "Is there a boat available?"

"I'll get one, Baird," Birnie said.

"Thank you, Cosmo."

"Captain Baird," Prendergast leaned back in his chair and surveyed Andrew through musing eyes. "I believe you have some business to attend."

"Have I, sir?" Andrew asked.

"You have, sir," Prendergast replied. "Two telegrams arrived this morning, Captain. One was about you, and one was for you." He lifted two telegrams from his desk. Sir Charles Crossthwaite had sent both, one mentioning General Windrush's involvement and marked confidential. Prendergast handed the other to Andrew.

"Thank you, sir." Andrew scanned the brief message.

Full pardon and safe conduct granted for Bo Thura. Bring him into Lower Burma at your convenience. Crossthwaite.

"I take it you'll be leaving us soon," Prendergast said. He glanced at his other telegram, lying face down on the desk. "You are relieved of any duties with the expeditionary force, Captain."

"Thank you, sir. I have a man to take to Lower Burma."

"Remind me," Prendergast demanded.

"The Burmese gentleman who informed us about the French intrigues in Mandalay and helped us avoid the ambushes on the river."

"Of course," Prendergast nodded. "Loyal Burmans will always be welcome. When do you wish to depart?"

"As soon as is convenient, sir."

Prendergast smiled. "That means as soon as you can. Do you require any men? I can spare a small escort in case of dacoits."

Andrew had already considered the possibility. "No, thank you, sir. I will travel faster alone, and British troops or sepoys may complicate matters."

"As you wish, Baird. I wish you luck."

"Thank you, sir." Andrew hesitated. "May I have some food, a Martini, and a supply of cartridges?"

Prendergast nodded. "I think we can manage that, Baird. I'll also arrange a boat to take you wherever you wish to travel."

"Thank you, sir," Andrew said. "Jamieson of *Little Salamander* knows the route to Yin Pauk."

"He's your man, then," Prendergast said.

JAMIESON CLAMPED HIS CIGAR BETWEEN STRONG teeth when he dropped off Andrew downstream of Yin Pauk.

"Be careful, Captain Baird," Jamieson advised as Andrew stepped onto the riverbank. He checked his kitbag and his rifle.

"I will," Andrew replied. "I'd ask you to wait for me, but I don't know how long I will be."

"It looks quiet," Jamieson said, "but looks are deceptive out here." He held out his hand. "Three sovereigns, Captain."

"Your prices are too steep," Andrew said.

"You won't need the money," Jamieson said. "A lone European out here is as good as dead."

"Thanks for the encouragement, Jamieson," Andrew said.

"Try to remain alive," Jamieson advised. "You are a good customer, and I always value your gold."

The track was familiar as Andrew pushed towards Yin Pauk. Men and women were busy in the fields as if their king had not recently fought a war with the British Empire. An elephant hauled a load of teak logs, and a group of men crouched at the entrance to a house, gambling and smoking.

Since his last visit, Andrew had learned a few Burmese phrases, sufficient to make himself understood if he spoke slowly. Stepping into the open clearing around the village to ensure he was seen, Andrew shouldered his rifle and raised his voice. "My name is Andrew Baird," he said in Burmese. "I do not intend any harm."

He heard the murmur of voices as women

quickly hustled their children away and men stepped forward to face this intruder.

"I am looking for Bo Thura," Andrew said as a man emerged with a *dha* at his waist and a musket in his hand. "He might be expecting me."

The man spoke too rapidly for Andrew to understand.

"Bo Thura," Andrew repeated. "I'm looking for Bo Thura." He waited, trying to look friendly as more men appeared from doorways or the surrounding fields. One man shouted something and a familiar scar-faced figure emerged from one of the houses. Aung Thiha grinned at Andrew and indicated he should follow.

"Where are we going?" Andrew asked, without receiving a reply.

Aung Thiha led him into a small clearing two hundred yards outside the village, where birds sang from a tree, and three women chattered while preparing food. A few ramshackle huts showed where Bo Thura had set up his camp.

Aung Thiha stopped, faced Andrew, and drew his *dha*.

"What the devil?" Andrew reached for his revolver until Aung Thiha laughed, and Bo Thura stepped from behind a bush. He looked older than the last time Andrew had seen him, yet still with the same wry smile and bright eyes. "Cousin Andrew! I wondered if you would come back. Have you any news?"

"I said I would return," Andrew reminded. "I have good news. Sir Charles has issued a free pardon and agreed to let bygones be bygones." He saw the relief on Bo Thura's face and produced the telegram. "Here, read this for yourself."

Bo Thura scanned the telegram, smiling. "It could not have come at a better time," he said. "Maung Thandar and Buda Sein have been pressing us."

"Even after they lost the war?" Andrew asked. "That's surprising."

"The British have allowed Maung Thandar to retain his position," Bo Thura explained. "Until they change their mind, he will continue to encourage his dacoits and persecute those who stood against him. Thandar will attempt to twist the British around his finger as he did with Thibaw." Bo Thura glanced around. "That means he will send his warriors against me, as will Buda Sein."

Andrew nodded, accepted a cigar, and took a deep draw. "You have the Chief Commissioner's pardon and my personal guarantee that you'll be safe in Lower Burma," Andrew said. "We'll have Upper Burma pacified in a few weeks, and then you'll be safe from Bhamo to the sea." Andrew looked around at the camp, with men and women milling in happy confusion. "How about your people? How will they fare?"

"Maung Thandar and Buda Sein don't know their names," Bo Thura said. "Some will stay as dacoits; others will return to their villages or move to Mandalay." He grinned. "As soon as Sir Charles realises what sort of man Thandar is, he'll get rid of him."

Andrew nodded, accepting Bo Thura's word. "Gather your possessions and whichever followers you wish to take with you," Andrew said. "The quicker we start, the faster we'll reach British territory." He looked around, "I know we've deposed Thibaw, but Upper Burma will remain dangerous until we have properly pacified it."

"I'll tell my people what is happening," Bo Thura said.

Andrew waited as Bo Thura gathered his followers into the centre of the camp and addressed them in a loud voice. Andrew listened, understanding the gist as Bo Thura told them he was heading south into British-controlled Burma and that they would be safer without him. Andrew could see the disappointment on many faces.

When Bo Thura finished, the crowd slowly dissipated. A few waited to speak privately to him and then drifted away.

"You'll miss them," Andrew said.

"They'll be alive," Bo Thura said. "If they stay with me, they may not survive."

"Let's move then," Andrew replied. "We'll find a boat and once we reach the Irrawaddy, we can catch one of the Flotilla steamers."

Bo Thura smiled. "I have a much smaller vessel than my old war boat, now."

"As long as it floats," Andrew said.

Bo Thura had hidden his boat in the undergrowth. High prowed and brightly-painted, it was only sufficiently large to hold four people. Aung Thiha and San Kyi eased it free and shoved it onto the river, where it floated as a symbol of hope for the future.

"We'll head for Kandaw," Bo Thura said. "It's a small village about twenty miles away. They know me in Kandaw, and we can plan what to do next."

"We head for British territory," Andrew told him, "and report to the first official we see."

Bo Thura shook his head. "They might not know Sir Charles has granted me a pardon. And how about my people?"

"I'll speak up for them," Andrew promised. "And I have Sir Charles's telegram in my pocket."

Bo Thura gave that wry smile that was so like Andrew's father. "Will a colonel or a general, or even worse, a civic official, listen to the words of a mere captain?"

"They'd better, by God," Andrew said, "or I'll have my father on them." He stopped, realising he was contemplating something he had vowed never to do, using his father's influence.

Burma is altering me.

"Don't waste time," Andrew said.

They paddled with the current, keeping to the centre of the river in case of ambush and watching every bend. Andrew sat in the bows with his Martini in his lap while Aung Thiha, San Kyi and Bo Thura paddled. Insects clouded from the undergrowth, and birds and monkeys chattered overhead.

It was evening when they arrived at Kandaw, with the light fading and the smell of cooking fires aromatic in the air. Bo Thura guided the boat to the riverbank, and they disembarked, with Aung Thiha and San Kyi smiling at the throng which gathered to greet them.

The headman welcomed Bo Thura and looked enquiringly at Andrew.

"He's a friend," Bo Thura said.

The headman faced Andrew, smiled, and ushered them all into his village. They ate a simple meal of rice with vegetables and stewed melon sauce, and the headman showed them to an empty house.

"We'll sleep here tonight," Andrew took control. "Leave before dawn and try to reach the Irrawaddy in a couple of days. There are plenty of British boats on the river, and we'll be safe."

He slept with an easy mind, knowing he was among friends and his path home was clear.

I'll see you soon, Mariana, and we'll sort things out between us.

"ANDREW!" BO THURA SHOOK ANDREW AWAKE. "Get up!"

"What's happening?" Andrew rolled from his bed, grabbed his revolver, and stood, dazed with sleep. He heard the brassy clamour of a gong, men shouting and a long, drawn-out scream.

"We are betrayed," Bo Thura said. "The headman has betrayed us to Buda Sein!"

Glad he had not undressed, Andrew followed Bo Thura out the door. He saw Aung Thiha slicing at a man with his *dha* and San Kyi running away, having given the warning with his gong.

A horde of men ran at Bo Thura, some with the jackets of the king's soldiers, others bare-chested, and all armed. Andrew fired his revolver, wounding the nearest man. The others hesitated, and Aung Thiha hacked a soldier down.

"*Pyay! Suuthoetko pyan htein htarrmaal!*" Aung Thiha shouted. "Run! I'll hold them back!"

"Andrew!" Bo Thura pushed Andrew to the village boundary. "Get out!"

"We can't leave Aung Thiha behind!"

"*Pyay!*" Aung Thiha shouted. "Run!" He jumped

into the middle of the advancing men, slashing right and left, laughing as he fought.

"Run!" Bo Thura said.

Andrew hesitated, firing his revolver into the mass. He saw one man fall and another stagger, holding his leg. He saw Aung Thiha slice a man's arm clean off and then parry a knife thrust at his throat. Aung Thiha turned, killed the knifeman, and shouted something Andrew could not catch.

He saw the headman at the back of the mob. Lifting his revolver, Andrew aimed quickly and fired.

"We haven't time!" Bo Thura shouted. "Run, Andrew!"

Andrew saw the headman spin around, holding his arm, and then Bo Thura shoved him ahead and into the forest.

The noise behind them rose and ended in a nearly painful silence.

"That's Aung Thiha gone," Bo Thura said. "He was a good man."

"He would have fitted in any British infantry regiment," Andrew agreed. "Where's San Kyi?"

"He'll catch up," Bo Thura said, pushing Andrew ahead. "He's the most agile man I have ever known."

They hurried on, with Bo Thura setting the pace and Andrew struggling to keep up. After half an hour, they left the path, and Bo Thura led Andrew into the forest, ducking under low branches and plunging through tangled undergrowth.

"How about snakes?" Andrew gasped.

"They'll run when they hear us coming," Bo Thura said. He paused when they reached a small clearing. "Wait."

Knowing that Bo Thura was his master in the forest, Andrew stopped.

"Listen," Bo Thura ordered.

They crouched beside a thick-trunked teak tree, with insects clouding around their heads and the bird calls harsh in the air.

Andrew heard the muted murmur of voices in the distance. He put his hand flat on the ground, then lay down to listen. "About a dozen men," he said. "It's in the vibrations."

Bo Thura frowned. "Who taught you that trick?"

"A frontiersman in the Natal Dragoons," Andrew said. "It might not be as accurate in the forest as in the African bush."

"It may come in useful," Bo Thura said thoughtfully. "San Kyi hasn't found us yet. I thought he'd be here by now."

They crouched as a group of hunters approached and walked silently past, looking to the right and left. Andrew began to stand until Bo Thura placed a hand on his shoulder and shook his head.

Andrew remained still as two more men padded past. Bo Thura lifted a finger. "Wait," he mouthed.

A few moments later, another two men passed, both carrying rifles.

Bo Thura waited another few minutes.

"This way," he said, heading at an angle away from the path. Andrew followed, admiring the way Bo Thura could move without making a sound.

They travelled for two hours, with Bo Thura following half-hidden animal paths in the undergrowth. He stopped at a small clearing, where trees overhung a small temple, and monkeys chattered all around.

"We can stop here for the night," Bo Thura said. "Nobody comes here."

"Will we shelter inside the temple?" Andrew asked, checking his rifle.

"No. The monkeys have made it their own," Bo Thura said. "They would tear us to pieces. We are safe if we remain outside." He glanced around. "I hoped that San Kyi would be here. We often use this clearing as a rendezvous."

They slept in a hollow in the ground a hundred yards from the temple, and apart from the ubiquitous insects and the chattering of the monkeys, nothing bothered them. Andrew woke at dawn to find Bo Thura scavenging for fruit.

"We're lucky the monkeys left us something," Bo Thura said. When he smiled, the tattoos on his face merged, yet his eyes wore Andrew's father's expression.

"How far are we from the old border with Lower Burma?" Andrew asked.

Bo Thura screwed up his face. "Seven or eight days if we are lucky."

"That's where we're headed," Andrew said. "There are police posts there and regular Army patrols."

"Maung Thandar and Buda Sein will undoubtedly have his men watching the river ports for me," Bo Thura considered for a moment. "I can't think of a better plan than yours, except the police posts only have a small garrison."

"It's a sanctuary," Andrew said. "The alternative is a much longer journey to Thayetmyo, which Buda Sein will be watching, or wait for a steamer on the river."

"The river which Buda Sein will have well-guarded," Bo Thura said. "He'll have every villager along the bank looking for us."

"Can you get us to the old border?" Andrew asked. "Without Buda Sein's men seeing us?"

"Can you keep pace with me?" Bo Thura responded.

They grinned at each other. "Lead on, cousin," Andrew said.

CHAPTER 34

UPPER BURMA, DECEMBER 1885 AND
JANUARY 1886

Bo Thura stopped without warning, holding up his hand. "Can you smell it?"

"Petroleum," Andrew said after a second. "Earth-oil."

"That's right," Bo Thura agreed. "Over this way." Moving quietly, he led Andrew to a small clearing with a crucified man in the centre.

"A message for us," Bo Thura said. "That's San Kyi."

Buda Sein's men had stripped San Kyi, coated him in petroleum, crucified him and left him to die slowly.

"He was a good man," Bo Thura said. "One of

the most loyal."

Andrew remembered San Kyi keeping pace with *Little Salamander* from Thayetmyo to Mandalay. Now, he was tortured, roasted, and murdered.

"Do you want to bury him?" Andrew asked.

"We'll leave him," Bo Thura decided. "Buddhists don't believe in burial, and a cremation fire would alert Buda Sein."

"Another good man gone," Andrew said. "Buda Sein has a lot to answer for."

"Buda Sein or Maung Thandar," Bo Thura added. He glanced at San Kyi. "Goodbye, my friend. Come on, Cousin Andrew."

Bo Thura moved faster now, threading through the forest without any sign of fatigue. Andrew lost count of the days as Bo Thura took charge, travelling by night and resting through the day. They bypassed villages or raided storehouses for food under cover of darkness, eased through tangled undergrowth on paths Andrew could not see, and listened to the sounds of jungle animals and birds.

Andrew learned to relish lizards and red ants as a nutritious meal, drank unfiltered water from muddy streams and watched as parties of dacoits questioned villagers with threats and violence.

"Can't we help?" Andrew asked.

"If we do, Buda Sein will return, destroy the village and massacre the people," Bo Thura told him.

They moved on, lean and ragged, spotted with

jungle sores and insect bites, until Bo Thura stopped at the edge of a man-made clearing.

"There," Bo Thura said. "There's the police post of Ban Hteik Chaung." He grinned at Andrew. "We made it!"

Andrew stared ahead, hardly daring to believe that they had reached sanctuary.

A Union flag drooped from a white-painted pole, with a small, walled encampment beneath. Andrew saw the colourful turbans of Sikh policemen and a smartly uniformed British officer.

Oh, thank God.

"Are you alright, Cousin?" Bo Thura asked curiously.

"Yes," Andrew replied. "Come on, Bo Thura, let's make ourselves known."

The Sikh sentry lifted his rifle when Andrew and Bo Thura emerged from the forest's edge. He shouted something, and a Burmese policeman ran to his side and called out a challenge.

"They want to know who we are," Bo Thura said.

Andrew nodded. "I bet they do. We're like two walking scarecrows." He raised his voice. "I am Captain Andrew Baird of the Natal Dragoons, and my companion is Bo Thura, a friend and ally of the British."

At the sound of a British voice, the officer stepped beside the Sikh. "Who did you say you were?"

"Captain Andrew Baird of the Natal Dragoons," Andrew repeated.

"Good Lord," the officer said. "Are you not the fellow who brought back young Mary Mac-Connacher from the dacoits?"

"That's right," Andrew said. "And this gentleman," he indicated Bo Thura, "rescued her."

"Good Lord," the officer repeated. "Come in. I am Lieutenant Hanley," the officer held out his hand. "Martin Hanley. What the devil have you been up to?"

"Buda Sein's men have chased Bo Thura and me from Kandaw to here," Andrew entered the police post with Bo Thura at his side.

"Good Lord," Hanley said for the third time.

Four buildings were within the compound, with the largest forming half the boundary wall and providing accommodation for the twenty Sikh and ten Burmese policemen. The smallest building acted as Lieutenant Hanley's office and living quarters; the others were a lock-up for prisoners and an armoury and storehouse.

"You'll need to wash, and you must be hungry," Hanley ushered them into his office-cum-living-accommodation. "I can't offer anything luxurious, I am afraid; we're a bit spartan here, but what I have is yours."

"Thank you," Andrew said. He sat down and closed his eyes, breathing in the smell of fresh coffee. Bo Thura looked nervous inside the police post until Andrew reassured him he was safe.

"Why is Buda Sein chasing you?" Hanley asked, looking from Andrew to Bo Thura and back.

"Buda Sein was one of Maung Thandar's accomplices," Andrew explained. "When Bo Thura refused to pay him tribute, he got annoyed."

Hanley frowned. "Bo Thura! I know that name! He's a notorious dacoit! A wanted man!"

"Not anymore," Andrew said calmly. "The Chief Commissioner has granted him a full pardon for helping rescue Mary MacConnacher, alerting us to the French interference in Mandalay and aiding us during the late war."

"Good Lord," Hanley eyed Bo Thura, immediately calmed. "You helped rescue little Mary Mac-Connacher, did you? Well done, Bo Thura."

They all looked up when one of the Sikhs shouted something.

"Don't be alarmed," Hanley said. "That's only my havildar returning with the regular patrol. Sukhbir Singh is a good man."

Andrew smiled. "I know him well," he replied. "We worked together before the war started. Sukhbir Singh is one of the best."

Holding his coffee mug in his right hand, Andrew strolled to the door to greet the havildar.

Sukhbir Singh arrived at the run. "Close the gate, Sahib!" he shouted. "The dacoits are all around us!"

As Sukhbir Singh spoke, a fusillade sounded from the forest.

"Good Lord," Hanley said and raised his voice, immediately dropping the façade as his professionalism took over. "Everyone to their positions! Rifles and forty rounds of ammunition! Sukhbir Singh! Take the east and south walls!"

"Here they come!" Andrew said as a horde of dacoits burst onto the maidan around the police post.

"Aim low, men," Hanley ordered. "Drive them back."

The Sikhs needed no encouragement as they ran to the outside wall with the Burmese police only a few seconds behind them.

There are too few men to defend this perimeter, Andrew thought. He joined them, with Bo Thura at his side.

"On my word!" Hanley said, watching the dacoits advance across the maidan. "By Jove, there are a lot of them. Wait for it! Wait! Fire!"

The police volley was as controlled as that of any British infantry regiment. Half a dozen dacoits fell, two to lie prone and the others to struggle and kick. The dacoits charged on, yelling.

Andrew aimed, fired, and saw his man fly backwards as the Martini bullet caught him high in the chest. He worked the rifle's underlever, pushed in a cartridge, and aimed again.

"Reload!" Hanley shouted. "Aim! Fire!"

The police fired, with Andrew and Bo Thura's rifles joining the general melee. The dacoits fired from the forest, with most of their bullets high.

We have time for one more volley, and then it will be hand-to-hand, Andrew thought.

"Reload!" Hanley shouted again. "Aim! Fire! Fix bayonets!"

As the police clicked on the formidable eighteen-inch bayonets, the dacoits turned and fled.

"Reload!" Hanley shouted. "Stand firm, Sukhbir Singh!"

Andrew saw the havildar halfway over the wall, preparing to follow the retreating dacoits.

"They'll be waiting in the trees, Havildar," Andrew said. "Ten or twenty of them for every one of us."

The police settled down as the dacoits occupied the forest, with both sides sniping whenever they saw an opportunity.

"What is your normal procedure when the dacoits attack?" Andrew asked.

Hanley reloaded his rifle. "They rarely attack police posts," he said. "When they do, it's in smaller numbers, more like a nuisance raid than a full-scale assault. This situation is highly unusual." He glanced at the sky. "It will be night soon, which might give them an advantage."

"Do the Royal Scots Fusiliers still patrol this area?" Andrew asked.

"They do," Hanley said. "One of their flying patrols is due here late tomorrow, and as soon as the Army appears, the dacoits will flee like snow off a dyke. We only have to hold out until then."

"It's me they want," Bo Thura said, stepping towards Hanley. "If I leave, they'll likely go away."

"You'll stay!" Andrew snapped. "We'll have to face the dacoits sometime. Buda Sein has been a thorn in our side for months."

The gongs began half an hour later, just as the sun faded.

"Scare tactics," Hanley said. "They hope to play on our nerves. Light the lanterns, Havildar."

"Yes, Sahib," Sukhbir Singh replied.

Hanley had placed twenty oil lanterns around the perimeter, each illuminating a five-yard radius. The lanterns also attracted moths and other flying insects that fluttered and burned their wings on the hot glass bowls.

"If you see anything moving beyond the lamplight," Hanley ordered. "Shoot." He translated his words into Sikh and Burmese.

Andrew nodded. He knew it was going to be a long night. He listened to the gongs, wondering if they were summoning more men or were only intended to intimidate.

Sukhbir Singh grinned at him. "They're trying to frighten us," he said and laughed. "Do I look afraid?"

"It would take more than gongs to frighten a Sikh," Andrew replied.

"I want three-man patrols to check the perimeter," Hanley said, "vary the routes and times, and don't leave anybody behind."

"I'll take a patrol," Andrew volunteered.

"Are you sufficiently fit?" Hanley asked. "You look like death's young brother!"

"I'm fit," Andrew replied.

The gongs continued, surrounding the police post with noise, disturbing sleep, and stretching nerves.

When Andrew returned from an uneventful circuit of the perimeter, Hanley asked, "Do you think they will attack?"

"I don't know how these dacoits fight," Andrew replied. He ducked as a rifle cracked and a bullet whined overhead. "It could be a long night."

"I could lead a sortie," Hanley suggested, "attack them rather than sit waiting."

"You'll be taking your men into their territory," Andrew replied. "The dacoits would cut them to pieces."

Both looked around as a dozen rifles fired together, smashing one of the guard lanterns. The police replied, aiming at the muzzle flares deep in the forest. A moment later, another volley smashed a second lamp.

"They're putting out the lights," Hanley said.

"Prepare a fire," Andrew said. "Darkness will give them an advantage."

Hanley looked at him for a moment, then raised his voice. "Gather anything that will burn!" he ordered. "We need light!"

As the Burmese fired at the lamps, smashing them one by one, half the police replied to the musketry, and the rest gathered tables, chairs, and spare furniture.

"Keep these patrols out!" Andrew shouted. "Watch for any incursions."

"Do you think they'll try to infiltrate?" Hanley asked.

"I would," Andrew replied, "and these lads are no slouches when it comes to raiding and small-scale warfare."

When the final two lanterns exploded in a welter of splinters and spluttering oil, the flames rose briefly and died. The darkness seemed total, enhanced by sudden silence as the gongs ceased.

"What now?" Hanley asked.

"Now we light the fire," Andrew replied.

He heard the warning shout from Sukhbir Singh, and then a volley of shots came from the forest, with bullets ripping overhead and crashing into the buildings.

"Return fire!" Hanley ordered, hurrying to the wall.

The Sikhs responded eagerly, with some standing

to get a better shot and others hurrying from quieter posts to reinforce the front. The Burmese police joined them, muttering to each other as they took their positions.

"Keep under cover," Andrew roared. He lifted his head, with his instincts, or perhaps his experience, warning him that something was wrong.

"Watch the rear," Andrew warned. "We've got too many men in one place."

Before Andrew finished talking, one of the Sikhs gave a long moan and collapsed, with a dacoit withdrawing a bloody *dha* from his back.

"Every second man! Watch your rear!" Hanley shouted. "The dacoits are inside the compound!"

The dacoits came with a rush, attacking the police from the rear. They killed the first man, a lithe Burmese policeman who tried to stop them, and thrust a *dha* into the back of a second Sikh.

Hanley lifted his revolver and shot one man in the chest, fired at a second, and gasped as a dacoit slid low across the floor and slashed at his thigh.

"You dirty hound!" Andrew shot the dacoit, saw Ajit Singh thrust his bayonet through another, and then more police joined in, shooting and stabbing with controlled ferocity. The dacoits within the post melted away while the firing outside intensified.

"Get them out!" Hanley ordered. He staggered as a bullet slammed into his chest, fired at the retreating dacoits, and swore as another bullet knocked him off his feet.

"Hanley!" Andrew leapt to his side. He saw Sukhbir Singh organise his men to eradicate the last of the invaders, and then the firing outside ended.

"I'm all right," Hanley said, smiling. "Let me rest for a moment to get my breath back. They've winded me."

Andrew saw the blood bubble from Hanley's mouth as he spoke and knew he was hard hit. "That must be it," he said. "Get back to your positions, men, and make sure all these dacoits are dead or in a cell. We don't want them coming back to life and stabbing us in the back."

"Light the fire!" Andrew ordered. "Keep it fed!"

The fire gave flickering light to the post, illuminating the men, from the bearded Sikhs to the smaller, stocky Burmese.

The gongs continued all night as the Burmese sniped without attacking. At dawn, they began to muster in the fringes, shouting insults at the police.

"They are gathering their courage for a final assault," Sukhbir Singh said. "Now we will see who the real warriors are!"

When one of the dacoits shouted something, the Burmese police fled, leaving the police even more short-handed.

"We're better off without them," Bo Thura said.

"We don't know when they will join the enemy. Look!" He pointed with the muzzle of his rifle.

Andrew swore when he saw the rising sun catch the yellow umbrella. "That's Buda Sein," he said. "He's come in person for the final assault."

"Here they come," Bo Thura said as Andrew lifted his rifle. "And there are more." He pointed to the right, where another force of dacoits filtered through the trees.

CHAPTER 35

UPPER BURMA AND RANGOON, JANUARY
1885

"Who the devil are these lads?" Andrew asked as the new force of dacoits arrived on the flank of Buda Sein's men.

"Trouble," Hanley said, struggling to his feet. Using a Martini-Henry as a crutch, he hobbled to the wall, dribbling blood from his mouth.

As dacoits began to fire from the trees, the two groups moved slowly towards the police post, with the gongs clamouring in the background and Buda Sein in the centre under his yellow umbrella.

"Ready!" Hanley shouted and coughed, spitting blood.

Andrew put a hand on Hanley's shoulder. "Permit me, Lieutenant," he said. "Present!"

The Sikhs aimed their rifles, facing their enemy without a trace of fear.

"Don't fire!" Bo Thura shouted. "Not yet!"

"What the devil?" Andrew asked. "What's wrong, Bo Thura?"

"Look!" Bo Thura pointed. "Look what's happening!"

The second group of dacoits had altered direction. Rather than advancing on the police post, they charged towards Buda Sein's men, fired their rifles and drew their dhas.

"What the devil?" Andrew asked again.

"That's Aung Thiha!" Bo Thura said, pointing. "Look!"

"Dear God! I thought Buda Sein's men had killed him!"

Aung Thiha led his force against Buda Sein's dacoits, slashing with their *dhas*. Taken by surprise, Buda Sein's men faltered. The advance stopped as they faced this unexpected attack.

"Sukhbir Singh ran to Hanley. "Permission to charge them, sir?"

"No," Hanley shook his head. "We don't know who is friendly and who is not. Stay put, Havildar!"

"Yes, Sahib!" Sukhbir Singh did not hide his disappointment.

"Stay here, Cousin Andrew," Bo Thura grinned as

he slipped over the wall. Andrew watched him march unhesitatingly towards Buda Sein's men. The fighting was intense as Aung Thiha pushed forward, with men falling on both sides. Bo Thura had nearly reached Buda Sein when Andrew saw the yellow umbrella begin to withdraw.

Aung Thiha reached Buda Sein first. Andrew saw the flash of steel as he lifted his *dha*. Buda Sein crumpled to the ground; Aung Thiha stooped, sawed at his neck, and lifted Buda Sein's disembodied head.

With the death of their leader, Buda Sein's dacoits fled, leaving their dead and wounded on the ground. Bo Thura embraced Aung Thiha, spoke briefly, and returned to the police post.

"Well, Cousin Andrew," he said. "Take me to Rangoon."

Hanley lifted a hand. "Hark!" he said as a half-company of the Royal Scots Fusiliers marched towards the post. "The flying column has arrived."

Andrew nodded and looked forward, where dead and dying men carpeted the open ground. "Thank God for Aung Thiha. Thank God for the *kyawal*."

"ANDREW," MARIANA TOUCHED ANDREW'S ARM and stepped back. "I have to talk to you."

They stood outside the Golden Pagoda, with the

rising sun reflecting from the roofs and the tinkle of temple bells in the breeze.

"This is a good place to talk," Andrew replied.

They were silent for a moment, both gathering their courage.

"When we were in Edinburgh," Mariana said quietly. "You asked me to marry you."

"I did," Andrew agreed.

"I turned you down," Mariana said, facing the temple. "I wasn't sure why I turned you down. I thought it was because of Elaine."

Andrew listened, allowing her to take her time. He did not interrupt.

"I was worried in case you only wanted to marry me for Elaine's sake," Mariana said.

Andrew slid his hand into hers, feeling her tremble. She was quiet for two minutes, ordering her thoughts.

"Yet, I knew there was more," Mariana said. "There was a shadow I could not fathom." She squeezed his hand, wriggled it free, and stepped away. "Andrew, if I had agreed to marry you on our wedding night, you would not be my first man."

Andrew took a deep breath. He did not interrupt.

Mariana continued. "When the renegades murdered everybody and kidnapped me, they did more." She remembered the horror, the laughing, mocking faces, the knowing, bloodstained hands tearing at her clothes, the leering, gasping men with urgent, demanding bodies violating her.

Andrew listened as Mariana told everything in an outpouring of horror that he knew she needed to cleanse her memory. He allowed her space to talk as the sun rose higher and yellow-robed monks began their day of prayer and meditation. The temple bells tinkled, somehow peaceful.

When Mariana stopped, she was no longer shaking. Her voice was unemotional as if talking had drained her of the past.

Andrew took her hand again. "You've been through hell," he said. "Could you not tell me this earlier?"

"No," Mariana said. "I had forgotten. Or rather, I pushed the memories away, stored them in some dark part of my mind and locked them in." She turned slightly, facing him with her eyes narrow. "Until something turned a key in the lock and released them all."

Andrew had to ask. "What was the key?"

"Stephen Jennings," Mariana replied.

Myat Lay Phyu stood on the pagoda steps, watching them without speaking. Her eyes were deep with knowledge.

"How did he do that?" Andrew guessed the answer.

"I shared his bed," Mariana told him.

"Did he rape you?" Andrew used the brutal term as

his anger rose. He could picture himself killing Jennings with his bare hands, tearing him to bloody shreds.

"No. He did not," Mariana replied. She lifted her chin. "I was compliant."

"Do you love him?" Andrew asked.

"No." Mariana shook her head.

Myat Lay Phyu had not moved. She held Mariana's gaze, unsmiling yet encouraging.

"Do you want to see him again?" Andrew asked.

"No," Mariana shook her head.

"I could kill him," Andrew said, meaning every word.

"Please don't," Mariana said.

"Will you marry me?"

"If you still want me," Mariana replied.

"If you want me," Andrew replied, "after I neglected you, leaving you alone with a predator like Stephen Jennings."

Mariana sought his hand. "I want to marry you."

"That is settled then," Andrew told her.

Myat Lay Phyu smiled and walked away, her feet making no sound on the stone steps.

"ANDREW, STAND HERE AND WATCH," MARIANA said as Than Than Aye approached Jennings outside Jennings and Stanley's office building. When Than

Than Aye slipped on the uneven ground, he instinctively caught him.

"Thank you, sir," Than Than Aye said, momentarily pressing against him.

"My pleasure, my dear," Jennings said. "You speak English very well."

"Thank you," Than Than Aye said, lowering her eyes demurely. "A kind missionary taught me." She remained at Jennings' side.

"He taught you well, I must say," Jennings said, eyeing her up and down.

"He taught me many things about your culture," Than Than Aye said. "Many things, sir."

"I can only imagine," Jennings replied.

"Do you know who that woman is?" Andrew asked.

"That woman is called Than Than Aye," Mariana said. "We're old friends."

"Are you indeed?" Andrew asked. "You'll have to tell me more."

"Maybe later," Mariana said. "A girl needs some secrets."

They watched as Than Than Aye slid closer to Jennings so her hip touched his. "I have heard that you are a kind man," she said.

"Where did you hear that?" Jennings asked.

"I heard you were good to girls," Than Than Aye said. She moved away again, pouting.

"Now, wait a minute," Jennings followed, putting a hand on her shoulder. "Where are you going?"

"Wherever you want to go," Than Than Aye replied.

"Would you like to see my house?" Jennings asked.

Than Than Aye widened her eyes. "That would be a pleasure, sir," she said. "I've never been with a European before."

Jennings smiled. "When I first saw you," he said. "I thought you were just another beautiful Burmese woman, but now I can tell that you are something special. You are like no woman I have ever met before."

Than Than Aye snuggled closer. "Thank you, sir. I am sure I can surprise you."

"Why are we watching this?" Andrew asked as Jennings ushered Than Than Aye into his Brougham.

"You'll see tomorrow," Mariana said.

"Tell me now," Andrew said.

When Mariana smiled, shaking her head, Andrew realised he was witnessing a new, mischievous side of her character.

No, he told himself. *It's not a new side. This is the old Mariana I saw before her abduction. Mariana is back to normal at last.* "I can wait," he said.

※

WELLS PLACED A FOLDED NEWSPAPER ON THEIR table at breakfast the following morning. He nodded to Andrew and walked on to another customer.

Mariana watched as Andrew glanced at the newspaper, lifted it, and read one of the articles. He looked across the table at Mariana.

"Did you know about this?"

"Did I know about what?" Mariana asked innocently.

"This!" Andrew prodded his finger at an article as he passed the newspaper to her. "Somebody broke into Jennings' stables and stole his horses while he was otherwise engaged." Andrew leaned back in his chair. "You and I know what he was doing. Our mutual friend Than Than Aye had him fully occupied. We also both know that Bo Thura is the best horse thief this side of India."

Mariana smiled slowly. "I said you'd see tomorrow," she said. "Stephen Jennings was proud of his horses."

"Bo Thura!" Andrew exclaimed. "Damn and blast the man! I went to a lot of trouble to rescue that fellow, and his first action is to steal the finest horses in Rangoon."

Mariana laughed. "I wonder if that was his plan all along," she said. "Was he playing a game with us?"

Maybe he was. Maybe my beloved cousin was pulling my strings like a puppet-master, working me to his advan-

tage as he planned to steal the finest bloodstock horses in Burma.

Andrew put the newspaper back on the table. "I doubt we'll ever know," he said. "Come on, Mariana. We must buy our shipping tickets."

As they left the British India offices beside the harbour, Mariana watched the launch steam slowly upriver, with the grey-bearded man in the wheel-house calmly smoking a cheroot. The flat attached to the launch floated light on the water as though it carried little weight, so they made good time against the current. She idly noted the name on the launch's stern, *Little Salamander,* and smiled when she saw a horse poke its head over the side.

"A bribe for Kiugkwek-li," Andrew had also seen the horse. "Now that Sir Charles has removed Maung Thandar from power, Kiugkwek-li is suitably bribed, and Buda Sein suitably dead, Bo Thura can resume the only life he knows." He placed the steamship tickets in his inside pocket and took Mariana's hand. "Come on, Mariana, we have packing to complete." He watched *Little Salamander* steam slowly upstream. "I wonder what Jamieson charged Bo Thura for that cargo. These two rogues are well suited."

YORLING CHAPTER 36

EDINBURGH, SCOTLAND, JUNE 1886

The sun eased through low clouds as Andrew walked under the portcullis and into Edinburgh Castle. The Governor had formed up the garrison as a guard of honour, with the men immaculate in their brilliant scarlet tunics and blue trousers. They presented arms as Andrew marched past on his way to St Margaret's Chapel.

Friends that Andrew had known since childhood packed the chapel. The garrison chaplain waited at the altar, Bible in hand and a benevolent smile on his face. Andrew's mother sat at the front, greeting him with a silent smile and a nod of encouragement. Andrew heard the echo of his boots as he marched the few paces to face the chaplain and slammed to attention as if he were before the regimental colonel rather than the Lord God Almighty.

"Relax, Captain Baird," the chaplain said quietly. "She'll be here."

"Yes, sir," Andrew realised how tense he was and stood at ease, feeling his heart thumping. He heard the murmur of the small congregation and wondered what they were discussing and how long he would have to wait before Mariana appeared.

What if she has changed her mind? She already embarrassed me in this castle. Is she going to do that again, jilting me at the altar?

As the thought crossed his mind, Andrew heard footsteps behind him, the heavy tread of a man with a slight limp from a wound in the Second Burmese War and the lighter patter of a woman. He glanced behind him and saw his father, General Jack Windrush, with Mariana holding on to the crook of his elbow. As Mariana had no surviving relatives, Jack Windrush acted as her father to give away the bride.

Andrew thought that Mariana had never looked more elegant in her flowing white wedding dress with the veil obscuring her face and two bridesmaids, chosen from the garrison children, holding her train.

"Face your front, Captain," the chaplain advised. "She'll be with you shortly."

Andrew obeyed, trying to control the surge of relief and the grin that threatened to split his face.

He heard the heavy footsteps halt behind him. The lighter patter continued for two more steps, and then Mariana was at his side, where she belonged. Andrew looked sideways as Mariana swept back her veil.

"Are you both ready?" the chaplain asked softly.

"Yes," Andrew replied as Mariana nodded.

Andrew felt as if he were somebody else, looking down as the chaplain intoned the words of the wedding ceremony. His father stood behind him, and Mariana was at his side. He could feel his mother's eyes fixed on his back and knew she was encouraging him, as always.

Memories of Zululand, the Transvaal, and Burma returned to him in an array of faces and incidents. He allowed his mind to wander and only returned when he sensed the chaplain's eyes fixed on him.

"I now pronounce you man and wife," the chaplain announced. "You may kiss the bride."

Andrew could not contain his smile as he turned towards his wife. He heard somebody cheer as he touched her lightly on the lips.

"Now we're married," Mrs Mariana Baird said.

"So we are," Andrew agreed.

He heard somebody call for three cheers, but the rest of that day was only a happy blur.

Andrew's house on Berwick's walls was warm and welcoming as he carried his new wife over the threshold.

"I have something for you," he said, placing her gently on the ground. "Wait here." He ran upstairs to his study, fumbled for the desk key, and withdrew the brown-paper-wrapped parcel he had placed there when Mariana refused his offer at Edinburgh Castle.

"What is it?" Mariana asked as Andrew returned with the parcel.

"Why not open it and see?" Andrew suggested. He watched with an indulgent smile as Mariana ripped off the paper.

"Books," Mariana said. "Leather bound with gold embossed titles." She held up the first. "Tennyson's poems, including the Morte d'Arthur and the Lady of Shalott."

Andrew nodded. It had cost him a small fortune to buy the books and have a bookbinder add a leather cover with gold lettering.

"What's this? Another *Morte d'Arthur*? By Sir Thomas Malory?" Mariana looked up quizzically.

"It's a copy of the Fifteenth Century original," Andrew explained. "You can compare the two versions. Malory's is much longer."

Mariana lifted the third and by far the slimmest book. She read the title. "*The Gododdin* by Aneirin," she said. "That's the poem you mentioned that day in Edinburgh."

"Yes," Andrew said. He had the heroic poem specially printed and bound for Mariana, with her name written inside, as she saw when she opened it up.

"Oh," Mariana said. "What a lovely wedding present."

Andrew nodded. He did not tell her the books had been intended as an engagement present. Some things were better left unsaid.

Mariana lifted the books, smelled the leather, and smiled. "Thank you, Andrew," she said and extended her hand. "Come with me." She smiled. "We've waited a long time for this, husband," she said, leading him upstairs.

HISTORICAL NOTE

THE KIDNAPPING OF MARY WINCHESTER

I based the kidnapping of Mary MacConnacher on actual events. The Lushais were a tribe that lived on the Northeast frontier of India, in the hill country between Bengal and Burma. They occasionally raided the British-run tea plantations to plunder and kidnap, continuing their depredations despite the British sending men on punitive expeditions.

In 1871, the Lushais grabbed a young British girl, Mary Winchester, who was reportedly golden-haired. The British sent an expedition to recover Mary, with men dying from diseases and accidents, as well as from brushes with the tribal warriors. When a relief column found young Mary, she was in perfect health, spoke Lushai better than English, and smoked cheroots. The Lushais were upset about losing her and asked for a lock of her golden hair as a keepsake.

As both Mary's parents were dead, she was sent to Britain to live with relatives. Sometimes, one wonders if she would not have been happier with the Lushais.

THE THIRD BURMESE WAR

The Third Burmese War was a short affair that the British won after a couple of skirmishes. However, the British found that occupying the country was one thing and pacifying or conquering it was something else. Dacoity continued well into the 1890s, with the British blaming any act of resistance on dacoits or bandits. It is possible that many of the perpetrators may have intended to remove British rule rather than simple robbery and mayhem.

THE IRRAWADDY FLOTILLA COMPANY

Rudyard Kipling immortalised the Irrawaddy Flotilla Company in his poem *Mandalay* when he wrote:
   "Come you back to Mandalay,
   Where the old Flotilla lay:
   Can't you 'ear their paddles chunkin' from Rangoon to Mandalay?"
   The Irrawaddy Flotilla Company was owned and

managed in Glasgow, Scotland with its headquarters in Rangoon. It operated from 1865 until the 1940s and, at one time, boasted the largest river boat fleet in the world. The ships were built in sections in Glasgow, sent to Rangoon and reassembled in the Flotilla Company's shipyard.

ABOUT THE AUTHOR

Born in Edinburgh, Scotland and educated at the University of Dundee, Malcolm Archibald has written in a variety of genres, from academic history to folklore, historical novels to fantasy. He won the Dundee International Book Prize with *Whales for the Wizard* in 2005 and the Society of Army Historical Research prize for Historical Military Fiction with *Blood Oath* in 2021.

Happily married for over 42 years, Malcolm has three grown children and lives outside Dundee in Scotland.

To learn more about Malcolm Archibald and discover more Next Chapter authors, visit our website at www.nextchapter.pub.

The Chill of the Irrawaddy
ISBN: 978-4-82419-473-2
Large Print

Published by
Next Chapter
2-5-6 SANNO
SANNO BRIDGE
143-0023 Ota-Ku, Tokyo
+818035793528

4th June 2024